Women, Converts & Azerbaijanis

Need Not Apply

P.A. Moses

To Fred Mathis, Moshe ben Avraham, of blessed memory. His simple request to read this book gave me the energy I needed to finish it.

Welcome to Jewish Germany

I am not sure what I expected when I first became involved in Judaism in Germany. I say "became involved" as I am not sure that any other expression such as "visited a synagogue" or even more haimish phrases like "went to shul" can describe one's relationship with a Jewish community in Germany today. Certainly "became a member" doesn't work as I could never even apply for membership even if I would have thrust cash toward a board member and cried "please let me pay!"

I say "became involved" because much like any nightmarish relationship where we hope for an ending with minimal open wounds yet are addicted to the drama, I gave heart and soul to an abusive lover that did not return my affection or understand my hurt. I thought that with the force of my will I could change what I found into my own utopian vision—that I could use my vast twenty-some years of life experience to show these backwater Jews what it means to be Jewish—that my simple positive attitude and down-to-the-root-of-my-soul Jewishness would magically transform the pathological reality in which I found myself into a Judaism I recognized.

Maybe I expected the promised renaissance. I had read the articles: "Jewish Communities Again Flourishing in Germany" and "First Rabbis Ordained in Germany Since the Holocaust." I guess it all started when at my very Reform shul in the suburbs of Philly we had once had a speaker that had taught for two years at the University of Potsdam, now the center of Jewish theological studies in Germany, who had spoken convincingly of Jewish rebirth in the third-generation aftermath of Hitler.

"Until the fall of the Soviet Union, Judaism in Germany was dead or dying." Stooped, gray and balding he spoke with a thick Israeli accent, a baritone like gravel, punctuating the incorrect syllable on every third word. "There were almost no 'German' Jews left after the Shoah. Most had either been killed or made it to America. A trickle had made it to Palestine in the thirties—the *Yekkes* like my parents—but just a few thousand even though they built every institution of importance in Israel today."

A few people coughed mildly, small pockets of Israeli expats whose parents were most likely not *Yekkes*, Israelis of German-Jewish descent.

"But the Jews that called themselves 'German' Jews in Germany at the fall of the Soviet Union were actually Romanians and Poles and Hungarians—those stuck in Displaced Persons Camps in Germany after surviving other kinds of camps all over Europe. Many tried to go home but had no home. Many tried to go to Palestine but were not allowed in by the British. Some even experienced pogroms and more death as they tried to lay claim to property stolen from them by their neighbors. As strange as it sounds, Germany was the best option, and the first synagogue services held after the war not led by American chaplains were led by these souls.

"They had been joined by a small trickle of Jews that came in over the decades, but even then, there were only a few. They had tried to create Jewish communities but for years could not entice many rabbis or cantors to work in the land of the Nazis. Yet with the fall of the Soviet Union, Germany sought to make *teshuva*, to loosen its immigration policy and to open up its gates to Soviet Jews."

The grumbling had become a bit more distinct. Saying such positive things about Germany was still not really in vogue. Many *Bubbies* and *Zaydes* in the community still refused to buy

5

BMWs and would not speak a word of what for some was still their mother tongue.

He continued, oblivious to the rumbles of resentment: "In the decade that followed, the dead and dying thirty thousand ballooned to more than one-hundred-thousand. Synagogues hired rabbis and cantors. New buildings were built. Even children of the German Jews that had fled to Israel began to return, open businesses and create a thriving subculture—thirty thousand in Berlin alone!" The speaker had begun sweating with his enthusiasm, gesticulating like a cheerleader to convince all of the great historical and moral victory. "Everywhere you can go to a klezmer concert. Every town has a museum and memorial. German schoolchildren visit synagogues and German civic leaders lay wreaths for Jewish memorials. Jews began living a Jewish life once again in what must be seen as one of the great miracles of our time. True *tikkun olam!*"

I was excited. His cheerleading convinced me. This *was* the repairing of the world–*tikkun olam*. Somehow I found myself much more deeply moved by the old *Yekke*'s excited exposition than I would have dreamed. I had to see this—be a part of it. Plans for graduate school in D.C. took a backseat to my Fulbright application and re-immersion in every German class I could take and still finish my B.A. at Temple University.

A year later, I received notice of my acceptance as a Fulbright Scholar in the U.S. Young Journalist program. I was on my way to see the renaissance myself! Certainly my academic topic for the year was a bit of a downer compared to his uplifting speech—I proposed to study and write on the anti-Semitic content of commentary sections of German newspapers, especially articles regarding Israel. I had become a bit addicted to reading the hate every time an article appeared about Israel online—not just from trolls but from left and right-leaning mainstream sources as well. As I brought the idea of working on this in Germany to my journalism advisor, she said it was brilliant, suggested I add either kosher slaughtering or circumcision to the theme, and signed my reference form.

I couldn't wait. I had done Birthright and had spent a MASA summer in Israel and had flown through Frankfurt, Amsterdam and Paris to see the Holy Land. I had traveled to Cape-Town and Buenos Aires with my parents and naturally visited Cancun and Toronto a half-dozen times each. But now I had earned a year in Germany. By myself. I visualized a year of tall bespectacled German boys not to mention charming, intelligent and engaging new friends from all over the world, groups of students talking seriously about world politics over a Warsteiner pilsner and hand-rolled cigarettes, weekends in Munich or Berlin or even Paris and Amsterdam, taking my above-average German to fluency, being completely fulfilled in my great European adventure, adult and independent!

And of course, I wanted to see this Jewish Renaissance for myself. More than that, I wanted to see it as a Jew. Something about this felt personal.

I guess you could call me religious. In Israel, I liked to introduce myself as a "Reform Super Jew" just for the shock factor. I have really only known one *shul* my entire life: my cozy suburban synagogue with a few hundred members and enough rich ones to keep the building in repair and the prayer books new. We had guitars and drums, a violin and a clarinet on Friday nights and non-lay-led services on Saturday only with a *bat* or *bar mitzvah* or a holiday. I have known exactly two rabbis in my life—the old Rabbi Applebaum of my childhood—clean shaven, cherubic round face, penetrating blue eyes and a counter-tenor voice that made every eye tear up for *Kol Nidre*. Then came the young firebrand, Rabbi Theresa. First job out of school, four foot

7

eleven, premature gray curls and bringing to shul every week a lovely slightly older Jewish lady named Irene: her life partner. No wonder that my *bat mitzvah* sermon, written somewhat worshipfully under her influence, was called "The Forgotten Women of Torah."

Certainly as an "out" Jew I always got "those looks." My features are those of my anonymous biological parents in China. Regardless of what my psychologist says, I don't think I have any negative feelings toward the family and culture that abandoned me amid the failed extremes of the "one child" policy of the late '80s. I have no memory of a parent other than the father and mother that brought me out of the Hunan Province. My birth-parents' lust for a son or negligence or whatever it was gave me David, Gail, an Anglo name that doesn't suck, a suburban Philly accent and a love of, nay, fanatical passion for baseball. Oh yeah, and my predilection to swear like a South Philly shipyard worker when annoyed. *Mom loves that.* It also gave me my religion, made kosher when my dad brought his recently rescued one-year-old to the *mikveh* to breathe in my face and then briefly let me float free in the water as I became adopted into both his family and the family of Abraham and Sarah. To the Andrea-identity I then could add *Devorah bat David v'Sarah* as my new inheritance. I truly do not have abandonment trauma. I love my life.

I later learned that my mother had stood outside the *mikveh* room, loving her daughter as always in her "I refuse to treat a child as anything but a person" manner, but with her actions, as my father loved to retell, clearly showing her distain for his "primitive" ritual. Had I been a boy I am not sure she would have allowed a circumcision. So, well, thank God for that. She grew up Catholic and ran to the Church of Academia as soon as she could escape my dogmatically Arch-Catholic grand-parents.

She tolerated my Friday evenings with Daddy and would even on occasion come along, somehow knowing the words and melody to every song. She cried at my *bat mitzvah* and then even harder at my confirmation at age sixteen when I led services myself. From my mother, I got my love of books and empowerment—perhaps even my sense of entitlement, if I am going to be overly honest. From my father, I found my soul-level identity, even if it was only recognized by other American Reform Jews and if it caused me to deliver at least once a month my "why I am a real Jew" elevator speech when well-meaning East-Coast *Bubbies* and *Zaydes* would look at my eyes, skin and hair and judge.

When I set off for my year in Jewish Germany I was ready to give my elevator speech and to struggle my first few months with my communication and comprehension. What I was not ready for was that German was the least of my worries, as I spoke it better than 99% of the Jewish community. What I was not ready for was that there was no homogenous "Russian-Jewish Culture," among the immigrants of the '90s—that instead there were factions sitting apart even on the Sabbath that hated each other. I mean hated. The Russians hated the Ukrainians and the Ukrainians hated the Moldovans and the Moldovans hated the Armenians and Georgians and everyone hated the Azerbaijanis and Kazakhstanis and Kyrgyzstanis, as they all had darker skin and the wrong accent when speaking the holy Jewish language: Russian. What I was not ready for was a rabbi who inspired me and was run out of town because of the threat he represented to both old German status-quo and new Russian hegemony. What I was not ready for were the fights and death threats in community meetings, the men talking, eating, drinking, using spray deodorant and then even shouting each other down in Yom Kippur services in the Synagogue with an open Torah Ark and the rabbi singing *Unatane Tokev.*

What I was not ready for was being met with bullet-proof glass and Russian and Ukrainian Jewish security guards that looked at my eyes, skin and hair, pointed toward the street and in horribly broken German said, *"Geh weg. Du bist keine Jüdin. Komm nie wieder zurück."* Go away. You are not a Jew. Don't ever come back

The University

If my first foray into a relationship with a synagogue had failed, surely my university program would embrace my scholarship and my obvious willingness to succeed. Fulbright scholar, valedictorian, full academic scholarship as a National Merit Scholar and Magna Cum Laude at Temple University—I had it made. They would see all of this and I would be a star.

First day of first class: Ethics and Journalism. The professor had written his name on the chalk board. Chalk board! Prof. Dr. Dr. h.c. Stephan Weissman. Ninety minutes of a frontal lecture. No discussion. The class knocked their knuckles against the desks in a sort of applause when the lecture had ended and we were all given a literature list with thirty-five separate entries—all German academic sources, of course. The prof was devastatingly handsome in a Daddy-issue sort of way, but as dry as aunt Elana's challah. This man was to be my Fulbright advisor.

I walked up to him after the lecture–big smile and every focus and intention of getting quickly on the inside of this man's "In" list for my year. In my best German I approached him with, "Dr. Weissman, I am Andrea Lewy, I . . ."

"Excuse me please. I am Professor Doctor Weissman. This is not America."

Two seconds and I blew it. I sweat only after thirty strong minutes jogging or when my foot is crammed down my throat.

Through the heat and dampness I swallowed as the Herr Professor Doctor stared at me with what must have been suppressed glee. *A lovely light frühstück. Jawohl!*

"I am very sorry," I swallowed. "I just got here and I . . ."

"Obviously, Frau Lewy. What can I do for you?"

"I . . ." I cleared my throat, feeling two-years-old and wishing I could crawl away. "Herr Professor Doctor Weissman. I received, um, I was told that you . . . " I *"duzed"* him without thinking, using the informal *"Du"* as opposed to the correct formal *"Sie,"* especially correct as Herr Professor Doctor wished to be known as Herr Professor Doctor and not merely Dr. Weissman. Certainly a *"Du"* would not be appreciated. His hidden glee deepened, I think, as I quickly corrected, *"Sie."* "I was told that you," *Sie,* "were to be my Fulbright project advisor and that I needed to set up an appointment with you to get approval for my project." In German, this was an incredibly complex sentence that I had been practicing in the mirror for days. But without the sweat pouring down my head. *Damn.*

"Yes of course," he replied. "You will notice that my official email and office hours are written on your reading list. I will look forward to seeing you during the correct office hours. *Auf Wiedersehen*, Frau Lewy."

Well, at least Germans pronounce my last name correctly, I thought, quickly follow by *shit shit shit shit shit.*

Two days later at exactly 14:25 I braved Herr Professor Doctor's office, properly obsequious, tail neatly tucked, cuteness subdued, and tried to resurrect my academic year.

"Yes, let's see." He decided this time not to dignify my German and instead spoke with me in nearly flawless, barely accented Queen's English. At least I would not mess up with *"Du"* and *"Sie."* "'Anonymous Hate in Germany: Anti-Semitic Discourse in Internet Talk-Back.' First of all, the title is atrocious. This sounds like a bad blog-post for the *Bildzeitung.* Except for the word 'discourse;' they would never use this."

He read the abstract silently—eyes unblinking behind the wire glasses, then lightly tossed the papers on the desk

"Yes. This will not work, Frau Lewy."

12

I swallowed. Nothing came out. The abstract and summary represented weeks of work and had been met with near cheers by my professors in Philly.

"Do you have any other ideas?"

I shook my head, wondering if tearing up a little might lead to compassion. At this moment, I wouldn't have to try hard. I wasn't even sure, however, that Herr Professor Doctor would understand human emotions.

"So why this subject anyway? You are one of these American Philo-Semites? We already have enough of them in Germany."

"No," I heard my voice reply with the correct tones for beginning my elevator speech. "I am Jewish."

Eyes. Skin. Hair. He made some sort of untranslatable noise in the back of his sinuses.

"Yes, well, maybe this is interesting material in the United States. But Germans are a little tired of this. Every time we listen to a Jew speaking in an interview, he is reminding us of why we need to hate ourselves and why we should open our pockets and buy him a new building. And now as well he tells us why we should allow his barbaric laws to mutilate children in an enlightened society. I think you need to rethink your project, Frau Lewy."

Yet more fantasies crumbled. This very reasonable looking man—albeit with no social skills—sat across from me without blinking or a single ironic twitch of the mouth and uttered what could only be a clear indication of this man's disdain for my people and religion. Had he only said this because my eyes, skin and hair did not *look* particularly Jewish? Then this was ok? Would he have said the same if Shlomo Goldstein had sat across from him with round glasses, a yarmulke and Hitler's fantasy of a Jew-nose?

I had originally meant to focus on articles about Israel in electronic media. Europe's popular disdain for the Jewish State had already been well documented, including the fascinating development in recent years where left-wing voices had historically joined the tone of right-wing rhetoric in extreme emotional and at least in my opinion disproportionate critique against Israel. Certainly I am no *Likkud* fan—never have been. I would also like to believe that my opinions of Israel are reasoned, educated and fair. I simply do not think one can make judgments based on such complexity with the information contained in headlines.

So for months I had already been sitting behind my laptop, combing *die Zeit, die Welt, Frankfurter Allgemeine, Spiegel* Online and anything else I could think to bookmark to look for articles about Israel with an open forum for readers after an article. For months I had been reading, translating, copying and categorizing my research into a spreadsheet. "Right-Wing Hate." "Left-Wing Hate." "Islamist Extremism Hate." Even "Jewish Self-Hate" had started gathering steam as the comments piled on. I had collected name of article, article summary, author, source, hyperlink—anything I could think to give me instant collated data to write my brilliant project as soon as I hit the ground—as soon as I got permission from my project advisor.

Then a few months before I arrived, a circumcision "scandal" hit the newspapers and then the radio, television and internet airways of Germany. The great irony of the whole thing, though, was that the event that began the hysteria had been a Muslim event and had nothing to do with the German-Jewish community.

As I understand the story, a mother in Cologne had had her three or four-year-old son circumcised. After being instructed to not remove and change the bandages for twenty-four hours, upon returning home the mother promptly inspected the wound and the boy immediately began bleeding. She returned with the son and the man that had performed the circumcision once more wrapped the wound and once more gave a warning, this time assuredly much more stern, that I imagine went something like: "I warned you so please listen to what I tell you and do not do this again."

Once again the mother removed the bandage immediately at home and once again the boy bled. The mother once again left her house with her son, but this time went to a hospital where a good and helpful German doctor called the police to report child-endangerment. Of course it was not the mother that was charged with the endangerment.

Somehow, although not entirely surprising, the mess landed at the feet of the collective Jewish communities who then had to defend legally and in the media their very different circumcision practice. *Mohels* began living under the very real threat of arrest, and until the Parliament stepped in there was true fear in the Jewish community that they would once again be beginning a massive emigration in order to find a land that would allow ritual circumcision.

As the articles started piling up, the vehemence and vitriol of the discourse shocked even me. After months of reading the aggression against Israel, I thought I was prepared for anything. Now I began to question if I should rethink my plans or if it was about to get too scary. Ok, honestly it wasn't ever a serious question of whether I would still go. As an aspiring journalist, the controversy as well as the work and research exhilarated me. I was ready. But Herr Professor Doctor sat across from me, still unblinking.

"I have really done so much work on this already," I pleaded. No, tears would not be difficult at all here. "Isn't there

15

any way that we can work on the title and maybe the content to find something that could save this?"

He stared silently, then, "No."

Nein!

The first tears started squeezing their way out. I definitely had decided against them, but they were making their own decisions.

"Listen, Frau Lewy." He leaned back and crossed his arms, looking somewhat humane and less . . . German . . . for the first time. "Instead of focusing on the evil Germans, why don't you look at your own community?"

"I am not sure what you mean."

"I mean there is enough drama in Jewish communities in Germany to fill many projects—and I promise you no one has written this yet. Go to the local *Gemeinde* and write about them."

Now the damned tears came freely. I nearly whispered, "But, em, I already tried to go and they wouldn't even let me in."

He laughed.

That son-of-a-bitch smarmy superior likely-to-be-anti-Semitic ass actually laughed. Guffawed.

"Yes. You are not so very special. Everyone that tries to go to these synagogues in Germany is not allowed in. Unless they know you—or you speak the right dialect of Russian. Here." He opened a ridiculously well-organized portfolio and handed me a business card. "The Rabbi there is American. Good man. He lectures here every month at the Uni. Call him, I am sure there will be no problem."

16

The Rabbi

Entering the synagogue proved at least slightly easier with a rabbinical blessing. Slightly. The next Monday, with a shiny new German mobile in my shaking palm, it took me several tries to get past the Russian receptionist who answered the phone and seemed to understand no German. On the third call, seriously the third freaking call, I finally repeated "*Rabbiner*," the German word for "rabbi," enough times to stave off another disconnection and, yay, get the sounds of a line transfer. I pondered while waiting how in brief days this synagogue had transformed and now appeared in my imagination as a walled fortress with be-accented soldiers hurling insults from on high guard towers as I pleaded for sanctuary. Maybe I am naïve, but aren't religious communities supposed to be welcoming and all that?

"Isaac Newmark."

"Hello, Rabbi?"

"Yes, speaking."

"Uh, hi." I swear to God that I never "um"ed this much in my entire life. Deep breath. No problems. This guy is American. Everything is fine.

"My name is Andrea Lewy." I slightly accented the last name. Normally I would assume that a dropped Lewy or Levi or Cohen or Katz or freaking Goldstein would be enough to stop any other need to explain or defend my Jewishness—at least until someone looked at me. But after two weeks in Germany and a bit of trauma, a quiet acidic rumbling in the deep of my

17

stomach warned me that nothing here was to be self-evident. Hence, "Lewy" got a bit of a shove from behind to the forefront. *Freaking Lewy, man, kosher in yo' face!*

I continued after the silence that followed my own silent pause and offered bona fides, "I am an American student on a Fulbright year here in the University."

"Welcome to Germany, Ms. Lewy. What can I do for you?" His voice sounded kind, but perhaps the kind of "kind" that is acted by a good actor. There was a hint of "you disturbed Great Rabbinical Thoughts" tiredness behind the gentle words.

I didn't want to make the same mistakes with this man as with the Herr Professor Doctor, but I knew nothing about him. How long had he served here? Why would he choose what must be the greater challenges of Germany over the hordes of communities in the States? Was he a bad rabbi who could find no work elsewhere? Or maybe he was some sort of non-Chabad Jewish missionary do-gooder with a secret passion for *bratwurst* and *hefeweizen*. Shit, maybe he was Chabad. Sure, he was American. His accent sounded somehow vaguely Midwestern, but he pronounced letters such as "r"s and "l"s and bit more European. Had he gone native? Was he still one of us?

I settled on the risk of assuming "American" and "not-Chabad." "Rabbi Newmark, I am really sorry to interrupt. I am sure you are very busy. I have only been here a few weeks, but I wanted to introduce myself. And, um, well maybe somewhat coincidentally I am writing my Fulbright project on Jewish communities in Germany." Now I am, anyway.

"Please call me Rabbi Isaac." He replied with a light chuckle. This was nothing of the *schadenfreude*-infused guffaw of the Herr Professor Doctor, rather a gentle, conspiratorial laugh. "Well, once again, welcome. Andrea. I am going to call you Andrea as there is way too much formality in this country and I avoid it when possible for sanity's sake. So please, Rabbi Isaac and Andrea, if that is ok with you."

"Sure," I answered not knowing what else to say. This certainly was a lot better than my reception at the university, but this style of conversation also seemed not really what I was used to in Philly or even my posh 'Burb. Maybe it was the mid-west thing?

"So you will come to *shul* here then, naturally." Not a question, a simple statement of fact. Yeah, he was an American rabbi.

"Um, sure, but—you see—that's the problem. I tried two weeks ago but the guy out front wouldn't let me in."

I heard a grunt that sounded a bit like "shit!" before Rabbi Isaac continued, this time with a very different voice. Annoyance? Bridled fury? "I am truly sorry about that. It's a bit of a crap shoot everywhere in Germany. Well, at least you got ahold of me. Do you have an email address and a *handy* number?" *Handy.* German word for mobile phone. Still took me a few seconds even if I had it in my head moments earlier. Hell, the words that *sounded* English were by far the worst. You should have heard the thoughts in my head the first time I heard a conversation about "oldtimers," before discovering this to be the German word for classic cars. Hilarious.

"Sure," I replied.

"Ok. Good. I am going to give you mine, and please send your contact information." He gave and then repeated his personal information then continued. "Ok—I will put your name on The List." I swear he capitalized the words with his voice. "But that is still no guarantee. If you get here and they don't let you in, then call my *handy* and I will come out to security. But that means you have to get here early for each service. I can't

19

help you after service has started. And even getting in once is no guarantee that that will work a second time."

Seriously, that had to be a joke. But still. . .

"*Kabbalat Shabbat* starts at 18:30 every week and *Shacharit* 9:30. You should probably be warned, though, that there is separate seating."

No I *didn't* know that. I mean, I hadn't even thought about that. I hated separate seating, which was one of the main reasons I declined most Chabad invitations during my time at Temple University and usually only went when travelling and had few other options. But, really, I just hadn't thought it through. In typical Andrea-the-idiot mode I blurted, "You're Orthodox?"

This time his laughter came through the cell connection as robust and un-bridled. "No, Andrea, I am Masorti—you are used to calling it "Conservative" in the States. But," he paused and drew out the poignancy of the word, "But the *Gemeinde* is 'Traditional' or at least considers itself so, even though I am probably the most *frum* of the bunch. You say you are going to write your Fulbright on communities in Germany? I think maybe you should pop by so that I can give you an emergency jump-start into the subject. Can you come by this week on Wednesday?" Which is how I found myself two days later in Rabbi Isaac's ridiculously cramped and cluttered office.

It had taken what felt like an hour to convince the, this time, female security guard to phone the rabbi when he came out on his own and waved her to open the gate.

Although he didn't look archetypically the rabbi, I had web-stalked the man after our phone conversation and found more than enough photos, articles and even an outdated online CV to have the social leg-up. Rabbi Isaac moved slowly, leaning heavily on the black cane in his left hand that immediately belied his CV-deduced forty-seven years. He wore American blue-jeans, what looked like an authentic Toronto Maple Leafs sweater and a thick-knitted black kippah on his thinning, salt-and-pepper hair. His face looked a bit like a man who had been destined to be gaunt and then had simply ate and drank beyond his genetic disposition, leaving rounded cheeks with a slight blush barely covered by a trimmed but patchy beard. He nodded at me quickly and wordlessly, his artic blue eyes behind round, gold wire glasses effortlessly seeming to lay bare in less than a second every secret that I had ever kept before turning to the guard.

He spoke a few words in what sounded to my ears like very good Russian to the woman. I mean, I use this term "woman" somewhat loosely but between envy and fear. At about exactly my 5'4" the guard looked somehow simultaneously like a short supermodel and someone who ate rusted metal for breakfast. "Valentina" I vaguely heard the rabbi call her then as well heard "Andrea Lewy" added to the Slavic mix, although my family name had become something like "Leh-vee-yoo." He then shook her hand with a *"bolshaiya spasiba"* and with a light touch on my shoulder invited me to cross the threshold into the stone courtyard. Almost as an afterthought, Valentina grunted at my backpack forcing the rabbi into a new confrontation that seemed to barely end with his victory and my right to keep my bag with my laptop and notebooks and all else that seemed appropriate for a meeting with a source in both my Jewish and Fulbright journeys.

Allowing me to possessively clutch my sanctified backpack, Rabbi Isaac at last somewhat apologetically offered his hand, proving his non-orthodoxy with a firm grasp and direct look in my eyes as he spoke the perfunctory "Nice to meet you." He half shrugged and hinted at an at an eye-roll back toward the security booth, seeming to either agree with my own churning emotions

21

or possibly allowing me into his own private windmill jousting. He spoke quickly and quietly in English gesturing with his head to include the greater building in his comments: "I would like to also take you on a bit of a tour of the building, but it will be better when there are less people in the building. Do you mind if we just head up to my office now to chat and see the synagogue later?"

I hadn't even realized that a tour had been on the docket, but now that I was "in" I was indeed curious, so I smiled my agreement and followed the rabbi as he turned and leaned on his cane.

Past security, a stone path with the building on the right and tall barbed-wire-topped concrete wall on the left led along non-comforting shrubberies and a distinctly non-synagogue atmosphere. It looked like someone missed a few bits of wall that had supposedly been torn down in this country.

As we reached a corner, the path turned right then led up a surprisingly long series of steps—with no accessible ramp in sight—to a jutting out entry way guarded by 10-foot tall weathered oak doors. Instead of attacking what must have been the tomb-like heaviness of the oak, the rabbi flipped open a cover to access a security keyboard and pushed open a much smaller metal security door off to the side. The sense of entering a medieval fortress rather than a shul just kept getting stronger.

Hating the silence, I tried to search for a little conversation for the journey. "Thank you for meeting with me today, Rabbi."

Without deviating from his path, he answered, "*Kol Yisrael arevim zeh lazeh.*"

I am not sure what it was about his tone but I stopped on the threshold. "What? I mean, what does that mean?"

"All of the people of Israel are equally responsible for each other. It means it is never about me, it is always about us. You

22

called, I made an appointment. It's that simple." He shrugged and we moved through the door.

At least the inside felt a bit more familiar. The security door led to a two-story vaulted foyer with the requisite children's arts and crafts—that is to say finger painting and bean-murals of menorahs, Pesach plates, various Chanukah symbols and other faded attempts to engage Jewish children in holidays-gone-by. Picture windows led to a walled courtyard that held the being-dismantled shell of a *sukkah* from the Sukkot holiday that I had just missed when the guards wouldn't let me in the previous week. That thought aside, the *sukkah* looked like it had probably been impressive, and beyond that the courtyard showed enough well-cared-for greenery to suggest a full time gardener or perhaps grounds keeper in addition to a community that could build a decent booth. Maybe everything wasn't that horrible after you finally got in.

I began walking forward automatically toward a glass door labeled "VERWALTUNG"–administration. In front, like a refugee intake office, sat an industrial row of stained chairs filled by mostly men speaking with each other at the average level of a shout and a few women aged between late sixties and late eighties looking like they were trying to ignore the men. Rabbi Isaac lightly touched my shoulder again and re-directed me from the scene toward a narrow stairway to the left, opposite the courtyard. "They put me in the attic, rather than give me the prime real estate in the *Verwaltung*." His voice *sounded* mild and joking. "Believe me," he continued, "it's a blessing.'

I followed the rabbi and the rhythmic click of his cane torturously slowly up two flights, past a couple twists and turns with at least three separate heavy fire doors, to a dead-end hallway with a slightly ajar door at the end emanating distinct sandal-wood incense. He gestured me inside and then closed the door completely, something that would never happen in the States. Maybe there was no problem with clergy and "improper touching" here. Maybe I should be nervous? Nothing felt off—just . . . different. I decided to settle on "cautious optimism," relaxed slightly and slid into the offered chair.

Without asking, Rabbi Isaac had placed a few tall glasses on the desk, rummaged in what looked like my own dorm fridge collecting dust now in my parents' crawl space, pulled out a green-tinted bottle of mineral water and poured us each a glass.

"I hope you don't mind the incense," he gestured at the small carved-stone egg emitting the admittedly pleasant smell. There was a large window tipped open from the bottom into what must have been the inner courtyard. The slight ventilation and the decent quality of incense seemed fine for me. I shrugged my indifferent acquiescence. He continued, "There is a slight smell of burnt wiring in here that I can never seem to get rid of. Incense helps."

I was still, truth be told, somewhat lost in the labyrinth we had traveled from the front gates to the end of the dark hallway.

"What was going on downstairs?" I blurted out absently, only belatedly realizing that I probably sounded a bit rude. "Sorry," I amended, modulating my voice further away from the sound of "paranoid, semi-hysterical college girl" that echoed inside my own head. "I mean, all the people shouting outside the office downstairs when we came in."

Rabbi Isaac blinked several times, staring at me without comprehension, and then fully settled into his own chair, lightly chuckling. "They weren't yelling, my dear." He took a long draught of his water and wiped his brow with what looked like a black biker hand kerchief. He leaned his cane behind his desk against the bottom of a massive white-board with half-erased Hebrew scribbles that I could barely make out. "That is part of

24

why you are here today. That was not yelling, that was Jewish culture in Germany."

He saw my expression and smiled. "I am not really trying to shock you. OK, never mind. I am. Let's start with you, though. I will know a lot better how I can help you if I know a little bit about where you are coming from, what brought you to Germany, what your Fulbright topic is and whatnot. Then I can explain what you saw downstairs."

"Well," I opened my mouth to begin, half expecting the omnipresent "um"s of the last week, and instead found myself recounting—somehow—my entire life story. I mean seriously. Non-remembered adoption through *mikveh* through earliest awareness through childhood and Hebrew School and *bat mitzvah*. He nodded at the right places and showed the appropriate looks of concern. He laughed at my humorous observations of the American education system and looked dutifully saddened by the death of a grandparent here or there. Was it genuine interest? My cynicism asks whether Shlomo Goldstein would as well get the same interest. And time!

Ninety minutes into the soliloquy I had finally reached Temple and Fulbright and then Herr Professor Doctor (to which Rabbi Isaac echoed Herr Professor Doctor's guffaw and quickly asked "Stephan Weissman?")

Indeed.

But seriously—ninety minutes and quickly moving in on two hours and I couldn't shut my mouth. Hopes, fears and silly aspirations. Who was this guy? I took a deep breath, reached for my own flattening fizzy water and downed the glass in one try. Maybe it was the ridiculous bald spot in his patchy beard on his left cheek that had so mesmerized me. Dammit. Rabbi Isaac promptly refilled both of our glasses, and only upon it being perfectly clear that I was boycotting his inquisitor's abilities to

25

draw out a single additional response, I was done. Except there really wasn't much left to tell. Boyfriends? Nope, he hadn't got that one from me. Too much vodka experimentation in Safed in the hostel room with Miriam-from-Manhattan after a lively women's *Kabbalat Shabbat*? Still mine!

His eyes and facial expression, however, betrayed neither glee nor victory. Instead he voiced his gratitude, as if I had just given him a gift.

"So now you are here. And probably really stressed at having just realized that nothing here is at all what you expected." He nodded my own answer for me. "Good, at least we got that out of the way early. It would have been much harder to deal with your disillusionment in several months. Now you actually have a chance of a meaningful experience, not just a hurtful one."

"So what's wrong here then?" I asked. "Everyone says that there is a renaissance going on here."

"Sure," he answered, "look at this." He opened up a file folder of newspaper clips and showed me one from *Die Zeit*, slightly yellowing and marked as 2006. *"Das Wunder von Potsdam"*—The Miracle from Potsdam. "This one was from the first rabbinical ordination in Germany since the Shoah. This is the one that got me here." He pulled out another, this time a full broad-sheet rather than a clipped front page. *"Kein besseres Land für Juden."*–No better place for Jews. This one had a picture on the cover of a younger rabbi, dressed well but clearly not orthodox, bathed in sun as a vision of a messianic figure to lead this dream. Or maybe the picture was meant for Germans instead of Jews—"Here is the Jew that will help you to no longer have to remember the crimes of your grandparents. Follow him as he helps you forget and tells you everything will be just fine!"

26

"It's all crap," Rabbi Isaac interjected. "You should see the ones that I am quoted in." He waved his hands in the air as if invoking some mystical newspaper from which to read, and then did the most spot-on German accent I have ever heard.

"U.S. Amerikaner Rabbi Isaac Newmark from Minneapolis, Bundesstate Minnesota left his position as Professor of Chassidic Studies at the University of Minnesota to lead one of the largest congregations in Germany. He also read the headlines and thought that he could change the world in a place where the healing of old wounds could become a visible reality and inspire the world with such aspirations." He dropped his arms and let his voice settle back into his own tones. "Unfortunately Rabbi Isaac hasn't changed much of anything." He took a sip of his water and settled back into his chair. "Do you know what a 'paid minyan' is, Andrea?"

"A what?"

"A paid minyan. I guess not. You're from a Philadelphia Reform community. No reason for you to know.

"When I first got here, out of the sixteen hundred some members we averaged about twelve men for each service and three or four women. Of course I also came from an American background, and even though I had read about paid *minyanim*, it never occurred to me that ten to twelve of the men that were there—meaning basically all of them—were paid a stipend in addition to a transit pass to show up for every Shabbos and holiday service."

I felt my eyes growing ridiculously wide. "You're kidding."

"I know, great, huh? It's true, though. Once I figured out what was going on, it was the first thing that I tried to change. There was this aggression at the beginning that I was just not getting. I mean . . . there is still aggression, but there was something specific at the beginning that I was just missing.

27

Turns out that the executive board of the community, made up mostly of non-Russian speakers, would regularly threaten these men—I mean yell at them in public and humiliate them—if they missed a service or didn't stay to the end of *Kiddush*. Worse, there are a few guys—you'll meet them—I am not telling you who they are as that really is *lashon hora*, but you'll figure it out. Anyway, there are a few of them that would take attendance—good Soviet behavior I suppose—and then report back. Created a bit of resentment, you could say. So the first thing that I really tried to change was to not require attendance. I told the board 'If you want to give them money as *tzedakah* then go ahead, but I don't want anyone forced to come to services or even feel like they are forced.'"

My head spun. I mean obviously I understood the meaning of the words, but in the two minutes that the rabbi had taken over for Andrea-the-garrulous it sounded like he was speaking a completely foreign language. Nothing that he had said made any sense whatsoever within the Jewish world that I knew.

He continued, "Typical American. I figured that I would rather not have a *minyan* and have a limited service that was made of people that wanted to be there than have a *minyan* of people that had been, essentially, coerced. I tried to explain many times that I wasn't keeping attendance, even in Russian as my Russian got better, but I don't think anyone really believed me."

"But did it get any better?" I asked, wondering more and more anxiously by the second what I was walking into when or if I was finally able to come to Shabbat services.

Rabbi answered with a shrug and a non-committal "eh."

"Most still show up when they can. Some actually like praying. Some are truly afraid of not being here. Some indeed come just for the vodka." He must have seen my look as he

28

grinned and added, "Seriously, Andrea, you really don't have any idea what you've gotten yourself into."

Going to Shul

I have to say that my anticipation of attending my first Shabbat service in Germany was a bit like the dread of shutting down my dad's old gas lawnmower. This analogy makes sense in the end—just humor me. Dad fancied himself a bit of a handyman, something that I am sure came much more from his father than his own more bookish nature as an engineering professor rather than, well, an actual engineer who makes things. This family curse, however, led him to tinkering with and maintaining old relics of lawns-gone-by that my *Zadie's* voice, while alive or the echo after he passed, would not rise in objection: "Would that I had had money to buy new such things!"

I was never quite sure if the overly-Yiddish accent and affectations were due to the thirty-some years he lived in Germany before fleeing in 1937 or his desire to fit in with his perception of American Jewry. He talked like an extra on a Saturday Night Live sketch and when my Dad was truly pissed at his father his *Yekke*-Yiddish impersonation was spot on.

Clearly I am trying to avoid thinking about that first Shabbat. So . . . lawnmower. At some point someone invented this cool device attached to the handle of a lawnmower that when held tight would allow a full current to flow through the engine and when released would as well release the engine. Safety first, you know. Of course before these modern advances, Jewish families like my father's suffered collective survival guilt which manifested as preserving dinosaurs where the engine could only be shut down manually—literally—by touching a small metal tab to an exposed spark plug to cut the engine. With the bare hand. The idiot duped into following the faded directions "touch

30

spark plug with metal tab to stop engine" had about a seventy percent chance of a massive jolt. Somewhere around age 10 I developed the Nike method–using forethought to touch the toe of my old gym shoes to affect the desired outcome. This still resulted in a twenty percent chance of shock, which resulted in further innovation after *bat mitzvah* of removing my shoe first and touching the tab to the spark plug with the toe of the shoe while holding the leather flap at the heel of the shoe with thumb and forefinger. But as any good rat scientist will tell you, once that fear of shock is there you will still flinch every time you get near that spark plug, no matter how reliable your sneaker technique. The Beast finally died one sunny Swarthmore summer, forcing Dad to buy a shiny new red and black Toro Personal Pace 22 Inch Variable Speed Self-Propelled Lawn Mower with Electric Start and 50-State Engine, whatever the hell that means. To me it meant I would often come home and find that Dad had mowed the damn lawn himself before I returned from yearbook club or city youth orchestra practice or dance during the years I obsessed about ballet.

It also meant that I should have evaluated much earlier in my life how productive a little well-placed sabotage can be.

I still flinch though when I look at a lawnmower just as I found myself flinching as I walked toward the guard towers of the synagogue building at precisely 18:15 one crisp October German Friday evening for an 18:30 service. With Rabbi Isaac's number floating underneath my thumb on my *handy* I had taken his advice seriously and showed up early enough to holler for help should those in the guard towers decided to ignore or forget that I was on The List.

It was back to Guard Number One, he who had so sympathetically calculated the variables and pointed to the road the first time I had tried to visit. In my mind I had taken to

31

calling him the "Czar" as Rabbi Isaac had informed me later on in our as-it-turned-out-nearly three hours spent together that this man was the One to Rule Them All in the guard towers. Moreover, he was clearly the cause of my oppression as I only wanted to show up at a damn synagogue and bloody find some freakin' Shabbat Shalom.

This time he didn't even come out of the booth. The security door slid open as the Czar gave a miniscule nod from the other side of the window to wave me through. I was perversely a bit disappointed. I had been getting hopped up on expectations for the shock of the lawnmower for hours if not days and now I needed to find a way to get rid of the wasted adrenaline.

I passed the odd ambling senior as I now expertly wove my way past moat and palisade, striding with perfectly feigned confidence until the wall of gawking Old Russian Dudes arrested my progress meters from the entry to the *beit knesset*, forcing me to adjust my angle and enter the left door, thankfully unguarded.

I knew from Rabbi's tour that I could have chosen to avoid this manifestation of the *other* entirely by taking the stairs up to the balcony and joining what Rabbi Isaac sarcastically described as Charming Old Ladies. Instead I chose to brave the main floor where during my tour I had been shown the twenty-one seat walled-off women's section that Rabbi Isaac had forced several years earlier into existence.

The wall of men blocking the first door and still following my progress looked more like Hollywood central casting for "Russian Immigrants" than actual people with that history. The throw-back clothing looked more like Paul Mazursky's vision of thrift-store Soviet deprivation than surely what would be found in a real closet. Yet there it was. Barely remembering to grab a prayerbook from the bookshelf between the two entries, I continued forward and through the archway, determined to study the clothing again later.

The *beit knesset* itself—seriously I hate calling it by the Americanized moniker "sanctuary"—had a bit of a high-school auditorium feel. Two double doors in the foyer led into a rectangular room with three sections of seating—left, right and middle.

During my tour earlier in the week, Rabbi Isaac had regaled me with a mystical and numerological explanation of how the architect had incorporated the number of rows, seats and windows into some universally resonant *gestalt*. By that time I was already so overwhelmed I didn't hear much more than that the numbers "seven" and "three" have particular significance and that Rabbi Isaac became childishly exuberant when he entered teaching mode. Not that there was anything wrong with it—quite the contrary I found myself, staring at the *beit knesset* now, wishing that I had paid closer attention.

Awareness of some sort of atmospheric shift in the room broke my zoned-out reverie. Sometime in the last five or five-hundred seconds much of the sound had dimmed as I had, in my moments of Kabbalistic-architectural contemplation, become the center of a distinctly voyeuristic piece of performance art.

From age seventy to ninety-five, the Old Russian Dudes left their various conversation-slash-arguments and entered into the great new sport of Andrea-gazing. I mean I am accustomed to this in Jewish circles, but for the most part I only had to deal with or ignore the surreptitious stares of disapproval from those that saw the tribal part of my tradition as one of primacy over the religious. Eyes, skin, hair. But this was different. My memory has reactions ranging from the collective licking of lips to several of the oldest ones collapsing in sudden heart pain.

Actually, I am pretty sure none of that really happened.

I am also sure, however, that I had never felt as naked in my life. That I was Jewish to my core meant nothing in this moment. My context in that collective licking of lips was solely that of a slightly-more-than-cute twenty-something Chinese girl in a black supposed-to-be-modest dress that I suddenly realized clung way too convincingly to hips that were beginning to look more like they came from Philly than Changsha, Hunan Province.

It seems I was saved by one of the gawkers, the only gentleman present dressed in a suit who came up and, shockingly, offered his hand and said with the voice of a Yiddish angel, "*Eyne gitte Shabbos!*"

"Shabbat Shalom," I offered back, maneuvering my positon to place this man's substantial frame between me and the still intake-ing-of-breath among the rest. "English?" he offered slowly in a nearly non-comprehensible accent. I assumed he was asking language and not nationality and answered back, "*Ich kann deutsch sprechen,*" I can speak German.

"Ah, *sehr gut,*" he answered back, the three words spoken in such a way to make clear that he assumed he spoke German well although the opposite most likely was the case. "*Ich bin,*" he tapped his free hand against his chest Neanderthal-communication style, still clutching my hand in his other. "*Ich bin Herr Adler.*"

"Andrea," I smiled back as convincingly as possible and wondered what it would take to pull my hand away without too much of a violent yank. "Shabbat Shalom," I repeated again like an idiot, not knowing how to continue this conversation. He smiled somehow simultaneously gently and possessively and continued in his broken German, "You are from?"

"America," I finished for him.

"Ah yes, America." He nodded with wisdom, gazing off into some unseen sunset of wealth and skyscrapers. "New York," he continued, the mere name of the city somehow clearly demonstrating his wisdom and familiarity with all things American.

As I began trying to think of both how to continue and escape from this conversation, he helpfully decided to explain my place in the greater Universe of his synagogue. "Women sit over there," he said in what sounded like German, but I was beginning to think he was mixing Yiddish and German. By now some percentage of the previous level of noise had resumed, so I began a game of what I hoped was subtle hand twisting meant to extricate my fingers from Herr Adler's still clasping grip. Yet he wasn't quite done with me.

"It is your first time here?" The question was code for, "Have you ever been in any synagogue in your life?" or even the more likely "What is a nice Asian girl like you doing in a place like this."

My fingers finally wiggling free, I decided to try at least to begin establishing my credibility with, in my best German, "It is my first time here, but I must admit that it is quite different than my own synagogue in the States."

Clever Andrea. Be an ass by showing how much better my German was than his while simultaneously saying "I am Jewish" without saying "I am Jewish." Problem is I don't think he understood a word. I started backing away with a somehow magically appearing bow as I offered another "Shabbat Shalom" and suddenly found my hand once again in his, this time being brought to his lips for a gentle kiss.

Not sure how to react, I giggled. I am pretty sure I blushed too, but no way I am going to admit that. "*Du bist hier sehr willkommen, Frau . . .*" You are very welcome here, Miss?

35

"Andrea," I reminded in a voice way too highly pitched. Belatedly I remembered my other bona fides and hastily added, "Lewy. Andrea Lewy."

Yet another kiss and blush and I somehow backed into one of the appropriate seats in the women's section, plopping down heavily right next to a woman maybe a couple years my senior, sitting there grinning at me unabashedly.

"You must be Andrea," she said and held out her hand. "Hi, I am Sabrina."

Looking gratefully at her and away from whatever was now happening with Herr Adler et. al., I belatedly realized she had spoken to me in clear English with a bit of a Marlene Dietrich sort of a German accent.

"I am," I answered, gratefully taking her hand and automatically adding, "Shabbat Shalom."

"Shabbat Shalom."

"How did you know. . .?" I kind of shrugged my shoulders and assumed she would figure out the rest.

"I had a meeting with Rabbi Isaac yesterday," she offered, "and he asked me to look out for you."

"That was. . . sweet," I answered searching for the right word yet with no hint of irony in my voice and no sarcasm in my soul. It *was* sweet. This already felt like a trip to the zoo much more than to *shul*. Thank God for anything, um, non-zoo-like.

The only problem was that now I needed to continue the friendliness.

This is the point where I must admit that I had been finding conversation difficult lately. What should I say now? Here is someone making an effort for whatever reason, it really doesn't matter, and somehow with age and some insane dawning self-consciousness it had been getting harder for me to engage in conversation with strangers. Super realization on a Fulbright

36

Year in which I am technically pretty much a diplomat for the U.S.A. But here I am next to a sweet woman speaking my own language, and now I am stuck.

Sabrina had black hair cut in a bob just about an inch longer than my own. She was a bit heavier than one was used to seeing here in Europe, especially among twenty-somethings, but she had a cute face in a pale Mediterranean sort of way and seriously smoky eyes so I instantly assumed some sort of Sephardic background. Her hand, still in mine, was warm and dry, the grip firm, and I nearly started weeping in the realization that in this moment I just wanted a girlfriend to hang-around with and to hell with all the stress of being a multi-kulti pioneer.

"Your English is great," I blurted out, settling on "everyone loves compliments" as my approach out of the myriad of other potential ejaculations ranging from "your eyes are *hot*" to "please, please, please be my friend!"

"Thank you," we dropped our hands and she smiled encouragingly. "I spent a year in the States in high school."

"Where at?" I asked curiously.

"Texas,"

"You've got to be fucking kidding me!" Seriously. I said that. No Philly prejudice in this innocent heart. I quickly looked around to see if anyone had begun approaching me to throw me out for my most un-Shabbos like statement. Seeing none I then quickly tried to read Sabrina, happily noting her chuckling rather than seeing a horrified response.

"We didn't have much choice. It was with AFS. I had asked for Montreal as I had studied French and had planned on doing a French *Abitur*. I also requested kosher. So of course, I ended up with a Southern Baptist family in Lubbock that loved barbequing pork ribs at least once a week."

37

My heart swelled. Her easy manner and the warmth in my body betrayed to me the releasing of a type of stress I had neither understood nor truly even acknowledged. But I loved this feeling—I guess I am going to call it "animation." I love this animation when you just kind of connect with someone. I mean, I had felt it also with Rabbi but it was different as there was no equality in that relationship. Just thinking about the levels of conversations in those few hours together still left me dizzy with the realization of the levels of my own personal ignorance regarding Judaism. But Sabrina. Thank you thank you thank you God!

Sabrina smiled and pointed at the *siddur*, the prayerbook, in my hands. "You might want to grab the German one, though, Andrea."

I looked down, not quite sure how I only now saw that among the usual prayerbook Hebrew characters appeared Cyrillic ones. Oops. I must have blushed more than the warmth in my cheeks indicated, as Sabrina was already standing up, grabbing my *siddur* and scooting past me without a pause, returning mere seconds later with an only mildly abused but very different looking prayer book with Hebrew and this time a clearly understandable *"Tefillat Amcha für Schabbat Kodesch:"* The Prayer of Your People for the Holy Shabbat.

I nodded and smiled my gratitude as the shift of the ignored din around me signified something moving through the throngs of Russians. I turned and saw Rabbi Isaac enter through the perhaps thirty people gathered like a crowd waiting for a politician to work a line. The men surprisingly looked genuinely happy to see him, greeting him with hearty handshakes, somehow unhindered by the cane clutched in the rabbi's left hand. I realized I was staring, and based on Rabbi's own words I just hadn't expected to see what seemed like a warm and genuine affection for the man.

Rabbi Isaac made his way down to the front of the hall, then worked his way back up to the ladies' section on the other side, eventually stopping in front of my row where he embraced Sabrina with a hearty Shabbat Shalom followed by most un-American kisses on either cheek. *"Alles in Ordnung?"* he asked her? She nodded and smiled, *"Baruch HaShem."* He smiled and turned to me.

"Shabbat Shalom, Andrea." I saw the working of his eyes as he ascertained which greeting to offer me—the friendly yet chaste and appropriate-for-Americans handshake from earlier in the week or the he-knows-pretty-much-everything-about-me appropriate European greeting. Seriously, it would just be awkward to be greeted differently than he had just welcomed Sabrina, so I leaned toward him with open arms and received the same seemingly appropriate European greeting that would probably get the man fired in half the congregations in the States. I would later find out that his greeting was also quite un-German and apparently reflected nothing more or less than how Rabbi Isaac greeted people. So much for my vast cultural knowledge.

"Welcome Andrea. Shabbat Shalom."

"Shabbat Shalom, Rabbi," I replied.

"You got in Ok tonight?" his head gestured slightly behind him, pointing to the Czar now thankfully far off in his guard tower.

"Yes thank you," I replied a bit stiffly.

If he had noticed, however, he gave no sign as he now worked the line in the women's section greeting the other eight-or-so that had by now gathered. As he then slowly worked his way back to the front I realized the service would soon be starting. Not wanting to lose the earlier animation with Sabrina, I was trying to figure out how to get contact info when she offered, "Do you want to come over for drinks after services? I don't live far from here."

I smiled my gratitude and acquiescence as Rabbi Isaac reached the front, threw a rumpled prayer shawl—a *tallis*—over his shoulders, stepped up to a narrow wooden pulpit facing away from the community and started singing a song without words. I was transported.

Rabbi Theresa couldn't sing. I mean seriously. She had a monstrous case of the tone-deaf-yet-loved-to-sing-along syndrome and it was the one blight on her otherwise stellar rabbinate. She relied on Bonnie, a guitar wielding cantorial-soloist to organize the other musicians and try to get the rather reticent east-coast jacket-and-tie Shabbat Jews to sing along with the latest opus that had probably been written for summer-camp rather than the more formal halls of a synagogue. But Rabbi Applebaum. Oh dear Rabbi Applebaum. What he lacked in the ability to relate one-on-one with anyone other than the, according to my father, seven-or-so rich donor families in the community he made up for with a voice straight from the *shtetl*. If you can imagine walking out into the town square of the most Anatevka-esque Disney fantasy of a *shtetl* and imagined the voice of perfect Yiddish loneliness in the middle of the night in that square, that's him.

Having picked up oboe in the 4th grade, the musical content of Judaism alone had begun pulling me to services each weekend more than just being a daughter that wanted to please her daddy.

But now the "Yai-dai-dais" of Rabbi's *niggun* nearly had me in tears as I both wanted to just listen and needed to learn the melody and sing with him. After a breathtaking peak accompanied by Rabbi banging the rhythm against the back of an empty row of chairs, the yai-dais's became words as his voice

40

now soared over even the loudly bellowing Herr Adler, leading me, the hapless elders and all others present through *Yedid Nefesh*. His voice, a clear tenor with only a hint of vibrato, not only hit each pitch perfectly and sung each word clearly, but somehow vibrated with a type of intentionality that, I must say, nearly made me envious. I didn't know how to pray like that.

But it didn't matter. I don't even have to exaggerate to make this story one worth telling. It was perfect. How could I have forgotten how much I love being at *shul*? What had I been doing the last few years?

Rabbi Isaac slowed his cadence to finish the melody then stepped up onto the raised *bima* and called out "Shabbat Shalom!"

"Shabbat Shalom," came the automatic response which included both my and Sabrina's smiling voices.

The rabbi continued in a deliberately clear, slow and punctuated German obviously meant to aid the comprehension of the mostly non-native German speakers. Hmm—I imagine that meant me too.

"No one here is ready for Shabbat."

That I had not expected. What kind of Rabbi says such a thing? I moved my eyes as far left as I could to gauge Sabrina's reaction, but she sat there with a smile and what I imagine a warm glow must look like so I decided to withhold judgment.

"I am not ready and you are not ready. But not only is that not a bad thing, it is completely expected—so much so that our Sages planned our Kabbalat Shabbat around this."

Ok, this was quite different from what I was used to, but it did seem as good an intro as any. At least I was paying attention. It even seemed that many of the Old Russian Dudes were paying attention as well.

41

Rabbi Isaac continued: "The reality is, right now we are still thinking about our week. If we just came from work we are still at work, if we are retired we are still more focused on that one struggle that is most in our minds this week. But it is ok. It is expected. It's is not even Shabbat yet. Before we accept Shabbat we have to first let go of the week, and that is exactly what our tradition allows us to do. The Friday evening service doesn't start with Shabbat—instead it starts with six Psalms, one for each day of the week leading up to Shabbat."

This was interesting. I had never really heard Shabbat described quite like this before. Come to think of it, I had to think hard in that moment to consider what would usually happen at a Friday evening service. I guess at my home *shul* we would have sung several songs to open the service and then pretty quickly get to the *Shema*. I am not sure we ever sang a Psalm for each day. Is that what they did at Chabad? Honestly I just couldn't remember and I felt a certain shame in that moment for not knowing. How could I have been to so many services and now I couldn't really say what went on there?

Rabbi continued: "Before each Psalm we are going to take a deep breath and then take a moment to think about that day. What happened that day that you are still holding on to? Is there someone that hurt you that day that you need to forgive? Is there someone that you hurt that you need to remember to call tonight and repair that relationship?"

He paused and seemed to stare down each person in the *shul* individually, including me. His eyes met and held mine and my memories flipped like playing cards being shuffled: The Czar, Valentina, Herr Professor Doctor. *Shit.* I didn't have to forgive Herr Professor Doctor did I?

"Deep breath, everyone. Now . . . Sunday."

42

He paused another five or so seconds and then stepped back down to the pulpit on the floor below the raised *bima* and once again began singing, his back to the congregation.

"Lechu neranena, neranena l'adonai . . ."

Some of the melodies I knew, some I didn't, but I tried to not only sing along with everything, but also to take the rabbi's suggestion seriously, breathe deep, and think about who I might have pissed off, needed to forgive, or some combination of the two.

"Shiru l'adonai, shir chadash . . ."

Funny thing was, it hit me after about Wednesday's deep breathing that I am not really sure how to forgive someone while sitting in the women's section, listening to rabbi and singing Psalms. Was I supposed to use this time to create mental stickies to go back to Valentina and say "I forgive you for being terrifying" or back to Herr Professor Doctor and forgive him for what, being German?

I was just going to have to find an opportunity to ask the rabbi about this. In the meantime . . . mental stickies.

At last we reached Friday and sang a vaguely middle-eastern sounding melody over the twenty-ninth Psalm, *"Mizmor l'David, Havu l'Adonai b'nei eilim . . ."* The melody proved easy to find my voice in and the assembled seemed to get into it as well, with Rabbi slowly driving the melody faster and at the end people were pounding their legs in rhythm while the rabbi beat a complex accompanying rhythm on the side of the wooden pulpit. The release at the end again felt, well, spiritual, as the congregation had been completely caught up in the unified vision. I had never before experienced this. And this rabbi thought that he was unsuccessful? This was awesome.

Into the echoing silence Rabbi turned back to the congregation and spoke quietly and firmly, a loud, carrying whisper easily heard by all but almost conspiratorial in tone. "Do you feel that?" Pause. "Did you hear that?" Pause. Once again his eyes made his way around the room, holding us each in his gaze. "Think now. Where were you when you came here tonight? How different did this room feel before we began? Now feel it. Now, we are ready for Shabbat!"

He turned back to his prayerbook and I barely noticed the *Lechah Dodi, Barchu,* and *Shema.* I clapped my hands absently to a familiar melody for the *Mi Chamochah* and stood when appropriate to pray the *Amida,* my eyes most likely glazed over as I should have been silently mouthing the Hebrew words.

What was happening? After the silent prayers everyone slowly sat. I did so as well but arbitrarily, without conscious volition. By the time Rabbi's voice once again joined the silence with a melody of *"Yih'yu l'ratzon"* I felt Sabrina's hand gently and kindly rubbing my back, obviously reactive to the unabashed tears streaming down my face.

"Are you OK?" She made her whisper convey appropriate concern.

I did my best to smile at her question and nod affirmatively, not trusting my voice.

Was I OK?

I didn't want to admit it, but homesickness had struck me hard. I was in a foreign culture inside a foreign culture with no friends, messed up expectations and no desire to admit I missed my mommy and daddy although I did. And then there was the University where I had assumed I would bathe in instant stardom. But what if I was really like the actor who wins the Oscar too early in life and then spends the rest of their career disappointing everyone?

I mean, it doesn't get more prestigious than a Fulbright. Ok, maybe a Rhodes—but really. What if I peaked out at twenty-two? I tried to remember the last time I had openly wept in Synagogue—really the last time I had openly wept period—and started to perhaps zero in on the problem. I was scared.

Judaism—or at least my identity as a Jew—had always been a constant as I burned brightly at Temple. But the last four years had also been defined by my lack of ability to say "no" to any group or project invitation. I loved and wanted the recognition that had started in high school and that meant that my time at Temple quickly swelled to proportions that drowned out pleas from my parents to come home a little more often for the weekend. The pace certainly made it easy to forget how much I loved *shul* on Friday nights.

I mean I talked about my Judaism all the time. Every friend had heard this or that story about one of my Jewish experiences at least three or four times. Being a cheerleader for my newly adopted Altar of Academia did not release me from the cheerleader obligations of my other identity as "Reform Super Jew." Three days into Orientation Week I found the Hillel booth in the SAC, signed all forms, smiled appropriately, and even went to some meetings at West Norris Street, usually when reminded last minute by chance running into a fellow Hillel-er on the Broad Street line coming back from Whole Foods in Center City or by chance rushing into classes at Annenberg Hall. Of course I went home for the bigger holidays and on occasion made it down to Rodeph Shalom on Spring Garden, but . . .

No!

Seriously? I had become one of those!

I used to mock the people that came to services only on *Rosh Hashanah* and *Yom Kippur*. On trips to Israel I would often hang out with the slightly more religious contingents of students, pitying those that claimed Judaism but relied solely on bloodlines and bagels to pass kosher muster.

45

I was certainly not one of *those*.

Why?

Because I talked the talk? Because my *bat mitzvah* nearly ten years ago pretty much rocked the house?

By now Sabrina had a legitimate look of concern. Rabbi had moved from *Yihyu* to *Oseh Shalom* and everyone had begun to join in. Under the cover of loud mostly tuneless Russian singing I once again reiterated to Sabrina the lie that all was well and snuck out the back of the *beit knesset*, heading quickly to the ladies' room.

Once there I began a series of profound self-recriminations whispered to the rhythm of the water I splashed on my face.

Seriously, in four years had it really not occurred to me that I went to *shul* roughly five or six times a year? For the first few splashes I gave myself the benefit of the doubt and assumed that in my busy schedule I simply must have gone on auto pilot and could not access what must be the numerous hidden memories of Friday evenings in the city at one *shul* or another or what must have been dozens of purposeful alarms buzzing Saturday morning at 8:00 sharp ensuring shower, scrubbing, maintenance make-up only and then the short walk to Hillel or the brief ride on the subway to Center City.

But of course it was all shit. Splash, splash. Absolute delusional horseshit.

Friday evenings were for meaningful conversation with whichever group that had both issued an invitation and had struck me as the one that I would feel the most interesting for the discussions that would go deep into the morning. Saturday mornings were for sleeping off the Fridays and then panicking over the projects that I had ignored during the previous days of social butterflying. Filial piety was easily assuaged by meeting with Dad once a week–every Tuesday to be exact—where we would play our game of "which food cart?" and then sit there with a meatball sub or tuna hoagie and I could feel like a good daughter.

Any potential guilt at withholding commensurate affection for my mother disappeared in my extra-special efforts to spend the majority of my time on my infrequent Swarthmore visits with her. In my mind this balanced the weekly time with Dad, and she as well seldom said anything to suggest my priorities might off.

Priorities.

If you had asked me at any minute during my time at Temple to list my life priorities, Judaism would have been at the top. I carried the Sim Shalom travel sized *siddur* and a book of Psalms with me everywhere I went. I doodled Stars-of-David with the best of them. I seriously could talk the talk but the more water I splashed on my face the more I realized that I hadn't been to *shul* in years yet all the while held the illusion that I was all that in the Jewish world. If you say something is your priority but don't really do it then how can it be your priority?

By the time I returned to the service, I had missed most of Rabbi's sermon. I settled with a tear-cleaned face back into my seat next to Sabrina, attempting to appear the type of person one would still want to take home for a drink rather than, well, an emotional train wreck.

Apparently it worked, as we both exited ten minutes later during the relative chaos of post service revelers moving to the social hall and made idle chatter in English for the ten minutes it took us to reach her flat and the other three it took to wind breathlessly up between six and eighty flights of stairs to her roof-level apartment.

I remember recounting to her with only a minimum of blubbering my ladies room revelations and then sharing with her more than one bottle of French wine as we both slowly mellowed and talked about important things that I assumed at the time I would remember. Finally, I do remember being tucked in like a small child and drifting into sleep on her couch.

What it is to Pray

The next morning Sabrina woke me up by setting a small French-press and white cup with saucer inches from my head on the Ikea end-table.

"Cream or sugar?" she asked as if my presence were a daily given.

"Just black," I grunted with my usual morning charm, trying to then lighten the asshole-ness of my light hangover with my most charming smile and a very sincere, "*Dankeschön!*"

I am sure I looked rumpled as I slowly moved to vertical to partake of the rich smell now pouring out of the French press. Sabrina had left to another room and inquired from the distance, "Is some bread and cheese ok? I don't have much but we can have some light breakfast."

"Sure, anything," I tried to mumble loud enough to be heard and grateful enough to be a decent accidental house guest, all the while deeply inhaling my fresh brew.

In what became, at least for my addled consciousness, an increasingly baffling volume of trips back and forth from kitchen to dining-room table I finally had enough initial caffeine to stand and stumble over to the table which Sabrina had somehow magically transformed into a buffet from a Four Seasons.

The "little" breakfast turned out to be a small supermarket assortment of jams and marmalades, a basket of what must have been fresh rolls, "*brötchen*" I guess they called them around here, and a covered cutting board displaying a French dessert worth of fine cheeses, each with its own appropriate cheese cutting knife, each shaped differently according to the density of the cheese. I kid you not—these Europeans are sophisticated as shit. On another cutting board sat freshly sliced tomatoes and cucumbers, and to top it off the last trip from the kitchen brought two soft-boiled eggs in highly ornamental egg holders.

While nibbling the feast and saying "thank you" in every way I could about every five seconds I reached a decision that felt holy and pure as it crystalized. During the rest of my year in Germany I would go to *shul* for every Shabbat service, evening and morning. I would make it the priority that I had previously said it had been.

Immediately I felt myself attempt to backtrack the promise. "But what about . . .?" my brain whispered, reminding me of concert posters and walls of social announcements at the University and in the *Studentenwohnheim* that had already begun filling my imagination with nights of wonder and the realization of my deepest fantasies of what it meant to live in Europe. Amazing how fast an internal voice turns to "But, but, but . . ." when it begins running counter to your self-illusions.

To bolster my quickly disappearing convictions I voiced my promise in between bites of one half-*brötchen* with the amazing raspberry spread and the other with butter and a slice of Emmentaler that tasted like it came that morning from Switzerland.

Sabrina stopped eating and studied me. I sheepishly realized that I should probably try and remember everything that we had talked about in several hours of wine-driven conversation the previous evening.

"Well why don't you just convert?"

For a second my always-an-outsider instincts threatened to surface and drown out a reasoned response to the apparent non-sequitur until I remembered at least a fragment of the previous evening's conversation.

Oh, that's right. Sabrina had at one point giggled—I am guessing sometime after the second bottle of wine neared its wistful end—when I told her with great authority that she must have come from a line of very beautiful Sephardic Jews. You know, smoky eyes and all that. It was inevitable that I would gush at some point.

The giggle turned into German version of "Golly, shucks" followed by the bombshell, "I'm not Jewish."

What had almost come out was, "But you look so Jewish" which would have been many levels of delicious reverse-hypocrisy coming from me. Clearly my gaping jaw was enough to encourage further elaboration.

"I have always *felt* Jewish," she had elaborated. "I know that doesn't mean anything, but I just remember always feeling a relationship with Jewish things and people and symbols. I didn't even have any idea that it was possible to convert until I bought the American book 'Judaism for Dummies' while I was in Texas. So I did what all good Germans do and I lived on a Kibbutz for six months in my gap year and everyone just assumed I was Jewish and I let them. At least on the Kibbutz they don't ask you what your grandparents had done during the war.

"I learned a little Hebrew, and when I moved here for work after University I started going to the synagogue every week or visiting synagogues in other cities like when I visited Berlin. Rabbi Isaac was already here so I had a little bit of a–maybe 'inaccurate' is the best word–view of synagogues in Germany. It took me nearly two years to get enough courage to ask Rabbi Isaac what I would need to do to convert."

"What did he say?" I asked.

"He asked me what I knew about converting." She laughed a little. "He likes doing that–making it seem like you are teaching

51

yourself when he is actually waiting to pounce with so much information that you leave feeling, what, *schwindlig*—dizzy?"

I think I had nodded both at the word and having already had the experience with the Rabbi and his "magic numbers."

She continued, I think after refilling both of our glasses. "So I told him what I knew and he asked me if I was crazy which is probably true and apparently a required question then gave me lots of books to read and now I have been studying with him almost two years."

Two years! "Um, does it always take so long?"

I think she shrugged and I am not sure that we pursued the conversation much further.

The caffeine hadn't yet fully hit my system, so in response to her suggestion that I convert I answered a predictable and I believe justifiable "But I am already Jewish."

Here is where either her several years of life experience on me or the genetic mutation that allow for "morning people" to exist put her at an advantage. She looked at me like the smart aunt sorely disappointed yet oh-so-patient with her prodigal niece. "Are you ever planning on living outside of the USA?" she asked in a level tone.

I let loose a meaningful "Um . . ." hoping to distract her and not have to face her question.

"Or what if you try to become a member of a conservative or even an orthodox Synagogue? What if you find a Jewish partner that is not American Reform and you wish to get married?"

Seriously, I was tempted to cover my ears, close my eyes, redden my face and start shouting, "I can't hear you! I can't hear you!"

This is where one of the cultural differences between the USA and Germany became apparent. I am sure that my face showed discomfort at the very least. In my usual circles, this is

52

enough to elicit a backing off and mumbled apology. Unless of course the uttered statement was a purposeful moment of cattiness meant to challenge the perceived pecking order of the social group, in which case an expression such as my present one would only show weakness and force me to tuck tail and back up two paces. Queue Wild Kingdom re-run music.

But no, not the Germans. Truth is truth is truth and I am pretty sure Sabrina had listened to my blathering about all things Andrea-Jewish for enough hours that her years of conversion effort were offended by my casual insistence that I should be universally accepted as *halakhically*—legally—Jewish even though the vast majority of world Jewry including Reform Jews outside of the States did not agree.

So my morphing from uncomfortable to mortified to victimized did nothing to release her meaningful hold on my eyes, as much as I wanted her to. But I had read about this. I had even had one of my few unpleasant conversations with Rabbi Theresa about this after some conservative Jewish relatives had shown up for one particular double *bar mitzvah* and tried to make a stink about the second boy, the one with the Jewish father but no Jewish mother, being called up to Torah. Theresa shrugged it off pretty easily when I asked her about it after the service and essentially told me to let rabbis worry about such things. This led me to some meaningful hours with Rabbi Google and the realization that I had never *really* been told in any direct way that my patrilineal Jewishness would never be accepted outside of American Reform synagogues. This pretty much sucked and led thereafter to exploring my exquisitely developed ability to ignore stuff that I "knew" but wished not to really "understand." I was Jewish! Case closed. Unpleasant thoughts tabled. Identity secured.

But there sat Sabrina and her smoky eyes and she wasn't going to let me get away with it. What *had* we talked about last night? Had we bonded that much? I looked again at the spread on the table, realizing the fresh *brötchen* could have only come from a morning-person run that sunrise to whichever local *Bäckerei* supplied such baked wonders. Sabrina was showing me a type of friendship that I hadn't really seen before—certainly not in terms of this type of hospitality. But I had started understanding that friendship around here also had something to do with truthfulness even if the truth made one feel uncomfortable.

Shit. Shit. Shit.

"I know." I finally uttered. It felt like a prophecy. "I know."

So here was the choice in front of me: fight to prove to the world the absolute legitimacy of my Jewish identity based on my sincerity and conviction or cross a few more t's and dot a few more i's in order to have a piece of paper that made that conviction stand up under legal scrutiny. This led of course to the thought that had been lurking since the first days of consciousness and therefore must be avoided at all costs: "Am I actually Jewish?"

What does that even mean?

I should have hated Sabrina. Isn't that what we usually do when someone makes us look at parts of ourselves we don't want to consider? I wanted to but she still sat there, relaxingly cupping her coffee while waiting for my conflict to somehow resolve.

"*Verdammt noch mal, Sabrina.*" "Dammit anyway" sounded so much better in German.

She shrugged. "You know they make it easy for *Vaterjuden.*" *Vaterjuden*? Ah, patrilineal. Pretty cool word. "At least Rabbi Isaac does. People like me," she didn't look in the least bitter as she said this, "study for a long time. But *Vaterjuden* get by much easier. I don't really understand why and I actually think it is a bit unfair, but that is how it is."

I think my face must have still been pulsing with its conflicting emotions, but now Sabrina shifted into some sort of conciliatory persuasion mode. "Seriously what do you lose? You just told me you wanted to go to *shul* every Shabbat and you spent all last night telling me that you were the worst Jew in the world while at your Uni. Go talk to Rabbi Isaac." She looked at her watch and shrugged. "Actually eat. If we leave in fifteen minutes we can make it for *Shacharit* services."

But, but, but . . .

In retrospect, I think this is how spirituality works. You tell the Universe what you intend to do and the Universe answers back, "Really? I'll see it when I believe it. Here, prove it."

That truly may have been the case, but I couldn't go back to *shul* in the clothes I just slept in and my dorm room was on the other side of the city, a good thirty-minute tram-ride from here. I voiced this to Sabrina who once again proved a kind of insufferable, "For every problem there is a solution" attitude that seemed to lie at an archetypical level in this country. "I have a closet. We are the same height. I was never your size but in the Uni I was thinner and I think we can make you look good enough for Shul."

I didn't sense any sarcasm in the words but I did squint at her to make sure she knew I was listening for it.

One more *brötchen* with cheese and cucumber later I had scrubbed my face and steeled myself to make my first public makeup-free appearance in years. Sabrina sized me up once again, handed me what looked like never-before-worn leggings and a perky green sweater that fell enough like a dress to make the outfit appropriate for shul. Fifteen minutes later we were sitting in the identical seats as the previous evening. Sometimes conviction comes much easier when it is part of a whirlwind.

The atmosphere and beginning of the service remained pretty much the same. It appeared that most of the Old Russian Dudes from the previous night had resumed their previous conversations while wearing their previous outfits. I think maybe a few new faces had joined the mix. I can't really be sure as I was having a bit of trouble with differentiation—something that I would actually never admit. At the appropriate time, meaning the very non Jewish Standard Time exact minute that the start of service was listed, Rabbi Isaac once again entered, made the rounds and greeted all. Once again he limped into the women's section, greeted us all with hugs and kisses, smiled warmly, and even offered me an extra wink that I interpreted as "You made it past the guard towers once again. Respect!"

Saturday morning services feel pretty universally different than Friday evening services. Friday evening seems much more meditative. One song flows to the next and before you know it the service is over and you just feel better. I am not sure if it is appropriate to say this, but to me *Kabbalat Shabbat*, the proper name of the Friday evening service which means something like "welcoming" Shabbat, feels spiritual while Saturday mornings have always struck me as more religious—more of a grind. I am sure that great Jewish spiritual leaders would read such a statement and shake their heads in discouragement at my clear ignorance or lack of evolved spirituality. And I don't even mean this in any pejorative sense. I don't dislike Shabbat morning services. Quite the contrary! It is simply that for good or ill there is always much more of a sense of fulfilling an obligation and much less of a sense of a *flow*. I know. My ignorance. But whatever, that is how I felt.

Worse, though, this was much more Orthodox than anything to which I was accustomed. Yes, I had been to the odd Orthodox service—Chabad is ubiquitous and there is always a *bar mitzvah* invitation that takes you to a synagogue whose name roughly translates as "House of the People of Truth" or "Sons of Jacob" or some such to sit in a balcony and feel slightly ill at ease. Those of us with Reform backgrounds prefer sitting next to and rubbing elbows with every gender at a synagogue whose name is usually roughly translated as The Temple of the Voice of the People or House of Peace or Living Waters. Different strokes.

The tradition to which my father introduced me and which formed my comfort zone is heavy on talking, singing, and reading alternative poetry or translations in English. It is from this perspective that I feel that the more one moved toward orthodoxy, the congregation's desire to take part only mattered for very little, until all that was left was a man standing with his back to me up in front, chanting through pages of Hebrew prayers far faster than my Hebrew ability could ever follow. I am sure that there were underlying values to this that I just didn't get. Feeling a part of what was happening, however, proved a struggle every time I found myself in this sort of situation. Add to that that unless you grew up in a *yeshiva* or received this sort of Hebrew from mother's milk, the probability of knowing where the prayer leader was in the *siddur* diminished quickly. Seriously, sit there stupidly flipping back and forth for a half-hour hoping that you can hear the *Borchu* or *Shema* and the desire to return so you can feel stupid again the next week is just not there. There must be a way I can find to back out of my promise to myself.

One thing that helped in Rabbi Isaac's *shul* was a low-tech novel solution born out of lack of a common language. Next to the small pulpit from which Rabbi led the services stood what looked like a wooden music stand with extra-large sized sheets of paper. Each sheet had two numbers in two bold boxes, with "Deutsch" written above the left number and "русский" written above the right. Every time Rabbi speed-prayed his way to the end of one page in his *siddur* he would seamlessly pull the top sheet down and place it on the slowly growing pile under his own prayer book. Even if you got totally lost or as happened to me more times than I will ever admit drifted into a land of disconnected daydreams, I could look up, smile sheepishly just in case Sabrina had noticed my vague stare into space, and flip professionally toward the correct page and once again pretend to mouth along with the words.

Overall the service felt a bit like the one Christmas hayride I had been lassoed into in high school by a well-meaning friend that assumed my Chanukah proclivities left me deprived of his high culture. Actually, come to think of it, I just realized he was trying to hit on me. Damn. He was cute too. Anyway, the drill was that some member of the twenty or so huddled under quilts and horse-blankets would begin whichever oldie-but-moldy the spirit inspired by bellowing, "Joy to the World," "Oh Come all Ye Faithful," or whatnot. The first verse would always be sung loudly and confidently. After that, one or two brave souls would mumble through the obscure second verse while the rest dropped out, looking surprised at their own ignorance. When the chorus once again rolled around, everyone would join back in, twice as loud as the first time with the "*In Exelcis Deo*" redeeming the mumbles. Then the process would repeat. Without the benefit of the spiked eggnog that made the evening patently hilarious for the grown-ups, I was stuck pretending that there *was* something charming about sitting in an itchy allergen for two hours. Moreover, my attempt to start a round of *Sevivon, Sov Sov Sov* was met by disapproving stares. Then I barely redeemed myself with a boisterous "Grandma Got Run Over" with which I faced them all by knowing every last word. I even imitated the voice quite well thank you—my little salvo in the War on Christmas.

Like at the hayride, Rabbi's beautifully executed prayer was punctuated by the few snippets known by those gathered, meaning the eight or so Old Russian Dudes that actually paid enough attention to belt out the "*Ki l'olam chasdo*"s or "*Yehei shemei raba*"s when they appeared. It all felt foreign and uncomfortable but with Sabrina next to me I had somehow already committed. Maybe I could get her to go with me to visit one of the liberal synagogues occasionally gracing the Jewish landscape of Germany. Rabbi Isaac was great but surely I could find something within an hour train ride that felt a little more . . . familiar and still keep my promise?

My reveries were interrupted by two men entering to what felt like a bit of fanfare from the back. First of all, the interruption itself, in the middle of prayer, was completely inappropriate. Seriously.

Rabbi Isaac had given me some warning regarding several of the folks I would run into as I began writing my Fulbright project. These two he hadn't mentioned and honestly I'm not quite sure why.

I looked at Sabrina meaningfully and then gestured my face back at the two slowly walking and talking in street voices with anyone who greeted them, seemingly oblivious to the rabbi up front *leading Shabbat prayers!* She leaned in and whispered in my ear, my inquiry obvious, "*Die Häuptlinge.*" I think that meant the "chiefs" but when Sabrina saw my lack of comprehension she continued: "*Herr Engels und Herr Platt. Der Vorsitzende und der zweite Vorsitzende der Gemeinde.*"

At this point I really don't think it's worth going into all the political and social differences between a community "President" and "Vice-president" in the USA and the kinda-sorta analogous "*Vorsitzender*" and "*zweiter Vorsitzender*" in Germany. What I can say is that responsibility is responsibility, and these two showed none. Not to mention the disrespect!

The show didn't stop as they reached the front row, noisily opening their own lock boxes built into the rows, pulling out their own prayerbooks—different from the one Rabbi was using, I should add—and then their own prayer shawls, making another show of swinging the *tallitot* around like bullfighters and audibly speaking the blessings that could easily have been mumbled *sotto voce*.

I would like to say it stopped there. Certainly, they did join in with the hayride chorus while still chatting to each other through the entire service. Occasionally I would look meaningfully at Sabrina, both attempting to gauge her reaction to see if she also wanted to join me in throwing objects. After the seventh application of the Andrea Death Stare followed by a glance back at Sabrina she leaned over and whispered once again in German, "*Du wirst dich daran gewöhnen müssen.*"

You'll just have to get used to it.

Jewish Sexuality

My second hookup in Germany at least left a positive enough memory to be mentioned in this space. This is opposed to the first encounter which shall be reserved for a future polemic on the social skills of Germans who use bed play to ask borderline anti-Semitic questions about Israeli politics. Peter, the mostly non-anti-Semitic latter, at least focused on the sweaty grunty mechanics and not politics, earning above-average marks in technical achievement and artistic merit.

In addition, Peter had going for him that one says his name "Pay-tehr" with the rr's in the back of the throat instead of the clearly less sexy "PEE-drr" in my less-romantic adopted mother-tongue. What he didn't have going for him was what was becoming a stereotypical inflexibility of life opinions and a seemingly universal inability to flirt. Seriously. The German verb "to flirt" is *flirten*. With all the delicious subtlety of the German language, they had to commit the heinous sin of borrowing a word from the English lexicon to fill a linguistic gap for a truly foreign concept. I count multiple verbs that have minutely yet connotatively important differences to express "to talk" between two or more people: *sprechen, reden, diskutieren,* and *unterhalten* to which we can add *plaudern, labern,* and *quatschen*—some of which I just had to look up and few of which I can *really* use correctly with the correct nuance. But no "to flirt," other than in borrowed form. Ontologically, this tells you enough about Germans to make you wonder how anyone ever continues to procreate.

So anyway, back to the point of Pay-tehr, the "hookup," and why I am bothering to go there.

First of all, sex is all fucked up around here. I mean, maybe the fuck-upedness of sex is ubiquitous, but it is a little hard to know for sure coming from, on the one hand, the United States of Puritanical America and on the other hand a minority religion with a well-deserved paranoid inferiority complex and a complicating commandment to "be fruitful and multiply." The assumption from the Bubbies and Zaydies on Day One is that you, the young potential child-barer in their midst, will indeed add more *kinderlachs* to the world and that this will be accomplished in a kosher heterosexual union with a doctor or lawyer.

Seriously, you don't even have to be anti-Semitic to utter these cultural stereotypes . . . what stinks is how true they are. What is tragic is that they are true even in the twenty-first century in a "Reform" community that somehow prides itself on being a bastion of progressive thought—most of the time that is the case, just not in the case of the being fruitful and multiplying thing.

If I am being fair, there is limited validity to this sort of hypocrisy. We just now have once again reached the pre-Holocaust world Jewish population. It took a lot of fruitful multiplying to get us here in roughly seventy years, and something tells me that Bubbies and Zaydies, the militant arm of this mitzvah brigade, use their medieval propagation peer-pressure to atone for a multitude of real and imagined sins from their past, the most depressing of which surely is survival guilt.

The conversation I wish I had never witnessed on the weekend of Rabbi Theresa's job interview is an appropriate case-in-point. Mrs. Kantor, seventy-nine going on Methuselah, had cornered the new rabbinical finalist and her partner Irene somewhere between Mrs. Schubert's I-can't-believe-it's-not-crack brownies and Mr. Strauss' an-old-dude-made-this matzo kugel.

"So how many children do you have?" Mrs. Kantor spoke-nay-bellowed with a voice like an out-of-tune trumpet, making her question the center of the now dimmed conversation.

"Neither of us are able to have children," replied the rabbi, nodding at her partner Irene without appearing in the least fazed.

Now in my book of ethics this is the moment where one nods thoughtfully and then moves on to another topic of inquiry. Maybe in my status of "adopted into the tribe," however, I am missing the crass gene which predictably led Mrs. Kantor to the follow-up question of, "well why not?"

I am sure Rabbi Theresa played around with multiple responses ranging from, "I am sorry, did you really just ask that" to "it is none of your damn business," but she earned my instant respect by smiling and lightly touching Mrs. Kantor on the shoulder saying, "Some things we just never fully understand. The blessing I have because of this, though, is that I have so much energy to give to the youth in the community. It's like in missing one thing I'm rewarded by something that for me is even better."

The ideal version of this tale ends with Mrs. Kantor becoming self-aware for the first time and Rabbi Theresa moving on to the rest of the questions waiting to be asked by the throngs. This being a synagogue, however, meant that instead Rabbi Theresa and Irene politely stood before Mrs. Kantor for another ten minutes while being regaled with an exhaustive list of every child bearing option for a lesbian couple with admittedly baffling against-all-probability two barren partners, finishing with the ultra-sensitive, "And you know that adoption is nothing to be ashamed of."

Dad, a very unwilling member of the rabbinical search community, later recounted after my steam-blowing-off session at the wizened age of eleven-and-a-half that the Rabbi's uterus had almost been the disqualifier. "How can someone without children ever hope to deal with all the children issues in a Jewish community?" seemed to be the dominant trope. As a not-yet-teen but fully aware of my coming from a non-traditional birth narrative I railed and cried and demanded that Daddy make sure that Theresa got hired. Justice and only justice shall you pursue, right?

Justice won out and it became my mission not only to support our new rabbi, but to be the best *bat mitzvah* ever, solely tutored by our childless rabbi, and prove that she kicked ass regardless of what Mrs. Kantor and her ilk thought of the Rabbi's uterus and subsequent life choices. And oh how I, the first *bat mitzvah* of the new regime, kicked ass. Oh yes, I led much of the Friday evening service, singing the blessings loudly and clearly unlike most of the boys that became suddenly way-too-cool when faced with their non-Jewish middle-school friends come to pay homage to our quaint Jewish traditions. No no—loud and clear plus flawless Torah reading plus ridiculous practice to make sure the melody was flawless. Then there was the brilliant sermon, no dry eyes, blah blah blah. The point is I became a cheerleader and contrarian on the same day, and I now must wonder how much this has affected me over the years.

But the underlying point, other than the fact I still have not really found my way back to Pay-tehr, remains the strange sort of regressive sexuality that the fruitful multiplying adds to the Jewish psyche. Theresa seemed to be at peace with her life decisions or situation and despite my curiosity I acted within my own emerging ethic and never asked how it came to be that two barren partners wound up together. Did they know this when they fell in love? Was this perhaps itself the *ontos* of their partnership? Was the stoic *nonchalance* a result of being barren or an expression that kids were never a priority? Rabbi Theresa seldom broke character and never regarding her uterus, always projecting the narrative-defying complete comfort in her absurdly and oft-judged status as non-child-bearer. But that truly did not minimize the explicit questions for every future child-bearer in the community and the implicit assumptions that we all had to deal with regarding the gender and religion of our future partners. A few friends and acquaintances that hailed from the West Coast that I met at various camps or Israel trips told a different story of more inter-marriage and less assumptions than my East Coast experience, but regardless my experience was my experience and as a type of outsider anyway, I resolved early, Rabbi Theresa worship notwithstanding, to move my life in the marry-a-male-Jewish-doctor-or-lawyer direction and minimize any future alienation that could have come from sexual and reproductive non-conformity. Of course I didn't call it that, but I have books upon books of poorly written poetry from age fourteen to nineteen in addition to humiliating posters of certain boy-bands that prove whether through nature or nurture, I indeed swallowed the Jewish heterosexual cool aid.

That could have ended the entire sexuality reflection had I at the point of moving to Germany had already found, wooed or had been wooed and formalized a relationship to Mr. Rightstein. Absent this, bad decisions made in the service of my sexual conformity were inevitably going to start me thinking about the sex stuff I had never really questioned.

Maybe it was the German surroundings that started smacking down my unchallenged fantasies. My Fulbright year coinciding with what I am told to believe in many a Cosmopolitan authoritative article are my most desirable years has begun to tempt me once again to consider certain assumptions about my sexuality—at least in terms of how sexuality relates to funneling our lives into relationships. Maybe I do feel that greater jolt of unreasoning follow-my-loins when in a meet-cute with a guy, but maybe that really is Bubbie and Zaydie with way too much influence. Maybe if I ignore that part that leads up to the fairytale kiss and focus on the years that come after, does my sense of sexuality change? If I look out over the modeling of my parents—a model that I am convinced is not only a healthy one but one worth emulating on many levels—then I see relationships to be massive amounts of planning, daily household business maintenance, needs negotiation, turning a gentle blind eye to the daily unintentional inflicted pains, and tearfully negotiating through the intentional injuries caused by very tired people who know how to draw blood from the ones they love the most. Part of me thinks that I "get" women, as if this sort of gross generality has any meaning, more than men and therefore the long-term same-sex relationship might have a better chance of success in the face of life reality as opposed to what a partner looks like that is going to satisfy east coast Jews and keep them from looking too hard at my eyes, skin and hair.

But maybe I am just so put off now at Pay-tehr's lack of having a native understanding of the verb "to flirt" or even maybe the Jewish guys I have met here during my coincidentally "most eligible years" that make me begin playing with images of celibacy.

I am obviously back to Pay-tehr, so let me please explain that I am not in his bed due to an arbitrary Jewish version of jungle-fever with a healthy dose of un-circumcised penis envy. First of all, I am already lying through my braces-straightened teeth when I started off by calling Pay-tehr "hookup number two" when the reality is that I saw a foreskin in person for the very first time during my real first hookup in Germany on the Jewish body of Boris-son-of-the-Czar. First of all, there is so much wrong here I am clearly having trouble being honest with even my own memories.

I am not even going to start trying to unpack the levels of fucked-upedness that led me to an unpleasant evening with the son of the man on my current most-hated-list. Revenge? Shit, seriously I said I was not going to analyze this. Anyway, fact remains that an extended conversation with one of the few Jewish lads in the community that I saw outside of the few services I had attended at that point led to a few more half-liters of Aventinus and its eight percent APV than a person of my body mass should ever try and next thing we are making out and next next thing I am pulling down are-you-kidding-me lavender fashion briefs to discover a real live foreskin on a Jewish lad.

I'm a good actor. I mean, my skills at Spock-ian emotional dissembling developed and maintained explicitly to prevent awkward social situations are nearly British in their epic-ness. But seriously if I didn't spring back as if the foreskin had hissed at me.

I once saw this fascinating exchange in a McDonald's in a train station in Essen while traveling through. The protagonist of the tale was not German, although she spoke passably enough. She was, however, clearly not aware of the fact that many train stations in that region have a single master public restroom, the so called and usually in reality "Mister Clean" where for from between seventy Euro Cents and a Euro you could enter and have a scrubbed cubicle all to your own. This meant practically and logically that McDonalds and Starbucks and every other symbol of American High Culture export that dotted German streets and train stations did not need to maintain a public restroom. So maybe when the woman in question asked at the counter for the location of the WC, the answer "We don't have one," did not satisfy. Yet surely the follow-up, necessitated by the look of desperation and confusion, should have cleared up the issue and more importantly cleared the counter for my McFlurry order. "There is a restroom down the hall in the train station."

The problem crystalized, however, as the ever-more-desperate woman attempted to convince the ever-more-frustrated girl at the counter that this was a McDonalds, which by definition means there must be a restroom. Even worse, after pointing down the hall and then explaining more patiently than I could have ever mustered that the needy woman needed to turn around, turn left, walk one-hundred meters, and then turn left again at the two-meter-tall universal male/female symbols for "please pee here," the woman walked out the wrong direction, still trying to argue her case that there must be a restroom in a McDonalds. By her definition of McDonalds, the *gestalt* of McDonalds must in its platonic form include a restroom. For the poor woman it was thus preferable to argue the case then to capitulate and actually pee where one peed in this part of Essen.

Much in the same way I gazed at Boris' foreskin.

In my universe, the platonic form of Jewish Man contains Circumcised Penis. No other possibility could exist.

My first thought, and oh yes this came out of Andrea-the-Appropriate's mouth, was, "You're not Jewish?" Luckily that ejaculation came out in English rather than German and so the slightly although not significantly less rude German follow-up sounded something like: "Wow, that's interesting."

Guys, you will have to help me here, as although I cannot say for sure, I am guessing that when the first reaction to exposing yourself in the midst of somewhat drunken bed-play is,

"Wow, that's interesting," the rest of the night is probably not going to go well.

At least Boris was not impressed with my tact, and a half hour later, after attempting to wipe out the memory of my unintentional emasculation, I was planting a chaste, sisterly kiss on the side of his cheek and sprinting out the door to catch one of the late bus routes. The "*Tschüss bis später*" that I spoke as I rushed out were the last words we ever spoke, if you do not count grunted nods when I had the misfortune to encounter him on campus or far worse when he filled in for the Czar at the security booth at *shul*.

But presence of foreskin is really not what I am trying to get at. The logical extension of my teen-age decision to not rock the Jewish Heterosexual Boat was that I would spend at least the plurality of my mating-ritual energy during my Fulbright year to see if my entrée into the world of Jewishly-responsible breeding parentage might just indeed come from a member of the tribe in the Old World, which based on the realities of German Jewish life meant dating Russian and Ukrainian Jewish men. After Boris, the blinders came off so quickly, though, that my youthful promises to myself and transitively to the World Collective of Bubbies and Zaydies fell away as I realized my only options were Jewish men from a culture so alien to me that I in my most multi-kulti fantasies could not recognize it as familiar.

So, Pay-tehr.

I mean, I kept my eyes open. As much as it sounds like I am revolving my life around partner-searching, this is not what it was. It is just that at early twenty-something I had allowed my perception of possibility to be so dimmed by the fear of adding yet another reason for Jews to reject my Jewishness that at some level I was always on the lookout to find the relationship that would remove the questions that my appearance elicited. Unfortunately, the fact that the genitalia of my potential Jewish mates available to me at this time and place did not conform with preconceived patterns proved only the beginning of the understanding that not only was this Jewish culture foreign to all I understood, so were the date-able men that I encountered anathema to my very American sense of progressive justice.

Take for example the general "Russian" attitude toward homosexuality. I mean this is pretty well publicized by now, but what the hell? I mean when a culture places its social policy with that of Iran one should look intently in the mirror. And if you think that the FSU Jewish community is in any way exempt from what qualifies as quant medieval wisdom then you haven't yet paid attention to a single word. In my world, this is a relationship core value. Any last "well I'll give it one more try" thought fell away quickly when confronted with the core value of so many of the men in the community espousing a self-evident homophobia that would sound just about right coming from the Westboro Baptist Church. What's worse, the more I had to swim near the bigotry the more I understood the nuances. In the Soviet Union, homosexuality had been considered a disease and was classified as such in a Doctor's handbook, even called 'homosexualism.' Apparently, a lot of the insanity I witnessed came from people even now believing it is possible to somehow 'catch' homosexuality—hence the law banning the propaganda of 'non-traditional sexual relations among minors' in Russia. On top of it all, being a passive homosexual in Russian popular culture signified the loss of virility and a lower hierarchical position. The more I learned, the more impossible a relationship would be with someone that had been indoctrinated in this way.

My mom and dad both had taken their opportunities to sit me down and talk about relationships and compatibility. In

70

retrospect it is all a bit charming. Most parents fret about the sex conversations. Mine fretted about how they could possibly break it to me that relationships where core values were not shared were bound to fail.

"Get the questions out of the way early, *Metukah*," my father had held my eyes like a master stage-hypnotist, willing me to hear his wisdom from two failed marriages before he found Mom. "I would like that you fall in love and experience romance. But no matter how good the romance, the relationship cannot last if you disagree on core values. You can ignore it for a while, but eventually your relationship will start becoming less about what you have in common and every day more of what you don't."

Daddy knows me quite well and easily replied to the obvious question in my narrowing of eyes that called bullshit on his statement.

"Yes, your mom and I. First of all, we share an underlying ethic about how people should be treated which to me is the central meaning of my Judaism anyway. You know me, my Hebrew is awful and for the most part I would be happy with three-fourths of the ritual cut out, but your mom supports my religious identity and my core value that any child of mine be a part of it. As she is not religious, there is at least not a competing active religion in the household. More importantly, we talked about all of this explicitly and asked frank questions of if this would work or not." Somehow it was far too easy to visualize such a conversation. I found myself occasionally fantasizing about what it would be like to feel so unafraid and so secure to have such a conversation with a partner.

This sort of conversation may not have completely rewired my own reticence to cause any sort of conflict, the odd gasping-at-the-uncircumcised notwithstanding, but why even talk about core values if you know before the conversation starts what the answer will be? All I had to do was watch how childless single late-forties Rabbi Isaac was treated to know this.

Sure, there was a surprising respect for Rabbi in general but that didn't stop the childish snickers when someone would bring up the question of his sexuality. I mean, how can it possibly be that Rabbi Isaac is standing up there, pouring every ounce of his being into every prayer every Shabbat and there is mockery and rolling of eyes because someone made a snide comment about the rabbi's lack of a wife? That is the focus? I mean sure I have thought of it myself. The more time I ended up spending with Rabbi the more I was aware of the complete lack of sexual tension. I am not being the vain one here and suggesting that I am so hot that any guy who that doesn't make a pass at me must be gay. OK, maybe in the slightest way I am, but this is certainly not the only conclusion one can draw. I have seen Rabbi Isaac on many occasions "shift his energy" as an actress friend of mine at Temple would say. With one group of people he would "seem" one way and then with a different group he would speak and even somehow look different. With me he could be quite familiar and even intimate, but I never in the least sensed sexuality behind that. I could just as easily postulate that Rabbi Isaac with his magical shape shifting ability simply learned the skill of projecting Rabbi-ness as opposed to sexual-ness when acting as a Rabbi in order to address one of the specific fucked-upedness of sexuality in the States. Perhaps that necessary life skill in the USA of being above reproach at all times in order to avoid even the inkling of impropriety when transferred to a European stage makes what was a career skill suddenly seem like asexuality. With his five years here in Germany, and according to the *lashon hora*-du-jour, the fact that he had never been seen by anyone out with a lady but had been seen at many a lunch or dinner locale chatting with one or another male friend, that asexuality could have no other local interpretation than "gay."

I mean maybe he was. But that is just my point—it doesn't matter. And the clear disdain I have for any that disagree is simply my way of shouting "core value." For all the other things I can look at my generation and yes even myself and have justifiable anxiety for the future, the fact that in the USA we as a vast majority look at homosexuality with a collective *"meh"* might just be the coolest victory for societal transformation since the Civil Rights movement. Sure I marched in Pridefest in Philly every year at Temple U partially because I was covering it for the school newspaper and partially because the party was truly that fun. Yeah, it wasn't Selma and on 12th and Locust you are kind of preaching to the choir, but dammit I marched, and my marching is to me this instant not only a symbol of how much I could care less with whom Rabbi shared his bed, if anyone, but as well how much the unevolved FSU mentality regarding homosexuality reached a point quickly that guaranteed any dating or hooking up done in Germany was most likely not going to be with my tribe-mates.

Moreover, this all seriously makes me want to find in the most contrarian way the hottest yet most clearly Jewish-in-the-Russian-eyes woman and make out with her or even worse hold hands and gaze adoringly at her as we walk into the synagogue for a *Kabbalat Shabbat* service. Unfortunately, as a non-dude this would probably arouse rather than offend which highlights the hypocrisy of this entire judging sexuality enterprise.

I mean seriously. The information about the fluidity of sexuality is out there and we still speak in terms of black and white, gay or straight. How is that still a thing? I know that being in full-blown Andrea contrarian-rant mode is coloring my rhetoric, but what in the end would it mean to my "label" if I were to have a fling with that Ukrainian girl I can't stop looking at at the Uni? What if I called the fling an affair? How about a relationship? What if as a serial monogamist I alternated between men and women for the next thirty years? What if I dated one of each gender at the same time? What if I ended up marrying a woman and stayed with her in a loving relationship the rest of my life but still had desire for men that I didn't act on? What if I acted on it? And perhaps most importantly, since all of these items can be a masturbatory fantasy for even those that have homophobic tendencies, what if my name was Andrew rather than Andrea and it was a man asking all of these questions?

All of this and we haven't even begun to touch on other subtleties such as trans- versus cis-sexuality or asexuality? What about the difference between romantic intimacy and physical intimacy? What about other potential continua like monogamy versus polyamory or even running the gamut from dominate to submissive? While we label people in the most black and white terms, our actual selves exist within multiple spectra of fluidity and the fact that I have never been taught this and am just now having to figure this out myself is really pissing me off because it feels way too heavy for one person to piece together.

So why even bother to think of all this? Well, here I am, next to Pay-tehr, and dammit I am just not sure anymore. My decisions to please my tribe have begun to wilt away in the presence of Boris and Pay-tehr and even the now mocking memories of every kiss and sexuality laced embrace and yes even love and sex that now cry to me and ask how much of the experience was me and how much was Mom, Dad, the Bubbies and Zaydies, Torah, apple pie, Philly Cheesesteaks and the good ol' US of A. Am I allowed to change? Do I even know who I am in the first place?

Women in the Balcony

I think I have found the antidote to being constantly annoyed at Rabbi Isaac's shul. Somehow this place is getting to me but it seems if I just focus on my Fulbright project and view every moment of insanity as the basis of a really clever chapter then I stay sane. Without this, I can far too easily imagine myself throwing objects at inappropriate times in inappropriate places.

Maybe I just have bad modeling on how to be angry and thus need such a crutch. My parents got tense on a regular basis but I have a feeling that if they ever went Full Shouting Match they left no clues behind for their daughter. So maybe I could use what I learned from Rabbi Theresa to figure out how to mold this burning feeling into a usable tool. She is usually a good place to start when it comes to mentoring and patterning. Unfortunately, I think I only saw Rabbi Theresa get angry once. Ok, I can't really believe I said that—I am *thrilled* I only saw her angry once as I am not sure a perpetually pissed-off Rabbi is a good thing. But I am talking modeling here, so back off. I learned from my favorite therapist in high school that finding a clear model from our memories and then visualizing ourselves acting as they had acted can help us develop skills without the messy trial-and-error required by real life. With that in mind, maybe remembering Rabbi Theresa's use of anger could help me out of my current frustration without solely resorting to journalistic distance.

So, to balance the budget, something according to my dad that is getting trickier and trickier each year, several members with deep pockets notwithstanding, we rented out our building on Sundays to a church. I must say I have mixed feelings about this. The more I have begun to learn about concepts such as "sacred space" and "intentionality" the more I wonder if there isn't some ethereal contradiction in groups with conflicting theologies and concepts of spirituality sharing space.

I don't know. Maybe I am way off on this. I know there is a project in the works in Petri Platz in Berlin to build a multi-use house of worship which will include a mosque, church and synagogue all under the same roof and connected by a long hallway. But even then there is not going to be a cross put up in the mosque or a Magen David in the church.

I have never seen what the church does for setup, so maybe this is a case of my fantasies running wild. Do they put up a temp-cross over the ark that holds the Torah scrolls? Should I even care? Maybe it is the fact that the church calls themselves "Swarthmore Bible Fellowship" and I am imagining speaking in tongues in the place where our cantor belts out "*Hinei Ma Tov*." Would I have a problem if it was a Unity or Unitarian Church— one of the more New Age-y far left Jesus-isn't-so-important-here sorts of denominations?

Anyway, one chilly February evening, I think I was seventeen at the time, Rabbi Theresa was presiding over one of her famous "Advanced Topic" seminars—three weeks in a row, one evening a week on a specific topic ranging from Kabbalistic Meditation to Biblical Archeology. By her fifth or sixth year in the community non-members were charged a hundred bucks in order to keep the numbers under forty—a steep change from the small handful that showed up when she started these. But Rabbi Theresa was one of those people who apparently never threw away a single class note going back to Hebrew School and had over years modified every class she took into a curriculum that made people feel like they actually knew something about their own tradition. She wasn't a brilliant extemporaneous speaker, but she could turn her notes into several evenings of truly interesting learning, usually well laced with her acerbic wit and continuous denigration of orthodoxy. I couldn't attend them all, but I really tried to catch two or three a year with Dad when my schedule permitted, almost always as the youngest present.

This said February evening, the back doors of the *beit knesset* opened about an hour into the two-hour lecture/discussion. This in and of itself was nothing unusual as our members were not exempt from operating on JST—Jewish Standard Time, meaning start times were fluid and flexible unless your family was of non-Jewish origin. Seriously, if it wasn't for converts and protestant theology students visiting certain services, no one would ever be on time for anything in the shul. Well, this time two that walked in, a couple somewhere between fifty something and too-tanned to make an upper-end educated guess, looked absurdly out of place.

"We're looking for Pastor Zach!" the man bellowed. No reason for the volume—our maximum occupancy read three hundred seventy-five and that applied only when the walls were removed from the social hall for the High Holidays. The rest of the time, the fifty to one hundred max that sat in the room enjoyed good acoustics and clear sight-lines. This tanned dude with the yellow pressed shirt, dyed hair with hairpiece, no coat and oh yes a deep-south accent saw no need to think about much of anything other than his immediate need. The fact that Rabbi Theresa stood in front of a pulpit with Hebrew lettering and a conspicuous Magen David, not to mention that there was something actually taking place, you know, a class, did not keep Mr. Inappropriate from bellowing out the question in what I am sure was a deeper version of the accent in order to react to the fact that our collective reaction was a silent "what the hell?" Seriously, sometimes the Universe must be sending us stereotypes just to ensure the ability to tell a good tale.

Rabbi Theresa to the rescue. "I am sorry sir, but we are in the middle of a class here." She wasn't nasty or anything. Her voice projected the usual firm confidence, her only concession to a Napoleon Complex, but certainly nothing antagonizing—also certainly not inviting a continued discussion. Good day, sir!

"Yeah, but I am looking for Pastor Zach."

You seriously cannot make this shit up.

Now totally curious how this would escalate I settled back in my chair at a good angle to watch the serve and volley between door and pulpit. At least Mr. Inappropriate's I-am-assuming wife had begun meaningfully tugging on his arm, realizing that her I-am-assuming husband had begun to engage in Unacceptable Behavior. At least that's how I read the tugging in that moment—I certainly allow for the possibility that I am completely wrong.

"Sir, this is a synagogue, not a church. Pastor Zach rents this space once a week, but he doesn't have an office here."

That was a pretty good answer. I filed tone and content away for future reference and possible use.

Mrs. Inappropriate took this opportunity to release her I-am-assuming husband's arm and start walking toward the pulpit. "Oh look, Bill. That's Hebrew written there!" she exclaimed both pointing at and moving in the direct of the ark. "What does it say?"

Clearly I either had misinterpreted the arm tugging or the Missus had a short social-appropriateness attention span. It wasn't clear to whom she was speaking. Logically the focus of the question should have been Rabbi Theresa as I assume the Mister spoke no Hebrew, but the question certainly lacked direction.

Volley back to Rabbi Theresa and I saw her uncharacteristically chewing on her lower lip. Yet before

79

whatever chewed-upon answer could come out, the Mister, not to be dissuaded from his original track continued with, "But Pastor Zach lives around here somewhere."

Here where? Wallingford-Swarthmore? Delaware County? The Greater Philadelphia Area?

"I am sorry sir, but I do not have any idea where Pastor Zach lives." The chewed lip apparently had underlying emotions, as Rabbi's undertones had taken on the distinctive timbre of stepping on broken glass.

"But this is Swarthmore Bible Fellowship?"

Actually I am not sure if it was a question or not, but I will give him the benefit of the doubt.

"This is a synagogue, sir, not a church." Crunch, crunch goes the broken glass. By now Mrs. Inappropriate had reached the stairs to the raised *bima* and, arm still outstretched toward the Hebrew, had begun making noises of disappointment that no one had yet translated the wood-inlayed text. Dad, warrior archetype invoked, had already left his seat and had placed himself between Crazy Lady and the Rabbi, somehow simultaneous making it clear he could dive in to protect me should the need arise.

Something of the moment must have finally penetrated Mr. Inappropriate as he now with the great pride of being clearly insulted huffed, "Well I *know* this is a synagogue." Then he clucked his tongue loud enough to be heard by all. Ok, it was a nice trick and I am impressed, but by this time people were barely breathing in anticipation so there wasn't exactly a crowd din to cover up the *tisk*.

With this he started trying to get his I-am-assuming wife's attention to leave this Place of Horrible Injury while she meanwhile ignored his meaningful gestures and continued her earlier train of thought with, "But it's Hebrew, Bill. Don't you think we should learn some Hebrew?"

"Sure Darling, whatever you want," he managed to say while seeming to simultaneously repeat himself, "Well of course it is a synagogue. Don't you think I know that?" *Tisk*. "Come one, dear." *Tisk*. "Tell me I think it's not a synagogue, I know what Hebrew is." *Tisk*.

By about the tenth *tisk* the two had finally left, ushered out by a simultaneous thirty-person exhale and some very uncomfortable snickers. But Rabbi Theresa wasn't quite done.

"Seriously. This is the thing. These two are going to now go tell all their friends about how evil the Jews were and this crap just makes me crazy!" She looked at everyone, face red and breathing heavy. "Sorry about that, everyone. But seriously. *Seriously*. Dozens of people here. Something obviously happening that wasn't church. Seriously people?" Crushed glass started fading. "Ok, where were we?"

I think that is it. This entire "Jewish" community—and yes I now feel it correct to use quotes around "Jewish" since I am having a hard time recognizing any Judaism—has started reminding me of those two looking for Pastor Zach. Exhibit One:

"He is an idiot. He has no idea what he is doing."

Old Orthodox Lady Number One nearly spat as she shook and cursed to the thrilled audience of Old Orthodox Lady Number Two who wore a look of profound disdain.

"Rabbi E_ would never have allowed that."

"It is like I am not even able to hear Torah anymore."

"This is not my synagogue anymore. This clown has turned us all into a joke."

First point: this conversation sounds much worse in German. I promise. Second point: the *schande* that they are bitching about, of all things, is the current rabbi's decision *four years earlier* to follow the triennial cycle of Torah reading. Now, I have to admit that all these details were filled in over time by Sabrina, and unfortunately did not at all help with my steadily decreasing self-esteem when it came to Jewish knowledge. I at least grew up understanding that the dividing of the Torah or the Pentateuch into sections had been done quite differently in Jewish circles then in Christian. Although all of our bibles also had chapter and verse, the important unit of organization was instead a *parashah* or a portion.

At least I knew this. I mean, everyone ever *bat* or *bar mitzvah*'d knew this, as we had to read from our *parashah* from the Torah scroll itself and then had to write some sort of sermon from the texts. I knew what a *parashah* was because I like every other shul-going-Jew has had to sit through an indeterminate amount of bad *bar* and *bat mitzvah* sermons that began with, "My *parashah* is x and in my *parashah* it says. . ." Seriously it is no wonder so many Jews end their religious education after age thirteen. But at least we all knew what a *parashah* was and we all explored our *parashah* with the generous help of rabbis, parents, grandparents and today I am sure Rabbi Google who was not quite as available for mine.

Anyway, my portion was *"Vai'era"* which from memory runs somewhere between chapters six and nine of Exodus and includes the God of the Israelites introducing God's-self to Moses and then concludes with the first of the plagues. At Rabbi Theresa's prodding I asked the question of what the women were doing while the men were creating plagues, which led to a seven minute excurse on how the Torah contains by necessity and politics more forgotten stories than written ones.

The reason I felt stupid in front of Sabrina once again was that I had mostly seen Torah read at Friday evening services, usually with a single block reading of five to ten verses. Of course we read as well on Saturday morning when there was a *bar* or *bat mitzvah*, but that was the only time I showed up for services at all on Saturday so I guess without thinking I just associated Torah reading with a nice, short and sweet shot in the arm two Fridays a month and didn't even pay much attention when I visited other synagogues that did it differently. That was them.

So the long and short is that in Orthodox synagogues, the entire *parashah* is read every Shabbat. This may not seem like such a big thing on the surface, but look at it practically. The first *parashah* in the Torah, for example, covers the first six chapters of Genesis. Do you have any idea how long it takes to chant six chapters of the Torah? Seriously, long enough that even on my best behavior I am going to want to start throwing stuff.

Apparently Rabbi Isaac either agreed with me or had other reality-based reasons and switched this community over to the triennial cycle. Practically this meant that Torah readings that once dragged on more than thirty minutes now took fifteen. According to Sabrina there are some really good reasons that are a part of Jewish tradition that allowed one to do this, but all I really cared about was that the already nearly three-hour services that I sat through were not *longer* than three hours. Seriously, who needed a better reason?

But, of course, once something had been done one way by a dude with a black hat then it was no different than if Moses himself had created the tradition. Hence, something that was meant to make services more accessible to the majority of the congregation that happened to have no Jewish education whatsoever was for certain segments of the population a sign that Rabbi Isaac was either *HaSatan* himself, an unlearned idiot, or simply not really a rabbi.

The decision to sit in the balcony instead of the *Frauenabteilung* on the main floor had been a clear mistake. Sabrina told me that she would be visiting her cousin in Berlin and without her anchoring downstairs, I seriously just wanted to see if I could focus on the service any better, as paying attention to everything Rabbi Isaac said proved occasionally challenging from among the din of Russian newspapers being read and constant conversation from those not reading or eating or, even worse, conversation when the chiefs of the community deigned to make an appearance. I figured that, like many theaters I had visited, the stage sound would go up and the audience sound would remain muted. What I hadn't clearly thought through was that from up here you could much more easily see the newspapers and eating and bullshitting. Not an improvement at all. Compound this with the bitter-old-bag brigade that scowled in disapproval at anything the rabbi said or did and my focus was shot almost immediately.

Truth is, I should have known better. I had already seen enough in the last weeks that the energy up here should have been predictable. I don't know, maybe I just wanted to be pissed off today. Maybe I wanted to know that my rising annoyance at "all-things-this-synagogue" had a justification stronger than "things aren't done my way here."

Regarding these particular Charming Ladies, I had already witnessed something that at the time I hadn't really understood. My first few weeks attending regularly, I had started going to every community meal with Sabrina after each morning service. Evening services had wine, challah, fruit, cakes and vodka, but mornings had full sit-down meals that had enough regularity and repetition that I had already labeled them A, B, C, D and VIP.

"A" consisted of two salads: a shredded carrot salad with various other veggies and then a tuna salad. "B," slightly fancier, provided pre-plated gefilte-fish-from-jar resting on exactly one leaf of romaine lettuce, accompanied by various other veggie items and halves of hard-boiled eggs covered in lines of mayo. "C," somehow already far and away my favorite, was described to me by Herr Adler as "*Alkoholiker Mittagessen*," or "Alcoholics' Lunch." Apparently it was so called because it was the perfect accompaniment to vodka. One feasted on the simplest of delights: skinned and boiled potatoes that were then braised in oil and onions, Russian-style herring with onions, pickles and the same egg-concoction as "B."

"D" I think was the I-don't-give-a-shit lunch of the angry cook consisting of hard slices of bread topped with dry sardines, smoked trout or sliced cucumbers. I think this one came out whenever the rabbi had allowed the *oneg* or celebration to go on a little too long the previous week. Seriously, on the best days this cook dude came out of the kitchen solely to scowl. Should the Rabbi dare to encourage, you know, activities like *singing* or *community building*, the scowl would deepen. I think his name was Shmulik, or at least everyone seemed to call him that, and Schmulik's favorite hobby was "get the Russian Security."

Rabbi Isaac had, per my calculations, about an hour after the service to lead *Kiddush*, lead the hand-washing, bless the challah, cut the two enormous and dare-I-say delicious challah loaves into slices—no tearing of a challah in a German community! —eat, try to inspire those present with a word or two of Torah or even better answer our questions from that day's service, and then finally lead the *birkat hamazon*—the blessings after the meal. In an attempt to be, you know, Jewish, he would also try to get a little *yiddishkeit* moving with some songs and banging on the table and even encouraging the Old Russian Dudes to belt out some of their Yiddish tunes from who-knows-how-deep in their memories. But damn all if this took more than an hour. I get that people have to do their jobs but am I the only one confused as to why the majority of those employed by the synagogue found nothing of value in Judaism? Schmulik had to clean up and the security guards had to go home and watch the St. Petersburg football club because at that one hour point the Czar or one of his henchmen stood in the back of the social hall tapping their watch causing Rabbi, while trying to appear to ignore the intimidating figure, to act rattled. If the Czar or Ersatz-Czar for some reason did not appear at the haunting hour, Schmulik would go get them. I mean I never witnessed him performing this ritual, but the clue of Schmulik and Czar standing together tapping their watches at the sixty-five-minute mark left very little to assume.

Describing the VIP meal now suddenly seems pretty unimportant. Well, for the record it came out only when ordered by Engels or Platt, usually when some other community president came to visit or an official from the *Zentralrat der Juden in Deutschland*, the central Jewish governing body in Germany, came for Shabbos. All in all, with the exception of "D," all were more than palatable and some were quite good. Of course every single meal came with a liberal amount of vodka, a chilled bottle supplied by the community sat next to Rabbi's place-setting often supplemented by additional vodka brought by the Old Russian Dudes to celebrate a birthday or commemorate a *Yahrzeit*. Rabbi would ritually open the vodka after all blessings were said and pour the majority of it into half-shot glasses set religiously on a silver tray. He would then assign one of us younger folk *sans* cane to walk the tray around.

There was a bit of an art to this. Trying to get in the good graces of the Old Russian Dudes, I brought the tray to them first my first time around. Each of the Old Russian Dudes took at least two glasses and many double that, meaning that by the time

86

I got to the other leg of the U-shaped arrangement of six large tables, there was no longer enough. Rabbi didn't get any, something that was such a sin that one of the Old Russian Dudes offered to give up one of his four. This led to the further humiliation of Rabbi limping into the murky depths of the kitchen catacombs to retrieve a half empty emergency bottle and take care of the rest that had been left out. After this, I always started with the Charming Old Ladies side of the table, each of whom only took one if they chose at all to participate in the Barbaric Russian Rite. After a little more experience I got better at giving stern looks at those back on the over-indulgence side that tried to grab for four before all had been served.

The act of me serving to begin with had begun to make me predictably popular with the Dudes, something I relished until I looked up the pet names they had begun calling me. The most consistent was *yablochko* which sounded sweet and charming until I found out it meant "little apple" and was a euphemism for my breasts. I guess some things are better left untranslated.

In retrospect, the vodka made some of the most unpleasant things which I witnessed or experienced in the community nearly tolerable. Perhaps I should carry that thought forward and expand it and maybe I can begin to understand and have compassion for Soviet Jewry. Perhaps, but not today.

For today, today I am thinking of anger and how even aspiring to write a great Fulbright project is not helping me with objectivity.

A few weeks ago, Rabbi Isaac committed the ultimate sin and *made another change*. To us mere mortals, the new placement of the hand-washing basin next to the rabbi as opposed to outside the social hall seemed kind of logical. I mean the sight of Rabbi limping on his cane followed by a dozen others with canes made the movement of the basin, a necessity for Jewish meals serving bread, a pretty smart but well over-due move. Add to that that the move must have saved at least five minutes of precious time and a win just doesn't get more obvious.

Way too much sense as it turns out.

Representing the Charming Old Ladies at nearly every function, Frau B_ normally sat joined at the hip with Frau H_ for any religious function. Both looked like they sucked sour-patch-kids for a living and both seemed to seethe with hatred for Rabbi Isaac, from what I can gather mostly due to the fact he liked what he did and did so with energy. I ascertained after much consternation that in their world, leading with energy and trying simultaneously to impart the energy to others qualified as a negative. If I hit a point in my life where this makes sense, I will begin another narrative to share this wisdom with idiots like me that find this the epitome of lunacy, but there you have it.

The day that Rabbi moved the wash basin, Fraus B_ and H_ left the balcony after the service in visible and inconsolable tears. Somewhere in mid-conversation with Sabrina, as we moved toward what would sadly be that day a "D" lunch, we both paused at the sobs and public woe and flagellation that met us.

The two of us were, as was becoming more common, among the last out of the *beit knesset* and into the social hall. Sabrina had a strong case of the schmooze gene that had me doubting more and more her story of not actually being Jewish. By the time we talked in length with anyone and everyone after a service, Rabbi would often already be singing *Kiddush* before we started looking for our seats.

This time, we had already missed seeing the Fraus enter the social hall then leave as Frau B_ noticed the basin's new location, run out to find the absence at the old, and then break down into tears at the humanity.

Sabrina and I watched as both women, holding each other upright like drunken revelers—just more, um, sad and sober—curse, complain and make their way out of the Synagogue. The next week, to her credit, Frau H_ had returned. It was, however, the last I ever saw of Frau B_ and her husband for that matter. The fact that Herr B_ was also one of the two *gabbaim* of the community, a position of great responsibility in Orthodox context as well as I think Conservative, made the loss problematic. Add to that that the two had apparently moved into the city several years before Rabbi Isaac arrived to be within walking distance of the synagogue and the drama of their departure became even more baffling.

Sabrina, much bolder or maybe just much more German than I had quizzed the Rabbi about this several weeks later in one of their individual meetings. She even tried to do Rabbi's voice as she recounted the conversation:

"Do you know anything about Frau B_'s or Frau H_'s background?"

Sabrina shook her head.

"Normally I would never talk about this, but it is actually a part of why I teach conversion the way that I do.

"Both of them are converts. This is in and of itself meaningless. In Jewish tradition and Law, converts are prized, honored and highly respected. A convert is a Jew just as someone born of a Jewish mother is a Jew. The only clue that is supposed to remain is the name. Since a convert's parents are not Jewish, the *giyur* cannot take on the name of their birth parents as a Jew. The Jewish name for one generation is then *Plony ben Abraham Avinu* or *Plonit bat Sarah Imeinu*—John Doe son of Abraham our Father or Jane Doe daughter of Sarah our Mother.

In most Reform and Conservative shuls today where both mother's and father's names are taken, it is *Plony ben Abraham v'Sarah* or *Plonit bat Avraham v'Sarah*."

Sabrina asked the logical question that has always bothered me: "What if the parents' Hebrew names actually are Abraham and Sarah?" Sabrina swears that Rabbi answered, "Sucks to be them." I am sure that the remembered phrasing had more to do with idioms she picked up in Texas rather than recalling perfectly Rabbi's words, but she swears it, so there you have it.

Rabbi continued: "The idea is that after conversion, poof, no one in the community ever has to think about it again except the rabbi. I have to for other concerns like filling out a *ketubah*, but that isn't really important here. What is important is that it never works out that way. Everyone knows who has converted and there is, quite frankly, discrimination. How much depends on the community or individuals, but it is always there even among converts themselves that can on occasion become, well, I guess you would say 'self-hating' converts.

"And to be completely honest, although there is no excuse for discrimination, the discomfort can sometimes be understandable. Converts learn their Judaism as adults and most born-Jews as kids, most of whom stop their education after *bar* or *bat mitzvah*. Just think about that. How do we learn at twelve and how do we learn as adults? How are we cognitively interacting with our environment and the information being thrown at us? At least from a straight knowledge perspective, converts often know more, sometimes much more about Judaism than the born-Jews in a congregation. No surprise that this can be unpleasant for some.

"But there is another problem, and that is the translation from non-Jew to Jew."

"What do you mean?" Sabrina had asked.

90

"Just what it sounds like. If you try to speak English when you are thinking in German, you may make yourself understood but it doesn't sound like English. Often times that is how it feels a bit with converts, especially in those first few months or even years of zeal and idealism that are usually challenged after one finally realizes that Jews are just as flawed as everyone else, and just as unable to live up to our own best ideals."

"I am not sure how that helps me understand Frau B_."

"I am getting there. Honestly, I was a little perplexed myself. I called her later that week and she hung up on me and she hasn't returned my calls since. I finally called a colleague who served off and on as an interim here while they were searching a new rabbi, me as it turns out. When I told him who it was he said, 'Oh, that's easy. She is one of the Catholic Jews.'"

Sabrina, herself from a catholic family, told me that she wasn't insulted but had had to hold back a reaction along the lines of, "What the hell is that supposed to mean?" To the milder version she actually said Rabbi replied, "My thoughts exactly. Then he explained it and it made sense. Frau B_ converted some years ago under an Orthodox rabbi in England when her husband was working there. Rabbi Kahn told me that when he was here, there was a constant battle in the balcony between the women that converted from Protestantism and those that had converted from Catholicism. He said, the point is that they never left their old religion behind, they just changed their vocabulary and way of speaking about the old things. Now here's the kicker: he told me that I should have expected the reaction. For Frau B_ the wash basin didn't represent a wash basin, it was scanned as a basin of water with the religious significance she knew as a child. In her mind, I moved the sacral basin."

After thinking about this for weeks now, I kind of get it, but it also has started pissing me off enough that I am losing sleep and it is becoming an obsession. That is what's going on here? This is why Rabbi has to constantly put up with a type of abuse usually reserved for Mets fans when they show up at Phillies games? Now I torture myself by forcing myself first hand to see how loathsome these people are?

It seems like getting angry should be a pretty simple thing requiring a minimum of thought. Here I am in the balcony having kept my promise to myself for going on a couple of months, and this do-the-right-thing thing keeps on butting up against people like the Charming Old Ladies and add to that Shmulik and the Czar and the poor behavior and lack of respect downstairs and I am pissed. But at the same time I am not really sure how to manifest this anger. One would think that when one hits their early twenties, becoming angry should feel natural. But this is maybe the first time that I have really been angry—an uncomfortable admission considering how many times I have acted angry in my life.

It is, truth be told, a bit uncomfortable to think of younger versions of myself and how *that* version of Andrea got angry. It is hard to recall many times when the "angry" was nothing more than an "I didn't get my way" mini fit or major pout. And to have this realization just adds levels of suck because now I have to admit things about myself that feel pretty uncomfortable. I mean seriously, how can one think such things about one's self and stay sane?

But there it is.

There is of course more to it. In my life I have been known to shake my fist and clench my stomach and rage appropriately to the ignorance I have had to deal with regarding people that talk about Judaism or Israel based on the authority of loud headlines and preconceived notions. That is a right proper indignation that I am not regretting. But the rest of my life has been pretty good. Not getting this or that and throwing a teen version of a tantrum does not qualify as a just practice of anger. Even over-acted frustration at the stupidity of this friend or that date is not really what I am looking for now as I seek to understand *this* anger and find a way to express it or at least get a full night's sleep.

Maybe in retrospect it is not help I need in directing my anger. The more I see of religious communities or the more I become aware of things I saw in the past and just filed away, the more I am beginning to understand misanthropy. Is this what Herr Professor Doctor was hoping I would find when he sent me back to this forsaken synagogue into an encounter with myself? If I figure out how to be correctly angry, I think I will have discovered some great truth of adulthood. On the other hand, if I can just stop from being so pissed off all the time I will have enough material for a hell of a Fulbright project.

Conversion

I put off my meeting with Rabbi Isaac a bit too long. Part of me frankly felt ashamed for going to a Conservative rabbi working in an Orthodox-ish synagogue, and wasn't I just disrespecting my own shul and family and even life if I now made some sort of acknowledgement that I had to convert?

Of course once Sabrina got her hooks into me, backing out of my intention was no longer an option. Here I was, living outside of the States and with some level of fantasy that my ex-pat status could become permanent given the right situation and in order to live fully as a Jew here, I needed to play by their stricter rules.

With a personal *handy* number, contacting and setting up an appointment with Rabbi Isaac proved as simple as it should have been from the very beginning. He asked no questions, merely spoke through what sounded like a smile and found a mutually empty timeslot on a Wednesday after I had once again braved a lecture by Herr Professor Doctor and put a few half-hearted hours into my Fulbright project. As had been more and more often the case, the security door slid open with neither hesitation nor objection, allowing me unbarred access to Rabbi's attic.

The Rabbi Isaac greeting of hug and kiss was now automatic and expected, and it occurred to me how much everything really had changed in a few short months, perhaps most especially my own sense of what constituted normalcy.

"Great to see you, Andrea." As always, Rabbi exuded sincerity and welcome. I am not sure it is possible for anyone to appear that positive that often, but either he faked that, he was that, or he put that on for only certain people. Maybe he didn't act so welcoming when sitting down to a meeting with the political leadership of the community. Maybe then he would lose the smile and sense of *Wohlgefühl* and would look them in the eyes and say, "Why don't you assholes show some respect in my services?" Or maybe I just enjoy imagining him saying that to them.

"Thank you, Rabbi. Thanks for taking your time to meet with me."

He laughed unexpectedly.

"What's wrong?" I asked. I wasn't offended, just wasn't sure what I had said.

"Oh, it really is nothing," he answered still smiling. "Just a reminder of some things I miss about the States. I haven't heard anyone call me just plain 'Rabbi' in so long that it surprised me. It sounded good and I guess I miss that."

"What do they call you?" Strange that I had never really paid attention to how I heard other people address him.

"*Herr Rabbiner*, mostly, but that is more a reflection of German language and culture than the Hebrew and Jewish nature of 'Rabbi.' Do you know what 'Rabbi' literally means in Hebrew?"

I still wasn't sure if I loved or hated it when he did that. At least this time he lobbed a softball. "My Rabbi or my teacher," I answered without the proud idiot smile that I somehow really wanted to show.

"Great!" he said as always without irony or condescension. "What about '*Rabbiner*'?"

I shrugged. "I would have assumed the same, but I guess by your question it is not."

He nodded. "If you look at German texts about Judaism, the word for 'rabbi' in German actually means *Schriftgelehrter*, or 'One learned of texts.' On some level, it has similar

95

connotations, but whereas 'rabbi' is essentially the personal choice to call someone 'my teacher' implying a relationship, *'Herr Rabbiner'* instead comes off more like "Mister Elevated Academic" and implies respect from a distance. Just when you called me 'Rabbi' I realized how much I loved and missed hearing that.

"So anyway, a bit off topic I am sure. What can I do for you?"

Well there it was. Better get it over with now. I swallowed, breathed deeply, steeled myself, fought several demons, suppressed an emotional breakdown, and ended up with barely more than a glottal stop and a gaping mouth.

Bastard grinned and let me off the hook. "You want to convert."

He held his hand up to ward off the look in my eyes of the woman terrified of presenting a mind that easy to read. "Sabrina already told me. Don't be mad at her, just think of how much easier it was to have me know than to have to overcome all the crap you are right now having to overcome just to be here."

Asshole! Seriously, that level of intuition is not fighting fair. I nodded dumbly, feeling about three, being flooded with massive relief at the same time. *Arschloch!*

Before I could formulate an appropriate response, he continued, "Actually, you don't need to convert."

Finally, stuck idiot-tongue located itself, "What? Wait a second, I thought . . ."

"No, you still have to go through the process of *Beit Din* and *mikveh* to be *halakhically* Jewish, but in Germany in the *Allgemeine Rabbinerkonferenz* we do not consider someone of patrilineal descent to need conversion. Instead we call it 'status clarification' and it is, well, we make it quite a bit easier than regular conversion."

96

"How so?" Good. Voice was completely back now and this was interesting. I had never heard of any of this before. I also had no idea what the *Allgemeine Rabbinerkonferenz* was, but in this moment I saw that as secondary.

"Well, where to start?" Uncharacteristically, Rabbi Isaac didn't pour forth an academic soliloquy on the given subject. "Well, let's start with you, first. What do you know about conversion?"

I was getting a little more accustomed to this method of questioning. It was an effective technique as much as it was annoying. I wasn't sure yet if I more liked the constant challenge of being on my intellectual toes or hated the feeling of constantly being tested. Luckily I had been talking to Rabbi Google quite a bit recently in order to fill in some of my knowledge gaps and feel slightly less the idiot. "Conversion" had been one subject I had boned up on.

"I know that conversion used to be easy." I made sure Rabbi was nodding. "I know that the first conversion to Judaism is considered to be the story of Ruth."

"And what formulation did she use to state her conversion?" That was a great jumping off point to the moment and conversations that followed, but honestly the fact that I zoned out so often should not be taken as any sort of insult to Rabbi Isaac.

Somehow he turned a request to become more kosherly Jewish into a journey from Ruth to Hillel and Shammai to Bar Kochba to Pogroms to the Holocaust and all compellingly had something to do with my journey. But even as I filed the words and thoughts away there was no escaping the absurdity of someone else giving me a piece of paper to tell me who I already was.

My first memory of Jewish identity goes back to being no more than three or four. From that hazy distance, every time Daddy says, "Do you want to help, *Metukah?*" of course I want to help because he usually only calls me that when he wears the colorful little knit cap on his head and his voice gets softer and all those lines in his forehead smooth out as he looks at me, arms open for me to climb into his embrace and wave my hands in tandem with his at the candles that he has just lit. The words at that time still sound funny but Daddy looks so peaceful when he says them and at that point the strange magic book he is holding is just another mystery that I am promised I shall one day understand.

Baruch atah Adonai . . .

Is that conversion? Crawling into Daddy's arms and trying to sing along with the words that remain nothing more than mumbled syllables? Wanting so much to be held and accepted when Daddy looks like *that*, regardless of the literal content?

I went to mass with Grandmother and Grandfather a few times. Of course one called them Grandmother and Grandfather, capitalized their names and acted and dressed quite differently than when going to *shul* with Opa and Omi. Both mass and temple involved various moments of choreography that separated the initiated from the uninitiated. In both versions I envied those that so easily answered "and also be with you," or "*baruch hu uvaruch shemo*" with equal ease. I assumed at the time that the definition of Catholic was knowing when to kneel without having to look around like I always did and the definition of Jew was one that knew when to bow at the waist and when to bend at the knees.

Even though I know intellectually that my real moment of conversion happened as an infant in the *mikveh*, my real first conversion must have been when I decided that *shul* was more fun than *church*. There is nothing meant to be universal about that observation—I assume that given similar birth situations some people must have experienced their Catholic grandparents as the "fun" ones and the Jewish ones as the ones where you were terrified to move your pupils at the wrong time. It just wasn't my experience.

As Rabbi continued, now talking about why traditionally a rabbi says "no" three times before allowing a conversion candidate to begin her studies, I almost giggled at the absurd image that popped into my mind, that of sitting in front of a *Beit Din* made up of both sets of grandparents, as of the last decade may all their memories be for a blessing.

Opa would speak with his exaggerated accent while Omi would occasionally translate the jumbled mix that came off his tongue. In my imagination they are demanding as proof of my Jewishness that I eat some more brisket as I sit across from them. Grandmother and Grandfather shake their heads disapprovingly at something as profane as food being served at something so religious. They have something different they would wish for me, especially as they failed with their own daughter. But they know they cannot compete with the smiles and laughter that Opa and Omi get out of me.

When did *they* convert?

My Opa, seriously named Siegfried Baruch Lewy and born in Berlin in 1915—did he convert at the moment of his *bris* or the moment that he fled without his own parents in 1937 with three snapshots and two silver candlesticks in his suitcase? Or was it when he met his American-born wife, fifteen years his junior, who according to my father convinced him to get married under a *chuppah* when he had all but abandoned his religion? Or was it when they gave birth to a son, named him David to empower him to fight off the unseen Goliaths of his time and invited hundreds to his festive circumcision on the Upper East Side?

Grandmother and Grandfather must not like that their only granddaughter loves *gefilte* fish and dips her pinky into Daddy's Manischewitz. But when they *converted* at their confirmations was that a choice or a foreordained certainty? And why did Mom dutifully fulfill her white-clad first communion promise and then later reconvert, bowing instead at the altar of academia? How the hell did that happen? What moment erased the absolute certainty of that white dress? When she took that off, how painful must it have been for Grandmother and Grandfather? Was it liberating for my mom or simply self-evident?

Mom scrupulously never rolled her eyes when as a child I reached for Daddy's open arms or as a teen when I began wearing that colored knit cap on my own head and had started reading from those funny pages with the no-longer strange squiggles. She must have seen the conversion happening, so much different than her own, but what allowed her to countenance my clear steps toward the type of ancient ritual that so contradicted the demands of her gods?

Sitting in front of this rabbi, part of me wanted an experience like being held in daddy's arms again, with the details of the religion so much less important than the feeling of it. Rabbi had kept on focusing on the difficulties. Sure, no way you could be the granddaughter of someone who barely got out before the Holocaust and lost everyone they knew and not be aware of the difficulties! At the same time, none of that story reminded me of my own life. The most unpleasant experience I had ever had as a Jew was the first time I had come to this shul. I wasn't here to ask to be something I wasn't.

"So, Andrea, this brings us back to my critical question from the Talmud: Why do you want to do this? Do you not understand

100

the state of the people of Israel?" He sat back, relaxed in his chair and smiled with his mouth but not with his eyes adding, "Are you crazy?"

I answered reflexively, truly without thinking. "But I am Jewish."

The harshness left Rabbi's eyes as he answered gently, "That is the only answer I would have accepted from you."

The sensation was still there. There really wasn't another answer, was there?

Aliens

I have absolutely no problems with self-image. None. I never grew up with "Don't eat that or you will get fat," or worse what would have been a deliciously ironic "clean up you plate—there are children starving in China." I grew up inside Whole Foods and probably saw my first ACME on a drive-by in Philly rather than as part of a destination. Meals were healthy, red meat occasional, soda never, and sweets consisted of berry deserts. My parents led by example instead of tyranny. Yes, of course I am fortunate to live in family that could *afford* to eat healthily— seriously how twisted is that statement—but aside from liberal self-recriminations from privilege I benefited from being bourgeois and grew up the type of healthy that at least gave me a fighting chance against the anorexic ideals staring at me from the newsstand.

This of course doesn't mean I don't fight certain fights and suffer from the insecurities that come from knowing I will never look airbrushed. And worse, reality intervenes to add more of what Vogue and Cosmo covers teach me are "flaws" to the ones already generously provided by nature.

About two months after my *bat mitzvah*, I got what we thought was simply a bad stomach flu—a really really bad stomach flu. I lay in feverish agony for days, listening compulsively to a rotation of Palestrina, New Age piano CDs and Renaissance lute music to keep calm and from ridiculously and dramatically moaning every other moment. I mean, it should have been obvious that I was sicker than the flu, but my mom had had the stomach flu the week before, and as my symptoms at least for the first few days mirrored those of hers, the shooting pains in my gut had been falsely but logically contextualized.

When I vomited black blood into the toilet on day three or four, the concern in my mom's face turned to horror and my dad proved his James Bond skills driving back roads at "I love my daughter" high speeds to get us to the emergency room at Crozer. Something like thirty minutes later they had me prepped for surgery. Sometime later, the clearly bent surgeon brought out a jar containing my engorged and burst appendix, reported the roughly two cups of poison scraped from my internal linings and that I would be on a morphine drip for a few days as the pain would be intense. My dad loved telling the story about the baby-fist-sized appendix but no one ever described how my parents reacted. I assume my mom at least wept in the mother guilt of not having magically known what was wrong. Perhaps she sat in silent shock. I do know that for years after she would look as if stabbed any time family conversation wound its way to the Great Andrea Appendix Trauma of 2003. Hell, on particularly, ahem, manipulative days I would even find a way to wind the conversation that direction myself in order to add the weight of psychic trauma to whichever request for material acquisition that my mother had just nixed.

Seriously, it was my own damn fault. Of course I knew far earlier than the Black Blood Horror that something else was wrong. I didn't imagine, of course, that it would prove to be so potentially deadly. But it turns out that I would rather pretend to be ok than to worry my loved-ones unduly. I have no idea where the insanity of this martyr syndrome came from, only that I still live daily with this shit and needed as well to be surprised by the contents of my innards before my instinct to live overcame the instincts to protect my parents.

I obviously at some point woke up, at some point heard the grim but martyrdom-empowering news that my peritonitis had left me about an hour short of the grave, and at some point no longer needed pain medication. Like resilient thirteen-year-olds tend to do, I bounced back, forgot most of the drama unless necessary to gain a nod of sympathy here or there after a dramatic retelling, and moved forward with minimal scars.

Fortunately, I was fully recovered in time for a long-coveted vacation to see relatives in LA, meaning lots of time with cousins in Malibu. I had impressed myself with the two-piece I got from Macy's at an end-of-season sale the previous year. It was yellow and green floral, cute, totally grown-up and made me feel special in a way I didn't quite yet understand.

After a little family tension and intense discussion my parents acquiesced and did not require return and exchange. . . which is why my father surely did not understand when he came home early that nearly-summer day to find his daughter sobbing after trying on the suit for the first time since the victory shopping of the previous autumn.

"Look," I sob-shouted, wondering why this usually wise man could not see my point. "Look! It's awful!"

In the sacred self-esteem space between the tied strings atop the bikini bottom and the lowest inches of my ribcage screamed The Scar. I mean, in my mind there was no skin left there, simply a gash thirty shades darker than my skin, drawing away every possibility of attention or appreciation from whatever assets genetics gifted me. My genetics as well had gifted me with an appendix quite a bit lower and stage right from the usual position marked in the textbooks elongating the expected one inch scar to a three-inch insult that now told my thirteen-year-old brain that I looked hideous. Malibu had already transformed itself from three weeks of fun and frivolity to a predictable disaster to be avoided at all costs.

"But you know it will fade. The doctor told you about that, *Metukah.*"

104

Yes, I know he did, but that was when it was still covered and after the bandage came off it was clearly still healing and since then I have been wearing my usual clothes and I guess I just really didn't want to see that but Daddy you just can't understand and nothing of this could be articulated beyond a mucus filled sob, "It'll never go away."

My father either channeled my mother or decided to stand up for his archetypal rights as an engineer and reasonably suggested: "Well, *Metukah,* let me just take you back to King of Prussia and we'll get you a one-piece to get you through the summer and until the scar heals more and fades more."

Of course the contradiction between simple logic and the pre-meditated disappointment implicit in my expectations kept me sobbing instead of arguing. I knew from long experience that my trump argument that made so much sense in my mind—*but it's* California*!* —would not engender more sympathy. I got in the car with him later that evening, found a sporty and shiny lavender number from Nordstrom that took away a slight bit of sob but did nothing for the assured impending doom of being the *only* freshman in high school on Malibu in a one piece. The *Schande.*

As it was, the summer was not exactly a disaster other than the fact that Uri Zilberman, the only openly Jewish boy on the beach *and* a junior, couldn't kiss worth a damn and made me secretly question my sexuality for the first time. This episode of questioning lasted until the very *not* Jewish Jason Park of Korean heritage somewhat erased that string of doubts my senior year. But at least that summer I could hide the scar and put off dealing with body and acceptance fears for a few more years.

So I have dealt with it but I don't like it. There are days that I stand and stretch in front of the mirror after a shower and love what I see, even without a little concealer here and a little toner

105

there. Then there are the days, in spite of my mother's best efforts to avoid body-shaming me and my father's best efforts to make sure I left home with no daddy issues, where every single flaw becomes the sole meaning of that moment of existence, screaming at me like the ads from the magazines that act as surrogate body-shaming mother and daddy-issue fashioning father. On these days The Scar, which has of course never faded that I can see, still looks like it takes up my entire midriff. Worse, it is one of those innies instead of outies scars, which makes everything worse by creating a fold-over several inches of skin suggesting more fat than I am going to ever admit actually being there. Moving down on *those* days in the mirror-view process of self-recriminations, stomach, hips and thighs all accuse me of the hours spent in the library instead of strapping on spandex and sweating at the gym to the latest Brittney opus. Moving up, I can never decide which breast is asymmetrical although I promise you it is one of them, and then further up my clavicles could poke the eyes out of any suitor. The beauty mark that could have been, well, beautiful had it attached itself one millimeter higher, instead looks like a bad lip piercing from a distance as it sits half-way between right upper lip and non-lip. My nose is ok, although I envy my K-pop idols—sorry, dirty secret here—and their far superior nose shapes as mine is a little too flat and the nostrils too wide. Of course the K-pop versions come mostly at the cost of a surgeon's knife, but I am just going to ignore that I know that. I do like the color of my eyes—I call it dark-stained mahogany and I dare you to contradict my label— but dammit if no amount of sleep gets rid of the suggestion of bags under my eyes and makes, especially on bad mirror days, the acquisition of toners, concealers and foundation a moral imperative.

Those days convince me that several boyfriend-slash-flings have been right in calling me a wee high maintenance but I swear it is only on *those* days. The rest of the time, thank you Mom and Daddy, the mirror grants me beautiful moments of self-esteem and deep conviction that in the right not-appropriate-for-synagogue kensie sleeveless crew-neckline brocade bodycon dress I *will* make you do a double-take and I *won't* apologize.

. . . which is why the shock of walking into the alien-filled Chanukah party was *that* bad. Where do I start?

In my "War and Conflict" course at the Uni, I sat next to a girl from Ukraine named Yana. Now, Yana also possessed the traits that I am choosing to call "alien" that so overwhelmed me at the party, but you must understand that one-on-one you can simply dismiss the empty pit of inadequacy that cannot be denied at one-on-one-hundred-twenty. I must admit Yana, about five-eleven, early twenties, strawberry blonde and with a perfectly positioned beauty mark not only took my breath away, she destroyed my for-sanity's-sake held belief that only airbrushed women look like *that*. So instead of introducing myself, holding out my hand in introduction or freaking asking her name I gushed, "*Um Gottes willen du bist schön!*" Dear God, you're beautiful.

Luckily, it turns out that Yana is also sweet and even later it turns out, a hell of a lot of fun to sip a wine with, so the ejaculation did not send her to a lower row in the lecture hall amidst backward *um Gottes willen* glances of disdain. Moreover, my somewhat memorable introduction led to a fascinating conversation including Yana's assertion that in her village, the Soviet government had deliberately relocated women considered even more extraordinarily beautiful than usual in order to breed, as it were, even more beautiful women. Yana provided no proof and I cannot find any mention of this on English language sources on the internet, but Yana swears it is true and this sort of eugenics program at least partially explains the Chanukah party. I once again received neither second-look nor assume-the-position demands from security as I made my way unaccompanied from fortress gates and guard towers to foyer to cloak room to second-floor social hall. I had worn your basic black dress—a Ted Baker flared cocktail dress with short sleeves and synagogue-appropriate modesty provided by below-the-knees hem. I wasn't exactly thinking of trying or not trying to stand out, rather looking appropriate *in the synagogue!* for what I assumed would be a party no different from the run-of-the-mill light candles, sing *Maoz Tzur*, eat *latkes*, eat *sufganiyot* and schmooze a bit parties ubiquitous at every synagogue in the civilized world. Instead I was greeted with ignore the rabbi as he lights candles, sing along with the two other people that knew *Maoz Tzur*, drink vodka, drink vodka, and sit alone at a table as I watched hundreds of aliens dance to the soothing sounds of Radio Vladivostok.

Okay, maybe I am being harsh. But my desire to be at least surface-modest had not prepared me to feel as if I had showed up for prom in strawberry shortcake pajamas.

The average female age in the packed social hall looked to be between sixteen and twenty-five. Fine, I fit in there at early twenties. But sixteen to twenty-five Russian and Ukrainian meant a critical mass of females that looked photo-shopped, springing fully alive from the cover pages Cosmo-if-you-look-inside-you-*will*-feel-like-shit-politan.

And I felt like shit.

The worst of the worst of the bad mirror days stared at me in my relative plainness. I stopped in the doorway, once more thirteen and once more confronted with The Scar. Only this time there was neither daddy nor one-piece to get me through the party, only the sensation that had to be true that I was suddenly, when it for months had meant nearly nothing to me, the least desirable person there.

I really need to stop here. It is beginning to sound as if this early twenties version of Andrea had built her ego solely on the ability win a mammalian pissing context with other preening females-of-the-species in an all-consuming quest to turn the heads of the male warrior breeders. Come on. I am still my mother's self-aware and my father's self-sufficient daughter. This has nothing to do with my shallowness. This has everything to do with the encounter with the other, and how the other, when presenting the mirror, often will show us that which we are not yet ready to explore. In this moment, this *other* showed me that despite my upbringing and clear priorities directed toward the library and away from the gym, I had a greater insecurity with my appearance than I had ever admitted to myself.

Maybe it is what my mother, when not poking at my somewhat-theistic father with her humanities-informed condemnation of theistic religion, deluged me with in the form of articles, anecdotes and lectures as to the effects of mass-media on the maturing self-image of any western girl alive today. Maybe the "Maybe it's Maybelline" and "How to Please Your Man in 20 Easy Steps," and "J-Lo's ass but without cellulite" had in spite of all intruded deeper than I ever could have imagined. An impending feeling of depression smacked me across the face, halted my steps, threatened tears and I hadn't even crossed the threshold.

Blessed Rabbi Isaac at least distracted me in the moment after seeing me standing there from between five and fifty minutes and compassionately moved in for a rescue.

"Chanukah *sameyach*, Andrea."

Rabbi's table stood nearest the door, so it did not seem odd when he stepped away from the conversation with the President's wife who he was clearly happy to get away from and came to me with a greeting and quick embrace and peck on the cheek. "Chanukah *sameyach*, Rabbi."

"Have you eaten?" he asked, gesturing toward the latke-laden tables on the opposite wall.

"Not yet," I answered, not really wanting small talk while at the same time realizing I should be grateful for the interruption.

"Tell you what, I'll do you a favor and accompany you to the table if you do me the favor of pretending we are having a deep and important conversation and I can at least for a while avoid going back there." He not so subtly jerked his chin back toward the *Häuptlinge* and their spouses.

"Deal," I said, settling on feeling ridiculously grateful for his intervention.

We made our way past what appeared to be surprisingly adept dancing from all ages to a table where my favorite asshole cook proved once again that providing surprisingly tasty and colorful food was not one of the challenges of this community.

Son-of-Czar tended the ad-hoc but well stocked bar and after a millisecond of locked eyes and an uncomfortable grunt of greeting I decided against paying a few Euros for a cocktail and settled for a tall class of fizzy water. Turned out it didn't really matter as full bottles of vodka were also available for purchase and were generously passed around, usually by middle-aged to older gentlemen, and I had enough in the next few hours anyway to give me bed-spins, even with my exponentially growing alcohol tolerance.

After a few more words with Rabbi including a few sentences of update on my conversion reading assignment, I parted ways with him and found an empty table to enjoy my latkes and develop my plan to escape soon after.

Midway through my plate and two *Na Zdaroviya!* shots of vodka later, my plans changed when Nataliya found me and with the warmest of Russian greetings sat down next to me. Which means this is as good of time as any to talk about Natasha, as the Nataliyas of the world were most often called.

Sabrina was already on her way to becoming not only a counter-balance to the denizens of the balcony but as well a German style friend. Shit, I need to explain that one too. Ok. There are essentially two words in German that translate into "friend" in English: *"Freund"* and *"Bekannter,"* or *"Freundin"* and *"Bekannte"* if you are talking women which on another note just pisses me off about German in general—three genders for nouns. Three. And seriously don't try to create some logic system to help you out. Other than a few blessed helpful noun endings like "-heit" and "-keit" which are always feminine, "-ismus" which is always masculine and "-chen" which is always neutral, there is neither rhyme nor reason. Seriously. Ask Germans to explain it to you. Have fun with that. And it all leads to such things as the obvious that man, "der Mann," is masculine—duh, I guess—and that woman, "die Frau," is feminine, but because of the "-chen" thing, "girl" is "das Mädchen" which is neutral. This leads to hilarity when literally translating such as, "The girl walked into the room and it was gorgeous!" How fun is that?

Anyway, friends. It truly didn't take long for me to embrace the German concept of friend. In America I think we throw out the word friend like we throw out likes on Facebook. Come to think of it, the 637 "friends" I have on Facebook . . . really? But if you say that someone is *"mein Freund"* or *"meine Freundin,"* it either means boyfriend or girlfriend or I guess what I am now going to have to refer to as a friend-friend. *"Bekannter"* is more like acquaintance, but seriously, isn't that what most of our friends are? "Hey, Jenny, I want to introduce you to my friend Rachel who is also good friends with John's boyfriend." Really? The question I ask now based on my new German language revelations is, "If I had a minor car accident and I needed to be picked up without having to call Mom or Dad at two in the morning and deal with *that*, which *friend* would I call?" Who is on that shortlist? If they are not on that shortlist, aren't they a friend and not a friend-friend, meaning truly an acquaintance but we can't say that in American English for some fear that feelings will be hurt? I don't think that there is any inherent insult in how Germans use language, I just think that there is something really useful about using a word that has real meaning as opposed to everyone you meet being a "friend" in the way that every new band is "genius." No, it is not and no they are not. So I meet someone once. Maybe we even sat next to each other at the bachelorette party, bonded, shared some laughs and more than the three obligatory selfies that got posted on our newly "friend" bonded Facebook relationship. They are not a friend-friend, barely even a friend, but I realize that by default I fell into the cultural norm of "Everyone is a friend" and I have already been changed by this German language idea. Perhaps that is partly why we travel other places—to add an idea or two.

So Sabrina with her hospitality and smoky eyes and challenging advice regarding my Jewish path was well on the way to *Freundin* status, but that was nothing compared to what developed with Natasha, although I am still not completely sure why, to be honest.

Hell, without understanding my more than twenty or so basic Russian words, I think the *Freund/Bekannter* dichotomy must

112

have existed with even more intensity within FSU culture—this gleaned from the time Natasha hugged me and kissed my cheeks upon parting from what became regular Sunday excursions and said, "You are like a Russian friend!" I had no idea what that meant at the time but it felt like I had been offered entrance into the holy-of-holies of a Russian soul and I knew enough to say, "*spaseba*" in return and look meaningfully in her eyes. Of course in retrospect I am an asshole because in order to even look at her in the eyes the first time I had to trip and fall on the uneven stone floors of the synagogue foyer.

I had seen Natasha before. Ok, it's probably more honest to say I had my eyes look in the direction where she stood on more than one occasion, and had in politeness once or twice practiced the odd "*zdravstvutye*" or "*privyet*" while walking by her on the way up to Rabbi's office as our meetings became more frequent. It wasn't that she was unpleasant to look at, quite the opposite, actually. She had what I call the sport-compact Russian type—less than five-foot-four, not-blond, and pretty as opposed to the alien type of somewhere over what seems like seven feet tall, usually blond and clearly airbrushed even though they were standing there right in front of me. Natasha had shoulder-length non-descript brown hair kept almost always in a pony-tail, light turquoise-y green blue eyes, and freckles right where they would play to the maximum cute across cheeks and nose. She seemed from facial creases about late-thirties although I later learned that she was actually thirty-three, and hardly showed from clothing outside the stress of the birth of a son followed six years later by identical twin girls.

Normally I would have, especially after multiple encounters, at the very least stopped and introduced myself in addition to the passing "*privyet*." The only problem was that Natasha dressed in sociological camouflage, in her case the light blue work uniform of the community's custodial staff. Yes, I told you: I'm an asshole.

So I will accept this as some combination of divine intervention and fate, if those are even two different things, that leaving the Rabbi's office one winter-must-be-immanent day a few weeks before Chanukah, that while in my usual act of not-noticing the custodian and distractedly fiddling with my *handy* that one of the woman-eating uneven stones in the poorly designed floor jumped up and tackled me. I mean at least it felt like it lying there with scraped and just-beginning-to-threaten-to-bleed palms feeling somehow betrayed by inanimate objects.

"*Alles ok?*" Natasha had left her custodial cart behind in what must have been a fraction of a second and was kneeling beside me, gently poking, prodding and inspecting all the while using very broken German to ascertain my condition. No one else had moved, not that it was any great worthy-of-notice fall other than my embarrassing squeak of surprise roughly three octaves higher than my highest singing voice. The several eternally arguing Russian Dudes paused their "discussion" for enough seconds to see if my clothing choice of the day made the fall particularly worth noting. Not particularly form-fitting 501s meant not really, and the "discussion" began quickly anew.

"I'm fine," I tried to say in several languages including a few repeated "*khorosho*" to stave off the embarrassment at being so intensely fawned over. Yeah, nice try. You try to get between an archetypal mother with practical experience and her object of mothering.

Her German was nearly unintelligible, but the communication came through clearly that I wasn't going to be un-mothered until completely cared for.

With a strength far greater than her frame would suggest, she pulled me to my feet and ushered me down a side hallway past

114

the cloakroom to the ladies' restroom. Leaving me with now decently bleeding hands under the water, she left and returned with her purse, more of a mother's backpack meant to contain every imaginable contingency item should a child be injured. As her *ersatz* child in that moment, I finally stopped internally struggling and allowed my hands to be cleaned, sanitized and bandaged as if I had suffered a war wound. She finished professionally and finally rewarded my patience with a satisfied I-told-you-so smile. "There. Better, yes?"

It was actually pretty impressive. Somewhere in the last few years I had begun to wonder if the mother-gene had passed me by. I had seen that certain look in friends' eyes when an infant was around. There was a glassiness to the look that I assumed I was supposed to have but couldn't quite replicate, turning my answers to the inevitable "Isn't he/she just the most precious thing that ever existed?" into strangled "um, sure"s. This woman didn't pretend anything, she just *was* and as she beamed at me I finally looked at her. I mean saw her.

"Thank you very much," I repeated in German and then Russian, and then let the dawning guilt for ignoring this person come out with an, "*Es tut mir so leid, dass ich mich noch nicht vorgestellt habe.*" I am so sorry that I haven't introduced myself yet. And seriously I was sorry. "Andrea," I held out my bandaged palms without thinking.

"Nataliya," she grinned and shook her head slightly at my outstretched hand and instead lightly grabbed my shoulders. "You are welcome," she said in an English far more accented than even her German.

I really didn't know where to go from here, but Nataliya did, as she was just about to get off work and plunging into this rabbit-hole I found myself thirty-minutes later in her flat, sipping tea and holding one of her two twin daughters on my lap playing

115

some sort of bouncy game that I must have picked up through the collective unconscious. As we had entered, an older and more world-worn version of Natasha had greeted me briefly, spoken some words of command to her daughter, and left the apartment for what I would later find out would be Natasha's mother's apartment across the hall.

Now the first challenge here has already been stated: how do you start a relationship with a couple dozen vocabulary words in common? Turns out pretty easily, if the chemistry is there. It is funny how you can stand in front of a hundred nearly identical people with identical backgrounds and education and even personalities, but one you will love, one you will hate and the rest will have little impact on you. There is probably something deeply spiritual in this, what we like to call "meant to be" although it is probably just as much a result of pheromones, good lighting and the amount of sleep we had before we met the people.

Beyond language I had nothing in common with her, other than that she decided to bandage me up and I decided to accept her invitation for hospitality. But how tea is offered and how children are introduced and handed over with instant trust offers a surprising amount of "conversation" if you are hyper focusing in order to make up for a verbal deficiency. I couldn't ask her about her life nor she about mine, but a smart phone with Facebook allowed me to give her a lot of "thousand words" testimonies as did her old-fashioned photo-albums.

For one thing, had Natasha who I had until today ignored because she was a custodian told me verbally that she had graduated from medical school in St. Petersburg there is no chance I could have processed the words. But seeing pictures of the lovely freckled girl in school plays and at track meets and in a gymnastics outfit with many pictures with medals told me

116

more than dialogue—as did picture after picture of the same girl, a few years older, in scrubs and then holding a stethoscope and diploma.

The obvious questions that could not be answered with words were then quickly answered with the marriage photo to a portly older gentleman with fiercely handsome features and a Hollywood-head of black hair. Then came pictures of a baby and pictures of a new apartment somewhere in Russia followed by an apartment in Jerusalem followed by an apartment in Germany. Interspersed were newspaper clippings in addition to postcards. At first these clippings would all be in Cyrillic—the articles probably about this play or that gymnastics-meet or that honor in Med-school. Later came more articles on the fierce gentleman, ones that showed him in the formal hat of an Orthodox cantor and ones that announced apparent hirings at synagogues in Russia and then Israel and finally in Germany, where I could finally read: "*Neuer Kantor für Synagogue x in Stadt y.*" Then came photos of another pregnancy, with lots of photos in hospitals with a desperately ill-looking woman, her freckles now creased in pain and worry, followed by a final crumpled article about the cantor—a hiring at yet another Synagogue, this one with him standing next to a blond German-looking, obviously pregnant woman that was just as obviously not Natasha. The final photos, back in Natasha's present, showed two tiny-but-perfectly-formed twins entering the world.

When I tearfully looked up after the journey and several refills of deliciously spiced tea, I realized I had fallen in love. Not in any way that I had ever fallen in love—not romantically or sexually or with any feeling of intention for partnership. Rather I had fallen into the love that is supposed to be inborn between you and your blood relatives. I had fallen in love with a narrative that broke my heart and had fallen into a kinship with a soul that had suffered and fallen profoundly—*she was a fucking doctor and now was a fucking janitor*—and sat there with a core of strength I really had never seen.

A few weeks later as she joined me at the table and lightly kissed my cheeks, she hollered conversation over the ever-increasing music volume with our now sixty-or-so common words in three languages. In lieu of deep conversation we had taken to talking caveman style and learning each other's language in the process as we walked a double-stroller through the snappy winter streets of our city. We sipped mulled wine in the local Christmas Market and learned vocabulary from simple object pointed, explained and then repeated until we had each mastered the other's word.

Here in the den of aliens, it hit me that her lined face with no trace of airbrush could not compete with anyone else there, except that she looked so much more beautiful. It could have been one of those feminist moments of overcoming mammalian predilection and patriarchal beauty rules to recognize true beauty, except that in this case it was real. This is what a Russian woman was. This is what a Jewish mother did to survive. These were the attributes to which I could aspire if I could simply overcome myself.

There were no taboos against Russian female friends holding hands or dancing together, so with her presence or support I forgot my alienation and found a strange sort of joy to the now pounding beat of Radio Vladivostok. Seconds of latkes didn't even look evil any longer as I started to wonder if there wasn't possibly something to be said for these Soviet Jews. Perhaps I had misjudged them.

Falling

"Are you ok?"

Rabbi Isaac looked pale with a steady film of perspiration beading on his forehead. He had already been in his office with another appointment when I came in, so it wasn't from the exertion of limping up the cement stairs leaning on a cane. Come to think of it, he had been looking a little drawn for our last several meetings. But every time Rabbi would begin teaching, you kind of just ignored everything else. He had one gear while teaching to a group or an individual— "full speed ahead."

Today something had changed. He just shook his head a bit at my question and then dabbed at his forehead with his black kerchief. Feeling a bit helpless I noticed none of the ubiquitous green bottles of German mineral water on the table, and jerked my head toward the dorm fridge in inquiry to which Rabbi responded with a non-committal shrug. Trying to channel either Sabrina's hospitality or Natasha's mothering I stood and squeezed carefully past the stacks of papers perched precariously on the file cabinets and pulled a bottle of "*Rheinquelle Medium*" from among the six stacked inside. I also tried to pretend I did not see the two empty Johnny Walker Blacks lining the back corner of Rabbi Isaac's desk adjacent the fridge.

As I grabbed a few cleanish looking glasses from the shelf and poured for us both, I began rapidly ticking off potential entre lines to break the rapidly mounting silent tension in the room.

A few uncomfortable sips later as about thirty potential lines were reviewed and rejected, Rabbi Isaac began speaking as if nothing unusual had been happening.

"I guess it is about time for the 'Chutzpah-Disillusionment' speech."

119

His voice sounded distant and he uncharacteristically refused to meet my eyes, looking instead at some vague point ten feet behind and to the right of my forehead.

"You don't really need it all. The chutzpah part simply is my admonishment to potential converts that you need to make your own way in Judaism. Did you ever see Chaim Potek's 'The Chosen?'"

I nodded. Who hadn't?

"Right. Well there is this scene—it has been years since I have seen it so I am sure I am getting the details wrong—anyway a scene at the Orthodox rabbi's house where everyone is talking and the guests are shocked that a younger boy at the table has to talk over everyone else to be heard. When one of the guests seems affronted by this, the *rebbitzen* responds that if you feel you have something to say, it is worth working to be heard.

"It's funny because it's true. I mean, maybe it is a bit extreme, but a lot of converts are simply way too polite and are waiting to be invited. To talk, to participate—you know. But it doesn't work that way. We are called to be hospitable, but not to be polite. But for so many that don't really get this or are never explicitly told this, people start feeling disenfranchised. Sure a community can be more welcoming or less welcoming than another, but at the end of the day, anyone that expects to be invited to be a part of active Judaism rather than simply demand to take part is going to be disappointed.

"I'm not too worried about you, so I haven't really bothered talking about this until now. You have quite a bit of chutzpah and I mean that as a compliment. I am not worried about you on that.

"But the second part concerns me. Everyone that converts to Judaism discovers what every born Jew realizes at some point—Jews can never live up to Judaism. Ultimately, everyone that practices Judaism—born, adopted or converted—as opposed to simply wearing the label as an identity—eventually has to overcome the realization that Jews are humans, meaning we all have the capacity to do great good but usually just suck."

Rabbi still hadn't looked at me, but as he paused to take a sip he finally met my eyes in apology. For what? Saying "suck?" The slight rant-y tone in his voice? I quickly checked myself and realized I was more fascinated than scared—although the fascination admittedly felt a bit like rubbernecking on I-95 to see the jack-knifed truck on the other side.

"Andrea, you are an idealist. This is mostly a good thing, but you are going to need to check the energy of your idealism. Where does it come from? From what I have seen you have a strong sense of what a Jewish community should be—what Judaism should be. That is in and of itself a good thing, but one: it can lead to disillusionment when you find out that none of us, me especially, can live up to your ideals—two: is it for the sake of the *gestalt* of Judaism or is it to fulfill your personal needs?"

It shouldn't be surprising that I started feeling more than a bit defensive. *What the fuck* is probably more like it. Now I indeed started feeling slightly unsafe, but wasn't sure how to react to these words and more precisely this version of Rabbi Isaac that I had never before witnessed.

"Part of this is your unique spirit—your Andrea-ness. Even though it will cause you pain, you need to keep up this idealism and soldier through for the sake of *Klal Yisroel*—for all of us. One person who cares will make more of a difference for Judaism than a hundred that just show up and a million that have just given up. Apathy is one of the biggest dangers to our future and it is not your problem as long as you don't give up when you are beaten down."

His eyes had a slight glisten and he hid the emotion with another sip and another dab from his kerchief.

"But there is another thing I want to challenge you with. When Gen Xers like me were growing up, most of us from the middle class saw this amazing explosion of materialism that few of us could access in our every day. I mean we had it good, but terms like Yuppies were usually applied in derision to the people in the movies while we would get a copy of the Sharper Image catalogue and lust over each of the gadgets that we just had to have. Our Baby-Boomer parents were also fully into that acquisition but had no trouble telling us 'no.' We hated that. I think my entire generation resented being told 'no' and so when we started raising our kids, the Millennials, we did so with this unconscious desire to never make our kids feel the disappointment that we did of wearing Nikes when New Balance was the only thing that the cool kids were wearing. The girls that wore Levi's were mocked by those wearing Guess until the style turned to Claiborne, and I think we channeled every ounce of our parenting into making sure our kids would never feel as ostracized as we did.

"But we really messed up. What is happening is that my colleagues at the Uni back in the States have stopped teaching anything that is controversial. It is actually one of the reasons I left and went back into congregations—not just the Messianic complex I obviously had when I came here and thought I could make a fu . . . a difference."

He had entered into some strange zone between rant and sermon, but with a frightening quiet and even tone of voice. It had become clear that the sublimated vitriol, however, had nothing to do with me. His focus still remained trained on that point behind my head and that person or thing was the one that should be afraid. Add to that that I have never heard a Rabbi say "fuck" or even almost say it and I felt that rather than a student in his office, I was the proverbial fly-on-the-wall listening to Rabbi's most private thoughts.

"I was tenured and therefore protected, but I had at least two non-tenured colleagues, one in Humanities and one in Philosophy, who were mysteriously not offered contract extensions when students had written letters of complaint. The problem? What the profs were teaching them made them feel 'uncomfortable.'

"This is like the great joke of Western entitlement. There are countries where honor-killings happen every day, even here in Germany. In America we go on the war-path when someone makes us read Salinger or Twain or Harper Lee and we cannot deal with how uncomfortable language makes us feel. So rather than deal with it, we remove anything that makes us challenge our own tiny little box.

"And here is the great joke. It has now trickled back up into my generation and that of my parents. The first time that I got a negative review from a course at Uni that my classes were too 'frontal' I wanted to spit. I am sorry, but if I go to a lecture on Mozart and I am not the Mozart expert in the room, my collection of Mozart chamber music does not entitle me to demand that my feelings about Mozart take precedence over the expert giving the lecture. Either I have something to learn or I can join a fucking Mozart discussion group."

Now he closed his eyes, possibly at the first realization at what had come out of his mouth as the almost-fuck had finally manifested as a full-blown-fuck. I was right as he opened his eyes and said, "I'm sorry. Truly."

I felt a mixture of anger and amusement. The anger came from the repudiation of my entire generation. There was a value in what he was talking about that he just didn't get. His

123

generation and older seemed to have this idea that if something sucked you had to endure it. I think what my generation was truly saying was, "Listen. Just because it has always been done that way doesn't make it right. I don't have to work at a job I hate like my friends' parents did. If I hate it then why not complain and get it changed? If no one is willing to change it then why not look for another job that better serves my needs." I wanted to start saying that until I realized that part of my desire to lash out had to do with the fact that my anger came from feeling incredibly uncomfortable. It sucked being the fulfillment of prophecy, and so for the moment I shut up until I could make my arguments for my own generation stronger. But as my second emotion was amusement at hearing a Rabbi drop an F-bomb, I decided to teach him a little about the values of my generation and let him off the hook for feeling "uncomfortable."

"It's ok," I forced a chuckle. "Seriously, I swear like a sailor in my normal life. Now in German too. You should hear what I have learned in Russian. No way you are going to offend me." Shock me, sure, but offend me?

His eyes finally locked on me. "I appreciate that. You may have noticed I am a little out of sorts today."

Yeah, you think?

That level of sarcasm probably would not have been appropriate, regardless of the boundaries Rabbi was determined to break with me today. I settled on curiosity instead of sarcasm and with as much compassion as I could infuse into my voice I asked, "What happened?"

"Disillusionment, my dear." He chuckled, the sound coming out choked. "One of my teachers once told me that rabbis write sermons for themselves—we preach what we ourselves need to hear. If it so happens that the message resonates with others, then so much the better.

124

"Anyway, I requested some time off because I have been a little tired recently, and was told that I was tired because I was too busy doing things outside the community. Technically my contract states that any rabbinical activity outside the *Gemeinde* needs to be approved by the board, meaning of course Platt and Engels. The question is: Do my lectures at the Uni and the speaking I do in public forums qualify as rabbinical activity or academic activity? Anyway, the powers-that-be told me to do an accounting of all my work. So I put together a spreadsheet of all my activities and hours. It is actually pretty hard, as clergy hours don't really fit into a nice box. If I teach one hour of a class for the community, then there is usually between one and two hours of prep time involved. Then do I count answering emails at 1 a.m. or the drive time to go to the house of a congregation member in preparation for the funeral of their mother? You add it up and it averages to between sixty and eighty hours a week, depending on if there was a funeral or a holiday in there.

"So when I turned that in, I was told to cut out all activities outside the community or I would be fired."

I jumped in, shocked, "Can they do that?" I had wanted to say, "You have got to be fucking kidding me!" but was not quite yet ready to match his apparent fluency with vulgarity with mine.

"*Jein*," he answered with one of my favorite newly-learned German expressions. "*Ja*" and "*nein*" together. As the best answer for most Jewish questions I had adopted "*jein*" quickly into my own lexicon. "I could take them to court for the German version of wrongful discharge and would probably win. But it would be a long battle and I am not sure I can really survive that right now. And you will love this, there have also been complaints that I spend too much time teaching converts." He laughed again, sounding even worse than the first attempt.

125

"What are you going to do?"

He shrugged. "Honestly, I truly don't know. I do need to cut back on my hours a bit, but the things they want me to cut out are the only things that are getting me out of bed in the morning. The worst part is, none of this is about what it seems to be about. There is an election coming up in the community and Platt and Engels have pissed off everyone at one point or another, meaning all the Russian speaking Jews. There is some stink that their reelection might not be as slam dunk as usual, and one of the ways they think they can please the natives is to bring in a Russian-speaking Rabbi."

"Seriously? Can they do that?"

"It's funny. I have actually been asking for an assistant for the last two years to help with the youth engagement. The only problem is that the only really good Russian-speaking candidates coming out of rabbinical school in Germany that don't already have a congregation lined up are women, which would be awesome if it would happen but also was rejected outright when suggested. The other possibility is to bring in an Orthodox rabbi. I am actually not against this in principle, except that no Orthodox rabbi would ever accept me as the *Mara D'atra*—the Chief Rabbi of the community let alone as an equal. Nor would they accept me as an assistant unless I agreed to operate under purely Orthodox interpretations of *halakha* even if I was willing to become the assistant, which I am not.

"But they can't fire me just because they need an easier path to reelection. They can, however, make me want to quit."

But you can't quit, I wanted to exclaim, until I realized that the exclamation came from a place of fulfilling my personal needs rather than thinking about Rabbi—the rabbi sitting across from me looking like he was fighting off malaria. Instead I felt the completely lame platitude falling out of my mouth, "Is there anything I can do?"

"Seriously, yes. Two things. First, keep on coming to my office weekly so I have something to look forward to. Second, keep on coming to services. Bring friends. When I was hired, I was specifically told that my job was to get more people into the door. That is the other part of it. If there were hundreds of people in here for every service, my job would be untouchable and Platt and Engels would feel more secure. For a while anyway that seemed to be happening but lately I have been losing people— regulars that I had brought in—and I am not really sure why and that is probably an even bigger existential threat to my job, if Platt and Engels want to hold something over my head. So come to my office and come to shul. Everything else will take care of itself, I hope."

With that we talked half-heartedly about my reading progress and went through some of my more pressing questions. Then he uncharacteristically shooed me out, mentioning that he had a funeral the next day and was meeting with one of the relatives in the next several minutes. By that time, I was emotionally more than ready to go. With all my defenses officially shot to hell, of course the universe would present me with a meet-cute of particular import while exiting the rabbi's office.

Now this is one of those great universal questions: are you allowed to go through all that love-or-lust-at-first-sight stuff when the person you bump into is the same person going in to a rabbi's office to deal with the death of, in Rafi's case, a grandparent? I mean the meet-cute part occurred with no Andrea-volition and therefore should absolve me of negative ethical recriminations. The stalking later is a different story, although I still maintain I am not really sure it qualified as

127

stalking, but the first moment comprised of classical girl-with-thoughts-elsewhere not hearing steps on the other side of the stairwell door knocking over the half-sweet half-dreamy man-boy entering from the other side.

Ok, knocking over isn't really accurate. I pushed the door open, not looking through the small portal while he was swinging it open towards him with the force of someone running a few minutes late. The quickly opening door pulled me forward off-balance and into the arms of one with surprisingly good balance. The back-wall of the stairwell helped a bit, too, as we ended up in a position more suitable for a lunchtime tryst after a smoking break than one suitable coming from and going to an appointment with clergy.

It's not fair to ask me to estimate the amount of time spent with my hands braced somewhere around his hips and his arms steadying me around me shoulders, but eventually I did what all folks with minor social anxiety do—I blushed, looked down at my feet, grunted a sort of apology in I'm-not-sure-which-language and somehow managed a nervous giggle.

Dude seriously smelled good—a mix of black worn leather jacket, mid-afternoon's time worth of daily perspiration, and what I later learned was Bulgari Man cologne. "I'm sorry," he said smiling, betraying a hint of accent behind perfect German.

"No worries," I finally looked back up, rather pissed at the blushing still happening that would be too apparent on even my complexion. "I was the one not paying any attention."

"You're American," he stated-not-asked switching to what now sounded like perfect and only slightly accented English. Not a Russian accent but similar—maybe Bulgarian? Were there still Jews in Bulgaria?

"Uh huh," I answered articulately then extended an only slightly trembling hand, "Andrea Lewy."

"Rafael Garayev." He accepted offered hand as I went through the minute calculations necessary to ascertain the number of seconds of clasping hands that would fall correctly in the Goldilocks zone of meet-cute appropriateness. "You are coming from the rabbi's office?" he asked.

Four point three seconds. That is my answer and I am sticking to it. Belatedly I did a quick mental outfit and clean underwear check, finding each item adequate for the time being. This wasn't some twisted old neurosis, rather a new lesson learned jokingly from Natasha. When language remains limited, friends will often discuss the wonderful absurdities that can be play acted. Natasha described in words and actions that every time she met a new man—one that of course stood tall and slim to provide no comparison whatsoever to her bottom-dweller ex—that she would go through the logical mental checkup of lingerie reducto-ad-absurdum: *What will be his first impression if he sees me with my coat off? What will be his first impression if I am stripped to my undies?* I don't think this was meant to be completely serious, but performing the quick check at least removed one element of potential stress from the near future. No wonder Russian women never left their abodes without being fully made-up—even if the trip led merely to an *Aldi* to pick up Möwenpick ice-cream and a bottle of fizzy-water.

I am going to blame the absurdity of these explanations and obvious twitterpation on chemistry. There are some pheromonal matches that simply overwhelm good-grooming, modesty or wasp-y mid-Atlantic-ness. We are lying if we refuse to admit that looks provide the usual initial entre into relationship *gedenk*-experiments. But sometimes looks or type or other preferences can be overwhelmed by something more primeval. I had heard about it and even thought that I had experienced it. If so, it had been a sub-par appetizer leading to a much more gourmet finish. Not that the looks were problematic—quite the opposite actually. Underneath the leather jacket he wore standard West-German urban camouflage—pressed fashion jeans, leather Italian shoes with overly pointed toes, button-down shirt, possibly tailored, with a patterned under-collar. His hair, tight black ringlets, had been controlled with a glistening metro-product that would have appeared Guido in Philly but worked just way-too-well with Rafi. He had a fully formed and perfectly cropped black beard and mustache, kept at about five-day's growth with not a single whisker longer than another. His eyes had landed at three shades darker and more reflective than my own mahogany, and where my skin looked consistently washed out in my genetically influenced fear of the sun—Malibu and bikinis notwithstanding—his glistened bronze and even, like a highly polished light walnut. Oh yeah—he had white, even teeth too. Bastard. Actually, the more I looked at him the more I became pretty sure that I had seen him before—probably at the Chanukah party or maybe at the university. But there is a profound difference between seeing someone across a room or campus with whom you have a chemical reaction and standing next to them—touching them. Besides, if it had been at the Chanukah party, I had *l'chaim*-ed enough vodka that night to give major bed-spins, so no way I can be blamed for vague recollection.

"Oh my God, you are going to see Rabbi now," I finally blurted, "I am so sorry. I mean Rabbi Isaac said he was meeting someone—meeting a relative of someone that had passed."

He nodded gravely. "My grandfather Avhat."

"I am so sorry," I repeated, searching my brain for the proper phrase of Jewish consolation. I wanted to whip out the appropriate Jewish phrase that I had been attempting to

130

memorize: *HaMakom yenachen etchem b'toch sha'ar aveilei tzion v'yerushalayim*—may the Holy Place of Being be with you among all the mourners of Zion and Jerusalem. But seriously, how the hell does anyone learn or say that, especially when it is needed? I think there is a shorter version for Sephardic Jews— definitely need to learn that one.

He shrugged slightly. "Thank you. It is ok. My father and my grandfather were estranged, so I have never really known him. But he lived in town and so was a member of this *Gemeinde* so he will be buried here in the Jewish cemetery. I am the only one that is close by and would come—my father won't—so I will talk with the rabbi even though I don't really know what to say."

Damn, that was a load. I couldn't tell if he was truly distraught and therefore letting me into a type of internal world that would normally not be presented in the post meet-cute bliss. He seemed somehow present and distant, and I knew I was keeping him from an important appointment now and had no way of getting to a next step without entering a type of inappropriateness that even Andrea-the-*gauche* was not willing to brave.

Well, hand to shoulder couldn't hurt, nor the look of sensitive understanding in my eyes. "I am sorry anyway. Losing someone is never easy. How do you say 'I am sorry for your loss' in Russian?"

That was bold. I had intuited some sort of Slavic in there, even though he carried none of what I usually associated with accents around here. Still, bold.

He smiled, hinting that there might be an astuteness behind the chemical exchange worth exploring. Maybe—in my experience the metro hair and this level of casual cuteness left a very small probability of high intelligence. But his language skills alone might signify his presence on the top of the bell-curve rather in the middle. He did add to the mystery by answering: "You say: '*Muiy soboleznuyem tvoyey utratye*' in Russian. But my native language is Juhuric."

I fingered my handy in my jeans pocket, anticipating a quick dash to the office of Rabbi Google. Unfortunately, I had also reached the end of any non-*gauche* delaying tactics I could imagine. Still he wasn't asking for contact info either. Idiot. Of course he had a wife or girlfriend. Well, no ring, but certainly a girlfriend. Damn. Ok, anyway, time to go and soak my head and let him deal with something much more important than my regression into pre-feminist doey-eyed-ness.

I shook his hand again, patted his arm again, and tried to repeat the mostly forgotten words in Russian that he had just taught. I got one or two right, so, well, go me. Giving a few last seconds of opportunity to see if *handy* number would follow I finally headed down the stairs with two hopeful glances back, only now starting to feel the sense of ridiculousness that I was sure would plague me for nights to come. You know—that feeling when you think of something you did and then clench your eyes tight, screw up your mouth and whisper, "Damn damn damn damn," to the ceiling above your bed.

But I did still have some stalking to do. I know, ethics. I would personally not really be comfortable with the thought of someone that I had just bumped into deciding to stalk me, but on the one hand I do choose my double-standards carefully and on the other I am not completely sure what I did qualifies as stalking.

There is really only one way out of the synagogue grounds—a block-long stretch of yellow-brick apartment houses. Once you reach the end you hit the first main street and here comes the decision: If I wish to find a spot to sit and wait for the man I would soon know as Rafi to come by, I would have one coffee shop to the left with tables outside and one bar to the right, also with a few tables outside, to innocently order, sit and pretend to study, only to be surprised when by complete chance Rafi would walk by, see me, and finally decide to stop and ask for digits. Today had been the mildest in a while, and Germans who would also sit outside in deep winter under the ubiquitous green blankets placed on chairs for that reason would even more so be gathering outside to enjoy a café or *pilsner* under the first promise of spring in some time. I mean, me sitting there looking like I was studying wouldn't seem *too* odd or obvious. Especially since I did have studying to do and had books in my backpack and I had the intention of stopping somewhere for a while on the way home. I mean just not here, but seriously, can you blame me for my flexibility?

I settled on the bar based on an intricately derived probability algorithm—meaning which direction had the more travelled transportation center had he walked. Had he driven, that side also had more city parking complexes. Seriously it was just a coin flip, but the "heads" meant "head to the right." I did and two hours and two pilsners and a lot of water later, Rafi walked by and indeed stopped.

"Hi again," he said mildly, still in English.

"Hey, what a surprise!" I said with far less acting skill than I would like to believe I possessed. He leaned over and looked at the book I had open in front of me, pretending to read. I kept my finger in my page so he could look at the cover. He read, "*Medien ohne Moral. Variationen über Journalismus und Ethik.*" Media without Morality. Variations on Journalism and Ethics.

"You are at the Uni?" I nodded and then in the heart-pounding boldest move yet, I nodded my head and gestured

133

delicately at the chair opposite mine. I had been rehearsing the hand movement on and off for the last forty-five minutes. And the verdict was . . . yes! He sits!

"Herr Professor Doctor Weissman," I said, trying to keep the irony to a minimum. "Lots of reading."

"Looks interesting," he said in a way that indicated that he may have indeed found it interesting. He caught the eye of the harried waitress and simply gestured at my nearly empty glass and held up two fingers. In magical German moments two more frothy pilsners materialized. We had already moved on into my program: Fulbright. And his program: Computer engineering.

I already knew from Rabbi Google on my *handy* that Juhuric happened to be a Persian-based language with a lot of Hebrew spoken in the mountains of Azerbaijan by a group known as Mountain or Caucasus Jews, the largest group of Jews in that region who were all descended from the ancient Persian Jewish society that dated back probably to the early second temple times. Of course I let him tell me about that, as too much knowledge at that point when I was supposed to be reading *Medien ohne Moral* would point much too obviously to the stalking that I am still not going to admit happened.

"My family still only speaks *Juhuric* at home and when we pray, but we refer to it simply as 'the Jewish language' at home, as if none other existed. Actually I am pretty sure my father thinks there is no other Jewish language."

To my inquiry as to how long he and his family had been in Germany, he answered, "Since 2003."

"Wait. No way. You speak perfect German. Most of the former-Soviet Jews here can barely speak German, let alone perfect English too."

He smiled, as if talking to a child. Ok, not really, but I felt a bit like an idiot with his answer. "Just because we are Mountain

134

Jews didn't mean we lived in the mountains. We lived in Baku, which is pretty developed, and my dad had a successful enough business that I went to private school. We all studied Russian, English, German and Azerbaijani."

Yeah, and I was proud of my German and how fast I was now able to follow Rabbi Isaac in shul. "Why did you move here? Antisemitism?"

He kind half nodded and half shook his head—his own version of "*Jein*," I guess. "Not really. I mean there is always some level of Antisemitism. But in our case my uncle had been out here for a few years—he was the one that had brought my grandfather. He was the older brother and when he died my father had to come up and take care of affairs. One thing led to another and the next thing my dad had sold his business to a Russian entrepreneur and came to Germany."

"I have never seen you at the Synagogue until today."

To his credit he didn't look at my hair, skin and eyes and ask why I would care about his Jewish observance. Instead, he answered in a tone of voice that echoed what I had heard earlier in the day from Rabbi Isaac. "When we got here, my father came to Shabbat services and was told at the front gate that he was Muslim and needed to go away."

I nearly spat my sip of beer. "Hey, I had the same experience!" I told him of my first visit to the community the week I had arrived in the autumn, which then somehow turned into my own family history and a lot more details that I hadn't intended. It wasn't as bad as my first meeting with Rabbi Isaac, but it was bad enough.

The problems that cropped up over the conversation were that I was ahead with the beer count and starting to feel a little squirrely and that initial chemistry thing had not in the least worn out. I ended up doing every unconscious mammalian thing

135

unsubtly as one does under such influences—grooming my hair, leaning forward, licking my lips. He held himself under a much better level of control, as I found out later he also had been experiencing pretty much the same chemical reaction since the stairwell. Well, he was a macho and I wasn't really accustomed to machos and at least this one not only had a high intelligence it seemed, he also asked a lot of questions, listened to my answers, and seemed to find me much more interesting in general than himself. He, however, wasn't sure how right it was to hit on a woman the day before his grandfather's funeral.

I probably should have been thinking such respectful thoughts myself. But I wasn't and didn't and eventually I had had enough beer to overcome any remaining shyness, inviting him to join me in whichever our apartments we would be able to get to the quickest.

Turned out that was mine.

One result of having such an intense conversation with a mentor followed up by such an intense sexual collision with someone that I wanted to get to know much better was that any lingering discomfort from the earlier conversation had been swept pleasantly away by the bliss of that oh-my-God chemistry. Add to that a real live circumcised penis and all was truly as was supposed to be.

Finally able to think back to the first part of the day, I felt for Rabbi Isaac, but was able to put everything in perspective. His problems were not my problems. I wished him all the best, but he had to take care of himself. I had enough challenges to deal with, and this was still my year. Rafi, cutely and quietly snoring next to me, his chest rising lightly with the peaceful breaths of deep sleep, was my present reality. Regardless of Rabbi Isaac's recriminations, I did have a right to determine my own destiny. As I snuggled up to the very warm naked body resting next to

136

me, my last negative feelings faded into a well-earned *Wohlgefühl*. Everything else would take care of itself.

Taking Over

I loved my hours with Rabbi Isaac. In spite of the occasional awkward openness, I say this now and will repeat it over and over because that love should have translated into loyalty.

At least I think it should have.

The punchline of this joke is the tearful conversation that Rabbi Isaac had with me only a few weeks before I returned to the States. I cannot yet bring myself to recount that conversation, but I deserved his rebuke and tears and even now I wince and cringe when I access the memory. Of course, looking back at the earlier diatribe about entitlement, the conversation is not only a punchline, it is an exclamation point. It is the realization that I alone was the sparkplug rather than the victim of the shock.

When I began the rebel movement, it had nothing to do with Rabbi Isaac. I mean, at least in my mind I repeated this but of course it had to do with Rabbi. He provided the intellectual and even spiritual animation that I needed, but as I had now gone full commitment on this Jewish community as the social center of my mystical year, some internal tantrum welled up and started making me think I indeed had the right to have the community fulfill my exact needs. I became a complete fulfillment of what Rabbi Isaac was trying to tell me, and I didn't see it. My chutzpah-disillusionment conversation with Rabbi had lasted an hour. The rabbit-hole, however, had been entered long before and in the weeks after our conversation started to bring about change.

If you think about it, it does make a little sense that I would justify my actions in the context of doing the right thing. I could even imagine I was *helping* Rabbi Isaac by taking some of the stress off of him. What it really meant is that I chose to hear from that conversation what I wanted to hear. But my actions did kind of make sense! Part of what this and seemingly every other Jewish community in Europe suffered from was a lack of positive modeling. This was Cognitive Therapy 101 and as my mom was a big believer that all humans should spend time in talk therapy, I had absorbed enough of the lingo to be dangerous.

I had begun to sense and then articulate to myself that the true underlying problem here was lack of continuity. Yes, it is clear now that all religious communities are a bit messed up. The fantasy is that we are supposed to bring our best selves into our religious groups and in reality we bring our worst while imagining it is our best. At least when there is institutional knowledge—when there are rules and regulations and committee charters and sensible contracts and term limits for board members, the damage that our worst selves can do is mitigated by a functional structure. At the very worst, a bad president will be quickly and clearly noticed by a board that has seen the modeling of a few good ones. Yet think about the institutional knowledge in a community such as this. Ninety-three percent of these folks came from the Former Soviet Union.

Ninety-three percent.

That means that out of the sixteen hundred members that had checked "Jewish" on their *Anmeldung* or registration papers when they moved to this area, somewhere near fifteen hundred of them had an absolute maximum of formal synagogue institutional knowledge that dated back to 1991. But even that is generous. First of all, the average age of the members, according to Rabbi Isaac, is around seventy. That is the average. That means that those few that came in that first wave still had zero modeling in synagogue life until their thirties or forties. Those that came in '94, '98, '01 or '04—well you can do the math. And to assume that there is any new modeling going on is still a pretty optimistic stretch. The thirty to fifty folks that showed up on good days for services were still at least half non-FSU. So how many of those fifteen hundred had any practical modeling?

If you want to take it even a step further, what kind of modeling did those very few that either had devoted themselves to attending or more sadly were paid to attend actually receive? The "leadership" of this synagogue was a fiefdom of several families, none of whom themselves had true German-Jewish origin—rather haled from the displaced-persons' camps at the end of the war. And it was like that everywhere else as well. Not too terribly far from here, the largest community in the region had a president that had served for over thirty years. Seriously? Is there a single right-thinking person that doesn't see a slight problem with this? So if the FSU Jews decided they wanted to observe and learn how to run a synagogue, their potential mentors were corrupt demagogues who interrupted every service they attended and ran the *Gemeinde* to serve their personal needs while I am sure under the illusion that they knew best for the rest.

Shit when it comes down to it, they were probably right. If you continue the thought of modeling and the question of the origins of our modeling into what some sort of political revolution from the FSU Jews would be, just look at the political structures they fled. The formal organizations as a possible model would have essentially been communist party meetings, chess clubs and the Red Army.

As I articulate this, though, I wish with all my soul that I was being facetious. But do a little research. And then do what I am doing, and project what a Jewish community looks like that is run by the best governing practices of the Communist Party of the Union of Soviet Socialist Republics or the Red Army. Or a chess club. Seriously, we would probably be lucky if the latter proved the dominant model.

With all this in mind, it starts becoming clear why anything not under the direct control of Rabbi Isaac felt zero percent Jewish, and even clearer why I convinced myself that starting a rebellion just might be a good thing for us all rather than the reality that I wanted a Judaism that didn't make me feel uncomfortable.

Regarding modeling, I had no hope for the Old Russian Dudes or Charming Old Ladies. But what about the Sabrinas of the world? In our little pockets around the *Kiddush* table after shul the three or five or ten of us between college age and middle thirties began vocally pining for a non-Chabad version of what Chabad did. I mean, there was a full-time cook here and a well-appointed kitchen along with seriously good facilities. Would it be so hard to get the community once a month to host a more festive dinner that didn't include a Czar-mandated hard ending time before any Joy of Shabbat had actually been experienced?

When I say that we "began vocally pining" what I really mean is I began manipulatively telling stories about Shabbos dinner at the Hillel at Temple or of our youth group services in Swarthmore or the various opportunities in Israel. Included in my stories were the provocative questions meant to cause folks to start talking to leadership about, "Why with so many resources are we unable to cater to the social needs of the younger community?" You should hear how awesome that sounds in German.

Knowing that Rabbi Isaac could not constitutionally resist singing or teaching, we, meaning I, either alone or through prodding others began encouraging more and more that *zmiros* be sung after the *birkat hamazon,* or the blessings after the meal. Then we, meaning I, either alone or through my strengthening band of minions would encourage Rabbi between songs to further expand on some subject upon which he had spoken that week in services. Of course the Czar or Sour-Cook-Shmulik or one of their cronies would still inevitably appear tapping a watch at some point, but I figured that wanting to do Jewish Stuff in a synagogue of all things trumped the watch tapping, and that such clear logic would eventually create the critical mass or crisis that would force the leadership into a duh moment of, "Well, maybe it's a splendid idea to let people celebrate the Sabbath after a Sabbath service!"

And of course underneath all this lie the assumption that my version of Jewish social behavior, projected through my desires, actions and the actions of my minions, would provide the spark to make this Jewish community suddenly start to feel Jewish.

It never really occurred to me that what I meant by that was "feel Jewish to *me*."

So at least I did try for a while within the context of the official *Einheitsgemeinde* of my university town. Yet every Shabbat the Czar still came, tapping his watch, and the rabbi would turn red and start looking nervous and the stand up, grab his cane and on his way out wish everyone a final "Shabbat Shalom" in his unambiguous sign for "Party's over, folks!" The last straw for me proved to be something that I shouldn't have even overheard.

Rafi and I had been dating, meaning having nightly sexual collisions, for a couple of weeks when Rabbi Isaac sent out an invite to several of the local Jewish youth groups on Facebook. The groups represented mostly university students from about a hundred-kilometer radius around our own town and were mostly convenience-groups to do this very thing: post about upcoming events with some sort of relationship to the Jewish world. This included informal beer gatherings all the way up to organized trips to various Jewish-Europe destinations. Obviously by using this medium, Rabbi was serious about tackling a new initiative. I couldn't help smiling, pretty sure my not-so-subtle pressure had pushed Rabbi in this direction. Seriously it was all good, right?

The announcement read in German, Russian and English: "*Beyachad*–Pizza, Beer and Torah. Come join us at our Community Center for our first monthly gathering of Jewish university students. This is an opportunity to not only get to know each other better, but as well to ask the hard questions and discuss our Jewish 'Now.' Bring a friend, your appetite and your curiosity. Pizza and Beer will be provided by us. Jewish togetherness will be provided by you!"

It was a pretty OK announcement. I thought a little tweaking here and there would probably have awoken a little more excitement. Nonetheless, I immediately wrote the date in my calendar, sent the link to Rafi, and RSVP'd for the two of us after a quick text and the predictable accompanying double entendres.

The gathering was set for a frigid Sunday after a pretty heavy snowfall that cancelled the earlier promise of spring. I arrived predictably first with a somewhat annoyed Rafi in tow to find Rabbi in the seldom-used youth lounge with a stack of cheese and veggie pizzas, various bags of what passed for potato chips in Germany and two cases of half-liter bottles of German beer, one local "alt" and the other a pilsner from up north.

Neither Rafi nor I, the starving college students, as it were, needed any encouragement to dig in and join Rabbi in a pleasant *l'chaim* as he grabbed his own bottle of Diebels and thoughtfully opened all of our bottles. I quickly suppressed my immediate nervousness at such lousy attendance at already fifteen minutes past the late afternoon official starting time, and

143

replaced it with a self-satisfied "I don't give a damn, there is beer, pizza and a rabbi."

Slowly and somewhat uncomfortably over the next hour more and more trickled in until a good two dozen twenty-somethings had occupied all couch and chair spaces and started making significant headway on the food and drink. I personally knew about half of the folks. Only a few actually attended synagogue here and some had come, even in the winter, from as far away as an hour ride by train. I knew that there was hunger for this sort of gathering, and my initial nervousness had fully given way to a bit of smugness.

Of course not everything could be roses and latkes. There was a little prick named Pavel that I had encountered at far too many Jewish gatherings in the region. Although he never came to synagogue, Pavel liked to show up at Jewish movie nights and beer nights and dominate the discussion. Usually his points of deep wisdom included everything that every rabbi in the area did wrong along with why women should remain perpetually barefoot, pregnant and uneducated. Occasionally he would offer learned discourse as to why Jews were the only created beings with a human soul while all other peoples and religions had an inferior soul more akin to that of animals. Someone once told me that this idea came from some 17th or 18th century Chassidic text, but the fact that that was the point that Pavel had gotten out of whichever text I think explains both all one needs to know about the little prick and why in my mind he is to be referred to only as "the little prick."

As he made his grand entrance, he surveyed the room with a scowl, refused to grab food or drink, and sat with his arms crossed as he said loudly in passible German, "Why isn't the language of this gathering Russian? We are all Jews here, aren't we?"

Up to that point, the conversation had been mixed German, English, Russian and even a little Hebrew. But there had been no formal announcement of a single language nor a need for one. Almost without thinking I slipped into and out of German and English and my growing Russian as the situation depended. Rabbi had been mixing his own communication and then providing good translations when needed in his side conversations. To his credit, he didn't throw anything at the little prick, instead just saying, "No official language—we have students here from all over." Then he used the opening as a cue to begin the formal program.

"On that point, how many here can speak and understand English?" Nearly every hand but the little prick's went up, even though I knew from a previous gathering that his English was no problem. Rabbi also seemed to recognize this—or more likely he knew or knew of the prick already—and with that Rabbi Isaac was off—holding court until you could begin to sense engagement and even a sort of trust.

The gathering had finally hit that spark moment of effortless conversation. Again, I smugly bathed in the sensation of my version of Judaism happening around me. Of course Rabbi Isaac's manner and natural presence when holding forth had offered the group the true catalyst, but at that moment I felt that I could finally sense the rest of the year opening up to the possibility of a tangible Jewish social culture. Only my beer-filled bladder could tear me away from the happy success of the event.

The timing of the break turned out to be a little too providential.

As one tends to do with a small frame and a sense of buzz, I lingered a bit in the WC, letting vaguely satisfied thoughts drift through my skull as I traced minor cracks in the wall and let my body relaxingly work through the liter-plus of pilsner. When flushed and washed, I started opening the door but stopped at only a crack when I heard somewhat stressed voices in the hallway nearby. Never one to miss a good moment of cloak and dagger I left the door cracked at a centimeter and tried to key into the conversation.

Evgeniy, one of the Czar's top lieutenants and frankly one of the scariest and most soulless among them, appeared to be arguing with Rabbi Isaac, pointing at his watch in the now clear universal symbol in this community for "I don't give a damn about your Jewish stuff, I need to go home and drink vodka." Two weeks of bed-talk with Rafi on top of five months in-country and my Russian comprehension had experienced a marked jump. Still, I could only really understand Rabbi's Isaac's Russian as he spoke it much slower. The gist was that the invitation had clearly communicated a gathering from 16:00 to 18:00 and it was now 18:10 and Evgeniy must have his vodka. Ok, not sure about that last part, but I am not really charitable right now. Sure, the invitation had said this and that, but in accordance with Jewish Standard Time, most had only arrived in the past hour and the spark point of social agreeableness had only been reached in the last twenty minutes. Surely a score of youth *wanting* to be in the synagogue fell into the Rabbi's mandate from the board to fill the synagogue with Jewish stuff and people consuming Jewish stuff and allowed for some get-out-of-time-constraint-free card.

No. Of course not. Evgeniy became more heated in his watch pointing. Seriously the guy had to by ex-military, ex-KGB, current Russian mafia or all-the-above and my one centimeter crack had started feeling about a centimeter too wide.

When I witnessed Rabbi Isaac's solution, the pleasant buzz threatened to become beer-sick and send me back to the toilet. It makes a sick sense, as Rabbi Isaac must have sensed the same thing I did, that this gathering represented a capital "I" Important movement in the direction of growing the size of the active congregation. Rabbi's explicit explanation that he wanted to eventually move these gatherings to post-*Erev Shabbat* gatherings once-a-month and the general positive reaction from the assembled crowd held more promise than I dared hope. To end this gathering now would threaten to extinguish the spark before it had fully created the sort of energy that would automatically bring people back for future gatherings and self-evidently become a *thing*. First Rabbi Isaac appeared to argue the importance of the gathering and its place in the board's mandate, to the predictable reaction of I-don't-give-a-damn. Next Rabbi told Evgeniy to simply go home, he would lock up. I had seen this argument fail before on Shabbat, and with a room full of people that were not regular visitors to the synagogue, no chance. Finally, Rabbi dug into his jacket breast pocket and pulled out a twenty Euro bill, handed it to the shrugging guard and then followed it with a second before Evgeniy finally relented and with a self-satisfied final tap at his watch indicating some implicit extension left to return to the guard tower.

What is even worse is that I found out much later that Rabbi Isaac had also paid for the beer, pizza and chips out of his own pocket. He had asked the powers-that-be to logically support this gathering. Somewhere in the process the FSU kitchen staff had refused to support the effort, and Rabbi Isaac had been told he could have water and soda from the kitchen stores in addition to the generous addition of bagged candies left over from last Purim.

I don't think that there is much more that I can say about this without devolving into medieval curses.

Anyway, despite the promise and the bribe, I think in retrospect something broke in Rabbi—that the Rabbi that I had met that said "fuck" to one of his students was quickly becoming the only version of this rabbi left. Predictably, this turned out to be the first and last gathering of *Beyachad*. For me it was the clear confirmation that I had to step up and take control of my own Jewish social existence and start using the same Facebook groups to organize my own similar gatherings. The gathering lasted for one more hour—I am guessing the going rate of time for a forty Euro bribe—while I spent the entire time plotting my next move.

Sabrina, who had not been able to attend, quickly agreed to help me as we began to organize our own Jewish existence outside of that pathetic community. Rafi, who after learning of my hallway eavesdropping seemed to hold in a truly terrifying rage, agreed immediately to help in addition to threatening to go to the board and try to get Evgeniy fired. Needless to say I made him promise not to do this, instead redirecting his zeal into starting our rebellion.

The first, obvious step was to "reward" communities within a logical radius of our home with our presence when they organized events that fit our criteria for Vibrant Jewish Life. Of course I always saw myself as remaining loyal to Rabbi Isaac, visiting him in spite of the board nearly weekly now as I threw myself into my "conversion" education with zeal. I chose to ignore the continued strain around his eyes and the look of sadness for the now more numerous weekends that I would spend at other shuls, including Chabad.

If there was an organized Shabbat service with a meal, we would sign up and distribute the information to as many people as possible. If there was an event that popped up anywhere in the region, we would re—post and re-tweet and re-blog in our effort to support *real* Judaism instead of this insane construct of these petty FSU marionettes that hadn't the slightest clue of our tradition or the smallest trace of understanding of "*oneg.*"

On the weekends where nothing was scheduled, we would organize a pot-luck either post Friday evening, post Saturday morning or both, and try to create at a rotating apartment what Shabbat was *supposed* to feel like. After not too long, a thirty-something Israeli couple with a guitar and drum joined our little *chavura* and added more voices other than Rafi and I that could recite the proper blessings for the appropriate parts of the night. If the Shul was going to deny us joy, then we would boycott meals A, B, C, D and VIP and instead make sure that those that wanted a Jewish life were not deprived by this "Jewish" community.

It felt amazing, and I slept every night secure and peaceful in the sense that I was participating and even leading that true *tikkun olam* in Germany that must have been lacking until my fortuitous arrival.

Old Russian Guys Revisited

After two weekends away, one at Chabad a few cities over and one glorious orgy of Judaism and debauchery-with-Rafi in Berlin, I returned to the community to find Gidal the *Gabbai* leading services but no Rabbi Isaac.

The absence caught me off guard not only in how unusual it was, but as well that I had had no pre-warning. Occasionally the rabbi would leave here or there for a conference or the like— come to think of it, I don't remember him ever taking a vacation—but always with many announcements in the weeks leading up to the absence. But then I hadn't been attending regularly enough recently to have caught the announcements, had there been any. As I took my seat in the downstairs *Frauenabteilung* I mentally checked off the last few months and suddenly realized just how scarce I had been. Even though I had been quite honestly having quite a bit of fun, the disconnect at having come to see and hear Rabbi Isaac yet having my expectations unfulfilled left me feeling a bit separated from my body—like a few too many glasses of wine after having already drunk a few too many glasses of wine.

After the brave women who chose downstairs instead of upstairs began filling in, I managed to dig into a few and get back at first, "*Der Rabbiner ist krank,*" the rabbi is sick, followed by the much more ominous pronouncement by an even more trustworthy source of gossip, "*Der Rabbiner ist im Krankenhaus.*" The rabbi is in the hospital.

Now I felt a bit ill. Rabbi Isaac's presence in this community offered something like the one relative you had in a distant city—as long as they were there, the city felt safe, even if you never saw that relative. Was that what Rabbi had become for me? Had he become my security blanket? My last few weeks—more than a few weeks—started popping a little more urgently into my mind until Sabrina's arrival gave me the excuse to shove the beginning moments of self-recrimination back under the service.

I asked her in whispered German, "Did you hear about the rabbi?"

"Just did," she answered, flushed as if having sprinted the last few blocks. "I just saw him on Wednesday."

"I know," I answered. "We didn't have an appointment this week but he sent me an email on Wednesday about my *Beit Din*."

As gossip passes in a Jewish community faster than can be explained by the laws of physics, over the course of the service and then *Kiddush* afterwards we would learn that he had collapsed with chest pain early the previous morning. Although some claimed it had been a heart-attack, the consensus seemed to be that he had some sort of stress-induced arrhythmia which had him restricted to his bed for the next several weeks. As the early information came in, I suggested to Sabrina that we see if there was anything we could bring him or do for him. Sabrina nodded, and then as the service such as it was had already begun, we decided to focus on the rubbernecking implicit in non-Rabbi services.

The sport did seem a little cruel, but you have to understand the level of dysfunction that Rabbi kept at bay by being, well, there. His professionalism covered up a lot of blight that only became apparent on the rare occasions of his absence.

One of the values in Judaism that I find powerful is that it doesn't take a rabbi or a cantor to lead services. Anyone can do it. Ok, not anyone. In an Orthodox community "anyone" would mean any Jewish male older than thirteen. I think you saw this

151

sort of thing at its most democratic more often in Conservative synagogues where the various parts of the service would be divided up weeks in advance in some places and in the moment in others. The fact that so many people were ready and willing to step up and lead prayer had always blown me away. We didn't really have continuous lay-leadership at my shul as services were pretty much the exclusive show of the rabbi/cantor team—but again that was more congregational aesthetic than necessity.

Here, I guess anyone with the right genitalia and parentage could also have led, except for the fact that pretty much no one could speak or read Hebrew—or knew anything about a prayer service other than the hayride version. *Gabbaim* would be chosen from either among the most learned in the congregation or from those that would represent the best political choices to have a leadership position. Depending on the congregation, a *gabbai* might greet people arriving, decide who received Torah honors, help with the Torah service including calling people up to Torah and correcting the reader or readers. In the case of this community—and from what I had seen in most *Einheitsgemeinden* in Germany, the *Gabbaim* were chosen from among the one or two in the community who knew anything about Judaism whatsoever.

As an Israeli, Gidal the *Gabbai* qualified automatically. A Kibbutznik descendent of German Jews, Gidal had moved to Germany enough decades in the past to make his German perfect. I still hadn't figured out if his wife was Jewish or not— she stood at what seemed half of Gidal's nearly seven stooped feet and barely spoke or looked anyone in the eyes on the few times that she had attended services with their teenage daughter, Aviv. Gidal often read the Torah for Rabbi Isaac, mumbling at breakneck speed through the verses—fast enough the make his perfect sounding Hebrew cover up for the fact, as I was learning more and more the farther I got into my own process, that he made a mess of mistakes and knew nothing about chanting. But he was Israeli and the Old Guard in addition to the FSU masses accepted that as kosher enough to make him head *Gabbai* and first out of the bullpen in Rabbi's absence.

The truly hilarious thing was how much more the Old Russian Dudes seemed to get into services when Gidal led. For one thing, Gidal led in a manner that everyone perceived as Orthodox. What that meant primarily was that he started the services as soon ten men had shown up rather than waiting for the official starting time as Rabbi Isaac always did. The paid Minyan Men, as I had begun calling the Old Russian Dudes in my mind, mostly came by public transportation and were thus at the mercy of bus and tram schedules. This meant that some of them regularly were forced to show up a half hour before the service was to begin. Previous Orthodox iterations of spiritual leadership in the community had apparently accommodated this with flexible service times. I mean I get it but didn't get it. An eighty-year-old being forced to wait around doing nothing certainly sucked. Yet at the same time, all service times were sent out in emails, pasted up all over the wall, sent out in the community newspaper, and were even published nationally online and in the print version of the *Jüdische Allgemeine*. Maybe I was just too American or too non-Orthodox to understand. Actually, it was when I visualized what it would be like to be a rabbi in a synagogue like this one—God forbid, I mean—that I imagined the possibilities of the hundreds of people that could come rather than pathetic ten that did. Come to think of it, I am not even sure I am on the right side of this argument.

Anyway, Gidal began the moment a tenth man entered what was now his domain, and as usual he mumbled like a champ through every prayer, stopping only when the hayride moments occurred. This thrilled Herr Adler as without Rabbi's dominant voice, he was now the alpha baritone and would take over every moment of congregational singing, usually turning it to a sort of shouted dirge.

Of course the one perpetual failure with no rabbi, other than the obvious failure of aesthetics, would occur during the Torah service. I had just recently learned that according to Jewish law, three Jews should always be around the Torah, meaning usually at the very least the one reading the Torah and then two *Gabbaim*. In this community, the second *Gabbai* had left after the Great Wash Basin Kvetching, and efforts to find another had been pretty awful, meaning that usually Rabbi just worked with Gidal and then would invite a teen, should any male teens be present, up to open the ark to carry the scroll. With three people around the Torah, Rabbi would not only not have to do much cane and Torah juggling, he would also have a buffer between FSU factions. When Rabbi was alone, or worse, when Gidal led alone, the cold war warmed up quickly.

Herr Adler, one of the two most dominant personalities, was a proud Ukrainian Jew. He also remained a charmer, grabbing my hand and kissing it at every greeting, trying to constantly engage me in conversation, and usually finding creative ways to brush past me whenever in transit from one synagogue space to the next. I know it sounds a little perverted, but it isn't quite as bad as it seems. Herr Adler had once shown me pictures of him in the 1950s. He had been some sort of competition dancer, and to be honest cut quite the striking figure. Photos of him mid-air, legs in a full split, hands touching the tips of both feet, wild grin of clear joy in his face, made me re-evaluate him as he was today

154

in his mid to late eighties. As soon as I realized that he still saw himself as that young dancer, I felt for some admittedly irrational and indefensible reason that it was ok to let me be the source of occasional adrenaline. I am not saying it was appropriate to let him rub my shoulders on occasion when he walked by, just that for the human behind the strangeness it seemed right, if not innocent.

Rumor had it that Herr Adler maintained two homes, one here and an apartment about an hour to the north in the location of another relatively large Jewish community where he served as a weekday member of a paid minyan. No one was clear if the woman in the other town was his wife or mistress or if it was the woman here, ten to twenty years his junior, who wore the official ring. Either way, it was kind of hard to dislike the man and pretty easy to feel a sense of grudging respect if not awe. I know that he constantly badgered Rabbi Isaac, constantly questioning him, often loudly and publicly, about every *halakhic* decision he made in service leadership. Several times I had witnessed a nearly feral look in Rabbi's eyes as he would explain with fading patience why this *haftarah* reading had been chosen and not that, and why no, Herr Adler couldn't lead services that week. (Herr Adler had once convinced Gidal to let him lead part of the service during Rabbi's trip to Belgium for a convention of Conservative rabbis. I had witnessed the debacle, and could only assume that Rabbi's weekly rejections of Herr Adler's requests had come from a similar incident at some point in the pre-Andrea past.)

Yet if Herr Adler, charming as he was, proved a problematic figure for Rabbi Isaac, the true nightmare sat up front on the right, right behind the Chieftains, dressed up in a nice cuddly grandfatherly figure.

Herr Grossman, ironically named with his barely five-foot frame, looked like the grandfather of your most Hallmarkstein

155

fantasies. A first glance would show a cherubic, aged Charlie Brown face with tiny round glasses and a perpetual two-day growth of gray fuzz. Like many of the Minyan Men he ambled around on a wooden cane, smiling "Shabbat Shalom" greetings to anyone passing him by in the foyer on the way into the *beit knesset*. The strong tremble in his hands and near humble downcast of his eyes made him seem precious and vulnerable, and the second hand that he would place over yours as you shook his made him seem gentle.

Herr Grossman was a Muscovite, second on the pecking order of the Soviet Union only behind Saint Petersburg—at least as explained by the half Ukrainian, half Russian Natasha. The Russians and Ukrainians would only band together in order to prevent the execution of ideas from Moldovans, the third group on the rung beneath Russians and Ukrainians (and I guess Belarussians, none of whom I had ever met in this community.) The Moldovans, represented by a third character in the weekly dramas, Dr. Likhtman, comprised a formidable minority among the FSU Jews in this particular community, although not an influential one as they had the great sin of speaking Romanian as their native tongue rather than Holy Russian. Of course Dr. Likhtman to my ears spoke perfect Russian, but on the occasions that he would be called up to read a text in Russian as part of the service, one could watch the inevitable mocking whispers from the other pockets of Minyan Men as they cut down his butchering of their Great Cultural Heritage. The fact that Dr. Likhtman had once, according to Sabrina, been a world famous heart surgeon either made no difference, or even made it worse. He had a circle of perceived Soviet-perspective *untermenschen* around him that worshipped him, but none could get past the Ukrainian or Russian gate keepers to rise up the pecking order.

The true provocateur in the drama proved to be Herr Grossman.

I had actually seen his *coup d'etats* early on in my German adventure, not really understanding what I had seen.

At one point the community had boasted a St. Petersburg Jew, Herr Landau, who had been—I found out much later—some sort of communist party boss back in the day. He also was the most hated man among the Minyan Men, lording over them his former status in addition to his current racial superiority. Somehow beyond my comprehension, as hated as he was the unspoken rules of Soviet culture meant that his tacit position of "highest" remained unchallenged. Highest what I have no idea, but there you have it.

One fine post-service *Kiddush* lunch, the relatively peaceful din of after-vodka conversation was shattered with Herr Grossman's trembling voice, shouting in surprisingly understandable German. "He is a horrible man. He is a horrible, evil man, and if someone doesn't do something about him, I am leaving and I will never come back!"

Coming from anyone else, this might have seemed self-serving and overly dramatic, but you have to imagine this diminutive, teddy-bear looking Old Dude standing and shaking his cane, looking as if he had just been stabbed by Brutus. It felt more than awful. It felt killing-a-mockingbird wrong and my mouth hung open trying to figure out what horrible person would dare to harm such a sweet old man.

At the outburst, Herr Landau from St. Petersburg stood up and released a tirade of Russian that led to the standing of the rest of the Minyan Men around the table and what looked like the imminent outbreak of a melee of canes.

Into the chaos sprang the surprising strength of Rabbi's voice shouting something in Russian that quieted every voice and plastered every eye on the supposed spiritual leader of the community. Rabbi Isaac continued into the silence, this time translating his own words back and forth from German to Russian. "This is Shabbat. Shabbat! This is our day of peace. Of Shabbat Shalom. What just happened is *Chilul Hashem*. The profaning of the name of the Eternal. This has no place, ever, for any reason, on Shabbat."

At this Herr Grossman and Herr Landau, both still standing, began simultaneously pointing at each other and pleading their cases.

"*Es ist mir scheissegal*!" thundered Rabbi Isaac. That does literally translate as "I don't give a shit," but you have to understand that it is much less shocking to hear a rabbi say "*scheisse*" in German than it would be to hear a rabbi say "shit" in American. Rabbi Isaac continued, still moving back and forth between languages. "I don't care what the problem is and I don't care who did what or who started what. This is Shabbat and there will be peace or I will be getting security to throw you out and make sure we have peace."

At this, Herr Grossman showed what looked like vulnerability, falling back into his chair and resting his head on the handle of his cane, slowly shaking his head back and forth. I would later learn this to be the devious genius of a predator.

With Herr Grossman's seeming capitulation, Herr Landau, secure in his rightful societal position, puffed out his chest and began spewing his litany of accusations against his frail rival across the table.

"Out!" Rabbi Isaac shouted, quieting the now completely shocked Herr Landau. I didn't understand the indignant reply in Russian, but am pretty sure it would translate as, "But, but, but . . ."

"Out. Now." Rabbi Isaac pointed again at the entrance and then stared down the gaping Russian. I can only imagine it would have been the same level of shock as a French President staring down a Russian Premier.

Slowly, with a few more attempts at self-defense to be greeted with Rabbi's pointed finger and uncompromising stare, Herr Landau tucked tail and exited the social hall. A dramatic smattering of applause accompanied the exiting, completing the scene for posterity. After a few minutes, Rabbi Isaac ambled after him to, as I found out later, talk to the security personnel and place Herr Landau on *Hausverbot*—a 'do not enter' list.

Several people, both Minyan Men and women, obsequiously surrounded Herr Grossman, appearing to ensure that no harm had come to the delicate octogenarian. It turns out that the obsequiousness had been congratulations for a job-well-done.

I pulled the story out of Rabbi Isaac much later, during a particularly manipulative moment where I convinced him of the utility of understanding the dynamic for the sake of my Fulbright research.

"All names will be changed if you ever write this up, right?"

I nodded. I had no intention of ever trying to deliberately piss of the Russians.

"After I put him on *Hausverbot*, I asked Engels and Platt to remove Landau from the paid minyan. You can't really kick someone out of the community since as you know we don't have traditional membership. In order for him to not be a part of the *Gemeinde*, he would have to commit an actual crime so that we could put him on permanent *Hausverbot* or he would have to essentially renounce his Judaism at the *Bürgeramt*—the registration office.

"So instead I got him off the paid rolls, figuring that he would stop coming to services, which is exactly what happened. He threatened to sue, and I think he might have even found some lawyer to call the office, but 'paid minyan member' has no standing in German law—it shouldn't have any standing in a synagogue for that matter—and so in the end he could get lots of people mad at me but not really do anything about it."

"But what did he do?" I asked, still at that point believing Herr Grossman to be a pathetic victim.

"Honestly, I am not really sure. I had a lot of people try to explain it to me, and I just tried to shut them down. It sounds like he had begun channeling an earlier version of himself as some sort of official from back-in-the-day, trying to browbeat others into God-knows-what. I seriously don't even care. Herr Landau had been the last of the Minyan Men chosen by my predecessor, and even among a group with little interest or knowledge in Judaism, he had neither interest nor knowledge—at all. He was there, I don't know, perhaps to reprise his role from his previous life. My experience with him pretty much consisted of him shouting out corrections to my pronunciation every time I spoke Russian, and then telling me after services that if I wanted to be understood, I needed to sit down with him before each service. 'None of them speak Russian correctly,' he would always tell me, referring to the rest of the Minyan Men. 'I am the only one that speaks correct Russian.'"

But if Landau had been the provocateur, then Grossman had been the KGB enforcer. From the beginning of his time in the Minyan all the way back to the early 90s, he had been the one to track attendance and then report any unexcused absence to the rabbi or board or whomever he had accepted as his *ersatz* handlers. The truly interesting part was that Grossman had not only been a *gabbai* before age and palsy had taken away his

160

ability to actually help in a service, he apparently had some skill and real knowledge. I tried to do the math. He was nearing ninety which meant he had been born in the twenties and so probably either fought in the war or had been in a concentration camp. At first I could not imagine he had actually been born in Moscow, as that had been outside the Pale of Settlement. I thought more likely, given his ability to speak and read Hebrew and once-upon-a-time read Torah and lead services, he must have spent a few years in a religious institution like a yeshiva before Lenin and his followers had completely done away with these structures. Then I found out that boys from the Pale were regularly pressganged after their *bar mitzvah* into the army, and that those few that survived the *twenty-five years* of service might indeed live in Moscow. *Seriously!* Either way, at some point he had moved from his shtetl to Moscow—most likely after the war as that had been the impetus behind most displacement—and then began his career as party official or whatever it was that led him to be this bitter old man in teddy bear skin. And I am not even completely sure I am wrong about the teddy bear part. I had witnessed moments of kindness from him toward many others—even a gentleness—so much so that it took quite of few incidents to remove the gloss and show me the deep anger underneath. It got so bad and frankly so obvious that I took to calling him Sméagol or Gollum depending on which one had shown up that particular day. Even the look was pretty spot on. I know, this is not nice, but I promise you that this was not a nice man. Most of the time.

To start with, he comported himself with the level of entitlement and lack of self-awareness that would make the worst of my generation proud. Most of the Minyan Men would whisper through services, 'whisper' being a relative term among older FSU Jews. As the service went on, the whispers that I

161

imagine had begun as "hey, how you doin'" sorts of things in their culture became biting commentaries about their rivals as they performed any duty in the service, the most common of which was being called up to Torah—supposedly the most sacred act and greatest honor in a Jewish service. The amount of times that Rabbi had to stop a Torah service and ask for respect for the reading of Torah had at the beginning embarrassed me greatly and eventually had just become a part of the spectacle. As a woman who had been called many times to Torah, actually knew the blessings, could chant from Torah with enough preparation and I think understood the magnitude of the honor of an *aliya*, it was hard not to look at that part of the service as anything other than a mockery of the true intent of reading Torah.

Part of Gidal's job, when he wasn't butchering Jewish prayer, was to hand out the Torah honors. This involved walking around the synagogue, usually in the middle of the most intense moments of Rabbi Isaac's prayers, and handing out between nine and twelve laminated paper slips, depending on the day. The first two said, "Kohen" and "Lewi," as in traditional Synagogues the first two *aliyot* would go to the decedents of the biblical priestly classes. If no Cohen had shown up, then a Levi would be required to take their place. If neither Levi nor Cohen were present in services, one of us shlepper Jews would be allowed. Herr Platt claimed to be a Levi, so when he deigned to show up, it was always just in time to receive his due honor. There had been a Cohen, some guy from Kyrgyzstan if I remember right, with a brood of four incredibly well-put-together sons aging from eleven to twenty-five. They had seemed cool and quite knowledgeable, but had disappeared a few months ago for some unknown reason. As for the other *aliyot*—seven total on Shabbat—Gidal's other job was to distribute the honors in such a way that two enemies never stood on the raised *bima* at the same time.

That is one of those things that sounds like a silly exaggeration and rests alongside now dozens of other items that I know will not be believed. Even as I observed what it meant when the *gabbai* or rabbi errored in this regard, I still wasn't really able to believe what happened as it happened. Maybe it is just the romance part of traditional religion—there are certain things that should be above being profaned by pettiness. When someone nonetheless profanes these things, it is nearly unbelievable that said profaning could be happening.

For a good 'for instance' we go back to our hero, Herr Grossman. Now, even though most of the Minyan Men despised this man already or transferred their anti-Landau sentiment after the *coup d'état*, the greatest animus still rumbled between Grossman and Adler. I mean, it is predictable. Now I guess why I still think affectionate thoughts toward Herr Adler comes down to his attitude toward Grossman. Adler *knew* that Grossman hated him—he just had to. And I *know* that Adler was not an idiot—occasional pain in the ass, yes, but idiot? No way. Yet he never acted as if Grossman got under his Ukrainian skin and he never acted any differently to Grossman than any of the other Minyan Men. He stood apart, sat apart—both acted and looked the proverbial island. So if Grossman would be called up to Torah, Adler would stand in respect at Grossman's shaky incantation of the blessings. On the other hand, and in blatant contradiction of I am sure hundreds of Jewish principles dealing with ethics, morality, decency and just not being an asshole, Herr Grossman would turn his back on Herr Adler on the *bima* in front of the open Torah and cross his arms until whatever version of Judaism he followed allowed him to descend from the *bima* back to his high horse. On the dear-God-thank-you rare

163

occasions that Adler had convinced Rabbi Isaac to let him read the *haftarah*—the reading of the prophetic texts after the Torah—Grossman and his Merry Men would point and mock how bad the reading was. I mean, it was bad, but that is immaterial to the horror of openly mocking someone during a service. One or two occasions that I can remember in addition to the ones that I am sure I still have blocked out, Rabbi Isaac was forced to either stop the reading, or stop the service after the reading to give a bi-lingual lecture on treating others as you yourself would like to be treated. I mean, seriously!

O the ways I could enumerate the moments of hypocrisy. I think my absolute favorite remains when Grossman had wormed his way into reading a Haftarah. I am guessing it was for a Yahrzeit or something, as that was usually the way they could browbeat Rabbi Isaac into getting their way. "Rabbi, today is the Yahrzeit of my dear mother. Please let me read the *haftarah*!" Well, Grossman's running commentary of services in the whisper-shout of an aging man probably would have helped a self-aware human to understand the karmic consequences of being a tool. Surely he would have no expectation that the congregation would remain quiet for his reading. In reality, the congregation did seem a little quieter. I would assume, however, that came mostly from the fact that Grossman was not among them adding to the din. Yet right on asshole-cue several verses into the reading, he stopped the quavering chant, glaring out at the assembled and their chutzpah of not maintaining strict silence. Several verses of reduced noise followed, followed by the predictable conversations within the synagogue once again starting up. This time Grossman's glare had been punctuated by a thundering smack on the *bima* followed by a growling pronunciation of, "*Frechheit! Ihr seid alle frech.*" Impudence! You are all insolent.

Of course, my absolute favorite Grossman-ism came one fine rainy Shabbat after services when I went up to the front to catch Rabbi before he hobbled off to *Kiddush* so that I could confirm how much the *Beit Din* was going to cost me. Grossman beat me to him and seemed to care nothing for the *Frechheit* I probably represented. Instead, he cared about making sure that even the rabbi would bow to his interpretations of congregational propriety.

"The men you call up to Torah," he spoke in clear if overly spat German, "are not circumcised. No one is circumcised. They lie and say they are but they are all *frech*. This is disgrace." *Das ist eine Schande!* "No one can read from the Torah if they are not circumcised. You need to check!"

Of course I didn't get to ask my question or hear Rabbi's answer to Herr Grossman's accusation. The image of Rabbi and Gidal holding up a *tallis* to block the view of the congregation of the eighty-year old men as Rabbi asked them to drop trou' on the way up to Torah had me barely holding in a guffaw. As I offered the image to Sabrina and recounted the conversation, the silly bug had been passed and we could barely keep a straight face the rest of the lunch. I doubled my vodka count that Shabbat hoping it would help and failed. Rabbi Isaac gave me a few pointed looks—not really telling me I was wrong to see the amusement, but rather to please make myself a bit less of a distraction. As curious as I was, I never did ask Rabbi how he had responded, but my vision, at least, never came true.

The rest of the Minyan Men personalities would manifest most clearly in Rabbi's absence. Mostly, the dominance of the Adler-Grossman-Likhtman power triangle in addition to Rabbi's influence kept the rest of the inmates in check, but with one missing warden, the crazy tended to creep out.

Two rows back from the front in the middle rows, always praying closest to Rabbi, sat Chayem. Although it certainly didn't appear to be the case as Chayem was in awful health, he happened to be the youngest at sixty-seven-ish. He looked a lot like a taller and more Russian, obviously, version of Dom DeLuise. I know—seriously blame my dad's taste in movies—at least I got to choose movies for Daddy-Andrea movie night every other week and got to subject him to a "Love Actually" for every "Smokey and the Bandit." Anyway, Dom Chayem had been a Red Army career officer. How and why he moved or if he had any family or friends remained hotly in dispute on my end of the *Kiddush* table. His demeanor, however, still betrayed what I am imagining to be a Soviet military esthetic. His favorite habit, for example, was to in what seriously must be a Soviet trope begin tapping his wristwatch violently as the clock neared whatever point his internal clock declared to be "too long." He was especially good at catching Rabbi's eyes when Rabbi would turn his head to offer some sort of explanation of a prayer toward the end of the service, or worse, when Rabbi would turn to ask for names to be called out for *kaddish*—the mourners' prayer. The violent tapping of the wrist-watch would often be accompanied by overly dramatic shoulder shrugs and hands held up in the air when the rabbi would not immediately comply with the order and stop the service on the spot.

To be fair to Chayem, our *Einheitsgemeinde* comprised a circle with about a forty-mile radius on our side of the Rhine. This meant some of the Minyan Men that lived in little FSU enclaves off of a trolley or train route would need several bus transfers and often more than an hour to arrive and return. Although I in my naïveté or idealism could easily claim that Shabbat should be trumping those concerns, I lived a simple fifteen-minute trolley ride from the battlements. And I was not in

166

my eighties. Yet wild gesticulations and violently meaningful watch tapping didn't seem the best solution. How about leaving before the end of *Kiddush*? I know, naïve.

One of the sweeter guys I knew only as Sasha the Lieutenant. I have no idea if he actually had possessed military rank. Rather, he sat inseparable from Dr. Likhtman and would be occasionally sent on errands throughout the service to pass on whatever wisdom or messages Dr. Likhtman needed delivered in his own covert attempt to obtain power. Amir, the one that so loved calling me "*yablochko*" in what he assumed to be a covert reference to my breasts, showed up later every week, sat in the very back with a newspaper and no prayerbook, and neither spoke nor understood a word of German. His bench mate, Yuri, had a paralyzed right hand and had been suffering along with the most corpulent of the men, Israel, with progressive dementia. Of course in spite of this, Yuri and Israel still received nearly weekly *aliyot* until they had reached the point where Rabbi had to say each word of the blessings individually and wait for the questioning repetition. In those moments, I usually vacillated between pity and anger—anger at Orthodoxy that these men qualified as the completion of a minyan and that I did not and would not even after finishing my own current 'status clarification' process.

All these personalities, characters and incidents in addition to the hundreds I am not yet sure how to tell would be pathetically hilarious and worthy of passing on in sheer mockery to future generations had it not been tainted by a tragic undertone. In the middle of the winter I went to my first Rabbi Isaac-led funeral. I had begun my conversion/status-clarification process and had been told clearly that any chance to witness a life-cycle event would be a requirement of my education. Rabbi Isaac even offered to drive me. This sounded like a pleasant offer as the community cemetery would take nearly an hour to get to by bus but a mere twenty-minutes by autobahn. Unfortunately, the Rabbi-mobile had been crammed with loud synagogue employees also wishing to pay their respects.

At least they seemed to get the mourning right, somewhat. Their presence in a place of mourning felt more orderly. I guess their mourning unlike their praying at least had been oft practiced, which itself felt sad and pathetic. But the small chapel at our cemetery filled up quickly, everyone acting with a sense of familiarity. I offered my seat to a grateful *Babushka* in black and joined the increasing size of the Standing Room Only section. The recently departed had been a member of the Minyan Men that I had never met. Herr Shlemovich had been diagnosed with pancreatic cancer not long after I started attending services. What I didn't know at the time was the Herr Shlemovich was the Czar's uncle on his mother's side, occasioning the first and only time I ever saw the Czar with either kippah or in attendance at a religious function. I don't know if it meant that the Minyan Men somehow also functioned as the cool kids, as Rabbi Isaac later explained the Standing Room Only thing to be a rare occurrence—among the duties of the Minyan Men was the requirement to be, well, the minyan at a funeral. Apparently they often were the only ones that showed up.

Rabbi Isaac gave his *hesped*—the eulogy—in both Russian and German, and suddenly, my reaction to the absurdity of these backward-seeming men felt cruel. Herr Shlemovich had been in a Nazi work camp during the war in Ukraine. His mother, father, two sisters and baby brother had been shot by one of the SS *Einsatzgruppen* as they rolled through the Pale of Settlement. Another sister, the Czar's mother, had escaped in some sort of forced march from Kiev to Kazakhstan, returning to find only a brother remaining from their entire extended family.

168

After this I paid a little less attention to my desire to mock and a little more attention to talking in limited words to these men. As much as people like Herr Grossman made it so hard to try and feel sympathy let alone respect, I tried. Then there were times I just couldn't escape the fact that I probably should just remain silent all the time and get over myself. Case in point, several times a year, during the High Holidays and during each of the Pilgrimage Festivals of Sukkot, Pesach and Shavuot, there would be a Memorial Service—a *Yizkor*. As very few people in the community could read the Hebrew to really pray the appropriate prayers, Rabbi Isaac did something that seemed humane. Unlike any other *Yizkor* I had seen where a book of departed might be distributed, Rabbi Isaac would walk around the synagogue, usually a close-to-bursting half-full for such services, and ask each individual present, men and women, if they wished to recite the names of their departed. After each name was spoken, Rabbi Isaac would repeat the name slowly, clearly and respectfully, so that every ear could participate and so that the sound of each name would echo just a second longer through the surprisingly silent room.

As Rabbi reached Herr Grossman, Herr Grossman's list took my breath away. Mother. Father. Brother. Brother. Brother. Sister. Sister. Sister. Sister. First Wife.

After each name, spoken clearly, Herr Grossman would distinctly pronounce: "*In der Schoah ermordet.*" Killed in the Holocaust.

These men were an absolute disaster. They had no respect for the rabbi. The presence of the women in services was barely tolerated. They knew nothing of Judaism. Nothing of Torah. They acted often like children and created an atmosphere anathema to spiritual or community growth. Yet what kind of anger management problems would I have if, like Herr

169

Grossman, I had lost both parents, a spouse and seven siblings in the Holocaust when I was roughly as old as I was sitting in that forsaken synagogue listening to men that I mostly despised? I had lost my grandparents, sure, but to the ravages of age. I declared my right to mourn within a haze of pathos while these people had seen tragedy that I could never understand. Then that doesn't even begin to touch the years after— "Jew" stamped in a passport declaring open season on a despised minority within the Soviet Union. Gulags and discrimination. Loss of religious tradition based on the whim of the politburo and Stalin's iron hand. My generation leaves our religions because they don't fulfill our perceived individual needs like a Whole Foods is supposed to fulfill my need for the most organic crunchy kale salad. How would I feel displaced in time and culture, fighting to claim the tiniest bit of my pride or connection to my hazily remembered origins?

And then there stood Herr Grossman, turning his back once again on Herr Adler. Gidal forgot to separate them for the Torah service. There is Herr Likhtman and his Lieutenant mocking those around them and once again Chayem trying to make his early bus through more wild gesticulations and watch smacking. And there is Herr Adler trying to charm me right before he explains to Gidal how the real *gabbaim* lead services in the other Great Synagogue that he attends. And there I am, trying to figure out if I can ever in any way be as authentically Jewish as these men who act so brazenly idiotic and know so much less than I do about anything you can learn about Judaism from a book. Can I ever pay for my Jewishness in a way that will give me the type of understanding that they have and that I am not sure I can ever grasp?

Ukrainian Funerals

My *handy* buzzed at about 22:30. That wasn't really late, especially for a potential booty call, so I grabbed the phone off of my desk, surprised to see Natasha's face pop up instead of Rafi's.

"*Privyet*, Natasha, *was ist los?*"

As Natasha was a pretty OCD creature of habit, meaning she would never call past 21:00, I asked her what was wrong assuming that something was wrong.

"*Mein Vater ist gestorben.*" My father is dead.

Although her German had improved markedly over the last few months of mutual language lessons, it took putting the sounds of her sobs and the nearly unintelligible German together to decipher the message.

"*Liebe Natasha! Es tut mir so leid. Ich bin sofort da!*"

I must admit, even if it is a little unbecoming, that I am proud that my reaction was to show true sympathy with my voice, tell her I would be over immediately, and then actually do as I had said. I know, what other choice is there? That is the humiliating part. I think I am telling this part of the story simply to make up for the fact that doing the right thing has been anything but self-evident in my life. I mean, is it my entire generation or is it just me who has such a selfish asshole default-mode?

Exhibit One: Being teased after school in the ninth grade. My best friend that year had been Bonnie Washington. Bonnie and I had bonded the previous year after she had moved up from North Carolina with her mom after a particularly brutal divorce. Her uncle, some sort of local real estate personality and life-long bachelor had welcomed his sister and niece to live with him until

Bonnie's mom could get her shit together. As a mixed race girl the two of us bonded over the fact that in our neck of the burbs our non-white skin made us unique. Add to that that she also was going through a ballet phase. This put us in the same after-school class and often the same car as our parents quickly learned the utility of car-pooling post ballet. I guess at that age these factors made friendship inevitable.

Even now I can't really believe I did this, even at age fourteen. Waiting for public transportation after school to make the several mile and sketchy traffic trek to the dance studio in the town of Media, two sophomores approached: Rick-who-preferred-being-called-Richard and Gerald the Golfer. Gerald the Golfer was well on his way to the PGA, as he would remind anyone given a two-second-flat pause in conversation. He dressed the part as well, a bit like James Spader from one of those '80s movies that my dad insisted we watch together for Daddy-Andrea night. Come to think about it, he kind of acted that way too, which was the problem. Richard, on the other hand, who when inevitably was called "Rick" by, well, everyone but me but would like a facial tick reply "Richard" automatically when addressed with one syllable, did not usually act like a modernized James Spader. Usually he was too absorbed with his budding online singing career, at that time limited to Myspace, to have much of any personality. Yet his talent made up for that, at least in my mind, as he sang beautifully and played every instrument on his songs from a basement studio that I longed to visit. My current scheme was to volunteer to choreograph one of his songs and then incidentally volunteer to perform for the resulting music video. The fact that I knew nothing of choreography and in addition to four years of ballet had only taken three months of jazz dance did not discourage my intentions.

James Spader, whose golf talent did nothing for me, did indeed have a personality. It sucked, but it was a personality. The particular suckiness that day involved racial epithets. As the recently released second film of the Harry Potter universe had sent most high school freshmen and sophomores back to the books to be prepared for the next to-be-published books and released movies, James thought that calling my mixed race friend a "mud blood" would be not only hilarious, but a great way to avoid getting in trouble for using any of the adult-recognized slurs. Funny how intent to hurt trumps the words used. In any case, Bonnie at that moment was not feeling very turn-the-other-cheeky and began to engage in a steadily escalating war of insults based on class and race. Bonnie showed no tears, rather a remarkable resolve and an enviable ability to sound more confident in her own insults the more her own heart bled.

I stood to the side, telling myself I was trying to think of how to help, while truly only thinking about how I could make sure this moment did not affect my chances to dance in Richard's basement. I would try to look sympathetic toward Bonnie and make it look like I stood with her injury while at the same time casting glances at Richard that I hoped appeared meaningful. Richard for his part shifted absently from foot to foot, waiting for his best friend to finish his foray into bigotry. When at last the SEPTA bus to Media appeared, Bonnie sat silently with arms crossed next to me and wouldn't meet my gaze. The silent treatment lasted through dance and then the ride with her uncle back to Swarthmore. Her uncle loved chatting with me about baseball so no parental figures had been let in on the tension. That night I received a simple text from my friend: "I would have stuck up for you."

In the moment I had justified my silence with a steady stream of excuses and justifications from, "She is doing just fine," to "I will only make it worse," knowing the entire time but refusing to admit that my silence had only to do with a crush.

I lamely apologized back my text and we remained friends, but the friendship never grew and certainly didn't last after Bonnie's mom, a few months later, found a job in asset management in Providence. The magnitude of my own selfishness came to me about three years later during *Yom Kippur* services after never having once seen Richard's basement. I guess that The Day of Atonement is when you are supposed to realize such things, although the fact it took me until my senior year speaks for itself.

Part of the *Yom Kippur* liturgy includes a series of prayers called, "*Al chet shechatanu lefanecha*"—for the sins which we have committed before you. Each time you say "*chet*" or "sin" you tap your hand on your heart. I always thought we were beating ourselves until Rabbi Theresa explained in one her Yom Kippur sermons my senior year how affected we were by the dominant culture in our understanding of our own tradition. Funny how Rabbi Isaac reiterated the same sentiment in my lessons with him years later.

"Think of what it would be like to walk into a Synagogue on *Yom Kippur* if you had never before seen a Jewish service. Here we have a whole bunch of people in white, standing, talking about sin and beating our chests. Some of us, me included I have to admit, even joke about this. 'Hey, Rabbi, how about you take a sample of that shrimp cocktail. It'll make you feel good!' Which is of course where I smile and shake my head and then sneak one a few minutes later saying to myself, 'Well, I'll just beat it out on Yom Kippur.' The problem is, sin isn't sin and we aren't beating anything."

174

Rabbis Isaac and Theresa had radically different speaking styles. Where Rabbi Isaac sounded about as close as one could sound to fire-and-brimstone Baptist as a Jew could probably get away with—or maybe as one preaching in German should get away with—Rabbi Theresa sounded like someone entering a personal and intimate conversation with a close confidant. The fact that she could pull this off in front of the packed house that would show up for *Kol Nidre*, the evening service at the beginning of *Yom Kippur*, demonstrated her mastery of her abilities.

"Sin, in the definition of popular culture, usually means something like 'an offense against God.' But the word 'sin' in Judaism is simply a translation from Hebrew of a very different word and concept. The word '*chet*,' which we translate as sin and say when we tap our chest, means 'to miss the mark.' Think about that. Think of how different the content of our prayers are when we pray, 'for the offenses we have given to You,' versus 'for the times that we have tried but have missed the mark.' The first one would require us to punish ourselves. How dare we offend God!" Here she pounded her chest, the thud echoing in the reverb of the microphone. "But with the other possibility, that we have missed the mark, would we truly beat ourselves while saying, 'How dare I be human?'

"According to our Chassidic ancestors, we are not beating ourselves at all. We are tapping at our hearts in hopes that they become open to change—open to hearing that we are willing to look at ourselves in the mirror, admit when we have injured someone. We are willing to make amends, and then are willing to make the changes needed to learn from how we have missed the mark."

At that point my inward gaze returned for the first time in years to the incident with Bonnie. What was worse, once Rabbi

175

Theresa had finished her sermon and we had begun the *vidui*—the confessional part of the service that contained all of the "Al Chet" prayers, a number of them jumped out and grabbed me by the throat: For the sin which we have committed before you with knowledge and with deceit. For the sin which we have committed before you by scheming against a fellow man. For the sin which we have committed before you by frivolity.

One of the elements of Judaism that I find psychologically healthy and one that I think every rabbi I had ever had has repeated is: "God cannot forgive you for a sin against another human. You must first make *teshuva*—amends—with the one you have injured and then you will be forgiven through the prayers of forgiveness on Yom Kippur." The confessional prayers were supposed to supply an exhaustive list of every way in which we might have missed the mark, so that what happened to me that night would happen to people like me that had so clearly missed the mark. Since I cried through the service my dad didn't ask questions when I requested an exemption to the family prohibition from using the telephone or computer on Shabbat or Jewish holiday. By my senior year, Facebook had replaced Myspace and although Bonnie and I were friends, that friendship existed as a typical Facebook one. At least through this medium I had her current mobile number and could call her and tearfully ask for forgiveness. A better person than I, Bonnie told me there was nothing to forgive and that all had been long forgotten. We talked a few hours and got all caught up, but distance and other distractions kept us from truly ever reigniting the friendship I had so stupidly and profoundly blown.

Perhaps my self-recriminations for that memory and my pride at how quickly I responded to Natasha's need wouldn't be so extreme if I hadn't repeated that pattern of self-serving mindless injuring of friends so many times after that. Missing the

176

mark indeed—I consider myself a professional anti-marksman. But Natasha was going to get the right version of me, regardless of the text I had to send Rafi fifteen minutes later on the tram that he could not come by that evening.

Natasha met me at her door, a predictable mess. The kids were already asleep and her mom back across the hall in her own apartment. I just wrapped my arms around her as she sobbed. At some point, an internal Russian Mother warning system kicked in and she realized she hadn't offered me tea. Normally nothing that I could do or say could keep her from playing a perfect Russian hostess. This time, however, I was armed with one of Rabbi Isaac's recent lectures in my conversion class about how a Jew should act when someone else is in morning.

"The job of the close circle of relatives is to mourn—nothing else. That means husband, wife, sister, brother, son, daughter, mother, father are the ones that are required to mourn. Everyone else, no matter how close you were to the person that died—maybe your cousin or grandparent, need to do their own mourning later. Especially for *shiva*—the seven days of intense mourning following burial. That means no cooking, no cleaning. You go to the house of the people in mourning. No thinking, just do it. You say nothing unless spoken to. You comfort through your presence, not your words. There is nothing that you can say that will ever make it better and there is no explanation that will have meaning—so don't even try. If there are thirty people there and you don't know what to do, then wash the dishes, welcome people that come in, clean the toilet, mow their lawn, take care of their kids, whatever."

With these words clearly burning in front of my eyes, I placed my hands on either shoulder, looked at her uncompromisingly in the eyes and said, "*Ya sdelayu eto.*" I'll do it. I'd heard enough Russian women say that, that it was one thing I was sure I could say correctly without butchering the language.

A few minutes later, tea service in hand with everything arranged exactly as Natasha had presented sacred tea to me dozens of times, we huddled together on her sofa as she curled into as close to a fetal position as she could as I put my arm around her.

Slowly the story came out in a mixture of languages. I had never really had the courage to ask about her mother's presence in Germany and the state or status or whereabouts of her father. I knew her father was Jewish from Ukraine and her mother Russian but born in Ukraine—such distinctions and ways of thinking were just now starting to make any sense to me. At some point the two had divorced and for years Natasha, who had moved to Israel and then to Germany to follow her prick-of-an-ex-husband, had been trying to get her mom a visa to move to Germany. As her mother was not Jewish, this had been hard. Only after the birth of the twins had Olga been allowed in, thankfully able to help her mother-of-three daughter right after her husband had taken off with the pregnant blond in the newspaper photo.

The divorce most likely had something to do with her father's alcoholism, something that seemed ubiquitous in Ukraine and Russia if Natasha's words were to be believed. It seemed that her father's death also related to the vodka, as the fifty-eight-year-old's passing had to do with either a heart attack or liver failure, depending how I interpreted Natasha's hand gestures and the miming of drinking a shot. Natasha herself wasn't really clear on what had happened, as the details from the phone call she had received from Ukraine earlier in the day were either sketchy or Natasha simply couldn't explain what she knew and how she knew it.

178

Now she was it. The body was laying in, if I understood her correctly, some storage shed outside of her father's home village and no burial—no decent burial anyway—was going to happen without Natasha's intervening. Of course at that time, the trouble with separatists in Ukraine had already begun. Even though the problems were geographically and practically far away from where we would be, the fact of conflict alone was why my parents were never told nor would ever be told about my volunteering to fly with Natasha. No way that my far-away parents would respect the subtleties of geography just as there was no way my friend was going to deal with this alone.

Luckily the ticket prices proved quite low as we found flights into Odessa via Vienna on Austrian Air two days later. After a train ride north along the Moldovan border to the birth and death town of her father, Boris, we arrived late in the evening at her father's apartment.

With our two modest bags, we walked the rough kilometer from the train station to her father's apartment. Natasha had only been there twice on visits, but somehow found her way beyond soulless communist-era tenements to her father's pre-war building.

The front door was, well, missing. A shriveled lady of about two-hundred-twenty years with a shrieking voice challenged our arrival from the apartment adjacent the non-protected entry way. The building itself bled graffiti and cement equally, making 'derelict' seem cozy. I imagined that Natasha, amidst the screeching and my steadily increasing adrenalin and terror, tried to convince the yelling corpse of her identity. I, simultaneously, had become suddenly aware now with my first minutes to think in two days that I was one of two pretty young women standing in the dark on a side street in the closest thing to God-forsaken

179

outside of the Shooting Gallery in North Philly that I had ever seen.

Eventually, a key changed hands as somehow Natasha made it past the guardian and we carried our bags up the five flights to the second-to-last landing. Some apartment doors had weak light emanating from under the intact entry ways while others clearly held either nothing or squatters, neither of which I wished to explore. Our plan had been to sleep in the apartment that night then the next day for Natasha to go through whatever paperwork or belongings she could, before we went to what qualified as a Jewish community to try and arrange for burial the next day.

Plans, however, change, as one finds out when the true cause of death and state of the apartment make themselves known. First of all, no flicking of the light switch would bring about light and judging by the freezing temperature in the barely-lit-by-moonlight room neither would the heat work should we endeavor to find out. It may have been early spring, but early spring in Ukraine meant little more than harsh winter in my book, and my warmest clothing to survive the German winter had met its match. Not sure how to ask Natasha what we would do next, I fished out my *handy* and found the flashlight app, encouraging Natasha to do the same.

Thank God that we saw the blood splatters on the wall behind the sofa in *handy*-light rather than daylight. Frozen blood pooled on the sofa where her father had apparently taken his own life three-days ago. Natasha stared emptily for long moments then ran to the kitchen where she loudly vomited into the sink. I really wanted to do the same, but somehow focused my now Hulk-like adrenaline rush into holding my friend's hair away from her face.

Finally, I gave her a bottle of half-empty water left over from the train and encouraged her to wash out her mouth. I

180

grabbed her again by the shoulders. "We need to get out of here. Where can we find a hotel?" It took a few repetitions, and luckily I knew "*gostinitsa*," Russian for 'hotel,' and could finally get my friend's eyes blinking rather than fixed in a ridged stare back at the living room. She finally nodded and I said, "Come on. Let's go."

Back down the stairs, back past the ghoul and back to the train station, we walked around to three travelers' pensions until we found one with a free room. Judging by some of the clothing choices of the ladies outside, I would bet real money that this particular *gostinitsa* had more hourly guests than nightly ones. The fact that the place was called *Gostinitsa Mir* or Peace Hotel did not tempt me to chuckle at the absurdity as I was by now simply too relieved to experience irony.

We placed our bags and found a food stand across the street where we ate things that have nothing to do with Jewish dietary laws. Believe me, every warm bite of meat and mushroom from inside the steaming *pirozhki* returned some of my courage although not my adventurous spirit. Truly, Russian friend or not, I was frightened by the extent of the unknown around me.

Not really possessing enough energy to talk, we returned to our room, once again ignoring the quizzical looks from the desk attendant. Natasha had grabbed a small flask of some sort of vodka from the kiosk outside the train station and we shared the bottle back and forth silently before crawling in bed together and holding each other to sleep.

The next morning, we made our way not to the building that functioned as the Jewish community, but rather the house of some functionary in the community. Because my Russian was so limited, I was never even sure when Natasha spoke in her native tongue or Ukrainian in which she was as well fluent. I could only

181

guess at the events of the next few hours, much like an anthropologist recording her first observations of a newly discovered tribe on some isolated island.

My first surmise was that Boris, Natasha's father, had not made himself popular with his fellow Ukrainian Jews. My clue came the spitting motion the functionary made upon hearing Boris' name. From what I caught and the brief barely-coherent explanation I got from Natasha, the functionary could not allow Boris to be buried in the Jewish cemetery without permission from someone else that Boris had pissed off, and I am pretty sure I heard the word "oligarch" batted around.

We grabbed a tram and went across town. I kept offering to pay for things, but Natasha had already nearly come to blows with me that I had paid for my own air fare. She had a small mountain of *Hryvnia*, the Ukrainian currency worth about a nickel a piece, and expertly negotiated the town even though she had spent so little time herself in Ukraine since her childhood visiting this or that relative.

The Oligarch and I am guessing member of unsavory elements in Ukrainian society could be found in the back of a cluttered machinist's shop on the edge of a dilapidated industrial district. Said Oligarch, shaved head, cigarette hanging out of his mouth and a pile of golden chains to complete the stereotype, eyed us both up and down in a way that was so anachronistic I didn't think anyone really did that any more, did they? Honestly, I was a bit shocked at how little attention I had received until I started scanning the people around me in our various aspects of our journey since we had entered the country. As the Soviet Union had been so far-reaching, the peoples within the country had been diverse. One of the, it turns out, relatively frequent genotypes that one would see were those with Han blood, ethnic Chinese and Russian or Ukrainian mixes, that seemed to dot the landscape. Of course they were mostly aliens, at least the ones that caught my eye. As I wasn't an alien and in my own eyes I could not stand up to the other women my age that I had seen, the eye-undressing took me by surprise, especially given the edge-of-civilization surroundings. Seriously, the fact that I survived this trip still surprises me.

Well, Mr. Oligarch looked but didn't touch, and apparently completed his promise from central casting by demanding compensation for his kindness of deigning to entertain the idea that Boris would be buried in sacred ground. This time it was Euros that passed hands—I counted several hundred that I know Natasha could not afford—and then we were off to the cemetery.

Continuing with the parade of stereotypes, the tall, thin attendant at the tiny chapel looked ridiculous, hunched over his workbench as Natasha gave whatever necessary information to ensure the pickup of her father's body to be placed in a coffin and finally buried. Without bothering to look up, Lurch clicked through a series of questions for Natasha. Immediately she began for the first time since the previous evening looking panicked, and finally brought me back into the conversation.

"He is asking about the box."

"Coffin?"

"Yes, coffin. He says wood but isn't that bad? Too cheap. I don't know if I can afford better."

"No, no," I corrected her. "It is supposed to be wood and simple. If it is not, it is not kosher." Thank you Rabbi Isaac.

Lurch wrinkled his nose at the sound of German in his personal Holy of Holies but still did not bother looking up. Natasha gave her answers and the questions kept coming.

"He says I have to pay the singer and the men," she said.

"The cantor, I guess," I said and she nodded. "That is fine, sounds like he is the one that leads the service here. You need one because there are some prayers that have to be sung."

"Ok, what about the men?"

"I think he means a *minyan*. I guess this is—I mean of course this is an Orthodox community. You need ten Jewish men total present in order for *kaddish* to be said. So, yeah, it's ok." I started really worrying about the cost and quickly said, "Please let me help pay though."

She gave me a quick look that shut me up and then returned to Lurch. I am pretty sure she didn't really understand what *kaddish* was, as she had only recently started coming to services and that was simply to spend some extra time with me and to have a break from being a single mother. Nonetheless, the fact that I knew or at least pretended to know what I was talking about seemed good enough for her. Of course I never really questioned if what I knew would apply here. I just kind of assumed.

More questions. "He wants to know if I want stones for the grave. What does he mean—the part with my father's name?"

"No," I answered, "I don't think so." Lurch raised his eyebrows slightly as I tried to mime the act of putting a stone on the grave mound. He grunted assent, barely nodding. I turned back to Natasha, "He means the stones to put on the grave."

"No flowers?"

"No, flowers are Christian. Jews put stones on the grave."

She seemed less pleased with this answer but seemed to follow my advice regardless. Lurch wrote out a quick sheet that seemed to be the line items: the coffin, the cantor, the minyan and then as well a chunk of cash to cover a bag of stones. I almost told her to forego the stones, that we could gather them ourselves, but at the same time I really did not want to buck local

184

traditions and imagined bad things happening should I recommend Natasha go around whatever the customs of this place turned out to be.

We went back to the hotel and tried to eat a bit, then had to go to the Jewish community to fill out paperwork. Of course it turned out that there wasn't really a community—certainly not a synagogue. In reality the rabbi for this town actually was a Chabad rabbi living two hours away in Chisinau, Moldova. I had no idea who the cantor was, if he was a real cantor, or if maybe he would also be travelling in. At least that would explain more of the volume of Euros that had changed hands. We walked to an unmarked building that looked more like a carriage house and pressed the lone buzzer. A few rapid-fire questions over the intercom proved our legitimacy and the door opened into a cramped hallway filled with stacked boxes of matzah from Israel.

A face peeked around an archway and gestured us forward into a room that held three desks, stacked with Cyrillic paperwork with official looking government stamps and what seemed to be travel brochures to Israel. The face belonged to the first non-stereotype we had seen. The woman introduced herself as Ilona and warmly shook both of our hands. Not much taller than I, the folds on her hands and face suggested an age of fifty-ish, although her shining black hair, pulled back from her noble oval face and her kind smile gave the impression of angelic beauty. Finally, I felt like Natasha would be taken care of.

I offered my name in Russian and tried to say I was a friend of Natasha's. I am pretty sure the meaning came through. Ilona then offered to take our coats and after hanging them up came back with a tray of tea and a tin of some butter biscuits that Natasha as well seemed to always have on hand. Munching absently, I relaxed and allowed my thoughts to drift. Ilona asked a huge amount of questions, taking all the notes herself. Occasionally I would be drawn back into the conversation.

"Why does she need a different name for my father?"

"His Hebrew name. They are supposed to use his Hebrew name when they pray at the burial and also for the gravestone later on."

"But he never prayed."

"It doesn't matter. Do you know his Hebrew name?"

"No, he was only known as Boris."

Boris, Boris . . . something that I had heard in conversation between some of the Old Russian Dudes and Rabbi Isaac popped into my mind. "Oh, his name is Baruch."

"Baruch?"

"Yes, Boris is actually a Russian variation of the Hebrew name 'Baruch.' What was your father's father's name?"

"Izrael," she answered immediately.

Well, at least that one was easy. "Tell her that your father's name was Baruch ben Izrael." She nodded and did so. Later she turned to me again. "Do I want a *hesped*? She says she needs to know details about his life to give to some man that says a *hesped*."

"Yes," I answered. "That is traditional. A *hesped* is the speech given before burial to honor the life and memory of the one you lost."

"But most of what I know about my dad is from my mom. It isn't very nice."

"Don't you have any positive memories of your dad?"

"Yes, but not about what he did. He didn't do much, I think. I have memories of him making me laugh."

"Then tell her that," I pushed. "They don't need a resume. They just need something meaningful to say to honor him. Tell them what you know about when he was born, what education he

186

had, how old he was when you were born, and then the things he did to make you laugh."

She nodded as if she didn't really buy it but seemed to comply and Ilona looked at her sympathetically as her voice caught several times.

About an hour later, another sum of money changed hands—this time significantly smaller than the previous amounts which made me think this was the legitimate burial fee as opposed to the "keep the Russian mafia happy" ones that had been paid up until now. Ilona ended up inviting us back to her nearby apartment for dinner, and my sense of this place and the people once again shifted from antagonistic to ambivalent.

Ilona lived alone. Pictures on the walls suggested a large family, but when pressed, she quickly explained to Natasha who later recounted the details that her husband had been a military officer who had died in Chechnya and her two children were both living in Berlin. Asked why she didn't join them, she made it clear that without her there would be no Jewish community left in the area other than in Moldova. I had heard this kind of "center of the universe" braggadocio often among the FSU Jews back in Germany, but somehow I believed Ilona. Moreover, if there were others, what would happen if someone other than the kind hearted soul took over? As sad as it was, I found myself hoping Ilona would stay here, just for the sake of . . . of what? The feeling that there was one place out here where one Jew still cared? Was that it? Was that enough to wish such an existence on someone?

Ilona spent a few hours cooking a feast for us and apologizing every five minutes for having so little. I am guessing that this was the simple truth, but that there was no way she was going to let her two guests see anything but full plates of chicken, potatoes and vegetables. We left well after dark with a

187

significantly reduced need for a flask of vodka than the previous night.

The next day—the day of the funeral and our last in Ukraine—warmed up a bit and by late morning felt positively balmy as the temperature moved above freezing. The funeral had been scheduled for noon and so we packed up everything by eleven and dragged our bags to the tram which would take us to the cemetery.

A few older men were milling around when we got there. In the sunlight, one could almost imagine that in the spring the place would be beautiful. Some of the gravestones appeared truly old while across the several-acre field one could easily see about ten mounds without a headstone, meaning they had been there less than a year. Next to them stood a fresh mound adjacent a newly dug grave—meant for today. Around the outer perimeter, about five or six dozen headstones had been placed against the property wall, a brick and mortar affair about seven feet tall that showed some signs of upkeep. I had seen orphaned headstones like these before in Germany—stripped from graves for a variety of reasons, usually having to do with Nazi desecration. I decided that at some point I would look up and try and find the Jewish history of this area.

About five minutes to the hour, a truck that served as a hearse pulled up through a driveway and then backed up to the chapel. Some of the younger of the men milling around, obviously accustomed to this as part of their duties as the Minyan Men, stepped up to the truck. Lurch appeared, dressed identically to the previous day in wool pants and a grayed overcoat, dragging along a metal cart. The six men at the direction of Lurch pulled the coffin, simple pine with no stain but a large inlayed Star of David on the top, out of the truck and onto the cart. Another man, after a sharp word from Lurch,

188

ambled into the chapel part of the building and came out with a black cloth also emblazoned with a Star of David which he quickly spread over the coffin.

When all was prepared, the men pushed the cart through the doorway into the chapel. No one had greeted us, but as we were the unknowns, the obvious assumption would be that one of us was the daughter of Boris. Natasha and I followed the twelve-or-so total men into the chapel where Lurch pointed to the right side and said, "Women sit there." Natasha tried to sit about half way back in the middle but I pulled her up to the front, whispering, "You are the family. You are supposed to sit up front."

The chapel itself would have been quaint with a few coats of paint, a good cleaning, and heat. The room, about forty feet long and thirty wide, held about sixty chairs in total: thirty on either side of a center aisle. The men all sat mostly toward the back and chatted with each other loudly in what I guess was Ukrainian. One of the men had a cigarette lighter and was currently engaged in lighting all of the thirty or so white candles in two black candelabras set in the front of the chapel. They looked a bit like dusty coat-racks, each about five-foot-tall, with the candle holders around the top bent in every direction giving a bit of a glittering medusa impression when all had been successfully lit.

The coffin stood in the center aisle, right between the candles and at the foot of a slightly raised dais with a simple wood pulpit. Natasha had not yet looked at the coffin, sitting instead stiffly, her eyes focused stonily at the empty pulpit, her hands trembling lightly. Her normally coiffed hair clung wetly to the side of her face. I was about to go and see if I could find anyone that looked like a cantor when a new set of footfalls entered from the back a swiftly came up to where we sat.

"You are the daughter," the man asked quickly. He appeared about sixty with a reddened alcoholic nose and breath that

189

smelled strongly of onions and garlic. I instantly disliked him on principle, but at least I could understand this one phrase of Russian. Natasha nodded in the affirmative to his question and he gestured for her to follow him. She gave me a panicked look so I also got up and went with them back outside the entry doors. Once outside, they begin speaking rapidly. He had a copy of the papers Ilona had filled out the night before and I think he was questioning her on several items. That was a good sign. Finally, he opened the satchel that he had been carrying at his shoulder and pulled out a dramatically long pair of scissors while saying a few more words to Natasha.

Natasha looked at me in horror as I explained, "It is called *kriah*. It is traditional and it is supposed to symbolize the pain of death."

"But this is my only dress I brought with me."

I knew Natasha had very little in the way of clothing. Most of her extra money went to buy clothing for her quickly growing children. It hadn't even crossed my mind that they might be doing this. In the States, *kriah* was usually performed symbolically with a ribbon placed on the lapel and then torn. This more traditional rite that we were faced with had always seemed to me to be a bit more like a barbaric way of destroying clothing. During one of our conversations, Rabbi Isaac had tried to convince me otherwise, talking about how sanitized our religion had become.

"Death is messy," he had begun. "Emotionally and literally. Judaism tries to get us to acknowledge the reality of death—to get us to actually deal with our pain instead of hiding it and deal with death itself rather than ignoring it. I think in America, death has started to be treated more like a failure rather than a natural part of life. Thus, we no longer tear clothes. Instead we tear a ribbon. We no longer sit on the floor for *shiva*. We sit in slightly

190

smaller chairs. We no longer take mourning seriously as the sole task of the mourner. We all need to mourn. Think of it this way—there is a finite amount of mourning that everyone must go through when we lose someone. Judaism tells us to get it out of the way—super intense for seven days when we do nothing but mourn. Then for thirty we begin functioning again—like going to work, but we otherwise remain in a state of deep mourning. Then for a total of three hundred days after the burial we move more slowly toward normalcy, but still do not attend celebrations. Over the course of the seven, thirty and three-hundred, you take the burden of mourning seriously and allow it to finally be released. But let's say that, like seems is becoming so normal, you mourn for a day or two then go back to normal life. You may be stoic and able to think you are fine, but the mourning that has not been done is still inside of you, meaning that instead of being completely able to healthily move forward with life a year later, you have the specter of all the un-mourned energy hanging over you. And it will come out—in dreams, in strong and unexpected emotions, in stress toward other relationships—it'll keep coming out until the definite amount of mourning has been mourned out.

"*Kriah* helps begin all that. Technically we perform it twice—the first time is the moment that we hear the news that a close relative has passed. Whatever we are wearing—our workout clothes or a tuxedo—we rip our shirt or jacket or blouse in that moment. Then before the funeral, we do it again.

"In the days or hours before a funeral, we get caught up in all the administrative details. The paperwork is numbing, and the second *kriah* begins the official mourning process—it is meant to force the tears to start flowing again."

Of course at the time of the explanation all had been academic, and my damnable imagination, instead of focusing on

191

the importance of mourning, had focused on all of the outfits that I would be comfortable ripping and those I wouldn't. Now I looked at Natasha and realized that other than the night she had called and the brief moment of sickness in her father' apartment, I had not seen her cry. She had indeed been numbing herself, and so I became Rabbi Isaac's surrogate voice for that moment, not believing for a second I had the right, expertise or knowledge to do so. But it had to be done.

"It doesn't matter. You have to do this," I told her. "It is your job to cry now. And then keep crying. I'll be with you. But you have to do this and you have to start mourning."

She looked at me with a mixture of trust and resignation. The garlicy cantor handed me the scissors, I imagine out of respect for Natasha's modesty. I knew Natasha had a black camisole beneath her black blouse. Apparently Russians and Ukrainians wear black to funerals, period, and nothing that I could say would convince her it wasn't necessary. Seeing that everyone else here wore black made me happy I hadn't convinced her. Gently opening her coat, I pointed to the top of her blouse, between the collar and first button. She nodded, and I turned to the cantor, asking, *"Brachah?"* Blessing? I hoped he spoke Hebrew.

He nodded and said quickly something that had no chance of being understood by a non-practicing Jew. Luckily the blessing was the same as what one says when you find out that someone has died. Rabbi Isaac had been drilling me for two months now on blessings, and for once I felt gratitude for the hours of head swimming.

"Repeat after me," I instructed my friend. *"Baruch . . ."*

"Baruch . . ."

She repeated carefully as I spoke slowly until we had completed the blessing, *Blessed are You, Eternal One our God,*

192

the only true Judge. With the sound of Hebrew her eyes reddened and as I cut a small starting point in her blouse and she ripped—first unsuccessfully and then with more force, you could see the anger transferring into her clothes. "Papa," she cried weakly as the material gave way.

The rest of the ceremony was not a complete disaster. Although perfunctory, Chazzan Garlic sang well and there were at least a few murmurs of appreciation from the small group for the words the cantor read from his notes to honor Boris' memory. After the *hesped* we stood and listened to a more than adequately chanted *El Male Rachamim*, after which we followed the cantor and the rolled coffin out of the chapel and onto the cold trek to the gravesite, about a hundred yards away. The cantor sung the entire time except for seven pauses where we all stopped briefly and then continued. I had heard about this and experienced it once with Rabbi Isaac, but had always wondered at the arbitrary-seeming nature of the ceremony, not to mention the torture in the cold or rain, should a funeral not have the good sense to be on a sunny albeit chilly day like today. But now in dialogue with a funeral as a real thing rather than a theoretical construct to be inconvenienced by, it all started making sense. You don't rush this. You let it become real for those that are in denial. Moreover, the discomfort is something that should be felt in this moment—not avoided. I could already hear myself telling Rabbi Isaac about my insights—about this entire experience—the next time we met.

Finally at the gravesite, there was none of the sanitized feeling of an American burial. No green tarps rested over the pile of dirt or around the hole in the ground. Instead of hydraulics, three blocks of wood had been set across the hole as well as three lengths of thick grey rope. After the cart stopped and the cantor motioned where we should stand, the six men that had

193

taken the coffin from the truck now lifted the coffin off of the cart and rested it on the slabs. The men, all wearing work gloves, pulled the ropes tight against the coffin and then at a vocal signal from the one closest Lurch, they all lifted as Lurch quickly pulled the planks out from under the coffin. Then slowly and actually quite efficiently the men lowered the coffin to the bottom.

By now, Natasha had been sobbing on and off since the *kriah* and rather than trying to say anything I simply held my arm around her—feeling helpless but understanding that helplessness was all that I should expect from myself in this moment. As the men stepped back, two workmen came up from behind the dirt pile. They started removing the metal platforms that had been around the hole to provide traction, half-tossing them onto the rows of graves behind this one. Then came the ropes: the first two came up easily, while the third had gotten caught on some hidden protrusion underneath the coffin way down in the hole. Seeing what was about to happen, I at least then knew what I could do to help. I swiftly turned Natasha away from the grave under the guise of comforting her by burying her head on my shoulder. Out of my peripheral vision I watched one of the workmen jump into the grave and heard the corpse rolling around in the casket as the workman jimmied the box until the rope could be released. Finally, Lurch and his fellow offered their arms to pull the man out of the hole, where by the sound of it he was standing on the casket in order to get pulled out. When above ground, I release Natasha. Seriously, there is no way she needed that as part of the memory of this experience. Getting real was one thing, but there is such a thing as too much reality.

Now the cantor walked to one of the shovels, said something quietly in Hebrew and then shoveled three scoops of earth onto the wood below, each sounding like a heavy boot thudding on a

194

wooden floor. Then the cantor placed the shovel back in the mound and motioned for Natasha. I helped her up to the pile and nodded encouragingly for her to do as the cantor had done. She had barely enough power left to lift the earth, but slowly as I stood near her to try and catch her if she stumbled, she fulfilled the obligation of burying her father.

She tried to hand the shovel to me and I shook my head, gesturing for her to instead place it in the earth. I would explain to her later that we don't hand the shovel off, as we do not hand our obligations of mourning off to another—each must fulfill that obligation themselves. I followed with my own three scoops and then each of the men who went back to talking slightly-too-loudly amongst themselves. Finally, all had scooped earth and I jumped at the sound of the workman operating the backhoe. Motioned by Lurch, we all stepped back as the vehicle moved up and noisily moved all of the pile back into the grave, leaving a rounded mound about a foot and a half high over where the hole had been.

Lurch grabbed a wooden stake with Cyrillic on it—Boris' name, and placed it in the ground at the head of the mound, then paused as the cantor stepped up and repeated El *Male Rachamim*.

This time the prayer sounded transcendent. Maybe the sun shining outside or maybe the contrast with the backhoe added some extra emotion, but now when the ancient-sounding melody came out of his mouth, it seemed to breathe with hope and meaning. He finished singing and then handed out small laminated cards to the men there. Confused at first, I realized this was for reciting the mourners' prayer—the *kaddish*—and as an Orthodox community they would not allow Natasha, a woman, to perform this obligation. Defiantly, I whispered, "When they pray, repeat what I say quietly."

If they heard our voices they were too polite or shocked to stop us as I helped my friend say, "*Yitgadal v'yitkadash . . .*"

When the last line, "*May there be peace*," had been recited, I felt a sort of platonic harmony descend over the ground and a sense of wellness rest in my heart that I had never expected. Lurch then walked up and handed us a crumpled paper bag. It looked heavy and I raised an eyebrow until all became clear. Ah—the stones. I took the bag from him and opened it to look inside, ensuring a sudden, complete and utter collapse of my sense of well-being.

The stones that Natasha had paid for were broken shards of another grave stone, with the break markings clearly fresh. Natasha's bribery had precipitated the destruction of one of the other gravestones on this cemetery, broken apart with a sledgehammer to fulfill a ritual but oh so clearly without a moment of understanding the meaning of the ritual. Feeling all blood drain from my face I thought quickly, then dug in and grabbed a small stone with no Hebrew letters to hand to Natasha, grabbed another for myself, and then commanded Natasha to lay hers on the mound. I followed her, then handed the bag to one on the minyan men and escorted Natasha quickly away.

"Come on, you are not supposed to stay at the graveside after you lay the stone," I said, hoping I was right and hoping much more fervently that Natasha would never understand what had just happened at the conclusion to her Papa's funeral.

Town Hall

Rafi kept uncharacteristically grabbing my hand. It wasn't that I minded, just that his affection usually presented itself as fully "on" or fully "off," and the fully "on" took place only behind private closed doors. This, well *normal* sort of affection never occurred in public, making it clear that the hand holding had little to do with establishing intimacy with his girlfriend of less-than-two-months and much more to do with his decision to speak publicly in favor of my rebellion and against the totalitarianism of the Czar and his minions. Power to the people, man.

The social hall had been reconfigured for town-hall, and it did feel a little shocking to see the room filled with about three-hundred as opposed to the usual twenty-to-thirty that stayed after a service. A table had been set for the chieftains up front in addition to a few others like the Czar and strangely enough Valentina-the-Supermodel. Rabbi Isaac was not counted among the Chieftains and it took a few minutes of glancing around to find him holed up in the far back corner nursing a glass of water and looking miserable. To be fair, he looked quite a bit better than when Sabrina and I had visited him in the hospital three weeks earlier. He then slowly seemed to improve as we took turns with others in the community over the next few weeks bringing him whatever it was we could bake or cook to try and fulfill our own vision of how a community treated a sick rabbi. I caught his eye, nodded, and received a pleasant nod and smile in return. Then I turned my attention back to the stressed hand squeezing mine, glad to see Rabbi Isaac finally back in the synagogue but momentarily much more focused on the hand in mine and the scene around us.

I gently kissed Rafi's cheek and made encouraging sounds to calm his nervousness. I am sure I did not succeed, but I loved his scent and in this moment I was simply so proud of him and so moved to have a boyfriend that had taken my cause and made it his own. I felt a sense of inevitable power in the moment—that all the trials and tribulations had led up to now and that this community meeting would lead to real change—that I was a part of something so important and so profound that made sense of every decision of my life up to this point.

Both chieftains began their spiels with empty self-congratulatory words about having such a strong *Gemeinde*. Herr Engels at least attempted a few words of Russian, and Valentina's place at the Chieftain table was quickly explained as she translated the German remarks that followed into Russian for the assembled multitudes.

A bit of grumbling started as Valentina began translating Herr Platt's words. I turned to Rafi with an inquisitive raise of eyebrows and he leaned in and whispered, "Her translation is bad. She is not really saying what they are saying." The frustration quickly mounted until Frau Hofstadter, a member of the community and professor at the Uni stood and offered her own services. "It is important that we understand everything that is said," she said in a clear German that rose above the din. "I can offer my services to translate for this meeting."

Of course such a sensible suggestion from a highly qualified individual could not possibly be met with acceptance, so she was ignored until she sat and Valentina continued providing the crap translation from and into German, in spite of her pathetic skills, for the rest of the meeting.

The rules of the community meeting were simple. The bi-laws of the community allowed for one gathering a year where the executive committee could comment on the state of the

198

Gemeinde and the members of the community could ask questions, add support or voice concerns. Up to this point, Rabbi Isaac would seldom comment on the political situation in the community during our weekly meetings, but a few days earlier he had let a little information out.

"They do this every year, but this year the scheduling is based on the upcoming elections. Once every four years a new board is chosen, but it is usually really just chosen by Platt and Engels and then voted in, followed by the new hand-chosen board turning around and once again voting Platt and Engels into their positions. The Russians pretty much have voted in whatever way those two want, partially because before every election they devote the community meetings to reminding everyone that they get money from the community only because Platt and Engels are generous."

I was actually pretty shocked—not to hear this news, as by now my righteous cynicism could allow for no more surprise— rather that Rabbi Isaac would so bluntly criticize. This was not only uncharacteristic, it almost bordered on *lashon hora*, the Jewish word for gossip that translated literally as the "evil tongue," something that Rabbi Isaac avoided with the sensibility of a much holier person than I could ever be. Not wanting to miss this opportunity I pushed, "Is that true? That people get money because of Platt and Engels?"

Rabbi shrugged. "*Jein.* As usual it's complicated. Most people in the community—about seventy-five percent—are on *Hartz IV.* You know what that is?"

I nodded. *Hartz IV*, ironically pronounced "Hearts Fear" was the social welfare program developed by some German business leader—if memory serves a former head of Volkswagen or something like that. Being on "*Hartz IV*" was German for "being on welfare." Except it was a bit different. Germany is what so

199

terrifies the American throngs—a true welfare state. That means that citizen or not, if you had residency you had certain welfare rights including housing and a monthly living stipend. Now, this does sound ridiculously generous, and I must say the American nightmares of "Welfare Queens" sprang to mind when I first drilled Sabrina about the system. It also explained why so many refugees from the various conflicts around the world sought out Germany as a landing place away from their various wars. Not only does Germany have the strongest economy in Europe—if you were lucky enough to land here legally, you would end up in an apartment and have some spending cash along with some sort of health care benefits.

I had assumed that the apartments would be along the lines of Philly projects, but the way that it worked, most apartment complexes were required to reserve a certain percentage for *Hartz IV*, which meant that you might actually end up on welfare in a pretty nice place. The clue to refugee/welfare density, however, came from the satellite dishes. According to Sabrina, pretty much the only folks with a dish on the balcony were those that were trying to get news and television in their native languages of Russian, Turkish, Arabic, Farsi and whatnot.

This year there was some sort of new intrigue in the standard "Vote for us, love us, fear us, because we hold the purse." I found this both confusing and nearly impossible to explain, but as best as I can understand, all of the *Hartz IV* members were going to have to start paying a fee to the community.

The separation of church and state that seems oft quoted but seldom understood in the States simply does not exist in Germany. The German constitution, the *Grundgesetz*, guarantees freedom of conscience and religion, but at the same time, religion is somehow regulated through taxes and official recognition. The only reason I really get any of this is that I had

200

already, in spite of everything, looked a bit into what it would mean to move to Germany.

Let's say I got a job working for a news service or international bureau in Germany and my contract set my compensation at fifty-thousand Euros a year. Since Germany has a significantly higher tax rate in order to support *Hartz IV* and other social services, not to mention the ongoing infrastructure projects and I guess probably Greece and Portugal as well, I would probably never see about forty percent of that sweet-sounding 50k. Then, of my roughly twenty-thousand Euro per year tax burden, eight or nine percent of that, depending in *Bundesland* or German Federal State would be levied as a "Church Tax" or *Kirchensteuer* depending on what "religion" I checked on my local registration or *Anmeldung* form.

If I checked "Catholic" then I would have roughly eighteen-hundred Euros taken out per year and sent to the national governing board for Catholics. They would then redistribute that to each of the sixteen federal states based on population ratio. The governing Catholic organizations within the federal states would then distribute that money to local communities, ideally based on population but apparently as often based on politics, to solely finance the local churches, to pay for the salaries of priests, and to cover any other religious costs such as religious schools, retirement homes, cemeteries, etc. And the Jewish community worked no differently.

Now, if everyone in a sixteen-hundred-person community is paying let's say a thousand Euros a year assuming a somewhat lower average wage than my journalistic fantasy, then that synagogue is going to have two full-time rabbis, a full-time cantor, a full-time religious school leader, several teachers, plenty of paid staff, new prayerbooks and a building that is staying in pretty good repair. But when more than three out of every four is on *Hartz IV*, well, let's just say that the Jewish communities do not have the religious staff to support the population. Keeping the very lights on comes from German subsidies.

Now I am not saying that is a bad thing. I wouldn't have a clue about how one would begin calculating the present value of the property lost in the Holocaust, let alone the unspeakable human cost, and from that perspective subsidies seem the least that Germany can do. But the ledger is going to hit a point where the fourth or fifth or sixth generation after National Socialism are going to throw up their hands and say, "Enough." The government, I think, is far from that point but I am pretty sure that the third generation populace itself is already there. All my wasted research for my original Herr-Dr.-Professor-nixed Fulbright project made that clear. There is indeed a vague sense of the costs in the collective consciousness of Germany and your average Thorsten or Anika on the street no longer really cares and certainly doesn't want to foot the bill.

If you just look outside you can see one of the hot button items. Not only do you need to pass through the guard towers to get in here, outside and across the street from the front entrance sits a car marked *"Polizei"* and it never leaves. According to some random article or another I ran into in my research, the official police protection became universal for every one of the 120-ish state recognized synagogues after 9/11. The protection had actually been at the request of the German government and not the Jewish community, but try telling that to someone looking at the budget. According to my notes it costs around one hundred thousand Euros a year for the twenty-four seven protection around the average synagogue. Do the math, then add that to the financial crisis caused by the mass immigration of a former Soviet population who either through age or lack of integration or lack of desire to learn the language became a non-working part of the population. And then add that to the new waves of immigration . . .

Germany wanted to do the right thing. I believe they really did. The Iron Curtain came down and they saw either an opportunity or a moral obligation or both and next thing you knew, the miracle had happened and there were once again Jews in Germany!

But we are now on the second generation of FSU Jews in Germany and the language skills are still pretty bad and the amount of families leaving the *Hartz IV* rolls appear far smaller than one would expect. Since FSU Jews make up more than three-fourths of the population and most communities have roughly the same number of three-fourths of the overall community on *Hartz IV* you start getting a sense of the financial crisis that is going to sound like the world's most annoying alarm clock for a whole bunch of people that are currently asleep.

Looking around the social hall at the relative throngs and the figures still wandering in and noisily finding seats it wasn't hard to feel disdain on top of all the other negative emotions I already harbored. The truth is that after returning from Ukraine, retaining any balanced perspective looking at these people sitting around me had become, well, not much of a priority.

Since *Hartz IV* recipients did not pay the church tax yet were still afforded complete use of the religious infrastructure provided by that tax including burial and essentially free use of the Jewish retirement home system, there was some attempt on the part of the German government to instill a sense of monetary responsibility. Every *Hartz IV* recipient who also had chosen membership in a religious community was required to pay five Euros a month of *Kultusgeld*—ritual money I suppose is the best translation of this non-translatable term—directly to the community. And here is the kick: the money was already a part of their monthly welfare check. That means that someone not a member of a religion would get the base monthly *Hartz IV* amount and religious community members would get base plus five Euros which was then to be paid to the community. It was kind of an indirect extra subsidy which sounded pitifully small, but if you add for this community the total is more than twelve thousand Euros a year which at least could pay for a burial or two. It seems like Rabbi Isaac does a burial about once a week, so maybe it's a drop in the bucket, but funding is funding.

The problem was, this was not a new requirement. This had been a part of *Hartz IV* from the beginning, but in order to continue "good will" from Chieftains, the community had simply eaten the five Euros. That all worked until the government, in what should be an ominous sign to anyone paying attention, demanded that the Jewish communities begin following the, you know, law—meaning everyone had to cough up sixty total Euros a year paid in whatever installments they could muster.

I didn't even know any of this was going on until one of Rafi's Ukrainian friends began ranting while out for a little after-Uni beer. I wish I could quote this all in German as truly "*verdammte Gemeinde*" sounds so much better than "damned community" and a good German rant is always lost in the translation.

"And then this damned community is trying to take away more of my grandparents' money!" I would like to think my agreeing to hang out with Bogdan reflected a growing sense of cultural relativism. Ever since Rabbi had told me that the "argument" I overheard from the Old Russian Dudes merely represented everyday conversation, I tried to ignore my own cultural bias and hear the aggression as something different.

Bogdan's girlfriend Melinda, a strangely mousy student from Lyon that refused to ever meet my eyes, seemed to take everything as normative except when I would attempt to act as an equal partner in the group conversation. Then her silent OCD rubbing of Bogdan's arm would stop and she would crinkle her forehead aiming somewhere in the direction of my not-beauty-beauty-spot on my upper lip.

"Wie genau tun sie das? Und warum?" How exactly are they doing this and why, I asked, resolving this time to ignore Melinda and her odd quasi glares of disapproval. Bogdan looked at Rafi and shrugged, as if asking his friend to explain the obvious to his halfwit girlfriend. Luckily, Rafi never treated me like Bogdan's expression indicated, and after a quick glare at his friend explained in English:

"Everyone in the community got a letter last week. It said that if they were not paying *Kirchensteuer* that they would need to begin paying sixty Euros a year or they would not be allowed to come to community events or be buried in the cemetery."

"That doesn't make any sense," I responded to the facts as presented. "Why would they do that?"

"Weil sie Idioten sind!" broke in Bodgan while rolling his eyes. I ignored the outburst and encouraged Rafi to continue. Rafi shrugged, "It is federal law."

"Is it a new law?"

"No, it has been around since *Hartz IV* started, but they are starting to enforce it this year."

"Well, sixty Euros a year doesn't seem that bad," said the American girl without thinking, seeing in my mind only my Dad's Synagogue membership dues of nearly four thousand dollars per year.

"Du hast wirklich keine Ahnung, oder?" You really don't have a clue do you?

That was, incidentally, the last time I joined Rafi in the context of this particular social group unless at least two other couples or four singles as well joined.

Rafi glared at his friend a bit more pointedly and Bogdan backed down, showing clearly who wore the alpha badge. I still wasn't sure about the beta in this group. Seriously, Melinda kind of freaked me out.

Rafi explained, "The *Hartz IV* stipend is only 438 Euros a month. That is pretty hard to live on. For some people, taking five Euros a month away is actually pretty bad."

In that moment I know I blushed enough that it could be seen through my Hunan complexion. Shit. I tried to imagine living off of 438 Euros a month and realized that I was the ass here. At least until more information came out.

Rafi continued, "There are a lot of people that are calling up and threatening to leave the *Gemeinde* because of this."

That was bad. One thing I did know was that the German subsidies were based on membership numbers—less people on the rolls meant a smaller percentage of the kitty would be distributed in this direction. Not only that, in order to no longer be a member of the community, it wasn't like in the States where you would just write a letter to your congregational president or whomever and say, "To Whom It May Concern: Please cancel my membership." In Germany, with the non-Church state separation, you only stopped paying *Kirchensteuer* or I guess *Kultusgeld* as well if you went to the local courthouse and declared that you were of no religion—essentially that you were no longer Jewish. It was pretty twisted and for a few seconds I felt a little compassion—at least until Rafi continued.

"But it is still pretty complicated. You only get the 438 a month if you are a member of a religion, otherwise you only get 433 a month."

It would have been a pretty cool dramatic gesture if I had used the opportunity to spew a good mouthful of *hefeweizen* over the table. This was still the first of my usual two after-Uni drinks and so the brain still functioned fast enough for me to grasp the joke and then lose my previous seconds of embarrassment or compassion.

"Let me get this straight." I said this in English as I really couldn't think of a good nuanced way to translate this wonderfully dramatic phrase from the English lexicon of Hollywood cliché phrases. "If I understand this right, then members of religious communities get a five Euro a month subsidy," shit, I didn't know the German word for subsidy either, "which one is required by law to turn around and pay to the *Gemeinde*. That means that they will have a take-home amount of 433. Now if they leave the *Gemeinde*, their monthly amount will anyway go down to 433, the exact same amount."

Rafi nodded, his face neutral. Bogdan took the opportunity to roll his eyes once again and dramatically shrug his shoulders as if to say, "I *knew* she wouldn't get it."

Apparently I was the only one who did, because at the town hall, the next forty-five minutes of speeches and responses after the Chieftains had explained to everyone how awesome the community was and why they were all one big happy family, every single person in the line to the microphone stepped up and said in Russian pretty much exactly what Bogdan had said at the pub several weeks earlier.

There are times you just wanted to scream. I mean, on the one hand, I have to admit that this moment bathed me in a particular sense of *Schadenfreude*. Watching Engels and Platt looking gradually more pathetic and uncomfortable as the speakers repeated the exact same complaints and then refused to hear or understand the admittedly bad repeated explanations of,

"We have no choice. This is the law," indeed felt better than it should have. On the other hand, this was just ridiculous. Rafi had gotten ahold of one of the letters from a cousin and showed it to me. The letter stated tersely in Russian and then German exactly what Engels and Platt continued repeating, that it was the law, we have no choice, blah blah blah. I sat there listening to the bullshit while visualizing a hundred different ways that the letter could have been better worded to explain what I had figured out in only a few seconds. Even now, all they needed to do, or so I thought, would be to show some sort of visual diagram explaining that if someone left the community they would get exactly the same amount of money as if they paid the five Euros as the law demanded. This shouldn't have been freaking particle physics. I didn't have any desire to make Engels' and Platt's lives easier, but there was principle here in addition to my sense of protection for my friends in this community. Moreover, I suppose I was also imagining solutions to the crisis as the atmosphere began to feel a little too mob-y for me, and mobs never turned out well.

I tried to catch Rabbi's eyes again, but he appeared to have found a particularly interesting something-or-other to read on his *handy* and seemed to have already checked out.

For a while the aggression had moved into cross-talk with very little formal process or translation in one direction or the other. I am not sure how many people heard or understood Herr Platt's most idiotic moment, as it was luckily for him untranslated. Herr Platt had obviously had enough when he slapped his palm on the table and let loose the tirade, "I really don't understand why this is such a big deal. When we went to Israel three years ago, half of you that are complaining right now showed up in the office with wads of mysterious cash to pay for the trip!"

208

Rafi actually snorted, he started laughing so hard. He buried his nose into my shoulder to keep from being seen or heard. "Is that true?" I asked loud enough that only he could hear.

He took a few deep breaths and replied, "Oh yeah. Probably. The *Arschloch* just screwed himself by saying it, though."

Somehow order was eventually restored and some sense of the usual chaos once again settled over the assembly. Rafi resumed his hand-squeezing and once again looked far too serious. Obviously he had begun priming himself for his own turn at the microphone.

I actually wasn't even completely sure what he wanted to say. I had tried to get details out of him at several points including the usually quite effective post-coital bliss of suggestibility. My guess was that he himself wasn't quite sure.

The general idea, however, we had discussed among our little core rebellion group and all agreed. Sabrina and I both knew from our conversations with Rabbi Isaac that his hiring had been specifically targeted to gaining a more active religious component to the community—he was to be a *Menschenfänger*—literally a "people catcher." Since the reconstitution of this community in the early 1970s with the somewhere around seventy or so Jews in the area at the time, the synagogue, as was typical, either had no rabbi or an Orthodox rabbi. The problem with "no rabbi" should have been obvious— that with so much non-contiguous institutional and religious knowledge, a professional Jew or two should be a requirement. The problem with Orthodox rabbis, however, especially after the fall of the Iron Curtain was, well, Orthodoxy.

Although about one hundred and ten thousand Jews registered themselves in Germany as Jewish and therefore members of communities, the actual number of Jewish immigrants since 1991, if they had been telling the truth about their Jewishness, put the number closer to two hundred thousand including the thirty thousand-ish "German" Jews here before 1991 but not including the somewhere north of forty-thousand Israelis that had begun creating an active subculture but had no relationship with religion.

Although these numbers come from an amalgamation of stories I have heard and articles I have read since the beginning of my Fulbright year, the reasons behind the numbers and the universal lack of synagogue attendance point to something else. I can clearly imagine the exchange between a newly arrived FSU Jew and an imported rabbi with a black hat and limited Russian and/or German skills:

"*Zdrasdvutye* Herr Rabbi. I am Jew. I would love to be part of Jewish community"

"Shalom Mr. Ivanikov. I will need to see your maternal grandmother's *ketubah* in order to make sure you are Jewish."

"What is *ketubah?*"

I can then further imagine the second level of conversation if it was allowed to get that far:

"But Herr Rabbi, my passport is stamped that I am Jew and my father was persecuted because of this. He could not go to university and although was very intelligent man, he was only allowed to work in building demolition. His father was sent to gulag."

"What about your mother?"

"My mother? What about my mother? She is Russian, not Jewish."

"Then you are not a Jew."

Any version of this conversation that comes to mind still winds up with a pretty clear indication as to why there is such a discrepancy between the number of "registered" Jews in

Germany and the estimated actual number of Jews and then the even fewer that involve themselves in services.

I mean, I am neither a Rabbi nor one that has ever harbored anything other than the most occasional fantasies of such a life path, but this is just not how such a conversation should go!

I imagine standing there as Mr. Ivanikov came in to maybe his very first real Synagogue and I imagine that I would say, after learning about his lack of Jewish "proof:"

"Welcome! Welcome! We are so happy that you are here. The doors of this synagogue are wide upon to you and your family. Yes, there are some technical details we need to work out to make sure that Jews all over the world also welcome you with such open arms, but we can talk about that later. First thing is come in and be welcome."

Maybe I am just a naïve idealist to think like this—you know—treating people with respect and acting as a conduit to their identity as opposed to a barrier. Maybe it's that I grew up with what so many Orthodox Jews consider to be "fake Judaism" that I can't help but imagine their acts in the absolute worst light. Either way, I think that the approach in my fantasies is probably not at all different than how Rabbi Isaac would deal with the situation. I already know how he treated and continues to treat me and others like me that fall outside of some Norman Rockwellstein version of Judaism, and it has carried with it echoes of doors as wide open as he can make them in spite of the synagogue's security detail and civilian leadership.

But at least that leadership recognized this problem at some point and brought in someone willing to act as if the doors were open. This would be nearly a generation too late for those first disillusioned immigrant waves, but surely it wasn't too late for everyone?

Except for the Czar and his watch tapping and Evgeniy and his taking of bribes to allow the Jewish community to stay open an extra hour for a fucking Jewish activity that was meant to *catch* people pinpointed a major problem: the leadership may *think* and even *say* that they wanted more people involved in the religious life of the community, but what if that meant that the involvement came from people like Rafi and Sabrina and me? Did that count? Moreover, were they even aware that regardless of Rabbi Isaac's actions, if you had to pass through the gates of hell to even get into Rabbi's welcoming hands, would you even be able to perceive him as welcoming if you were already pissed off by the time you managed to get inside the gates?

That's where Rafi came in. Fluent in Russian and German in addition to his lovely nearly accent-free English gave him an opportunity to articulate the case: if the Chieftains wanted more people and more involvement, they were going to have to take away some of the gatekeeper role of the Czar and then work with the Czar to shift the mindset from its current state of either "Only Russians Count" or "Time's Up!" Judaism. Three more quick squeezes after a lull in bodies moving toward the microphone and Rafi stood up and took his place.

"My name is Rafael Abramovich Garayev. I am a member of this community since my family—my Father, Mother, Grandmother and older sister moved here in 2004."

My heart caught. He spoke German slowly, clearly and beautifully, and then even better translated himself at the end of each sentence into just as clear and beautiful Russian. Unlike most, he stood and spoke directly into the mic and brought the assembly to attention as everyone present could thankfully both hear and understand him.

"My father and mother are both Jewish, and for us being Jewish is very important. Like everyone maybe we do not come

212

to synagogue as often as we should, but we love coming and especially love services since Rabbi Newmark became our rabbi."

It was a bit shocking to realize, but I am pretty sure that that had been the first time the entire afternoon that the rabbi of this Jewish community had been mentioned. I resisted the impulse to see if Rabbi Isaac was among those that now had begun paying attention.

Rafi continued: "I think that having a positive and lively Jewish community is not only important for one part of the population, but for everyone. There are many groups in our community that are supported by the community—the *Senioren*, the *Junioren*, the Chess Club, the Maccabee athletic society, and many others."

I always got a bit of a chuckle from the group names. The *Junioren* or the "Juniors" would obviously imply folks maybe my age, but it was actually for thirty-five to sixty-year-olds. Originally, according to Sabrina my fount of all institutional knowledge, the Juniors had been a twenty-five to forty group, but rather than graduating and leaving the infrastructure of Saturday night dances and "let's see who can sneak the most *treyf* in parties" to the next generation, they redefined the "Juniors" to be middle-aged and pushed the age of the Seniors up.

"But the best way to ensure the future of the religious community is to support religious activities for the next generations, especially for teens and for young adults."

There seemed to be some general assent to Rafi's words. I looked around and tried to ascertain the mood. Maybe it wasn't the best day to speak with all that had already happened, but the Chieftains seemed to be listening and the Czar and Valentina did

213

not seem overly perturbed by Rafi's hijacking of their translation monopoly. Maybe he was going to do it!

"But that has been very difficult."

My attention back on Rafi, I watched him swallow and I guessed that this was where he would present the crux of the problem. I flushed with pleasure when his next words proved to be nearly the words that I had spoken to him in defense of our cause the previous night.

"Being a Jew means having a relationship with Shabbat and having a relationship with Shabbat means that celebrating Shabbat takes precedence over everything else. But that is the problem. There is a large group of between ten and twenty young adults in the community that come regularly to services and then after join the Rabbi here in the social hall to celebrate *Kiddush*. In many communities around the world, this is the most important part of the communal celebration.

"Even in this part of Germany, there are some places including Chabad that are full of younger people because there is no limit placed on this celebration. We celebrate and then eat and drink and sing and many people come to these Shabbat evenings. There is a hunger for this and many more people that would come if we had such a celebration here."

At this point, somewhat surprisingly, Herr Platt grabbed his own mic and interrupted, "Then what is the problem?"

I sat about thirty feet away from the Chieftains' table, so I could not clearly see Herr Platt's facial expression. His antagonistic tone, however, immediately took me aback. It was out of place especially as even with his clear annoyance he had not once up until this point interrupted a speaker. Apparently Rafi felt the same as he sounded slightly less sure when he continued.

"The problem is that for many months we have been trying to encourage this type of celebration, but every time we try, security comes in after an hour and stops the singing and tells everyone they have to leave."

That wasn't strictly true, as the "tell" part came from dour expressions and violent watch-tapping, but the point remained accurate. Unfortunately, the Czar took exception to the characterization and in the most rapid emotional escalation I had ever witnessed had jumped to his feet and shouted in Russian, "That is a lie. He is a filthy liar. I have never done any such thing and neither has anyone else."

This is where things get messed up in my memory.

First of all, no attempt by anyone could at this point restore the translation. Anything I know about what was said, from the first accusation of "That is a lie" up until Rafi being physically thrown out of the synagogue grounds and being put on permanent "*Hausverbot*" comes from piecing together different versions of the story from different Russian speakers over the next weeks.

What was clear was that as much as the Czar took umbrage to the accusation that he regularly did exactly what he did, it in no way compared to Rafi's reaction to being called a liar. I knew he had a temper. This never in any way had been directed toward me. Ever. But I had heard his phone conversations or bar conversation quickly turn into the sort of ranting that includes veiled threats and not-so-veiled curses to whichever objects of his ranting were foremost in his mind at a given time. With me he had always channeled that passion in ways that proved, um, constructive. I knew he had a temper, but now he frightened me.

Various accounts have the first death threat thrown by Rafi and others by the Czar. It is my bias, probably, that has me choose the account where Rafi responded to the "Liar" accusation by suggesting that the Czar repeat the accusation outside to his face without all of his friends around. That either at this point or some later point in the shouting the Czar commented that he would shoot him in the head with his gun is not in dispute, nor that he at this point refused to refer to Rafi by his given name and instead began calling out various epithets including, "*chyornyi*" which I knew to mean "black," "*chernozhopyi*" which must be some variant of black but Natasha blushed when I asked her later to elaborate. The most common and vehement shouted words by the Czar and then others were "*chyortov azarbaidjanets*" which means "devil's azeri" and which sounded so hateful that I did not pursue any further understanding.

Within seconds Rafi was being restrained, and after a violent shake he held his hands up in retreat and indicated he would walk out on his own power. Two of the Czar's henchmen played escort and maybe it was only rumor that had him being dragged in a scuffle outside for the last ten meters until being shoved over the threshold of the sliding security door and told that the police would be called if he was ever seen again. I of course didn't witness any of this endgame as I sat mortified and rooted in my seat while everything went down.

We as humans, I think, harbor pretty grandiose illusions regarding how we would react in stressful situations. Maybe it is the everyman-becomes-hero fantasy that has us thinking we would be the one taking down the bank robber or thwarting the airplane terrorist when in reality most of us are so shocked by such extreme events that we take an infinity of moments for our brains to register that something is happening that requires a response. As a Temple student, I knew this intimately from several harrowing experiences in North Philly. My self-delusions suggested I would always act correctly. Contrary to my self-image, however, I always seemed to freeze until someone else stepped in. It's not an attractive reality, but it is the one I must admit and the unfortunate one that came into play in the void left where Rafi should have been standing.

So, although I should have known myself and have been better prepared to step up and be a *mensch*, I froze and stared at the emptiness. Then small details and whispers of responsibility began creeping in. I still had his scarf next to me. Had they let him at least pick up his jacket from the cloakroom? Shouldn't I be up at the mic right at this minute defending him? He was in the right. Whatever had been said, the Czar had clearly attacked first in response to the deadly sin of daring to criticize while having dark skin and coming from one of *those* republics. This was my fight and shouldn't I be up there now?

Or more, shouldn't I have jumped up next to him while it was happening? Show everyone that I stood by with moral outrage on the side of right? Or what about making sure that I ran after him like some southern belle, fluttering my own scarf as I protected the dignity of my man with my swoon. Or what about the bad-ass chick standing up and saying "Threaten me, you cretin. Try throwing me out you petty marionette!" Even though I didn't know what had really happened I could have guessed and stood and defied and then thrown the bird and shouted "screw everyone" in this shameful joke of a community. Was this the bus stop with Bonnie and James Spader all over again and I am still the same shitty person that I swore had been left behind?

I began reasoning only after it was all over—as order began returning and the Chieftains huddled with the Czar showing Serious Facial Expressions to the assembled masses. Only now I texted, "Wait for me, I am coming," and then surreptitiously snuck to back of the room and tiptoed out to the cloakroom where Rafi's hanger still held his jacket confirming that Rafi was out there somewhere in the should-be-spring late winter chill in a button down and nothing else.

No reply to the SMS, I tried calling when I had passed the outer palisades. No answer and then no answer again as I knocked on his apartment door and then no Rafi as I let myself in and left his jacket on his place on the sofa where he would see it. I tried a few more pleading texts of "I need to know you are ok" before giving up and heading back to the Uni and my own apartment.

Maybe it was shame that kept him from responding to my texts that night or maybe it was my own in the next days as I found out more of what had been said and simply had no idea how to hold onto a relationship with a man that had been part of what sounded like serious death threats being leveled at a Jewish community meeting. Maybe I stopped trying to contact him as I became less sure of anything, leading me to pick up my things at his place during a time when I knew he would be at class, leaving his key on a conspicuous corner of the table in the entry hall. Maybe it was just the shame that beneath this all I had manipulated him to speak on behalf of my needs, and rather than admitting that I had somehow been the cause of this and who knows what else, I decided to keep staring at that blank space in the social hall where someone special scared the shit out of me and made me look at parts of myself I had no desire to see.

Natasha tried to help some, her wisdom explaining that I had done nothing wrong. Rather, she clarified that Rafi having been physically overpowered in front of his girlfriend would have made him unable to face me again from humiliation. I mean I got that—he was my first macho from a part of the world that I have to admit I really didn't understand. But I could have helped, couldn't I? Did I even still want to?

Either way the relationship was over as sure as any illusion that I could fix this community.

Jewish Holidays

"Damn, Andrea, sorry but I need your help."

Rabbi Isaac, somehow simultaneously leaning more heavily and pathetically on his cane than usual and moving faster than appropriate for the five minutes before the beginning of a festival service, grabbed me by the shoulder and maneuvered me off to the side away from the knots of grey-heads gathering in the foyer in front of the main entrance to the *beit knesset.*

"Sure, whatever," I replied as we reached perceived safety and he released my shoulder. I was becoming accustomed to last minute tasks. Rabbi Isaac really did seem to be struggling more with what I finally learned was his osteoarthritis, and I had become one of several people, mostly young women and mostly his conversion students, that he asked to retrieve the odd forgotten prayerbook or sermon notes from his office.

It actually felt quite nice to help and be included. The rabbi had a way of communicating with people he trusted with the subtlest eye movement, raised eyebrows or head/neck gesture: *please go close the sanctuary door* he might gesture as an overly-loud Russian discussion began outside in the middle of a sensitive prayer or quiet part of the service—or—*please introduce yourself to that new person I have never seen and welcome them* on the rare occasions that someone unknown and not on The List made it past the battlements.

"I need you to sit up front and turn the pages."

By "pages" of course he meant the A3-sized loose pages on the music stand up front with the page numbers for the most commonly used German and Russian prayerbooks. The only time that Rabbi Isaac needed help for what seemed to be an automatic action as he prayed was for special services that required a lot more intricate and a lot less automatic cantorial work. The answer, however, was usually a grumbling Gidal who moved the music stand over to his chieftain-chair and half-assed and occasionally on-time turned the pages.

The rabbi must have seen me flick my eyes into the *beit knesset* in search of the *gabbai.*

"I just got a text from Gidal," he correctly read my glance. "Sick. Not coming in. Anyway, I can't do it today. We are using the *Machzorim* for *Pessach* and there are too many jumps in the service for me to pray and turn pages and try to keep the service to under three hours."

"Sure. No problem," I shrugged a nonchalance I did not feel.

As usual he read my nervousness and replied to it with, "I really appreciate it. You are the only one here this early with good enough Hebrew to keep up."

The task looked easier than I thought it would be. I had personally reached the point months ago where I could keep up with Rabbi even without the page numbers and even if I was often using my own *Sim Shalom* from my one time at a Conservative summer camp instead of the provided community *siddurim*. But Rabbi still prayed *fast* and we would be using a prayerbook I had never before used, the special one just for Passover with the numerous additional prayers for the holiday.

I was still a bit high from the *Seder* the previous night. Maybe I was so accustomed to the community bullshit that I had entered the night with no expectations. But instead of yet another evening of, well, the usual, the around one-hundred-twenty that packed into the social hall not only seemed to be on their best behavior, they as well shockingly seemed to pay attention to Rabbi's words and then the quick translation from one of the Russian social workers. As we reached deep into the retelling of the entire Exodus story, Rabbi had challenged us all and I had stayed up half the night pondering his teaching.

"I think these words are the most important in the entire *Hagaddah*—maybe even our entire tradition."

Rabbi spoke uncharacteristically into a microphone in order to not have to shout in the hangar acoustics, allowing him to use a much softer tone than he usually needed to be heard giving a sermon. The voice was much more that of our one-on-one sessions and I found myself soothed into a meditative state."

"*B'chol dor vador, chayav adam lirot et atzmo k'ilu hu yatza mimitzrayim.* In every generation each person must regard himself or herself as if he or she had come out of Egypt."

It was nice not even needing to actively listen anymore to

absorb the words in German. At least my dream of becoming a fluent speaker of German had been realized this year. That was something, wasn't it?

"I think sometimes we react to the contemporary interpretation of our texts as a bit of a fiction, like we don't really have the right to transport words and concepts from thousands of years ago into a relevant language of today.

"From my perspective as a rabbi, I always feel vindicated by this passage. *B'chol dor vador.* In every generation. It is not just my crazy ideas—the text explicitly tells us what our obligation is when we explore our tradition. In every generation, each person must regard himself or herself as if he or she had come out of or was currently in the process of coming out of Egypt.

"The text is not relevant because it is a "holy" text—the text becomes relevant through our efforts and actions. If we read this story as some sort of history book about events that took place more than three thousand years ago, we miss the point completely. Every generation must read this as if it *is* us.

"What does that even mean? You see, that is what is so hard about this. We are taught to think so literally that is hard for us to see this symbolically. I have never been closer to Egypt than the Negev in Israel—how in the world can I possibly imagine myself coming out of a place I have never been?

"But that is exactly what the text does not mean. Egypt is a symbol. A metaphor. And I don't even have to make this up. The word for Egypt in Hebrew, *Mitzrayim*, can literally be broken up into 'from narrow places,' so a real meaning of this text is: 'in every generation we have the obligation to regard ourselves as if we are escaping from narrow places.

"So what Egypt are you coming out of today?"

Rabbi Isaac paused and took a long drink of water as he waited for the amplified translation to echo through the hall, then he continued, "Or maybe we first need to define Egypt or even slavery today. If I replace 'Egypt' with 'slavery' and ask 'what slavery are you coming out of today?' then transporting our Pesach story into the present might seem easier.

"At the symbolic level, slavery means anything that determines our daily actions and decisions other than our own personal conscience and consciousness. This most obviously includes all of our addictions."

I was already a bit buzzed at that point. The rules for pouring wine on Passover included that one had to drink at least the volume of an olive each time a glass was blessed—seriously, don't you just love these sorts of rules—and that you couldn't pour for yourself. This evening Sabrina and Natasha flanked me and were apparently feeling frisky. I am sure the overflowing glasses that they had been pouring me had nothing at all to do with the kind of depression that I had slipped into with the loss of Rafi and the continuing resonance of what had happened a few weeks earlier. From Rafi to no Rafi in a blink was bad enough. Maybe worse, it was starting to hit me that no one outside of Jewish communities in Germany were ever going to believe that any of this had happened.

I knew this for a fact. I had begun limiting what I communicated to my parents via email and especially Skype to "yes my Fulbright project is going well" and details only of museum visits and the occasional lecture. It seems that when you tell your parents that you are having a swell time and then you work up a giddy excitement worthy of a Golden Globe about the visit to the Archeological Gardens in Xanten or the Kröller-Müller Museum over the border in the Netherlands that you play into your parents' hopes and they have no reason to assume their fears. I am guessing that a story that my boyfriend had threatened the life of the chief of security of my German synagogue, that he had been threatened as well, and that he had been permanently thrown out would most likely fall more into their "fears" bucket rather than that of "hopes."

I had received further details a few days earlier from Rabbi Isaac. In our first one-on-one since The Incident, we had barely talked religion. Instead, the town hall seemed to tear down a major wall surrounding the rabbi and what he would discuss, and he spoke about a long list of unbelievable things that had already happened to him, most of which I would have called bullshit on my first few months here. Even now I kept having to remind myself of my own experiences to not automatically assume hyperbole.

My favorite crazy Rabbi Isaac story was about a man, whose mother had passed after a long illness, who requested to meet the rabbi at the cemetery for debriefing rather than the family's home or rabbi's office, as was usual. Rabbi Isaac recounted: "Although that request was a bit strange, the meeting went well.

224

The man seemed well-read and well-spoken and I was able to take many more notes than usual in order to give a good *hesped*. Usually it's like pulling teeth. Anyway, we get to the end of our time and he breaks down crying. Not really that unusual, but usually in my office with tissues it doesn't seem awkward, but standing on the steps of the chapel at the cemetery, well, everything felt a bit awkward.

"Then, he stops crying as quickly as he started and then puts his hand on my shoulder and gets his face inches from mine. 'Rabbi,' he says, 'I know that you are a good man.'"

It was hard not to chuckle. Rabbi Isaac's Russian accent and comedic affectations could probably get him an audition with Lorne Michaels.

He continued, getting closer to me in order to act out the drama. "'And I think you know I am a very good man. So I will tell you something important about what I do.'"

I knew that Rabbi Isaac had grandparents both from German-Jewish descent and Slavic-Jewish decent. Maybe he was that good of an actor or maybe he tapped into a deep well of his ancestry, but with the accent and mannerisms in service to the story it seemed that his countenance had changed. Suddenly his resemblance to some of our Old Dudes in the community became uncanny.

"'You may know, *Herr Rabbiner*, that there are many people that do not like the Jews. So I tell you what I do. My friends and I, we take care of them.'"

My eyes must have widened in the universal look for, "You are not saying what it sounds like you're saying, are you?" Rabbi broke character only long enough to tell me with his eyes that what I thought I heard matched what I had been meant to understand.

225

Back in character he finished the macabre soliloquy: "'So if you ever have anyone that is bad to you, you know to call me and we will take care of them.' Then he handed me a business card for a shipping company and I returned the next day to do the funeral."

"Did you ever call him?" I asked, somehow believing the pretty out-there story.

"No. But he called me three times," Rabbi chuckled. "I let it go to voice mail and he never left a message. I guess after three times he figured that I really didn't need anyone off'd by him or his former KGB buddies."

"But he wasn't really ex-KGB was he?" I asked really not wanted to step out of my Stepfordstein view of the world for the sake of the story.

Rabbi Isaac involuntary fluttered his eyes in the direction of the guard towers. "Andrea, there are a lot of people in this community with ties to groups that we would rather they didn't have."

How did he stay the Rabbi here? He was basically pissed on on a regular basis, and if his eye fluttering and story were not drama or paranoia then how could he stay here? I even started to feel a prickling at my spine and resisted the impulse to start checking the office for bugs or hidden cameras. I then looked at Rabbi's cane and thought of his earlier absence with his heart problems and suddenly saw the inevitable conclusion to his decision to remain the rabbi here. Didn't he realize that this was *his* Egypt? Seriously, this place was going to kill him. Why was he still here? This beautiful speech about slavery had become only tolerable through a wine buzz—this man used his heart and body to feed the dream that he could help others out of their slaveries while he wasted away and couldn't see his own.

226

Each word of Rabbi's Pesach challenge became more poignant as I started seeing his own pain more clearly. "But slavery is more than addiction and addiction is more than the need to drink or take a drug. We can become addicted to people, to drama and to negative thoughts. We can become addicted to controlling others and having things our own way. The eternal truth of Egypt is that we are always there and seldom coming out."

Looking around I felt shocked with how much people appeared to be listening. "It can be the simple things. I cannot get out of bed in the morning without drinking a pot of coffee. My daily routines and even my apartment are set up in order that an automatic coffee maker deposits my Egypt in front of me every morning. Even with heart problems I still pump this into my body every day and feel panic when there is not enough in my flat.

"And this is all I am willing to admit. Maybe even to myself. When we look at ourselves in the mirror, are we willing to admit that there is even a single thing that's holding us back? Are we willing to admit that we have work to do on our own lives? Are we willing to admit when it is our actions, our Egypts, that are hurting others around us? Or are we admitting only to the things that allow us to cover up our true addictions and our most devastating entanglements."

Hardly bothering to cover up the clear irony I grabbed a bottle of wine and refilled several times. A few more sips and I could at least pretend to ignore some of the thoughts that had begun to bubble to the surface.

I guess the wine is why I ignored any strangeness occurring during the festival service the next morning. Hangover in place, a depression that I choose to call mild and a Rabbi that I had

227

begun fearing that I was going to lose, and I barely had enough energy to focus on more the prayerbook and the page turning.

After the service, head finally mostly clear, I made my way into the social hall for my date with another sheet of matzah, the hair-of-the-dog kosher-for-Pesach potato vodka, and leftovers from last night's VIP *fleishig* meal.

Halfway there after dozen hand-shakes, hugs, kisses and "*Chag Sameyach!*" greetings I realized I had left my backpack under my chair in the front of the *beit knesset*. I quickly excused myself from the small migrating circle of greetings and trotted back and down the aisle. I didn't think much of seeing Rabbi Isaac enter the side room off of the front followed by Herr Engels until the shouting began.

"*Das war eine Provokation!*" I heard Engels' clear voice shout. That was a provocation. "*Unsere Gemeinde ist eine Einheitsgemeinde und nicht eine von Ihren beschissenen liberalen Gemeinden.*" Our community is a community synagogue and not one of your shitty liberal synagogues.

This went on for a bit as I stood shocked, rooted into place, trying to figure out what the hell until it became clear. It was about me. Somewhere in there I heard the terrifying sound of Rabbi Isaac as well raising his voice, as he returned in German, "There was no provocation. Gidal is sick, you were not there at the beginning of the service and there was no one else there that was either willing to turn pages or who could read Hebrew well enough to do it. Andrea was the only one able and willing, and the service is more important. She sat up there alone, did a great job, and made it possible for people to follow the service."

Engels tried to raise his voice higher, but I imagine he must have as well felt a bit of shock at the wrath in Rabbi's tone that said, "For once you will listen to *me*."

Vaguely I stroked my memory to try and figure out if something other than the obvious, me, had happened to set this off. There was the usual obnoxious late entrance by the Chieftains and their continuous dialogue. This had become so *de rigeur,* though, that it barely registered. But thinking back, I guess Engels' father, one of the original founders of the post-war synagogue, had made a rare appearance and seemed agitated. That made me the agitation and I guess further that Herr Engels had some individuation-from-Daddy issues. It would be amusing if what I was hearing wasn't so disgusting. That unmitigated asshole was yelling at my rabbi—at my teacher— because he wanted to help this community experience services in the best way possible. Moreover, asshole, this *was* an *Einheitsgemeinde. Not* an Orthodox *Gemeinde. Einheitsgemeinde* at least theoretically was supposed to mean that Orthodox Jews and Masorti Jews and Secular Jews and even we *beschissene* Reform Jews were all to be serviced by the same religious community. In practice the service served only to fulfill the fantasy of 'authentic' Judaism—meaning the Chieftains' and even Russians' limited-perspective understanding of what constituted Judaism. But these assholes drove to shul, ate bratwurst and shrimp the rest of the week, barely knew anything about Jewish tradition, showed up to no adult education but yet demanded an Orthodox appearance to satisfy Daddy or some ignorant wet dream of Judaism or both.

Somewhat lost in my thoughts and the shock of the moment, one of Herr Engels' tirade comments shot me back to awareness. *"Und noch schlimmer, sie ist eine verdammte Nicht-jüdin! Verstehen Sie, wie peinlich das ist? Was hätten wir gemacht, wenn orthodoxe Gäste uns besucht hätten? Was dann? Zeigen wir jetzt, dass wir nicht nur liberal geworden sind, sondern dass wir zusätzlich offensichtliche Nicht-jüdinnen hier reinlassen?"*

And yet worse, she is a damned Non-Jew. Do you know how embarrassing that is? What would we have done if we had had a true Orthodox guest come for the service? What then? Are we showing the entire world now that not only have we become liberal, but also that we let people that are obviously not Jewish into our services?

I had seldom felt true fury and the only thing that kept me from running into the side room and delivering a few bitch slaps across Engels face to make me feel better was the realization that Rabbi Isaac's job was right now, in this moment, on the line. Maybe even more than the fury, it just hurt. Herr Engels' tirade sounded a bit too much like some of my own emerging imposter-complex issues.

Wanting to hear more—desperately needing to hear Rabbi's defense of me—but knowing that to be seen when they emerged would open up a whole new crapstorm, I soundlessly grabbed my bag and then made my way *en pointe* back out as if nothing had happened.

At Sabrina's worried look at my pallor, I whispered a quick, "I'll tell you later," and we wound our way up to the social hall.

I could barely even look at Rabbi Isaac as he came in a few minutes later. All clichés aside he looked aged, defeated and as if he could barely move save for inching himself forward on his black cane. It was nearly impossible to remember that this man was not yet fifty.

I decided to hair of the dog it and grabbed a few extra shots of the special-for-Passover potato vodka. The pleasant buzz allowed me to focus intently on nothing more than my own matzah and plate of Seder leftovers. I am sure that everything tasted delicious but I had little desire to taste or to hear what sounded like Rabbi's half-hearted and mostly defeated attempts to engage his community in discussion about this holiday. Egypt indeed.

Natasha, Sabrina and I walked back to Natasha's place where I absently played with the twins and gave a Reader's Digest version of my eavesdropping. Bless them, they both said the appropriate things with the appropriate sounds of outrage. I heard and appreciated, yet could not get the feeling out of my gut that Herr Engels was somehow right. My trip to Berlin in two weeks in order to convince a *Beit Din* that they should accept me as equally Jewish as they were seemed now both farcical and fruitless. The closer I got to what had seemed months ago the most important moment of my Jewish life now felt like an audition for a school play instead of a spiritual fulfillment. Eyes-skin-hair. No one was ever really going to buy this and I wasn't sure how much I wanted anymore to defend something that seemed so much further away than when I had in blissful ignorance begun.

After crying myself into a half-sleep I dozed in fantasies. In some I simply screamed myself hoarse at these idiots and in others I escaped to China to live in a tiny village where my looks would provide a passport to unquestioned identity acceptance. The angriest of them had me dressing up in camo and Zhang Xixi'ing these idiots who through the luck of their birth could judge me and make me feel like this without ever having to look in the mirror themselves or understanding a single thing about the religion they had the privilege to be born into.

Cried out at last, I let myself step into the last and silliest fantasy: that when I awoke my self-identity would once again be as firmly rooted as it once was.

Beit Din

So the absurdity should be clear by now. Although I still stand by my decision to go through with this and although I still think that Sabrina and Rabbi Isaac suggested this course of action with the best intentions and although I attest that I was and still am of sound mind and body, what the hell was I thinking?

The potential implications had already swirled around in my brain in between awkward affairs and even more awkward breakups, but until I sat waiting outside the room where the *Beit Din* was to be held I didn't really carry everything to logical conclusions.

What if they said "no?"

Was I still a Jew? Was I ever a Jew?

How can someone be raised a Jew, be educated as a Jew and fully embrace the entire Jewishness of it all and be asking the existential question of if someone else's words can unmake such a self-evident reality. Yes, I get the legal issues. You can't have an academic engineer for a father and the rare renaissance-woman academic and badass for a mother and not get that there are rules and processes and gateways into and out of everything worth getting into or out of. I was fortunate to be accepted as a Jew by the traditions if not explicit "law" of American Reform Judaism. To be fair, though, the 'they' that in my mind represented American Reform never attempted to sell that this was a universal solution which one should expect the rest of world Jewry to accept. Maybe it felt like they had tried to sell it as such when you learned about it as a kid. Maybe it just felt like it if you never fulfilled the Jew 101 responsibility of asking questions.

I mean, I did finally look all of this shit up. The fact that my conversation about the implications of my Jewish identity in the larger world with Rabbi Isaac was indeed my first conversation about this made me wonder if I had been betrayed. Were Rabbis Theresa and Applebaum complicit in some vast Reform conspiracy to rob youth in their synagogue of awareness of the global questions regarding identity, belonging and authenticity? The official words read: "The Central Conference of American Rabbis declares that the child of one Jewish parent is under the presumption of Jewish descent. This presumption of the Jewish status of the offspring of any mixed marriage is to be established through appropriate and timely public and formal acts of identification with the Jewish faith and people." They are indeed good words, but I did have to look them up and I didn't know they existed until I did.

If I am being overly introspective, my own perceptions go back to my central identity battle—my looks. I have spent so much time dealing with *those looks* when encountering my looks that the fact that my mom is not Jewish and has no interest of ever becoming Jewish never seemed to be the battle, even though for the larger world it was the only battle.

"Frau Lewy, Sie dürfen eintreten."

The slightly-too-short-to-be-an-actual alien popped her blond perfection into the holding room where I had been now sitting for nearly ninety minutes ruining my manicure. She found the one that must be Frau Lewy based on my furtive attempts to gather my wits and belongings as well as my quickly sweat-soaking blouse and motioned me to follow her across the hallway into the mysterious inner-sanctum of Great Jewish Decisions.

The first thing that struck me was the presence of five rabbis rather than the three that I had expected. I approached and sat in

233

the offered chair opposite the imposing group and quickly had the first mystery solved through introductions.

"You are Andrea Lewy," the center rabbi spoke rather than asked in perfect American-sounding English. In front of him rested a sheaf of papers, the end-result of one of the most difficult homework assignments I had ever had. The easiest part sat on top—my questionnaire and passport photo. Name of Applicant. Requested Hebrew name. Name of Mother. Religion of Mother. Name of Father. Religion of Father. Current religious affiliation—and so forth. Filling out paperwork in German does rightfully possess a Kafkaesque feel, but at least I had breezed through that part up until the 'gulp' moment of, "Please attach 1000 Euros fee for *Beit Din*."

That had occasioned an are-you-freaking-kidding-me but much more polite email to Rabbi, who had responded with what seemed to be sincere apologies. "I usually warn people. Sorry. Lots on my mind. The actual fee is from zero to a thousand Euros depending on what you can afford. As an Uni student you won't be expected to pay the full amount, but the fee does pay the cost of getting the rabbis to Berlin—so pay what you can." In truth, as an American Rabbi he would know that growing up in Swarthmore probably meant that I did not come from a poor family. In comparison with other Swarthmore families it did occasionally feel like it, but as an academic family we fell into the middle-middle of Swarthmore economic society, even though that probably meant upper-middle class most any place else in Pennsylvania. Maybe it was adoption guilt, something that my therapist promised me is a real thing when I brought this up with her in high school. She assured me that it was my adoption guilt that drove me to try and live as independently as possible and feel shame when asking for money. Nice to know— still didn't help with the feeling and still influenced a lot of

234

decisions. Most of my graduating class had Dartmouths and Yales and Stanfords on their resume, even the occasional Penn, fully funded by their families. Even though my parents had promised to, as they said, "make it work" wherever I should choose to go, I had heard enough muffled night-time discussions about finances—often times probably exacerbated by dance lessons or a better quality oboe for City Youth Orchestra or whatever that made me choose Temple. With a Professor Daddy discount and in-state tuition, I got through on scholarships and work-study; in my case stage-managing at Rock Hall for student and faculty concerts. I always knew that I would need to go to grad school anyway and thought at that time I could get some sort of teaching assistant position, so to see my parents not have to pawn something for me to have a cooler sounding undergrad resume I chose a destination slightly less Ivy League-y.

Because of all this, I had also developed a bit of pride in not asking for money from mom and dad for every-day expenses. I had a still-as-of-now unused "no questions asked" emergency credit card with a two-thousand-dollar limit from my Dad's Credit Union, and with some personal savings and my Fulbright stipend I had lived comfortably. Meals in the Mensa for students ran a ridiculous three-ish Euros and were pretty damn good, and if I really felt poor and wanted a beer, a half-liter of *Bitburger* at the corner store cost 79 euro cents, 15 of which would be returned when the bottle was returned. A thousand Euros represented sticker shock, and I felt a sincere sense of guilt if I couldn't pay the full amount. After some soul searching I wrote down that I would pay 360 Euros, the Jewishly meaningful "double-chai times ten" that you're just going to have to look up to understand, and blushed as Rabbi without comment signed next to that amount and then stamped my document in further homage to Kafka.

Now in front of the four men and one woman, looking very much like a slightly smaller Supreme Court session, I wished that I had been able to cough up the full thousand, even if the entire money concept had started my internal dialogue asking questions around conflict of interest—if I pay, what happens if they say no? Are they more obligated to say yes with a larger donation?

The questions made me feel sick that I would ever even think such thoughts. I didn't know how a *Beit Din* worked in the States, but this was not the States and for the first time I wondered what Rabbis in Germany got paid. Because of Dad I knew what Rabbi Theresa got paid—a little over one-hundred-twenty-thousand a year when she got hired—something that apparently could grow significantly for rabbis in much larger synagogues. Considering the completely different system here—these rabbis were state and tax sponsored—something told me that they probably did not even make half of what an American rabbi would make. In a feeling that had become more and more familiar, I felt ashamed of my own judgmental thoughts.

Beneath my intake form and payment amount rested a stack of what I knew to be thirty pages. Hoping that these rabbis had printed everything out double-sided I thought back to the soul-searching of the questions. My third session with Rabbi Isaac, I had been handed an English and German printout entitled: *Giyur* Program for Rabbi Isaac Newmark. Page one consisted of thirty-six short answer term identification, ranging from *Yom Kippur* to *Megillah* to *Regalim* to *Nidah* (the one term I could not identify without looking up.) These had been quickly written and discussed, Rabbi Isaac commenting on how easy this part was for people that had spent a lifetime in shul. The second page, however, contained a "choose seven of the ten following" which included "How does Judaism define G-d? What are your views

236

of G-d? How do you explain the phenomenon of anti-Semitism? What are the major causes and origins of anti-Semitism?" The one to three pages suggested for each question hardly could dent the mass of thoughts that each question brought. It was probably beneficial, as annoyed as I had been at the time, that I had not known until the week before the *Beit Din* that the essays were not for Rabbi Isaac alone, but also for those arrayed before me.

And those arrayed before me intimidated me. To their credit, I am pretty sure none of them eyes-skin-haired me—of course they also had what qualifies has high-esthetic in the world of international relations in front of them in the form of a clipped-on passport photo. I guess certain surprising features might already have been discussed.

After receiving my assent that I was indeed said Andrea Lewy the same man continued: "I am Rabbi Herzfeld, these are my colleagues Rabbi Klein and Rabbi Harlow." The man in the center that had spoken looked between sixty and seventy with a striking shock of white hair—movie-star swept back underneath a blue-patterned, tightly woven *kippah*. He nodded to the balding man on his right with the tiny, very German wire-framed glasses—Rabbi Klein—and the diminutive woman of about sixty on his left with extremely tight graying curls and who looked to weigh no more than ninety pounds—Rabbi Harlow. He then gestured to the two younger men, one looking in his thirties but quickly balding and the other about my age but built like a walrus. "These gentlemen are our colleagues from the progressive rabbinical seminar in Potsdam, and will be observing if you have no objection."

He didn't really phrase it as a question, so I started shrugging until I realized that would look very teenagerish or American or both, so I quickly followed up with, "That is no problem." Hoping to earn a few extra points I added in German, "But if you would prefer, I have no problem speaking German."

Rabbi Herzfeld smiled in the perfect mimic of a kind grandfather and answered back in English, "It is ok. We all speak English relatively well, and as your materials are all in English, we can always use the practice.

"All of which brings us to the question, Frau Lewy, 'Why are you here?'"

I opened my mouth, but as sometimes happens in manuscripts to cheaply written films, nothing came out. Why indeed?

Rabbi Isaac had even warned me that this question would come. "Either you go into the *Beit Din* as a Jew or not. No one can make you Jewish, only agree that that is what you are. The *Beit Din* is not a test of knowledge, although some knowledge questions will be asked. It is an attempt to figure out who you think you are and who you really are."

But that was just the problem, wasn't it? Who was I? Had they asked this question the day of my *bat mitzvah* or confirmation or after a visit to Hillel at Temple or on Birthright or even when I stepped off the plane in Frankfurt or even when I realized I couldn't hook up with Son of Czar due to my foreskin preconceptions I would have answered. "Jew! Jew! I am a Jew. My father is a Jew and raised me Jewish and every act of my life has had my Jewishness either written all over it or at least influenced how I see it. There has never been a period of my life where the synagogue or the holidays or Shabbat hasn't been as self-evident as the fact my parents are my parents. I am a Jew." Except for now I wanted to say, "So just get it over with, dammit. I need you to wave a wand and make people believe it as much as I do." As much as I used to. Shit.

So instead I went for the honesty of the moment, realizing soberly it might disqualify me.

"I don't know," I answered and was rewarded with various expressions ranging from curiosity to shock. I am guessing this answer wasn't in the book of usual opening gambits. Rabbi Herzfeld looked as if he had begun searching for a way to derail my courage so I continued into the framing of arched eyebrows. "At almost any time in the past months I would have answered, 'I am here so that you, an official Jewish body, can agree with me that I am indeed Jewish, and help me to achieve a level of legitimacy that I don't currently have as a patrilineal Jew.'"

It was Rabbi Harlow that astutely broke into my introspection. "What changed?"

Again I felt powerless to offer much more than a shrug. The level of honesty that bubbled out after the shrug, however, shocked even me. "I realized that it doesn't matter what kind of piece of paper I have. No matter where I go, people are going to look at my eyes and skin and hair and never really believe that I'm Jewish, no matter what my story."

More arched eyebrows, this time with the beginning of uncomfortable throat clearing from several present. Rabbi Klein covered up his discomfort by flipping meaningfully through my paperwork. This one was certainly not going the way they had envisioned, I am sure. I know it wasn't going the way I had imagined. My mouth was still moving though.

"It is something that I have never doubted. Had never doubted. My Jewishness. I had a *mikveh* when my parents adopted me, I had a *bat mitzvah*, I went through confirmation, I went on Birthright. Even my Fulbright project is Jewish-themed. Then I got to Germany and realized that what for me was so obvious and without question was not *halakhic* and would never be accepted if I chose to remain in Europe, for example. I found

239

a rabbi that I loved learning from who decided to sponsor me, and I realized how much more I needed to learn about my own tradition and how amazing it felt to learn these things as an adult instead of a child."

Now Rabbi Herzfeld echoed his colleague's question. "So what changed?"

Germany, I thought. This place was Jewish before it was German. Jews had come up as either slaves or traders or artisans with the Romans and city charters in the Rhineland dated official Jewish communities back sixteen centuries. I had touched the nearly two-thousand-year-old *mikveh* baths recently unearthed in Cologne. I had attended services in Berlin at the non or not-completely destroyed synagogues dating to way before the Shoah—synagogues that had held the first female rabbi ever, Regina Jonas, and the exploration of modern liberal Jewish thought. I had walked past dozens of memorials and statues, seen plaques on wall after wall and house after house of which great rabbi or Jewish thinker had lived where, and stumbled over the ubiquitous *Stolpersteine*, tiny brass memorials buried in the sidewalks of many German cities that listed the Jews that once lived at that address, when they were deported and in which camp they were murdered. I had prayed and danced and sung in holidays and celebrations now all over this country, in *Einheitsgemeinden*, Chabad shuls and even a few of the liberal ones. I could at times feel the ghosts of the Jews that once so impacted every facet of society and without whom Germany itself was not really Germany. I had felt over and over that profound hole and even tried to have some tiny part of filling it.

But . . . I had to come up with some answer . . .

"What changed was moving here. Most of the Jews that I have met are . . . insecure . . . about their Jewishness. Everyone has a different story. I mean who am I to judge? Everyone has

240

the right. But the Russian Jews had three generations with no contact to their own Judaism, and so it's like they brought with them the one thing they knew. Maybe it was one home tradition. Maybe it was one song they had learned. Maybe it was just one photograph or just their name. But because there is so little left, if the Jewish communities in Germany that they moved to didn't practice that one tradition they knew or sing that one song they knew, then they would act like they were betrayed. Instead of trying to learn more, they try to either remake what they had found into something that felt familiar to them." That thought made me go white. I stumbled forward, "Or they would try to tear down the communities because they couldn't handle being made to feel non-Jewish when their entire lives had been one persecution after another for being Jewish.

"Then we have 'German' Jews. It seems like that identity is about building a museum to how it was or at least how they imagined it was before the Holocaust, and then they try to tear down anyone that tries to make any changes to move forward with the times because it is some sort of desecration of the memories of their long-dead ancestors. So we have ghosts running the synagogues instead of breathing Jews.

"And then we have the converts. In Germany everyone knows exactly who they are, and for some reason even though they became Jews they never became Jewish. The converted women sit in balconies and judge everything based on their harshest Catholic or Protestant ideals while the men lord it over the born-Jews that they have so much more knowledge.

"It is like everyone at their core is terrified of their own level of authenticity and so rather than looking at their own lives they try to tear everyone else down. I always felt authentic until I saw myself through the eyes of an entire Jewish society that had no sense of its own authenticity. If these people who survived the

Holocaust or whose relatives died in the Holocaust can doubt themselves so extremely, then how can I ever—me—with this hair and these eyes and this skin—how can I ever be sure of what used to be so obvious to me?"

Here I stopped. I felt a little like Mookie having just thrown the trashcan through the window. I fully expected to be thrown out. Seriously. I had even in that moment begun revisiting plans to return soon to China so that I could start rebuilding an identity that I imagined wouldn't be so incredibly *hard*. And painful.

Rabbi Herzfeld saved the day, as it were. He stared at me with a slight squint and then started laughing. There was nothing cruel about the sound. Nothing mocking. He smiled and leaned forward, patting me gently on the shoulder. Then he leaned back and shook his head slightly. "I don't have any more questions."

There had been a few more questions, regardless. I am sure there was some rabbinical rule regarding minimum-questions-before-sufficiently-frisked status could be reached. Rabbi Klein seemed mostly interested in the objective test questions: What is your definition of *halakha*? What month is it in the Jewish calendar? What is the next major holiday? (My answer of 'Shabbat' made everyone grin and nod in approval, and then led Rabbi Klein to repeat the question with the addition of 'Other than Shabbat . . .") Thank heavens—I mean I guess seriously in this case—thank heavens for Rabbi Applebaum and Rabbi Theresa and especially all the hours with Rabbi Isaac. I was able to answer confidently and authoritatively.

Rabbi Harlow seemed a bit off, though. I am not really sure what the deal was. I suppose there could have been a 'good cop bad cop' thing going on or she might have had a bad batch of Kosher-whatever that morning. Her first question seemed to be an attempt to question my legitimacy from a motivation perspective. "Why would you want to go through a *Beit Din* in Germany and not in America? Wouldn't it be more appropriate for you to convert where you are planning to live?" First of all, I am status clarifying, yo. Second of all, how do you have any idea where I am planning on living? Several of my most Philly-mouthed retorts came within about two millimeters from leaving my lips until I had the bad cop revelation and responded instead as honestly as I could: "I never considered until I lived overseas that I might not stay in America the rest of my life. Then I had to really think about my Jewish status for the first time and so I approached Rabbi Isaac. And, maybe even a bigger reason is that I have really thought about the nature of my relationship to Judaism for the first time since being here. It seems appropriate that since Germany . . . changed me . . . that I would put the exclamation point on my journey here."

That seemed to satisfy everyone else, but Rabbi Harlow glowered. Ok, seriously I am not sure she shot me a dirty look—I was still annoyed enough at the question and her tone and her body language that I stopped giving her the benefit of the doubt. Maybe the problem was that something I had done had caused her already to do the same to me. Anyway, her next questions seemed more perfunctory, so I gradually chose to forget. At last the rabbinical students were asked if they had any final thoughts or questions. Rabbi Klein had already begun filling out the blank spaces of a Hebrew document, and my heart started racing with excitement. Student One declined to speak but Rabbi-to-be Walrus asked me what my favorite mitzvah was. Through my giddiness I didn't think before I answered, "That a man is required to give his wife an orgasm on Shabbat." Well, Andrea couldn't stay hidden for long. Germany being significantly less prude than America made the answer well received—appropriate chuckles and 'clever girl' looks came from around the table.

243

Some communication must have passed between the Rabbis that I missed, for now all had passed the Hebrew document back and forth and signed. Rabbi Herzfeld spoke, "All that leaves us with just a few final items. I think you have been honest with us in a way that was probably hard on you. So I am going to be as honest back to you. If you hadn't shown awareness of how complicated your path was, I would be concerned. Yes, you are patrilineally Jewish, which makes this process usually very direct—are you aware of what it means to be Jewish and are you willing without hesitation to devote your spiritual, religious and cultural energy to the good of *Klal Yisrael*? Of this I have no doubt. The fact that your lineage comes through adoption is also not complicated, as adoption in our religion is in most cases identical to birth. The one exception is that an adopted Jew may choose at *bar* or *bat mitzvah* to freely renounce. Since you had a *bat mitzvah*, it is clear that even at that time you chose this path without hesitation. My concern is not with your identity or sincerity, rather your sensitivity.

"I sense you are a leader. Judging by your essays you also are a fine writer, if a little too journalistic for my tastes." He smiled and actually winked, showing the words to be mere levity. "People that are such natural leaders will be drawn into leadership positions wherever they go. With you, I can imagine you will serve in many leadership capacities. I can also imagine that you will be tempted to join the rabbinate at some point. I think what you are beginning to understand is that no matter how much you know and how solid and true your self-image is, there will always be people that doubt you. The sad thing about Judaism, is most of the time us Jews cannot live up to the beauty of our own tradition. You are right, the more uncomfortable one is with their own heart, the more they will try to tear you down to quiet their own demons.

"I think it is clear that you have learned these things now, which is why I and my colleagues have not hesitated to sign your *te'udah*. But it doesn't get easier from here, especially for someone like you. You will never be universally accepted. That is wrong, it is unfair, it is against the *halakha*, but it is also true. Do you understand that Ms. Lewy?"

I nodded slowly, feeling somehow transfixed. "I do now."

"I see that you have chosen—no I mean I see that your Hebrew name already is *Devorah*. *Devorah* was a warrior who fought against impossible odds. You know the saying *nomen est omen*?" I nodded—funny my mom would say that on occasion. He continued, "Seems your Hebrew name already contains deep truths."

He looked at his colleagues and then handed me the document that they had all signed. The right side was all in Hebrew, with all the blank spaces filled in like date and place and of course my name and the Hebrew signatures of the Rabbis. On the left hand side all the Hebrew had been translated into German. Rabbi Herzfeld pointed down to the bottom, a small passage in German quoted from the book of Ruth. "Please read the passage, *Devorah bat David v'Sarah*."

I pulled the paper toward me, wetting my lips and forming the intention with my throat to make my German sound as clear and authentic as possible. My throat caught a little. All the adrenaline and fear had started to fade, and now the rest of the emotions had begun threatening. I cleared my throat and spoke through the growing lump, "*Wohin du gehst, will ich gehen, und wo du weilst, will ich weilen. Dein Volk ist mein Volk und dein Gott ist mein Gott.*" For wherever you go, I shall go. Wherever you live, I shall live. Your people shall be my people and your God shall be my God.

"Only one thing left to say then, Andrea. Devorah. *Mazal Tov.*"

The Alternatives

There are only so many times that you can get burned before you finally get wise and change it up and then usually end up doing something that really gets you burned. You know, it is the old cynical "no good deed goes unpunished" utterance that so pisses off my mom when it comes out of her sweet daughter's mouth. No, it's not that, it is actually the lawnmower all over again. But this time it is the nightmare version where instead of replacing the sparkplug-of-death version with the Toro Personal Pace 22 Inch Variable Speed Self Propelled version, Dad replaces it with the wood chipper from Fargo and throws me in. Too brutal? Too soon? What, I am not allowed to get this mad?

So let's get it out there. The insanity is not just in Rabbi Isaac's synagogue, if truly one can call it "his" synagogue. Anyway—it is not just his community that is messed up—it is all of them. It seems so true that I am starting to wonder if all synagogues in all the world are this damaged. I mean, I seem to remember what appears in my memory to be functional, non-pathological *shuls* where I could sit next to my father and we would be able to follow the service seriously and still laugh at how badly Mrs. Kagan sang even when she thought she should be opening at the MET. I seem to remember people staying after services for what must have been hours—schmoozing with Rabbi Theresa or old Rabbi Applebaum and each other, still ringing with the after-effects of a provocative word or Torah or the collective huddling of safety at those times when the events in Israel or our own country gave us all the need to congregate just a bit more. I remember not being afraid to sing, not being afraid to have knowledge, not being afraid to have ideas, not being afraid to simply walk in the door.

The fact that the high from the *Beit Din* could be so easily and quickly threatened added fuel to the fire. Sure, there was the concern for Sabrina. Her path as a conversion candidate with no Jewish background whatsoever had made her appointment directly after mine last twice as long and included a private discussion between rabbis before a final decision could be made. I had sat waiting on the bench, right outside the *Beit Din* room, hoping to catch something more than muffled German from beyond the heavy double doors. Looking at my *handy*, mine had taken a total of twenty-five minutes, even though subjectively I still couldn't decide if it felt more like five minutes or five hundred. So when after nearly forty-five minutes the door opened I wasn't sure if I should pop up in excitement. I waited to read her expression and got nothing.

I stood up and grabbed her hands. "Everything ok?"

She shrugged. "I don't know. They asked me to wait outside a few minutes. They didn't do this with you so I am a little nervous."

'Nervous' was clearly an understatement. Her hands trembled and she appeared on the edge. What was I supposed to say? It's going to be ok? If they were in there now discussing how to say 'no' it certainly wasn't going to feel ok. So, I just held her hand until the door opened again. "Frau Weber."

This time, five minutes later, rather than confused or strained, Sabrina—excuse me—*Jael bat Abraham v'Sarah*—looked beatific. This time both of our tears—the good and happy kind—mingled freely. We had been told to hang out until someone came to take us down to the *mikvah*, so we returned to the social hall, sipped passable coffee and munched on butter cookies while comparing notes.

Sabrina had been mostly grilled on being a single woman. Maybe I was wrong, but I can't imagine that an American *Beit*

Din would have asked these sorts of questions, but mostly she had been pushed to confront what would happen "when" she met a non-Jewish man and wanted to marry him. Totally non PC, but after talking it out, both of us got where they were coming from. As I had discovered, the chances of partnership with a Jew in Germany were . . . problematic. Ok, downright dismal if you count hissing foreskins. After determining that Sabrina had indeed been Jewishly well-educated over the previous years by Rabbi Isaac, they had moved on to trying to get her to admit that she would up and leave Judaism with the first tall, blond and skinny Jürgen-the-Catholic that she met. "I kept telling them that I chose this path knowing how hard that was going to be. Yes, I want to get married, but no, I am not willing to compromise my faith. I guess they finally believed me."

Still not sure how I felt about that type of questioning—I mean were men given the same line of questioning? —we finally were gathered up by a sweet and vaguely Slavic looking woman in her forties wearing a crocheted *kippah*. She introduced herself as Liora, one of the local rabbinical students. She would be our witness for our *mikveh*.

Down to the basement we went, like stepping into an ancient catacomb ritual. Rather than creepy, it was warm and well lit, with women's changing rooms clearly marked to the right and signs sending men down the left hallway. As the *mikvah* ritual was performed completely in the nude—not even rings or even nail polish could get between you and the water—all *mikvaot* were separated for modesty.

Sabrina and I had both been getting steadily giddier, the magnitude of the moment becoming clearer the closer we drew to the water. We asked if we could also be present to watch each other. Liora assented and then the only competition became which of us cried harder when we finished the third of the three immersions and the third of the three blessings. No false emotions were needed. The water welcomed me in with its warmth, going up to my neck at the deepest part. I closed my eyes and held my breath, tucking myself into a fetal position and then just let my body slowly drop to the bottom. When I felt I needed breath many seconds later I didn't rush, rather floated back up, emerging and uttering the words of my first blessing. *"Baruch atah Adonai, eloheinu melech ha'olam, asher kid'shanu b'mitzvotav v'tzivanu al hatevila."* Blessed are you, Eternal One our God and Sovereign of the Universe, who has sanctified us with the mitzvot and commanded us concerning immersion. Then I went down again, all fear that I would forget the blessings gone—feeling more steadily cleansed and elevated. I returned to the surface, looked for a quick nod from Liora and a very warm smile from Sabrina as I pronounced the second blessing: *"Baruch atah Adonai, eloheinu melech ha'olam, shehecheyanu, v'kiyemanu, v'higiyanu lazman hazeh."* Blessed are you, Eternal One our God and Sovereign of the Universe, who has kept us alive and sustained us, and enabled us to reach this time.

Finally, one last time I floated down and felt the entire universe for the tiniest of moments contract into that pool of rebirth. The tears already began mingling freely, joining the other living waters of the *mikveh* and maybe even the tears of other women as we tied ourselves to traditions so old that we had lost the origins in the misty distance. The third blessing took so much longer through my emotions, yet eventually did come out. *"Baruch atah Adonai, eloheinu melech ha'olam, asher kid'shanu b'mitzvotav v'tzivanu al tevilat gerim."* Blessed are you, Eternal One our God and Sovereign of the Universe, who has sanctified us with the mitzvot and commanded us concerning immersion for conversion.

Sabrina and Liora both wrapped me in a towel and embraced me, Liora in short moments already feeling like a close friend, a friend-friend, and then we watched and both of us cried for Sabrina as she seemed to be shedding a false skin and emerging each time more herself than she had ever been.

Liora waited for us to get dressed and then took us back upstairs where she asked us if we would like to perform some *mitzvot* with her. She winked when explaining they would be subversive egalitarian *mitzvot*. We both grinned and entered into one of the small synagogues nestled in the Berlin Jewish Center. First Sabrina took three prayer shawls off the wall and we all said the blessing together, Liora demonstrating the proper way to wrap oneself in the *tallit* and what to do if one wears a shawl-style half size one versus how to place the longer *tallit* on your shoulder should you wear a full-sized one.

Next we each said the *Shema*. Liora asked if we wished a prayerbook which of course neither of us needed as we recited the words so deeply etched in our hearts from so many services. Finally, we stepped up to the ark and Liora pulled out a Torah which she passed to each of us, asking our Hebrew names and offering us each a blessing while holding the scroll, "May the one that blessed our ancestors, bless as well . . ." We all cried again, Liora now fully a part of the emotions, confiding in us that she had converted to Judaism twenty years early. I looked at this woman that helped to add the most exquisite frosting onto a singular day, and told her what I believed in my heart—she was going to be an amazing rabbi. She was exactly the kind of person that Germany needed. We finally left the building, accepting Liora's invite to a beer at a pub about a block away, where she asked about our future plans and I excitedly told her about what I had been practicing and what I would be doing in the next week.

So the thing I haven't talked about yet was the little secret I was keeping for when I got back to the States. As part of my conversion lessons with Rabbi Isaac, he had asked me if there was anything I had specifically wanted to learn, beyond what was in the group lessons and the individual instruction. It seemed like he was already covering so much more in each class or session that I couldn't even think of what more, but then I remembered something obscure that he had done one day off the cuff.

Somewhere around February—it must have been because there was a decent amount of snow on the ground—a family had come to visit Rabbi Isaac from Israel. I never figured out the entire dynamic—Rabbi hugs everyone so the fact that he embraced father, mother and two kids like long-lost family didn't seem very important. I missed the explanation, but somehow the woman was one of Rabbi's cantorial teachers in Israel, and in order to honor her or impress her or show off or whatever, that week he sang the *haftarah*—the reading of the prophetic texts that follows the Torah reading—with a melody I had never heard before. It was almost otherworldly. I remember being moved by the vaguely middle-eastern sounding trope and then I forgot about it in whatever drama followed the service that day.

"So what about it? Anything come to mind?"

It was already getting near enough to my *Beit Din* that I was just happy to see an end in sight. *Nope, let's just get through it.*

What came out instead was that vague memory of that February service: "What was that melody you used that one time—you know the middle-eastern sounding one when you read the haftarah?"

"The *Baghdadi* trope you mean?"

I had no idea so of course I nodded. He responded by humming a few phrases of melody without words.

"Yes!" I leaned forward over his desk. "That's it!"

"Well sure, I mean your Hebrew is good enough but I am not sure that I have ever heard you chant. What did you do for your *bat mitzvah*?"

I still found it a bit crass to have to acknowledge the reality of having already had a *bat mitzvah* while I was nearly ten years later preparing to convert. "I had to chant Torah and *Haftarah* in Hebrew. I have read Torah a few times since—it was kind of a big deal in my *shul* for teens to continue reading their *bat mitzvah* portion when it came around the next year." I tried to think if I had done much else to make my experience seem grander than what it was. "That was about it though. The Torah melody was similar to yours, but I think the *Haftarah* was like identical to the one you usually use."

He seemed to think about it a few moments, absently scratching his hypnotic beard bald-spot. Finally, he reached to his right and pulled out his calendar. "What was your *bat mitzvah* portion?" he asked.

"*Emor*," I answered immediately with the name of the portion towards the end of the book of Leviticus. "Easy to remember with all of the holidays in it."

"That's just a week and a half after your *Beit Din* this year. How about we learn the trope using the same text you would have had for your *bat mitzvah*?" He started speaking faster, ideas flying, "and then maybe we can have you read that for the clandestine service that week?"

But the clandestine service wasn't enough. When Sabrina found out that I was learning that melody with Rabbi Isaac, she suggested that we actually do it in a real Shabbat service.

"Listen, we just go to Stuttgart. They have the egalitarian place there with that one German lady as the Rabbi—you know gray-haired one that was on that awful debate show on ZDF? I know the *gabbai* really well—you really should celebrate and you can't really do that here."

So the Shabbat afterward, Rabbi Isaac walked back to the women's section and gave Sabrina and me a public blessing for our successful conversions, reiterating the Hebrew name that had already been mine since my child-hood *mikvah*. Then on Monday morning we gathered a few more than a dozen of the outcasts for a morning service where we—the two of us who had just survived the ordeal in Berlin could be called to Torah as grade A USDA choice wholly kosher Jews. And then, even though it totally was not traditional to do so on a weekday, Rabbi Isaac had me read the *haftarah* that I had so lovingly and intricately prepared—the *haftarah* that had become a surrogate savior to make up for all of the losses up to this point. And then we laughed and cried and did some morning vodka *l'chaim* with a bottle of Absolut that Rabbi snuck from the Shabbat stash in the kitchen and life was good.

That Friday, Sabrina and I took the train down to Stuttgart and played dorm buddies, bunking in a single bed in a *Hauptbahnhof* business hotel— "business" meaning of course "just the business, no luxury for you." And then we went to one of the few *shuls* in the land where men and women sat together. And yes it was that same Rabbi Harlow from my *Beit Din* and yes the energy did seem a little off, but the *gabba'it* called me up for the last part of the Torah reading and as a fully halakhic Grade A Kosher Jew I blessed the Torah and wept and was overwhelmed and then took my station up there to then chant the words of the prophet Ezekiel, "They will teach my people the difference between the holy and the profane," weeping the entire time with the so well earned magic of all of it. It was like something else took over my voice and the weaknesses in my singing I always felt were gone and I felt transported in that way that only so seldom happens. I had embraced my Judaism and it embraced me and everything up until this point was just . . . worth it.

And then came the accolades and the *yasher koach* congratulations from the community and then lots of smiles and questions and *why the hell* hadn't I gone to the Uni here and why the hell hadn't I been in this shul all along and then in a perfect, barely accented English the rabbi taps me on the shoulder and motions me into the corner.

"Why did you use this Sephardic trope?"

The question jolted me out of the moment in its caustic abruptness.

"I, uh, it was just what I had learned with Rabbi Isaac."

"It was *completely* inappropriate!" She whisper-shouted enough to knock me backwards but not attract the attention of those blithely still eating *challah* and enjoying their not-utterly-ruined Shabbat Shalom. "This is an Ashkenazi synagogue. Such things are simply not appropriate. And moreover, had I known that it was *you* coming to read this weekend I would never have allowed this. You are just a brand new Jew. You have no right to try and lead anything. You need to spend your time now learning how to be Jewish and not putting yourself up front and disrupting services."

I would like to say I had a great answer. I would like to say that I clearly and concisely articulated that I had been an active Jew my entire life, but being in Germany had encouraged me to make my identity universally recognized. But . . . but . . . she already knew all that! She already had heard my entire history.

I would like to say that I calmly mentioned that I had read flawlessly, pointed out the warm feelings of those in the community, how they reacted with living breathing interest and how what I had done had caused questions to be asked and curiosity to be aroused and maybe even had inspired someone else to take on the task of jumping in and participating. I would truly wish that I could have made the correct argument about how according to Jewish law that once "converted" the convert is as if they had been born Jewish and why don't you know that since you are a Rabbi?

Instead I froze and then turned and ran out of the door, wanting to keep running across the border and then across the ocean until I could get away from this nightmare and back into the arms of a Jewish community.

I mean an American Jewish Community.

No, I guess I meant what I said.

I have no idea what to call these German communities any more, but "Jewish" just doesn't seem to fully encapsulate the insanity.

The Second Affair

Clearly, I am spending too much time contemplating from between the sheets while lying questioningly next to a bed partner.

This is where I wish for a little more chutzpah. I am sure that if I possessed just a bit more, then I would ask a male partner if they experience the same sort of self-recriminations and navel-gazing in which I seem to find myself. I am not even going to speak for other women, as this is an area where I don't even feel bold enough to ask my female friends.

Mom and I always had a real-life version of what Time-Life movies suggest to be the epitome of mother-daughter relationships. Mom said that I could talk with her about anything and to her credit even on those few occasions when I am sure she was shocked, she still barely blanched and continued the conversation in fulfillment of her promise and aspiration. But the sex talk was limited to sex talk. Nothing that happened to my body ever crept upon me in spite of or more probably in reaction to her own very different upbringing. Breasts and periods in my early teen years were well documented family expectations. From what I gather, for my mom in her childhood they were the pure instruments of Satan.

Even the mechanics of who does what and what goes where and why had been presented and discussed with my mother's blunt academic style, much as I imagine she spoke with her seniors regarding their various graduation projects. I cannot tell you how grateful I am for this. My job from pre-*bat mitzvah* on was to constantly refute, correct and dispel friends' fantasies and illusions culled from internet chat rooms and idiot boyfriends whose sexual education came from YouPorn.

At least the condom thing posed no similar problem in Europe as it did in the States. With the exception of my flirtations with the FSU, the much more liberal sex education in Germany made the purchase of condoms un-interesting as opposed to the frightful "will they think I am a slut if anyone sees me at the CVS" that accompanied teenage prophylactic shopping in my part of the world.

But with all the academic knowledge and honest conversations with mom, I still cannot in my most remote fantasies imagine asking her, "How many times can you have good sex with someone before the potential wrongness of what you are doing outweighs the feeling?"

Maybe I should back up a bit, because this expensive hotel room in Dresden and this man next to me did not just occur. I mean, I agreed to come here and I am pretty sure I leaned forward and instigated the first kiss that led to a quick car ride and a not-so-quick evening of what I will without shame call hot bliss. Incredibly, the beginning of this tale begins much more mundanely in the office of Herr Professor Doctor.

I had gotten used to the much greater formality of German university life pretty quickly. Compared to my culture shock in the Jewish community, even the most marked differences at the *Uni* felt positively tame. Even Herr Professor Doctor grew on me. The alien foreignness of his demeanor on Day One eventually felt familiar as one said "*Sie*" to all professors, rapped your knuckles on the table in a salute-cum-applause for all lecturers, and showed up for official conversations only at proper listed office hours. It turns out, however, that you can easily call a professor by their first name and say "*du*" to them after you have sex with them.

My Day One intentions of getting on my Fulbright advisor's good side never in any way contained an intention for a liaison. I hadn't even worked up any good-old-fashioned crush energy over the course of the year up to this point, rather I tried to be as culturally relative as possible and learn to try and appreciate what Herr Professor Doctor—what Stephen—had to offer.

Neither first night nor the morning after held self-recriminations. Maybe it was shock. Maybe it was being treated like a delicate vase. Maybe it was the fact that his knowledge of the grunty mechanics far out-weighed, well, pretty much anyone. Maybe I just felt like I had pulled off the coup of the century. I just don't know. I woke up to an even more bourgeois sort of hospitality than what I had experienced with Sabrina and a gentler sort of feeling of being cherished than what I felt from Natasha. I felt like I could see what relationships might feel like if I just waited long enough for my own maturation to catch up to my aspirations and the maturity level of my partners to equal, well, this.

Of course the Herr Professor Doctor part was a front. OK, maybe not a front, more of a societal requirement. When you went to work you wore a uniform, and Herr Professor Doctor just happened to be Stephen's. He didn't exactly say this, it was more that as soon as his hand began fumbling for buttons and mine was more-than-gently grabbing the back of his sandy-blond hair that I met the real Stephen.

Partially, there were no self-recriminations as the first morning moved seamlessly from waking to coffee and breakfast and sharing the sort of intense conversation that made me feel like an unquestioned equal, to a mutual shower followed by another bout of hot bliss. He dropped me off at my place on the way back to the Uni without awkwardness and with the polite request to cook for me that evening.

The evening turned into a second and then an opera and dinner in Cologne the night after and then a night of me cooking for him my one and only specialty the night after. He insisted I try single-malt for the first time and regaled me with tales of culinary travel, his apparent hobby outside of academia that he pursued with a type of religious fervor. I had no idea as to the nature of the romancing and if it contained either goal or end-game. Fully in the rabbit-hole for three weeks, broken only by weekly outings with Sabrina and Natasha and clenched teeth enduring the deteriorating atmosphere at Shabbat services, I uncharacteristically rode the wave of existential bliss and suppressed any need to question or define. In class he was simply who he needed to be in class. Outside of class I felt, despite the psychological challenge of the age difference, treated with more respect than in any relationship I had yet experienced.

I have to be honest with myself and admit that part of the energy I threw into time with Stephen had to do with avoiding shul, if not Rabbi Isaac personally. Around the time that I had had my first round of bliss, I had witnessed a pretty epic meltdown—something that I still wasn't sure how to handle.

The incident began innocently enough. Sabrina had been off and on dating a doctor from Berlin. She spent enough time there with her cousins and attended the egalitarian *Neue Synagoge* enough that a long-term friendship with a member there had begun transforming into something more suggestive. I, of course, knew pretty much every intimate detail and quite frankly liked Avram more than a bit—that is to say I liked how he treated my friend. His birth name and professional name remained "Christian," which he stopped using in Jewish communities after his conversion about five years previous. For some people this is not so necessary, but Avram looked much more like a Christian or Sebastian or Ullrich than an Avram. At easily six and a half feet, short cropped sun-blond hair, blue eyes and at no more than one-fifty or one-sixty, there was no Avram that I had ever met that looked like this—a statement that I, Andrea-whose-birth-name-had-been-Xiaofang, make fully aware of the stupid irony.

Avram finally removed the last barrier to me approving of him without reservation when he decided to come to our little corner of Germany rather than simply expect that Sabrina would be the one to travel. Naturally this would include Friday night in the synagogue followed by Shabbos dinner at Sabrina's with a few other members of our coterie. I had been planning on meeting Sabrina and Avram early, just to give him the rundown of the synagogue—meaning pointing out where it was safe to sit in addition to giving a mini-tour. I had been running a bit late, however, as I had also invited an acquaintance from one of my classes—Yana of "first alien encounter" fame, who had become my regular lecture buddy and who had been mentioning interest in coming for quite some time. She hinted at some deep dark hidden Jewish ancestor, but I had simply told her she would be welcome any time, and explained how much better it is to go with a guide—not only to understand the liturgy but as well to just get in the door.

When we arrived, still about five minutes before the start of service rather than my habitual fifteen, Sabrina stood outside with Avram and another younger couple that had been coming more and more often to shul and our social add-ons. It didn't really hit me at first that the Czar stood outside the sliding security gates with them. As I started to move forward to greet Avram with a hug, the clear anger in the conversation stopped my advance and shifted me into "paying attention" mode instead of whatever half-aware, half-half-crush on Yana state I had been in.

"This has never been a problem before," Sabrina sounding like she tasted blood. The Czar looked simultaneously relaxed and menacing.

261

"It is new rule," he replied in his never-improving German.

"From whom?"

"*Vom Vorstand.*" From the board.

I knew Sabrina well enough to hear from a few words to know that whatever they were arguing about had her on the edge. Gambling that something bigger needed to be headed off, I turned my body away from the conversation, grabbed my *handy* and quickly shot off a text in all caps to Rabbi. <<SOMETHING WRONG AT GATE. PLEASE HURRY. –A.>>

"That doesn't make any sense!"

"You can come, they are not on List."

"But they have been here a dozen times!"

Starting to figure out what had happened and trying to figure out how I could jump in, Rabbi came around the corner moving about as fast as I had ever seen him move. Going straight to the Czar he asked, surprisingly mild, "*Was ist hier los?*" What's going on here?

Sabrina answered before the Czar could begin, "We just got here and were told that visitors had to have been pre-approved a week earlier and that they need to pay ten Euros to get in."

What? Rabbi Isaac seemed as shocked as I felt, and he responded back to the Czar the German version of "Says who?"

"*Der Vorstand.*"

Rabbi Isaac had gone visibly crimson. The Czar tried to add something else but Rabbi had already tucked his cane under his armpit, pulled out his *handy* and held his index finger up to block whatever the Czar had been about to say. The situation obviously sucked on many levels, but the level of fury that had appeared without transition in Rabbi's voice, color and posture seemed . . . extreme. I gave the very confused looking Yana a quick look of apology and inched closer to Rabbi hoping to hear both sides of the exchange.

"Engels," came the clear sound through the maxed speaker.

Rabbi Isaac quickly explained. "I am standing at security and was just told that you had ordered that no visitors were allowed in the Synagogue unless they had been approved at least a week earlier and that they had to pay ten Euros to get in."

"I never said that," came the reply. Thank goodness for older folks keeping their phone volume up way too loud.

The Czar had already begun shaking his head. *"Nicht Engels. Platt."*

"Sasha is saying it wasn't you it was Platt. What's going on?"

"Give him to me," came the reply and Rabbi Isaac quickly handed the *handy* to the Czar.

Now the voices were muffled by the distance and the *handy* having been pressed more tightly to an ear. The Czar listened without nodding or changing facial expression, repeating several times, "Ok. Ok Chef."

After the last nod, Isaac took back his phone and once again I could hear the other side. "I'll talk with him later. The board had talked about keeping costs down for Kiddush. Sometimes we have too much and sometimes too little. But I didn't tell Security to change anything. I am sure Herr Platt didn't either, but I'll talk to him." The voice sounded what I had begun to call in my mind "German Matter of Fact." Bombs could be dropping but the voice of German Men shall never change. Unless a girl dared to sit in the front of the Synagogue, of course. Asshole.

Rabbi Isaac pressed disconnect as the Czar was already opening up the gate and saying, still toneless, "You can all go in."

"No wait. Not yet." Rabbi tucked his phone away and once again wielded his cane. "I'm not sure any visitors are welcome here. I want to know first what is going on."

"Nothing. I am doing what was told."

"So then someone is lying!" Rabbi shouted this, everyone, me included, stepped back several paces in complete shock. It didn't get better as he continued even louder in German, "*Verdammt noch mal*, I am so sick of this crap. It's my job to get people inside, and since the beginning of my time here, you have done everything you could to prevent that."

Not surprisingly, the Czar answered back with perfect innocence. "I have no idea what you are talking about." The last time someone had questioned the Czar he had publicly threatened to shoot him in the head. I found myself slowly backing up another few paces.

Seemingly oblivious that it was now past time to begin the service, that he was yelling at a sociopath and that a steadily growing audience had gathered to rubberneck, Rabbi continued, now having slipped the bit.

"What about Wednesday? I had an appointment with the man from Krefeld and you wouldn't let him in. I had to get a call from him an hour later, after I thought he had skipped an appointment, to find out you wouldn't let him in."

"He was a Muslim," the Czar replied evenly.

For a second Rabbi stopped and indeed his mouth hung open. Funny how in extreme emotions we do fit our Hollywood stereotypes of appropriate reactions. Then: "He was a Jew! What the . . .? His family was from a well-known group of Jewish leaders in Georgia. His wife is Jewish and they have three children—one getting ready for *bar mitzvah*. They had a possibility of a job up here and wanted to check out the synagogue to help them choose between us and several other communities. But not now. Now we have lost another potential family. A good family. Just like all the others you have sent away. And how many don't I know about?"

"He looked Muslim," the Czar answered, some emotion finally creeping into his voice. "His Russian didn't sound right."

"Is this a joke? His Russian didn't sound right? It is called a *verdammter* dialect."

"What am I supposed to do when someone looks like *that*?" The Czar shot back, sounding as if he thought his pronouncement should end all argument. I swear he flicked his eyes at me briefly as he said, "*that*."

"You are supposed to let him in!" Rabbi's voice dialed it up even more, something I didn't think possible.

"He didn't have a Jewish name."

"His name was Yitzchak!"

The Czar shrugged. "It is my job to keep you safe. To keep this community safe. There are people that hate Jews and want to kill us." Now the Czar had begun raising his anger to begin matching Rabbi Isaac's. "You don't know how many threats we get. You don't know how bad it is. I am doing my job."

"It's not your job to figure out if someone is Jewish. Ever. That is my job or when I am not here the job of the *Geschäftsführer* or if he is not around the job of the board."

"It is my job to keep you safe. I don't tell you how to do your job, you don't tell me how to do mine."

"But I can't do my job because of *this*. Do you know how many people have stopped coming to services, and when I have called to find out where they went they tell me about being stopped at security? How in the hell can I do my job if there is no one sitting in the synagogue?"

"Then they are lying to you."

Rabbi Isaac had both hands raised in punctuation and now lowered them both, shaking his head and beginning to pace back and forth like a feral animal. "Well, you heard him. Visitors are not welcome here. No one is welcome here unless you are acceptable to security or have a Jewish name like 'Boris.' No sense coming in, you are not welcome."

He didn't look at us, keeping his eyes on the Czar instead. I knew that he was being facetious and was not really telling those gathered to go, but at the same time, looking back at the now horrified Yana and the expression on Avram's face mixing confusion and indignity, I wasn't sure if I wanted to subject myself to this community on this evening. Seriously I wasn't sure I could bear to watch Rabbi.

Rabbi had already turned to the gates and without a backward look stumbled back to the waiting fifteen to twenty people gathered inside. I caught Sabrina's eyes and tried to gauge her needs and desires. She sort of shrugged, I guess telling me that she knew even less than I did where to go from here. "All right, you heard him. We are not welcome here. Let's go."

I wasn't sure what I would accomplish. I had no idea if I had signed my own *Hausverbot* or if all would be forgotten and would go back to its normal dysfunction the next morning or next week. I knew in my case I would never again invite a visitor. I knew as well that I would rather try to salvage some sort of Shabbos at Sabrina's with the waiting bottles of wine and the challah that Sabrina had baked earlier that day than to stay here.

I did go to shul the next week, soon after my tryst had started, and was let in through security with no comment. Sabrina had been so humiliated she needed a bit more time before she would join me. I personally found it hard to look at Rabbi without seeing how stooped he stood and how much he had aged. I didn't blame him—quite on the contrary I think his rage had been justified—but after his sickness earlier in the spring, his argument with Engels that I had eavesdropped on and

266

now this, the man with such mental vibrancy that had first welcomed me looked hollow. It broke my heart to hear his words as perfunctory rather than sincere and the fact that I had entered my last few months in Germany had me withdrawing my energy from this forsaken place.

So, pulling my energy back from this insanity of my until-now dominating Jewish focus and back into one more purely German made some sense. I needed an *ersatz* to the intense Jewish focus of my German life, which probably for some therapist would explain the chutzpah of my leaning forward and kissing Herr Professor Doctor—Stephen. The bliss of the resulting night became a fling and the fling became a tryst and the tryst had begun communicating the hints of being a relationship.

I had no idea what the rules were around these parts for such tryst. I assumed it to be forbidden, but Stephen never counseled nor asked me to refrain from talking about what had happened. I somehow felt anyway that I should respect that we were still committing some forbidden act and I told only my two aforementioned female confidants, both of whom I made promise secrecy and both of whom seemed willing to at least tolerate what I am sure counted as an item of disapproval to both.

On the fourth week I accepted Stephen's invitation to go to the lecture of one of his mentors at the University of Dresden. We packed bags for two nights and he purchased first class tickets on the high speed train, the ICE, where he ordered us both surprisingly pleasant dinners and a bottle of Bordeaux to make the five-hour trip seem like nothing. The occasional odd glances meant nothing as I embraced this strangely fulfilling moment in time. Or was it the embracing of a pure escape rather than a true fulfillment? If there was a difference did it really matter as I sat

267

across from Stephen and laughed at a clever observation, while he then listened attentively to my rejoinder and smiled back in pleasure and approval? Only the cultural divide between east and west finally led to what in retrospect would be the inevitable questioning.

Actually the entire day started off brilliantly. Outside of our own corner of western Germany Stephen let himself become fully, as strange as it is to utter the words, my boyfriend. We walked through the stone streets of the beautifully rebuilt *Innenstadt* playing at window-shopping and early spring café hopping. The walking for the first time included hand-holding, a ridiculously pleasing sensation of intimacy and normalcy.

The strange looks that I would expect—that of an obviously older man in an intimate relationship with a clearly younger woman—seemed slightly more pronounced in this city deep in the heart of former East Germany.

Seriously, for me glances and stares are usually pretty easy to ignore. Live a few decades in a Jewish community in Pennsylvania looking closer to Japanese than JAP and you are either going to stop coming, go crazy, or learn to ignore it even if the ignorance implicit in such stares deserved a little focused yelling now and then. I was actually getting a little bit used to not being stared at often in Germany, surprisingly enough. My Uni sits within an easy day-trip from Düsseldorf which boasts a significant Japanese population. In addition, more and more students were coming from Japan, Taiwan and South Korea to attend university in Germany and walking down the streets of Berlin, for example, it would surprise you how many people look in broad strokes like I look. Sure, conflating Japanese and Chinese to someone in, well, Japan or China and you are going to get as good of a reaction as conflating the French and Germans in France or Germany. But one thing I am familiar with

268

is western ignorance surrounding Asia and Asian peoples. I think my all-time favorite ignorant-ass question is, "What kind of Asian are you?" This is usually asked on the street as part of an attempted pickup rather than part of a long conversation or a friendship where digging into each other's ethnic past is part of sniffing each other rather than part of being borderline racist. In Philly, I would usually answer the question with my best "I am now ordering a cheesesteak at Tony Luke's" accent with a shrug and, "The South Philly kind." For anyone that laughed and showed any level of self-awareness, I would allow the conversation to continue. Anyone that kept digging would henceforth see my less social side. Did I say that politely enough?

But now a few strange words and phrases began chipping away at the hot bliss as we walked here or there or sat and sipped here or there. The word I most commonly heard sounded a lot like "fishy" and made no sense, although I did hear other phrases, usually uttered by groups of two or three women walking near us in the other direction as they passed, saw Stephen and then my eyes, skin and hair and would sniff, snap off some phrase and then pass on by. It didn't happen often and as I had never walked hand-in-hand with Stephen in a western city, I wasn't even sure if there was enough here to be concerned about.

Back in the hotel room, buzzing a little from the in-total liter of Radeberger Pilsner that I had just finished in the town center, I took off my jacket and scarf and casually asked Stephen, "What's a fish?"

Stephen finished removing his own jacket and deliciously tasteful dark purple striped scarf and wrinkled his nose at me in confusion, looking over the rims of his glasses. "Fish? I am not sure what you mean."

"I don't know. I heard it on the street a few times. From people passing us by. It sounded like 'fishy.'"

He stared silently for a few moments and then straightened his skin and smiled. "Oh. Not 'fishy.' *'Fitschi.'* They thought you were a prostitute."

What? Ok, no reason to leave an interjection left inside in such a moment. "What?"

"It means 'Fiji.' *'Fitschi.'* It is for Asians in Germany the equivalent of calling an African in America a 'nigger.'"

What? I mean, again, seriously? I looked at his face to try to ascertain his own personal opinion of what for me was not a neutral sensation. Of course he was speaking German Matter of Fact in the moment and that shit was impenetrable. I think the appropriate thing was to gulp but I had no saliva so I only managed a squeaky, "And you are ok with this?"

He shrugged, turning back to the important task of hanging up his jacket, carefully wrapping the scarf around the back of the hanger and then returning the entire get-up neatly to the wardrobe. Finally turning around, he wrinkled his nose again, probably noticing the flames flickering from my eyes and acid dripping out the side of my lips.

"Why should this bother me? You are not a prostitute."

Again, seriously? I was beginning to lose any sense of place. I wanted to begin a Rabbi Isaac-worthy rant but held back at Stephen's absurd calm. The angrier I became, the steadier he looked back at me, head slightly cocked, waiting for whatever meaningless objection I would try next. I decided to breathe twice and then try for obvious clarification. "But don't you think it's inappropriate for people to say such things?"

Now he looked at me with utter confusion. Seriously, this guy had to have an IQ of north of 150. I had read both of his books—somewhat worshipfully—and had seen him as a regular guest on WDR broadcasts that needed subject-matter expertise on any number of media-related issues. This guy simply knew his shit. In contrast to the States where the "Professor" title appeared often at universities, in Germany you had to have completed a doctorate and then a post-doctorate to even be considered for the title. Every department at a German university had really a maximum of one or two, almost always men— which is a completely different rant—and always *über* experts in their fields. That meant anyone with a mere Ph.D. could only be a lowly "*dozent*" at Uni—a word that translated roughly as "instructor." This guy sitting across from me looking as if I had sprouted a third ear actually had gravely undersold his qualifications when berating my American ignorance on Day One. His demand—before I had begun sleeping with him, I guess—that I refer to him as Herr Professor Doctor had been generous. He had two earned Doctorates in addition to an honorary one given by the Sorbonne. The Sorbonne. His business card actually listed his full and correct academic title as Prof. Dr. Dr. Dr. h.c. Stephan Weismann. I mean *damn*. And this guy seemed confused by my righteous stare.

He walked toward me and put his hand on my shoulder. A nice hug and "I am sorry for being an insensitive prick" would have been nice. I felt like slapping the hand off but let it be for the moment. "Andrea, they are just ignorant *Ossis*," he said, using the derogatory term for those that had grown up in the East. "They don't know anything. They see a German man walking down the street with a beautiful young Asian woman and they think one of two things: You are a mail-order bride or you are a prostitute. None of this affects you, though. Their assumptions don't make you either of those, they just show that they are ignorant."

Here come the but, but, buts again. "But it is offensive!"

"Sure," he said without changing his tone. "So are many things." He saw me try to argue again, but I truly had no place to go if he didn't just get why this was wrong. I mean, he didn't even know that you were supposed to say "The 'N' Word" rather than actually uttering the "N" word itself.

"Andrea, I am sorry to say but this is not America. One has the rights in Germany that are listed in the *Grundgesetz*, but none of those include the right to never be offended. You are not only a racial minority, you are also a second minority as a Jew. People will always be ignorant. Is that supposed to affect you? To make you think differently about who you are? If you are called a prostitute from ignorance when you are not a prostitute, how does this reflect on you? It only reflects on ignorance. If you let such things define you then you are giving power to the ignorant. In America you have taken this idea of PC way too far. The second you shut down offensive speech, then there is no longer anything such as free speech. Your libertarian radio personality Neal Boortz said it well: 'Free speech is meant to protect unpopular speech. Popular speech, by definition, needs no protection.'"

Ah, but now I had him. "But then Germans are the biggest hypocrites because it is illegal to own a swastika." There, take that genius.

"That is different," he said, completely unaffected.

"How in the hell is that different?" I had really been trying to not raise my voice, but he wasn't going to get away with an arbitrary differentiation.

"In every system of government where free speech is protected, the rights to free speech end at the physical safety of others. How do you say it in America? 'You can't yell fire in a crowded theater?' The swastika for Germans is like yelling fire.

There is no free speech usage of the swastika that is not simultaneously an incitement to violence. I think that is hard to understand if you are not German, but with our history, there is no way that the displaying of a Nazi artifact could ever be free speech."

The ass made way too much sense, and what was worse we were now way off the topic of my indignation. Even worse than that, he had a better vocabulary and grasp of English than most of my American friends. Asshole. I sighed, hoping it sounded dramatic, and then sat on the bed. He followed me down and I leaned my head against him. To his credit he shut up and let me process.

I was pissed. I was pissed because some idiots on the street made assumptions based on my looks and then said offensive things to me—things that I am pretty sure I would not say to others. I was pissed because in my book of "How Things Should Be" which includes circumcised Jews, good Rabbis that are allowed to do their jobs and boyfriends that defend the honor of their girlfriends, my experiences of this year contradicted Andrea's Justice. The only conclusions that I could come to were either that I was wrong about what was just and fair or the rest of the world was. There were just so many things wrong with this picture—the way the Czar had clearly been undermining Rabbi, for example. But what if he truly meant what he said—that he was protecting the community? I mean, he did it stupidly and destructively, but obviously not from his perspective. What made my perspective right, that I was American?

If a professor at Temple ever uttered what Stephen had just explained to me they would be fired. No, worse, they would be ostracized. I mean talk about sleeping with the enemy. What was I saying about who I had become that I now leaned my head against his shoulder—that I had decided in any small way to

273

consider his unacceptable words. Wasn't it the job of a boyfriend—a partner—a teacher—to create a safe space for their partners—their students? Or was it? Stephen could care less about my indignation. I mean he wasn't insensitive to my emotions, just in this case he saw no need to feed into what he apparently saw as an American weakness. But wasn't it a strength? Wasn't calling racism "racism" and bigotry "bigotry" a step forward?

I mean, the one time I had taken a road trip down to Nuremburg, I swear I found a place on the main street called "*Mohren Apotheke*" or the Moor Pharmacy. Moor, I knew from my initial Fulbright research, was one of the derogatory terms used in Germany for people of African descent—kind of their own little 'N' word. Displayed proudly in the window were a line of specialty products in blackface. Literally—just like out of some horrific pre-War uncle Remus sort of nightmare, they had bottles of shampoo and shower gel all wrapped up in little racist packages. Let's be honest—I am kind of proud of the fact that America would take a look at that and call it "wrong." It was wrong. It was offensive and was I some sort of ignorant puppet of political correctness to find it important to recognize how backwards this was?

I still wasn't ready to give up. Maybe I would never be a Prof. Dr. Dr. Dr. h.c. but I'm a Fulbright Scholar, damn it! I have a brain, too. I lifted my head and tried to choose my words in a way that rose to his discourse. Not just his—Rabbi Isaac's and Rabbi Theresa's and my mother's and my father's . . . "Different cultures have different thresholds for what they find offensive. I understand I have no right to impose my values in another culture." I scooted a bit away from him so I could look in his admittedly compelling eyes. "And maybe legislating away insensitivity is neither practical nor particularly ethical. But insensitivity to other cultures is also the first step to dehumanization. It's not right what people on the street said about me today—not because it should affect me—even though it does—but because it shows that Germans haven't learned as much as they think they have since the Holocaust. The Holocaust didn't begin with Hitler, it began with denigration and then dehumanization. Every time we let it be ok to see someone as less than us, it becomes easier to do it the next time until the words that shouldn't bother me—that maybe do come from just ignorant people—become the way more and more people see people like me. The Asian—the Jew. It really doesn't matter. Maybe we can't legislate it—maybe we shouldn't. But shouldn't we call it out? If we recognize that a swastika is incitement, then where do we draw the line? Why is one incitement illegal and the other tolerated?" I almost continued by calling out his use of "*Ossi.*" Didn't he denigrate an entire group with such a word? How was he better than those that called me a prostitute? It would have been a good argument but even my newfound strength seemed to have limits.

Stephen raised his eyebrows a bit and smiled. "That's better." It wasn't patronizing. Coming from anyone else it would have sounded like an owner of a puppy patting Wolfy on the head for waiting until the walk to relieve itself. From Stephen it sounded . . . collegial. "That is why I am here with you. I know that hurt outside. But Americans are starting to tear themselves apart with headlines instead of substantive debate. The left. The right. It is not about good ideas or bad ideas it is about good and bad—even worse, good and evil. And now this mentality is coming more and more into Europe like McDonalds and Starbucks.

"I don't know how much time we have together. I know you are leaving soon and we are not talking about tomorrow and that is ok. But you know I don't just let any student kiss me." He smiled a particularly surprisingly wicked smile. "From the first day you put up with me pushing your buttons about your Fulbright project I saw a human being with real potential. Do you know how few of these I find? Students come to Uni and choose journalism as one of the 'easy' majors. I get people who can't put two sentences together and wouldn't know a lead if it rained on them. I like you.

"But Andrea, do you know how many times in the last month that you have told me about everything you have done to improve the life of Jews in your community? Improve them how? So that it is comfortable for you? Yes, institutional Judaism in this country is nearly a complete failure, but that is not your fault. Are you sure it is your responsibility? Does American Judaism work for Russians? Should it? Rabbi Newmark is a good man in a bad situation. He is the one responsible for the religion—the spirituality of the community. Not you. Have you helped him or hurt him by making your own little America in his back yard?"

I just stared at him at the unexpected rebuke, ready to lash out. Then the tears that had been held back so many months ago finally started coming. No one can bear to look in the mirror that intensely. Stephen just held one up that I couldn't escape. I hated him-fucking hated him for it. And I loved him for it, but knew how finite that would be. I had been prattling on about my great deeds of social justice. He always listened and asked questions that showed he cared about my life. I loved how he made me feel. But he knew me better than I knew myself and there was no way I could deal with it.

I can't hear any more. Please stop.

"The fact that you recognize how hard it is to make good law and to dance between cultural morality and universal ethics is why I love being with you. You are complex, Andrea. I cannot even begin to understand your background—your challenges. Everything—your adoption, your ethnicity, your parentage. But here you are in Germany, surviving. Thriving. Arguing with you professor. And quite well, usually, I should add. I have always just needed to know as well that you were not only clever but also self-aware."

He didn't seem to mind after as I held on to him tightly that my emotions ran the gamut. There is probably some right thing to say or do in such a moment, but I felt exhausted and stretched thin. It wasn't that the room or even the city felt unsafe, it was rather that there was nothing I could do to un-hear Stephen's words or my thoughts. Had the world always been this dangerous or was it only the awareness of what was happening that made us feel threatened when nothing had really changed?

The Election

There is a scene from what I suppose is a now infamous Israeli musical that just needs to be seen by everyone in my opinion. The movie *Kazablan* came out in the 1970s, clearly an interpretation of West Side Story yet with a distinctly Israeli craziness. I think every Jewish teen that has ever spent more than a weekend in Israel has been subjected to the film, seemingly there to educate about history when in actuality it provided little more than mockery material for the next days of bus rides. Except that the film still rocks. Anyway, regardless of the perceived absurdity, in retrospect there is a scene of pure prescience.

At one point in the film, the slowly formalizing community of Sephardic exiles in Israel need to make the decision on whether to stay in their failing community or to move and try to integrate into an already established community, yet one where they would surely be strangers. Without established hierarchy, however, the community resorts to a clearly foreign decision-making methodology, "Democracy."

Hijinks ensue. The villagers clearly know nothing about the democratic process, and instead enact their ignorant—yet hilarious—perception of democracy:

---Is this a democracy or isn't it?

---Of course it is!

---(What's democracy?)

---Democracy means everyone does what they want.

I think in America it is a little hard to have this conversation. Capital-D Democracy lives up there on the top shelf of Americana concepts like hot dogs, John Wayne and the half-ton pickup truck in Texas—you simply do not disparage at the risk of societal ostracization. Yet Kazablan shows through comedy and dodgy song-writing the true folly—that enacting the tenants of democracy within a group that has never experienced even the smallest elements of it is doomed. There is neither background nor infrastructure to enable a decision through vote. Winston Churchill's axiom that democracy "is the worst form of government, except all the others" works only if democracy is the natural outgrowth of all systems that came before it. Alright, I am totally stealing this from a conversation with Rabbi Isaac, but it makes sense. You don't order "five star" spicy from a Thai restaurant when the spiciest thing you have ever eaten is a bell pepper. Not even three or two stars. You do not introduce most people to opera through Parsifal and you do not try to acquaint most people with ballet by taking them to a performance choreographed by Pina Bausch. Yeah, I will argue the superiority of abstract to romantic, challenging to white-bread and Wagner to Rossini all day long, but I am never going to try to do this by throwing the uninitiated into the fire to prove an aesthetic point. The neophyte is simply going to walk out the door and go back to China Emporium Asia Delights in your nearest South Jersey strip mall and order Americanized Kung Pow chicken for the rest of their lives. Sure I may have maintained my personal militant aesthetics, but I have lost the convert. Bravo me.

So hopefully I don't even have to try and explain the disaster that "voting" represents in a German Jewish community comprised nearly completely of FSU imports for whom democracy is no more real or understood than it was for the poor settlers of Kazablan. The best possible but still hideous outcome is that sheep will follow the expectations of the most experienced in democracy—meaning the will of the hegemony of the several non-FSU Jewish families that have maintained until now iron-fisted control through their superior knowledge of the system. The worst case, of course, would be that the disenfranchised try to begin practicing their own version based on their own Soviet fantasies about the nature of democracy.

My first clue as to how this would play out came with panicked phone call from Natasha. OK, panicked doesn't really do it. My clearly distraught friend could barely breath through her tears as she kept repeating, "They came. They came."

Here is where members of quaint American Reform communities will no longer be able to suspend their disbelief. The drama may be extreme in our board meetings and rabbi search committees and certainly in our religious practice committees where those of us with a slightly greater interest in tradition fight for a food policy that explicitly bans pork, but these dramas are not life-and-death existential. Opposing sides in these debates at their very worst lead to split communities, but not to threats of reprisals. In our effete world of idealized Judaism, such things must simply be misunderstandings or exaggerations.

"They came and brought The List." In German she had indeed said "*die Liste*" but it took me a few questions and repetitions to extract context and meaning.

"The List" turned out to be a slate of candidates. In my every-day-more-sane-and-seductive home synagogue, board members had hard defined terms of office. Every year, a quarter of the board turned over so that every four years there was a completely new body. A committee of both board and non-board members selected a slate of potentials, then called up candidates to see who could be guilted, shoe-horned or simply convinced to serve in the thankless job of steering Jews very set into their ways through the next leaky roof, search for Hebrew School

280

teacher or God-forbid capital campaign. The shoe-horned candidates would then be voted on at the next congregational meeting, and all of this process by law is transparent, documented and easily available online in pdf format with a simple search of Rabbi Google. Sure, in such a system there is still room for corruption, usually in the form of a saboteur with an axe to grind. But the transparency of the rules and stability of the community tends to mitigate the damage from those most hell-bent on damaging. At least this is how Dad described everything over an intense Skype session, but I have no reason to doubt him.

"*Was ist passiert?*" What happened? I repeated the question several times until it became clear that I needed to be there. So with an "*Ich bin gleich da!*" I stripped off comfy sweats and hoodie and threw on pleasant-spring-day appropriate jeans and light jacket. Arriving at Natasha's flat I once again repeated, "*Was ist passiert?*" until the story slowly took the patchy shape of a tattered quilt, woven through stress, sobs, and simple lack of words in German to explain.

About two hours later, the Czar, Son-of-Czar and Valentina-the-mini-model buzzed through my boiling vision as I pulled out my handy and called Sabrina.

"Did you hear what they have been doing?" I mentioned Czar and Son-of-Czar by name, even though Sabrina had been long used to my nicknames. "Have they come to you?"

"No," I had caught her at work, so she asked me to hold on while she went out to a stairwell to speak more freely. "I had heard something from Tatiana last night." Tatiana was one of the nicer and younger Latvian women that hung with us and chose to sit downstairs on the rare occasions she came to services. "But she was pretty vague about what happened."

"Ok. I'm with Natasha. She's pretty upset. Sasha, Boris and Valentina came by earlier today with a list. I guess of candidates. I have it here." Even though it was all in Cyrillic, after trading language back and forth now for months with Natasha, at least names were not hard to read. Deciphering full sentences was another thing. I read the list for Sabrina, adding the occasional correction to pronunciation that Natasha mumbled from leaning against my arm. "This guy at the top, Vladimir Revutsky—have you ever heard of him?"

Neither Sabrina nor Natasha had, which was a bit weird. The way these lists usually worked was you stuck your top candidate at the top and then worked your way down. But this wasn't a parliamentary slate, as far as I knew. Living in Germany had at least helped me demystify one of those great mysteries that you are supposed to learn in comparative politics but never really grasp. In places like Germany you don't vote for people, per se, rather for a party or a slate. One vote for CDU or SPD means one chance at a seat in parliament. The more votes, the more seats and the more people come off the list, starting at the top, and sit in government. Of course it still was about the people, because when Germans despised the top name on a party slate, that party obviously got fewer votes. It didn't quite rise or sink to the level of American media popularity contests, but there was some relation.

For the Jewish community, I had thought that you just voted directly for potential board members, not a slate, so maybe I was missing something—maybe the unknown name at the top of the list was incidental and not meant to reflect the grand pumba-ski. "Should I ask Rabbi?" I continued with Sabrina, patting Natasha. "I mean it sounds like they came in here and said that they were going to harm her kids if she didn't vote in the election for the listed candidates."

That wasn't exactly what Natasha had said. The three had knocked politely enough. As Natasha was a paid staffer in the community, she knew all three security personnel well. She had thought it strange, but had no reason to hesitate with welcoming them in and offering tea.

The Czar had refused the tea for all, but had accepted the sofa and pulled out an envelope with Natasha's full name written on the outside. "Open it," he had commanded.

Natasha did as she was told and pulled out the List. "You are planning to vote in the election." It had been a statement rather than a question. Natasha was a bit vague in how she had responded, but I imagine her as shrugging and offering the Russian equivalent of, "Yeah. Sure. Why not?"

"Good," the Czar had said. Son of Czar and Valentina had not accepted a seat, something that had bothered Natasha a great deal. Instead they stood on either side of the door with their arms crossed. "Read the List," the Czar had commanded. Natasha had complied and read through the ten names. When she had finished the Czar continued: "Every voter can vote for as many as seven candidates. There are twenty-three in total. You will pick seven from this list. The only one that you must choose is Mr. Revutsky. You will not vote for anyone else not on this list."

Again, Natasha could not clearly express what she had done, but I imagine the words to have been a bit strange. Then again, depending on what she remembered from her earlier life maybe not so much. I imagine her looking back at the Czar, questioning and then looking again at the exclusively Slavic names on the List.

She did explain to me that she had had the chutzpah to ask "why?" She didn't say chutzpah, rather had said in her slowly improving German, "*Ich war so dumm.*"

283

The Czar replied with something like, "We really like your children. We think it is our duty to protect them at the kindergarten." Message received. Soon after they left, leaving the simple words floating in the living room until Natasha had been able to call me.

Sabrina and I agreed that I should be the one to call Rabbi and that she would come over and sit with a still shaking Natasha. It hit me as I listened to the ringing that I had not spoken to him outside of "Shabbat Shalom" since the Epic Meltdown and really not so much since the *Beit Din*. Had I even thanked him? Of course I had—at our clandestine service I am sure I did—lots of hugs, lots of tears—but still . . .

"Hi Andrea."

"Rabbi. Hi. Did you, um, can I come in and talk to you?"

He sounded tired but that had been his normal state for so long it barely registered. "I have time now."

"I'll be there in fifteen minutes."

Guard towers. Moats. Palisades. I once thought my observations to be clever until I had become so used to them that I could ignore them and try to find my own perceived safe space within stone and armored-glass security. Evgeniy-the-bribe-taker manned the gate and let me through with no problem, and within minutes I sat where I had sat for so many months, sipping from the same glass poured from the same green bottle of Rheinquelle as Rabbi had the *Menschligkeit* to smile lightly and pretend that I was a better human than I was starting to suspect I actually was.

"What's wrong, Andrea? It sounded urgent."

I nodded, feeling my chest quavering at the delayed-reaction fury I felt at seeing my friend in tears. "Did you know what is going on with the elections?"

He looked at me evenly, paused, and asked without inflection: "Which part?"

284

"The List."

He sipped some water, his voice still unchanged when he responded with, "Which one?"

"What do you mean, 'which one?'"

"Last I heard, there were three."

"Three?" I guess my reply had been more a word of exasperation than a question.

"Herr Engels is trying to take power away from Herr Platt, so he put out a list mixing his German and Russian allies but trying to push out Platt. Apparently Platt has been making deals with the Security folks to get them more influence—which probably also means money but I am not really sure. Engels is now completely at odds with Sasha from that night with the issue about guests coming in. He actually tried to work with me. I described everything that I knew had happened—information I have just recently been putting together at how many people have stopped coming to synagogue because Sasha or someone else in security didn't want them there. So Engels actually did the right thing and created a mandatory training for Security. I can imagine they weren't too happy. So now I think—I don't know I'm just projecting—Engels' play is to get people on the board that are subservient only to him so that he can wrest power from Platt.

"Platt on the other hand—here is his list." He handed me a slightly crinkled piece of community letterhead with names typed in both German and Russian. "This is the only one I actually have yet. You see that Platt has himself first and Engels second, so either he doesn't know about Engels' little coup or is playing at something else.

"The third list is Sasha's. He has been trying to get rid of his direct boss, our *Geschäftsführer*–you know, business manager, right? Like an executive director in America but with a lot more power and total control of the purse." I nodded. The *Geschäftsführer* here, Herr Lubinsky, was an author of some repute in Germany—a historian of the Jewish families that had returned from exile or hiding after the Holocaust. He represented one of the oldest Jewish families in a neighboring community. I liked the guy although he did not often attend services and I had only had a few conversations with the seemingly gentle sexagenarian. "Anyway, the two don't get along and Sasha wants the job, so he is trying to put his own guy on the throne."

"Who is this Vladimir then?"

Rabbi shrugged. "Your guess is as good as mine. Never met him. He has never been to synagogue, as far as I know."

"And he wants to be president of a Jewish community?" My voice rose in an incredulity that I know by this time I shouldn't have felt. Seriously, why did this shit surprise me anymore?

Rabbi shrugged again. "Herr Lubinsky says he owns a trucking company that operates out of Kiev and several cities in the North Rhein, but he lives here. He is pretty well off, I imagine."

"Well, they're threatening people!" I finally found an indignation that I felt needed neither subtlety nor nuanced discussion. This was just wrong, plain wrong and utterly wrong.

Rabbi Isaac stared at me, almost coldly. Finally he said, "I know."

He knew me well enough to know what was about to come out of my mouth—the just questions of what he planned on doing about this—great and all-powerful rabbi. Looking at his severe expression I just shut up.

He filled the silence by making the narrative worse. "I have been getting phone calls for about the last week. First the social

workers and now people in the community that trust me—
usually ones that I have worked with for family funerals or
people whose weddings I have performed. Funny how that
works. Many people have been in tears. Apparently, some
permutation of security personnel has been going through the list
of members—most of whom have never even seen the inside of
the synagogue—and either made some sort of threats or gave
gifts. For the people already pre-disposed to listen to Sasha's
people, they get a bottle of vodka. For the people that aren't as
sure, they get threatened."

How could this man just say these words so coldly? Wasn't
he the rabbi? "Rabbi . . ."

He held his hand up and stopped me. "Andrea, who do you
think these people are? What power—what influence do you
actually think I have? You have been here for almost a year,
have you paid attention to anything that is happening? What do
you think happens to me if the Russians win? Do you thing they
want an American who speaks German as their Rabbi? What do
you think is going on here?" He slammed his hand down on the
desk, causing me to jump. For a moment he glared at me, an
alien haunted and unhinged, then he sat back and sighed the
demon out of him. "I am sorry," my once-again rabbi said, tears
in his eyes.

We watched the election live. Well, kind of. The community
had set up a real-time internet site to track the votes as they came
in as a sham of transparency. Sabrina and I had gone to the
community meeting, about half as full as the one where I had
lost Rafi, to hear the now twenty-one candidates speak. Two had
not collected enough signatures and had dropped out. Natasha
refused to come with us, and had begun looking for other jobs in
the area after having begun losing sleep and wrestling with

nightmares when she was able to nod off. For Sabrina and for me it was like watching a train wreck. Valentina once more did her horrid job of translating—this I knew well because when Vladimir-the-Czar's-Stooge got up to speak, he mentioned quite clearly that the community needed a Russian speaking rabbi, none of which had been translated. Even with my limited vocabulary I could understand it, and Rabbi Isaac, sitting once again in the back and who surely understood it would not pick his eyes up from his handy to meet mine when it was said.

The Russian speakers mostly gave CVs instead of speeches and then told what Big Problem they intended to fix—no youth engagement, no senior engagement, not enough entertainment, not enough jobs for Russians, no one should need to pay *Kultusgeld*, and so on. The German speakers spoke much more eloquently, practiced in their calls to tradition and reminders of how much they had done for the community.

In the end, Sabrina, now a member of the community as a real registered tax-paying Jew, had chosen from what the two of us figured were the least of the evils and then watched the votes coming in. Unsurprisingly, the turnout was great—about fifty percent. The board would consist of the top seven vote receivers with two non-voting alternates. The top vote getter would be assumed to be the new *Vorsitzender*, to be voted in by the new board within a week of the election or within three if the vote was contested. The *Vorsitzender* would then choose the *zweite Vorsitzender* and then the new reign would begin. For a couple decades this had been Platt, Engels, or a member of one of three other families that had been the founders of the present community after the war.

Herr Engels faired the best of the old guard with seventy-five votes out of eight-hundred or so cast. Herr Platt had received twenty-three. Stooge-of-Czar netted six-hundred fifty-four and within twenty-four hours of being officially voted in by the new board had sent a letter to the congregation, explaining why he felt forced to fire the ineffective Rabbi Newmark and why the community would immediately begin their search for a real traditional Russian-speaking spiritual leader for their Glorious Community.

The Aftermath

My most enduring memory of the last weeks in the Jewish community would prove to be one of the most pathetic. As one could imagine, the stress and insanity of the overall situation—which part of the situation, just take your pick—led to a lot of poor behavior. In a congregation filled with poor behavior, a drop in standards could get downright ugly. To Rabbi's credit, he showed up on the weeks when there wasn't another rabbi brought in to interview, and also to his credit, he mostly pulled back from the more and more accusatory sermons—as righteous as they had been—that had highlighted the steadily declining mood in the synagogue for months. In some ways, it seemed that he had been rejuvenated. Perhaps, for someone with severe heart problems because of stress, the prospect of having even a forced relief from that stress may just have been liberating. The only problem was that no one else had been liberated.

The election of Vladimir-Stooge-of-Czar had given permission to the Russian speaking Jewry to discard the last of the respect for Rabbi Isaac's authority that had held them at least nominally in check. Chayem's watch tapping become more obsessive and violent as Herr Adler's insistence that the Great Rabbi in his other community led services correctly while Rabbi Isaac did not as Herr Grossman simply became a worse version of himself, if possible.

A couple weeks before the end which would then be only a couple more before my return trip to Philly, Rabbi had actually walked out of a service. Everyone had been unusually quiet until after the Torah reading. In traditional communities, a "*Musaf*" or an additional "standing" prayer or "*Amidah*"—the central prayer of the liturgy—would be prayed at the end of the service in order to reflect the additional sacrifice performed in the Temple back in the day. The *Amidah* acted as an *ersatz* for the temple sacrifice—a pretty damn good replacement as I had no desire to see temple sacrifice ever as the center of my religious practice— and the obligation of a traditional Jew was to pray an *Amidah* for every mandated sacrifice. This meant three a day on normal days and then four—the three plus the *Musaf*—on Shabbat and festivals. For morning and afternoon services, this would start with a silent *Amidah*, a chance for those who cared to pray through the liturgy once on their own, followed by the cantor's repetition of the same prayer out loud. This was most definitely not how I had grown up, but after nine months I had become used to the pattern, even finally finding my own spiritual voice within it. Surprise of surprises. I had even begun wondering how I would feel going back to American Reform practice. Would it be like a pair of comfy jeans or more like an unexpected culture shock?

Rabbi Isaac usually had mercy and davened at light-speed through the cantor's repetition, as the *Musaf* usually hit nearing the third hour—yes you heard that right—of a Saturday morning service. The more I had read about and discussed liturgy for my "identity confirmation" the more I realized how precise Rabbi was in ensuring that Jewish Law was followed. If he skipped something, it truly was an optional part of a service in spite of what the Charming Old Ladies would have each other believe. One of those items of precision was that once you began praying the Amidah, you kept your heels together for the duration—as the Talmud put it, "Even if a snake crawled up your leg."

That Shabbat as Rabbi's pure tenor began spinning out the Hebrew faster than most could follow in a race to the end, an argument started between Herr Grossman and Dr. Likhtman. Ok, maybe argument is unfair, as 'fistfight' would probably be more accurate. I had missed the beginning, nose buried in my own prayerbook as I mouthed the words as fast as I could, more successfully than ever starting to achieve Rabbi Isaac-like speeds that would have once seemed unreachable. The sounds of scuffle stopped Rabbi's words and jerked my head up as I saw Likhtman's Lieutenant stepping in between his patron and the Russian Enemy as if they were twelve and in a playground.

Not having seen the tussle part, Rabbi kept his feet planted and turned his neck. Essentially, if he moved his feet or said anything to interrupt the prayer, he would feel compelled by his interpretation of Jewish Law to start the prayer again from the beginning, something that assuredly no one in the community would wish.

Somehow, the silence clued the dueling partners into the fact that their idiocy had affected the service, and so they continued to fulfill the mentality of twelve-year-olds by pleading their case— sounding like a broken-German Russian-accent version of "But mommy, he hit me first."

Rabbi made violent shrug and pointed at the prayer book, I am sure attempting to say, "If you make me say something, I have to start again. Grow up and shut up."

Of course both gentlemen continued with the mommy-he-hit-me-firsts so that Rabbi stepped out of his stance and said in Russian something about having to start again. More 'mommy mommy' followed until Rabbi bellowed out in German, "Enough!" which finally stopped them.

"This is a synagogue. A synagogue! Have you no respect? We are in the middle of prayer. Prayer!"

The 'mommy mommys' started up again quickly to be squashed by and even louder, "*Es ist mir egal!*" I don't care! "We are in the middle of prayer, I have to start the *musaf* over again, and I don't care about what happened. Be quiet now or leave the service.

More mommy mommy.

Rabbi stood on some combination of shock and fury and finally ripped his *tallis* off of his shoulders. "This is *over*. I don't care what happened, but obviously no one has interest in being in a synagogue. I'm *done!*" And with that he threw his *tallis* unfolded over the pulpit, grabbed his cane and without looking or deviating to the left or right, left the *beit knesset* and I imagine went up to his office.

Everyone in the shul kind of looked at each other in confusion until the rest of the Old Russian Dudes began shouting at each other. Dr. Likhtman, the only one who seemed to be affected by what just happened or his part of it had gone pale. He simply turned from the shouting, left the *beit knesset*, grabbed his hat and left the building. Sabrina and I both discussed going up to check on the rabbi, but truly felt helpless and quite frankly uncomfortable. Not knowing what else to do, we decided to stick around to see if Rabbi Isaac would come down to *Kiddush*.

Herr Grossman at least had the decency to leave without trying to plead his case any longer, also grabbing his cane and hat and leaving with huffs and puffs of indignation.

We sat in the social hall and quietly chatted with our neighbors after Gidal had led the *Kiddush* blessings. The gathering seemed about the most sober that I had ever seen here. Maybe something—the vision of a scuffle followed by a rabbi walking out in the middle of services—had finally penetrated some level of the stone coldness wrapped around these damaged men. At some point Rabbi Isaac hobbled into the room and everyone went silent—well more silent than they had been. I felt like standing at attention as if a *rebbe* from antiquity had entered our presence. For a moment it almost seemed as if that figure

293

shone out from beneath Rabbi's shell, until the illusion faded and only a mostly broken man leaning on a cane was left.

Still not meeting anyone's eyes, he went up to where Gidal sat in the position of rabbi and spoke a few sentences in Hebrew. Only then he looked around at everyone else but said nothing. Instead he walked the length of the U-shaped tables and ritually touched everyone on the shoulder. When he brushed mine I lost it completely, only to be quickly followed by Sabrina and several others.

Two days later I had scheduled what qualified as an early meeting with the rabbi in order to go over final questions I had for my nearly complete Fulbright Project. At the ungodly hour of 9 a.m., his hands gripped the American-style coffee thermos more in the manner of raptor-talons than rabbi hands. I knew and I am positive he knew that he barely functioned before 10:30 and at least a liter of caffeine, but at 10:30 he had open office hours, which usually meant a decent line of various people with various problems and which definitely meant that this was the only time this particular week that I could get my last questions in before a quickly approaching deadline.

I had once asked the rabbi what people talked with him about in his open office hours. I mean, most people spoke such poor German that I cannot imagine there being much depth possible. Yet there was always a line and never enough time.

"It really depends," he said. "I mean, you have to be ready for anything. I think the most common is that people want me to write a specific prayer for them and for their family. They want a prayer to help deal with whatever sickness or family crisis. They usually won't even say what the crisis is, just that they need a real Jewish prayer to help them out."

The plaintiveness of his answer had floored me. It was so hard to picture these people as having that kind of spiritual

294

connection, but this sort of behavior showed the type of respect if not trust that I imagined only in the most religious of communities. But wasn't that what I did here too? Maybe it wasn't asking the magical *rebbe*-guru to heal me, but all the hours of proverbially sitting at his feet, readjusting much of my Jewish self-image based on his teachings—wasn't I doing about the same thing? Asking him to help me become complete?

This morning's meeting had been scheduled for a few weeks and I really did have a deadline otherwise I am not sure I would have had the courage to come. Yet he greeted me with warmth and friendliness as he always did, lighting incense to cover the ever-present electrical smell and pouring fizzy water to keep our throats moist for conversation. He had clearly aged and every movement showed the events of the last months, but he was still Rabbi Isaac in all that mattered to me.

"So, how's the project?" he asked casually.

I dug my notebook with the questions and clarifications that I had prepared for the meeting, opening my mouth to say "It's going great" and instead hearing my mouth speak, "Oh my God I am so sorry what's happening!"

He looked at me with the stony version of his eyes that had been coming out more and more before that dissolved in the tears that filled his gaze.

"Andrea, I . . ." He swallowed and then pulled out some tissues and tried to discretely blow his nose. "Andrea, I need to get something off my chest."

"Sure, anything Rabbi."

The sides of his mouth twitched in at least the beginning of a smile as he said, "You are way too eager. People getting things off their chest is seldom pleasant."

My chest clenched at this, but I waited without speaking.

"You need to know—wherever you go, wherever I go—I want you to know you can always contact me. You know, Skype, chat, old-fashioned phone calls, whatever. Regardless of what you do, I will always consider myself to be your rabbi. I know that sounds strange, but I am proud of you in so many ways. You have worked so hard, you . . ." The tears came back now pretty intensely but he spoke through then. "You weren't here for *Yom Kippur* this year. I think you got here right after Sukkot was over." I nodded that he was correct. "So you never really heard how I teach *Yom Kippur* and *teshuva*."

I nodded, wondering where he was going. I thought back to Rabbi Teresa's teachings that had so affected me regarding the *teshuva* I had had to make with Bonnie. I started trying to figure out what Rabbi was about to make amends for.

"Well, it's probably good you weren't here for Yom Kippur." He chuckled and for a second he seemed closer the man I had met when I first came here. "Grossman got into it with Gidal and Platt while I was praying *Unetane Tokev* in front of the open ark. I couldn't do anything but stop and stand there until the powers that be realized that this was one of the single most holy moments of the liturgy and maybe not the best time to act out. Not that it was terribly unusual, but not the best first impression, I would imagine. Anyway, when I actually have the ability to teach the High Holy Days and I have an audience willing to listen, I usually give people the image of a bank account with a hundred dollars in it. Let's say a hundred euros here. It doesn't seem like much, but that hundred euros in the account will be replenished every day and always be enough to pay for what we need."

I nodded. I wasn't entirely sure what this had to do with *teshuva*, but the image seemed clear enough.

He continued, "But we can put little bunches of the money in escrow accounts that don't replenish. These escrow accounts represent everyone that we need to forgive or need to ask forgiveness from. Over the course of time, we damage our relationships or are a part of others damaging us. Any time we wake up with a memory that we can't get rid of or anger at someone that doesn't go away-maybe even a sense of shame at something we have done or a thought form we can't get rid of, that's another escrow account. Then this just builds up over time—our relationships with our parents, teachers, siblings," he shrugged, "our religious institutions. The older we get without ever having reclaimed the accounts the less we have to live on."

Faces and thoughts went flashing in front of my mind. Herr Grossman came first. I had been so furious with him since the weekend I could hardly sleep. Actually all the Minyan Men were in there. And then the Czar. Big time. Asshole. Then the rest of security and the Charming Old Ladies and even Stephen although we still shared a bed. I loved what I felt with him but hated the thoughts he had opened up in me and the sense that I no longer knew anything. Then the list started flipping faster—friends that had betrayed me and teachers that had been hard to deal with. My parents were in there too—maybe not as big as I imagine some would see their parents—maybe only a few dollars in my escrow account—but certainly I had a few unhealed injuries. The number of people that came to mind in a blink shocked me until my mind settled on the surprise image of a faceless woman in China who had clearly shown she didn't want me. With that thought my eyes began to moisten dramatically and match Rabbi's.

"Pretty soon your account is empty and then what do you do?" he asked rhetorically. "You start paying with your own body. We still need some cash each day, so if we can't get it

297

from our account we are going to get it from our bodies. Here, I'll prove it to you—who is the first person that came to mind when you just now started going through your memories."

I still wasn't really thrilled with him reading me so easily, but I answered nonetheless, "Herr Grossman."

At that he finally smiled through his tears. "Yeah, me too. That one is going to be a hard one for me. Ok, think of Herr Grossman, picture him, and now tell me where in your body you feel him."

"My back," I answered without thinking, feeling a throbbing in my middle back where a heavy backpack would press.

"Right, now think of Rafi and tell me where you feel him."

Sometimes I forgot how much I had told this man. We didn't have father confessors in our tradition but damn if I hadn't been using this man as one for the last year of my life. Well, I felt a pressure on my chest and could hardly breathe as Rafi's face floated into my mind so I pointed to my heart, not trusting my voice.

"Exactly. Now think of Sasha."

Seriously, I hated this. "My stomach," I answered through gritted teeth.

"How are you sleeping lately," he asked.

"I'm not," I pleaded with my eyes to get him to stop.

"Ok. It's ok. You get my point." I nodded. "So maybe it is pretty New Age-y sounding and it's certainly not scientific, but at least we can agree that stress makes us sick, and at the very least all of these unhealed memories contribute to stress." I nodded. Of course they do.

"So my first point is that even though you have done so many great things since you got here, I know that you are leaving here with almost everything in escrow." He gestured his neck back at his cane. "I don't want you to end up like me,

298

paying for your convictions with your body." He saw my expression change and continued, "What you think it is normal for a forty-eight-year-old man to have his entire body riddled with osteoarthritis? I have been financing the attempt to build this community for years with my bones. My orthopedist tells me I have the feet of a seventy-five-year-old. Lesson for you, do as I say, not as I do. I have always been a better teacher than a doer."

"So what do you do? I mean what do I do?" All the various pains in my body and ways in which my body had stopped functioning and digesting and moving correctly now screamed their protests unambiguously. Yeah, it all sounded a little too-mystical-bullshit for me, except for the fact that it made way too much sense.

"Well, in Judaism we have the High Holy Days," he answered. "Ideally we should be in the process of reclaiming our accounts every day, but even though most spiritual traditions implore us to live in the present, we seldom do. So we have these special holidays—*Rosh Hashanah* and *Yom Kippur* and the month of *Elul* leading up to them both to get us to start trying to identify all the junk. The really cool thing is that this is not even a new interpretation of our tradition. The Talmud talks about the meaning of the *shofar* and why we blow it on the first day of *Elul*. It says 'Wake up! Wake up!' It is a call for us to start becoming aware of the *teshuva* we need to make—of the junk that we need to dump and the relationships we need to repair."

Again I asked, "But how?"

"Awareness first. Make a list. Draw a picture of yourself. List number one contains all the people you need to forgive. List two contains all the people you need to make amends with. List three has all the thoughts that you are stuck in—all the head trips and 'I'm not good enough because' bullshit that we tell

299

ourselves. Then we figure out if we can feel any of those people or items in our body and draw a little line from the unforgiven name to the part of your body so you become aware of what it is costing you. That's the easy part."

His eyes were beginning to clear up as he entered the passion of teaching. I really wanted, with all my own pain, to just keep him in this moment as he looked like the *rebbe* at whose feet I had sat now for so many months.

"An Episcopalian pastor once told me one of the greatest truths I ever learned about forgiveness. He told me, 'Most of us wait until we feel like we can forgive someone before we proceed with forgiveness. The problem is, forgiveness is an action, not an emotion. You forgive first, then you feel it, not the other way around.'

"So there are a lot of ways to do this. The easiest I have ever found is to combine this exercise with *tashlich*."

I loved the fact that he no longer asked me arbitrarily if I knew the meaning of a Hebrew term that he threw out. Now he assumed that I knew and if I didn't know I would ask or look it up. He was right, and that was a major change. In this case, nothing to look up. *Tashlich* was the *Rosh Hashanah* ceremony of 'casting away.' You would leave services on the first day of Rosh Hashanah and go to a body of water, digging into your pocket for any lint or more commonly-placed breadcrumbs that symbolized your sin and then 'cast' it away into the water—the modern-day remnants of sending the scapegoat into the wilderness.

In spite of his trust in my knowledge I still nodded so that he knew I understood.

"What I recommend is that you write each name on a tiny piece of paper, and then hold each name up and think of that person and see them in your mind and feel them in your body

300

and then you say, 'I forgive you.' Do this over and over and then put these slips of paper in the pocket of what you are wearing to *tashlich*. Then you go through the thought forms and think of each one, realizing that it is a lie and say, 'I am through with you. I am over this.' Then what is left you start making phone calls or visits. You don't wait. You fix that relationship. You call that person up and say 'I am so sorry, what can I do to make amends?' and then you do it. Life is too damn short and those relationships need to be repaired and you need that money back in your account."

The names and faces flipped through my mind again. But some of these people. Damn. Seriously. The Czar. Herr Grossman. That inhuman asshole in Ukraine that destroyed one Jewish gravestone to make some cheap Euros and completely profane a sacred rite. Did these people deserve my forgiveness? I decided to ask Rabbi the question.

"You know, the funny thing about our tradition is we are not required to forgive. We are required to go to others and ask forgiveness, but when they come to us, we get to make the decision to forgive or not. We are not obligated. But the reason I teach *teshuva* like I do is so that you ask the question if holding back that money from the account is actually worthwhile. Is being pissed off at someone worth letting it eat at your own body? Isn't that the definition of 'they win?' Do you really want to give people like Sasha that level of power over you?"

He gave me a minute to think through what he had said, and then he continued when I looked back up. "All the slips of paper you take with you to Rosh Hashanah services and feel them in your pocket as you listen to the shofar, and then after at *tashlich* these are what you cast into the water. I even shout to myself when I do this, 'I don't need you anymore. I am free.'"

He noticed my look of skepticism. "Listen, there is nothing about this that is easy. But the longer you let it all build up, the harder it is to get rid of later. Think about the metaphor of the 'Gates of *Teshuva*' that slowly close over the course of the High Holy Days. It actually all makes sense. The gates being open means that you are in the midst of the process of making this inventory of all the relationships you need to repair and all the escrow accounts that you are using to lock yourself away from yourself. So let's say you go through all this—making lists and forgiving and letting go and talking to others—and then you decide that you are not going to let go of that one thing or that one person. Ok, fine. But when it all comes around again and you make another list—after you have hardened your heart and chosen to leave that one thing in escrow, what are the chances that you will be able to forgive and get that back the next year? And then the next? That is what it means by the Gates of *Teshuva* closing at the end of *Yom Kippur*. Our entire liturgy is designed to get us to wake up, pay attention and do some real healing, but if we get through all the special prayers and melodies and still haven't paid attention or done the work, the chances of doing it next time are even less. Basically, until you reach a complete breakdown or crisis that forces us past—well really past our egos—we are just going to let that fester and poison us more and more each year. You want an example? Just look at the Minyan Men. Herr Grossman? Pity him instead of hating him, because that is what a lifetime of true horror—held onto and never let go of—looks like."

I had thought that I always had taken the High Holy Days seriously, but I had never heard it presented quite like this. I started thinking about how many names would be on my list and tried to figure out why I had never actually encountered this. Yom Kippur always felt like the most beautiful ceremony with the most amazing melodies, but I had never had such a direct, well, homework assignment. Moreover, feeling my acid-filled stomach and temper so close to the surface and my days of crap for sleep and even my innate trust for this man, I wanted to take his words seriously, even if it felt like simply too much and too frightening of work. But still, beyond all that—why was he telling me this all now and with such emotion? He was that worried about me and what this community had done to me?

Reading my mind as usual, he continued: "I can see it in you. I pay attention, you know. Not just to you—to everyone. It's just that not everyone will let me in. I am *Herr Rabbiner* here, seldom a rabbi and almost never a *rebbe*. For whatever reason you let me in right away and asked me with your trust to be your *rebbe*. So I can see what this year has cost you. And I really need you to promise me that you are going to go through this exercise."

I nodded, but felt numb. Sure, I thought. Why not?

He continued, "Which is why I also have to forgive you."

That one jerked my head up.

"You may have noticed that most of my money is in escrow, and before I leave and you leave I need some of that back. But because of how much you have confided in me, I feel that I cannot arbitrarily forgive you without talking to you first."

His hands had begun shaking enough that he put his glass down immediately after trying to take a sip. His voice came from the back of his throat and I knew that I wanted to run and not be present in his emotions.

"You once asked me if there was anything you could do to help me—around the time that things were first starting to get bad. I had said two things: keep coming for weekly meetings and keep coming to services. I know that this is not some ideal synagogue for you—hell what place in this country is an ideal

303

synagogue for anyone? Maybe there is one—there are seriously some amazing rabbis in this country that could stand up to the best in the States but will never get an ounce of credit. But no way that a young Jewish woman is going to find her perfect spiritual community here. I knew that. But you asked, and I also told you that my job depended on keeping people in shul."

Maybe the easiest thing now would be to hold my hand up, stop him, and tearfully make amends for what I knew was coming. This had been the bottom of the sinking feeling that I had been ignoring for months. But maybe I needed to hear it from him. If I had ignored some voice inside me for this long even though I knew that this speech would someday come at me then maybe I deserved whatever vitriol I was about to receive.

"Listen, Andrea, of course I am not trying to say you are the reason—at all—that I lost my job. That is not what this is about. I think we all can see that none of us had any control over anything. But . . . I needed you."

Now he had to pause as his voice caught and his breathing became labored. I felt steadily more like stone. I felt like I was once again getting the phone call from Bonnie hearing, "I would have stuck up for you."

Except this was worse. So much worse.

"It wasn't just that you left, you took everyone with you. The weeks that you chose to go to Chabad or somewhere else, you didn't just take yourself or Rafi or even Sabrina—every young couple that I had been cultivating was now gone.

"I chose to not say anything. You really had to figure it out for yourself. And I know you didn't deliberately try to harm me, but I could have really used that energy. I am maxed just doing the basics—the number of funerals alone that I do is nearly a full-time job. I don't have the energy to do the sorts of outreach that you did—social media, dinners. But what I felt was that what I could offer simply wasn't good enough, so without regard to the needs of the community, you took care of your own needs."

God I wanted to slap him. It wasn't just about me. It was for his community! The people that came to Chabad or chose the dinners or Shabbos excursions that Sabrina and I had organized were hungry. They were desperate for anything that felt Jewish. It had nothing to do with him it was this broken community. He had to understand that! The fact that he had landed in a bat shit crazy synagogue didn't mean that we all signed up to help him out of it. I mean, why was he coming to me now? What about Rafi? He did some damage. Why not Sabrina? She was with me every step of the way.

Still reading my mind—*still* godammit—he continued, "I know you weren't alone. But I don't have any anger toward anyone else. And yes, that's probably not fair. But you weren't just a leader—you *are* a leader. There is a social contract. Maybe you are not quite there yet, and I am not saying I am blameless. I should have been more explicit. I should never have assumed that you understood the situation here. But it was that something in you that I trusted—that something in you that I cultivated knowing the fruit that you would someday bear. Even though I bear a lot of the blame because I should have just had a direct conversation with you, I just wanted you to come to the realization on your own that it wasn't all about you."

All about me? Where did he get off with that kind of assumption, that it was . . .?

And even if it was, what did it matter? Wasn't it my right to have the kind of community that I wanted?

And even if it wasn't, look how much good I actually did. There was now a group of younger Jews in the area that were much more engaged now than they had been before. And Sabrina was going to keep up with it all.

And even if she didn't, none of this would have in the end made any difference because it was Sasha, the Czar and his lunatic cronies that had been sabotaging the rabbi. How could I be blamed for that?

Except for those words that Rabbi had spoken to me the first time I had met him chose this moment to pop back into mind. *Kol Yisrael arevim zeh lazeh.* All the people of Israel are responsible for each other. It was why we needed a minyan to pray certain prayers, to read Torah, to have a funeral. We were all responsible for each other and it was never about just one of us.

Which of course I knew.

I knew if from the first time that Rabbi had asked me where I was the previous week and I had answered back with innocent glee that Chabad in Düsseldorf had had a wonderful dinner and we had been there until one in the morning singing and singing. I had meant it mostly to hint that others in Germany were managing to pull it off, so why couldn't he? More mean-spirited I meant it to light a fire under him to get him to work just a little harder to satisfy the needs of the younger families. I mean to satisfy me. You know, just get this man who spent a month in the hospital to work a little harder for Andrea-the-Just. Don't look at the pain in his eyes when you say how great *those other Jews in the other community* do it. You know, the ones with seemingly limitless money, rabbis and interns to organize such things. *Kol Yisrael arevim zeh lazeh.* But you, Rabbi Isaac, work just a little harder so that I can feel just like I felt every other time I spit on my own Judaism by going to this or that instead of the perfect Judaism wrapped up in a nice little bow in the thousands of well-funded Hillels and synagogues all over

America. You know, the ones that had unbroken traditions and chains of leadership and finance and supporting congregational and rabbinical and cantorial institutions. Those were perfect but you would rather get an invite to the cool-kids' table and do the Temple Poetry Slam or Bruce Lee Movie Night or Center City Bar Hop. But when you really need it. . . when you are really alone. . . when you start doubting everything about who you are and where you are and if maybe everyone that has ever looked at your eyes, skin and hair and judged maybe wasn't on to something—maybe then, when you don't find the community you want and instead find the one you need—the one that makes you look in the mirror yourself and makes you earn what has just been given to you—then you decide to recreate the shul you stopped going to or the Hillel you never went to while this guy who is now openly weeping in front of you for your betrayal— who gave you time that his heart meds say he really didn't have—who just asked you to please be present—no for him you turned your tail and justified it as his fault or the Russians or Herr Grossman or does it even matter? *Kol Yisrael arevim zeh lazeh* and for you it was just about you.

Sobbing, then and only then could I understand what those words meant and even more what it meant to say. "I have offended you and hurt you. I am so sorry. Please tell me how I can make amends."

A Bit of a Finale

Poetry would have been a full synagogue for Rabbi Isaac's final Shabbat. The thirty-two that I counted at least included a few more than the recent dwindling into the teens, but still left me mutely full of rage.

New signs in both Russian and German for the offerings of the new rabbi had been gleefully posted everywhere. Sabrina, Natasha and I all stopped and read one in the foyer, working hard to find everything about it to mock and curse. Turns out that wasn't especially difficult.

First of all, the service times had been changed. This wasn't such a big deal, I guess, but the Old Russian Dudes got their way and now the Saturday morning services would once again start at 9, guaranteeing participation only by the sept-, oct- and nonagenarian crowd that would actually come that early. I mean, everyone gets accustomed new things, but I was in no mood to challenge my own prejudices in this case. The kicker, though, turned out to be the new programming:

"Men are welcome to meet with Rabbi R_ before services for Torah Study in Russian and in German. For women and children, we are happy to offer an exciting evening in the community kitchen to learn how to bake challah."

The three of us vacillated back and forth between mute agony and the steadily growing volume of our curses when we once again found our voices. Sabrina particularly took this hard. I was to head back to the States in three weeks while Natasha could frankly live without services. For Sabrina, however, this was a disaster that essentially locked her and all like her outside the gates. When Rabbi R_ had visited for his final interview several weeks earlier, we had all shown up in order to watch the train wreck. And it was indeed the train-wreck of a rabbi leading impersonal prayers without any interaction with the community. Sure he had a nice voice—a beautiful one even. But what he did only worked in synagogues filled with people that had begun drinking their Jewish prayers with mother's milk. These people needed guidance and help understanding the forms of the tradition that had been ripped away from them for more than three generations. Sure the Minyan Men kind of reacted well to him. He looked the part with the black hat, long black coat and black velvet kippah. He looked the sort of authentic that people think is the exclusive authentic of Judaism had their interaction with the complexities of Judaism been limited to Yentl and Fiddler on the Roof. But even though they shook his hands passionately, as if overcome by an ecstatic messianic fervor, they likewise lost interest in the service five minutes after the soon-to-be new rabbi had plopped his own prayerbook on the pulpit—not one of the ones used by anyone in the Synagogue—and began davening through the service without guidance or page numbers. Sabrina and I followed along bravely and stubbornly, refusing to be cowed by the violent looks of the balcony-brigade at the *kol isha*—the voice of the woman daring to interfere with the sanctity of clueless men rumbling like the hayride through the two or three prayers they knew.

Of course we had to endure those stares from the balcony. About five minutes before the beginning of the service, one of the lesser-seen security personnel—one that according to Sabrina refused to go to services because Rabbi Isaac was not Orthodox, came down the aisles and informed us all that women were, out of respect for the rabbi, not allowed to sit downstairs for that service. Only the fear that we would under this new regime be bodily thrown out and never allowed back in moved us like docile creatures, albeit with healthy doses of the evil eye, up into

Jewish Purgatory. Our rebellion came in the form of voices that the rabbi must have been able to hear from up front.

So, I guess that the step back into the glorious shtetl days of the nineteenth century or the more modern rhythms of Williamsburg or B'nai Brak shouldn't have surprised us. But for Sabrina, that bright and shiny conversion certificate that she had polished in tears would be meaningless for this leader of the Jewish people. Her years of learning would amount to nothing under the yolk of this rabbi and she would be relegated to the kitchen when she only wished to be present in a synagogue and pray. Sure she would still go to Chabad and sure she could take the hour train ride to the nearest Liberal community. Word had it they were getting a part-time student from the liberal rabbinical school in Berlin to come next year. But the way it worked, Sabrina could only be a member—could only be fully enfranchised here. Rabbi Isaac's pink slip left her and so many others without a home.

At least today we could settle into our usual chairs, pretending with our placement and actions for a few more minutes that nothing had changed. On cue, right on the hour, Rabbi Isaac entered from the back and walked around, greeting all present. I pretended not to feel the dampness on his cheek as he hugged me what normally would feel way too hard and tonight felt entirely correct. His hands shook as he reached to Sabrina and then Natasha and then limped his way down to the front.

He spent much longer than usual under his *tallis* as he wrapped it around his head. When he came out his face looked dry, his eyes clear, and his voice betrayed nothing other than the joy of Shabbat as he started his *niggun*. We all sang and prayed along as if prayer suddenly mattered. Even the men, usually so detached from the content of what happened in this room seemed

310

to sense in contrast to the soon-to-be-rabbi that this man in front of them had given them something that they would not soon see again. Rabbi Isaac's voice only shook when he exited the silent prayer with a rendition of *Yihyu l'ratzon* that we had never heard before. "May the words of my mouth and the meditations of my heart be acceptable to you, Eternal One, my Rock and my Redeemer."

Instead of stepping up to the *bima* where he had been delivering his sermons since he returned from his illness, he stepped deep into the rows of congregants, surrounding himself with the men that he had tried for so long to engage and within reaching distance of the women that he had so briefly been able to enfranchise.

"Final words," he pronounced carefully. "Usually we don't get to choose them. Few of us get to choose the time and place of those moments where we have the opportunity to try and communicate those things we find most important. Few of us ever get the chance to ask the question, 'For those gathered around me in this moment, if I only had a few moments to give to them what I believe most important, what would I say?'"

He had placed his hands on the back of the chairs in front of him, his white knuckles clear even from meters away.

"Luckily I am not alone in this. *Chas v'Shalom*, God forbid, that I should compare myself to *Moshe Rabbeinu*—to Moses— but the one similarity is that we both knew the time and place of our final words."

I searched his face for signs of deeper or rather darker meaning to his words. He was the one who had taught me more than anyone before to always look for the multiple layers of interpretation for anything worth interpreting—the surface, the symbol, the allegory and the hidden mystery. Was this a *remez*— hint to an even greater and much darker impending departure than simply moving back to America? I looked but could truly only see a white knuckled version of the man that I had in my own way loved and betrayed and then loved again.

"This week we read *Parashat Devarim*, the first portion in the book of *Devarim* or Deuteronomy. What most of us don't think about is that the entire book of Deuteronomy takes place over one day, the last day of Moses' life."

He had now started entering his rhythm. He was a gamer. I can't imagine his inner turmoil, but when he would have been justified in shouting curses he chose nonetheless in that moment to be, well, himself.

"Moses had been forbidden by the Eternal to enter the Promised Land. For a sin that most of us look at as minor, this man that we know from the end of *Devarim* to be the greatest of all prophets as he knew the Eternal face to face is forced to stay behind rather than step into the place that he had worked for the last forty years of his own life to help his people reach.

"So he had one day. He had one day to step up on a rock, look out at the faces that he would never see again, and try to find words that would make a difference.

"How do you do that? Not only how, what do you say? Do you scream? Do you extol? Do you warn? Do you teach? How in the world are you supposed to choose mere words to encapsulate what you know to be the most important things? Moses could see the abilities as well as the weaknesses and self-destructive tendencies of his own people. How do you turn that wisdom into not only the most important words to say, but as well the words that they would—that they *could* actually hear?

"At the end of the day, Moses was human. He showed his humanness his entire life as he fought with his own personal vice and ultimately the one that caused his downfall—his anger. He yelled at his people. He threatened them and listed all the curses

312

that they would endure should they continue to act exactly as he feared that they would act.

"When he wasn't yelling he was retelling the tale of the last forty years—but of course this time he told it differently. He changed a detail here or there to help his make his point. He focused on the aspects of their relationship with the Eternal that had more to do with reward and punishment than what had been reflected in previous parts of the Torah.

"But then he also did what you would expect a good leader to do—he tried to prepare them for the future. What do you do when you go to war? What do you do when you select a king? What do you do when you are tempted by the ways of other cultures? Last words.

"But then the end. Oh what an end. After one of the most brutal sections of Torah, the poem *Haazinu* which excoriates the people of Israel over and over for their obstinacy—after getting all of that out, how does Moses finish?

"With a blessing.

"This is one of the great truths of our tradition that we seldom mention. Much of our law is caught up in the practical— what do we do in any given situation from a legal standpoint? But Moses gives us the ultimate example of what it means to be a leader. A prophet. A mensch.

"It should have been him entering the Promised Land, I am sure he was thinking. Who are we to blame him? Which of us would blame him for wanting to light one last fire or shoot one last parting shot? But instead, he blesses us—we the collective people that could never be worthy of a Moses. We get to move forward—he stays behind—and he blesses us anyway. 'Surely the Eternal loves His people,' he says.

"I don't have enough chutzpah to compare myself to Moses other than to say that I have some idea what it means to depart before I am ready. And like Moses, I have so many things to say that it would take a book to say them. I want to yell at you all for every moment that we have hurt when we could have healed. I want to show the list of good things that could come if we would just take our tradition seriously and its call to love our neighbors as ourselves rather than look at the differences that separate us. I want to hurl out the warnings of what will happen to this community if we do not start overcoming the worst of ourselves—the parts of us that need to tear each other down—mock what we don't understand—be unforgiving for small slights. I want to retell our tale from our years together and try to help you all see what I see—how far you—how far we have all come. Maybe it doesn't seem like it, but for all the things that are causing us pain today, we have come so far, made so much progress, learned so much about what it means to be a community.

"But I've done all that. If you have heard any of my words over the last years, then you know that is what I have been saying. If you heard it then, you don't need to hear it again. If you haven't yet heard me, there is nothing—truly there is nothing any more that I can do or say that will make any difference.

"So with every fiber of my being wanting to curse—with every bit of strength I wish that I could scream so that the pain in my heart could be clear to all—the pain that I must go and the pain that I will always feel like I have abandoned you—I will instead offer a blessing.

He held his hands up in a strangely ancient gesture. For a moment he just stood there, clearly fighting emotion that had taken his voice. After long moments he continued, "I have no words of my own, so I rely on those of our priestly ancestors. That no one leaves without the blessing, the only words I have

314

left, my final words, I offer the blessing that we may all hear, understand, and with the help of the Eternal begin the work of blessing others instead of cursing them—the only work that matters:

"Yevarechecha HaShem Yishmerecha. Ya'eir HaShem panav elecha vichuneka. Yisah HaShem panav elecha, veyasem lecha shalom."

The ancient words of Hebrew he sang with his lifting tenor, letting each individual word ring and then echo, willing each word to remain present. After each line, some in the community that knew the liturgy tried to respond with the appropriate *"Keyn yehi ratzon,"* so may it be, although our words felt pathetic against his emotion.

Now he looked at the Minyan Men, but not with the anger that I was still dealing with. Instead he gave them a type of absolution with his tear-filling eyes as if signing his gratitude for his time with them as he continued in their language: *"Da blagoslovit tebya Gospod' i sokhranit tebya! Da prizrit na tebya Gospod' svetlym litsem Svoim i pomiluyet tebya! Da obratit Gospod' litse Svoye na tebya i dast tebe mir!"*

A few of the Minyan Men seemed to get it. Chayem of all people, along with Dr. Likhtman, wept unabashedly as Rabbi's voice cracked. Sabrina, Natasha and I all had been holding hands, and we felt each other trembling. Now Rabbi Isaac closed his eyes, as if unable to hear these words in the country that he thought he could help save—help heal the wounds of the Holocaust by shepherding the rebuilding of a religion that had been in this country for a millennia and a half longer than it had been Germany. *"Der Ewige segne dich und behüte dich. Der Ewige lasse sein Angesicht leuchten über dir und sei dir gnädig. Der Ewige erhebe sein Angesicht zu dir und gebe dir Frieden."*

Now rabbi too wept openly. The German seemed after nearly a year like my own language, and I took the last words as my blessing, but he gathered himself again and stared at me, right into my soul like he had so often, and finished with my own language and his: "May God bless you and keep you. May the face of the Eternal shine on you and be gracious to you. May the countenance of the Eternal be lifted to you, and may all of your paths be paths of peace."

Epilogue

Kol Yisrael arevim zeh lazeh. The words kept echoing with me. Even after I made amends by promising Rabbi that I would never forget his hurt should I encounter such a situation again, I still tried to put the pieces together and really understand myself. Why? Why had I acted that year as I had? Why did I always see my own needs as the only ones of any importance when so many people around me clearly also had needs.

What did I really think that I was doing? Staging a rebellion? Becoming the *Moschiach*? Playing rabbi?

Now, with enough time past to be back in a country where Judaism is a self-evident reality as opposed to what seemed to be a purely racist and cultural phenomenon meant to exclude the incorrect accent and skin tone, I must admit that, yes, in all honesty, I did have a bit of a messianic complex in addition to my inherent selfishness.

First thing I did after moving to D.C. to begin grad school was to find a synagogue. Ok, not the first first thing—I got an apartment and a therapist first, but back in therapy and in shul and as far away from that dying community as possible, it was easy to see how naïve and selfish I heed acted. It came from the best places, though. I promise. Rabbi Isaac always talked about Torah as the mirror, and with all my heart I promise that I am taking blame where blame is due. I am not going to sit here and say what happened is only your fault or their fault. I was there, I tried to show everyone, to my shame including the rabbi, what Judaism really was—which of course meant Judaism as I defined it and as I had learned it. I made life difficult when I didn't get my way and pouted with appropriate batting of eyelashes when I thought I could manipulate others to my view.

317

So why would I do such a thing? I have beat my head and argued in my best impersonation of "disagreeing rabbis" with my lovely atheist Jewish psychologist to try and zero in on my motivations and to balance out those things for which I must–somehow–make *teshuva*. Or I suppose I can just say to the superimposed faces in my memory of that community, "You suck. I did nothing wrong there. *You* beat *your* heads and make *teshuva*. If you even know what that means, assholes."

Anger. Yeah. That is a part of it. Overwhelming sadness too. Guilt. Self-recrimination. Disgust. Therapy has been so very fun.

I am angry, sad and disgusted because a bunch of people that call themselves Jews, and technically qualify as such yet haven't the slightest clue about the most miniscule aspect of Judaism, took over a building that at times had been filled with people giving every bit of their hearts and souls in the best ways they knew how in order to flip the bird at Hitler and rebuild Judaism in Germany. Yeah, they were outcasts and converts and a few Israelis that were sick of missing Pesach and needed something more Jewish than their Magen David pendant and their *sabra* accent. Yeah, scattered around Germany there were other Anglos and Americans that had experienced the self-evidency of Judaism in other places, and wished to transport their model of Judaism and pound the hell out of that square peg. Yeah, there were *Yekke* families like museum curators that wanted to recreate from half-formed memories and barely-informed fantasies the "*Gemeinden*" that stood and then burned before the darkest years of the Shoah. And yeah, there were people–good, beautiful and amazing people–who too spoke Russian yet wanted to live fully expressed Jewish lives. We all gathered and prayed and plotted and cried and complained and drank vodka and rejoiced and still thought we were making progress until everything crumbled around us and we all stood outside the

318

bullet-proof glass of the guard building with an Orthodox rabbi inside that would only let us in if we baked challah and sat in the balcony.

The memories became more immediate than usual around that first Thanksgiving back. I saw Rabbi Isaac on Skype and decided to buzz in. He was living back in the Twin Cities, teaching once again at the University. He looked tired—no—he just looked defeated. Maybe over the glow of a laptop screen we all look a little bit drawn out–a little bit transparent. But I sat across him for enough hours and watched him wildly draw his emerging thoughts on the already crowded whiteboard to know the difference between that man and this. For months I had witnessed his passion and nearly silly excitement over the smallest Jewish concepts. Now I heard someone going through the motions of being a rabbi, instead of one who still believed that title meant something in his life.

"Are you in a congregation?" I heard myself ask. I had never heard him give a *drasha* in English. I wanted there to be at least the idea of a synagogue that I could in my fantasies go to and hear that just once–to know that that part of the community in Germany wasn't destroyed.

"*Jein,*" he answered as usual with one of his favorite expressions. Ja und Nein. Yes and No. Just like the desire to rebuild Judaism in Germany coupled with the practical reality that seemed to make it impossible

"*Jein.* I am working with a network of small congregations. I lead maybe one service a month and the odd funeral when no one else is available. It's nice, except for I have heard that more people will find themselves available in the summer than in the dead of a Minnesota winter. What the hell, eh? The dead deserve respect even when we're freezing. I can do that much."

319

I wanted to cry. I wanted to tell him again how unfair everything had been. I wanted to tell him that he hadn't failed. I wanted to hug him and tell him not to give up. I wanted to explain to him that people here in America got it and they would be able to hear what no one wanted to listen to back in Germany. I wanted to say I am sorry I am sorry I am sorry please can you still be my rabbi. Please don't leave my life.

Instead I just sat there in a lengthening uncomfortable silence that as usual, as the rabbi, he was forced to fill.

"Have you found a synagogue there in D.C.?"

"Yeah. Conservative, though."

He chuckled. "My bad influence, huh?"

"Sure."

"And school? Do you have a good *Doktorvater*—um—thesis advisor?"

"Sure. I mean, she's cool. She's a little too hard-core editor for my taste. You know, style over substance. But it's good. Lots of access to libraries in D.C."

"Good. Good."

More awkward silence. Was my friendship with this man meant just for the time that we went to war together? Is that it? Were we comrades in arms and now with the battles over and the war lost, we had nothing more to say?

He absently scratched his head. I couldn't really tell over the video quality, but I think—I am pretty sure he wasn't wearing a yarmulke.

"Do you have any plans of going back?" he asked. No need of course to ask where. Germany. His home. His only home, in some strange way.

I shrugged. "I miss the beer." I thought that would get him to smile a bit. He at least tried. I'm sure it was just for my sake. "I am heading to Israel next summer and wanted to spend a few

320

weeks in the Conservative Yeshiva. I am flying through Frankfurt. I thought I might take a couple of days. See Sabrina and Natasha." And maybe Stephen. Still no resolution there.

He nodded, picked up what looked like a Bic pen and absently began chewing on the blue end.

"Do you . . ." I didn't even know what I wanted to ask him. Why did I need to try to get him to talk about something that he clearly did not want to talk about? Did I think I could now save him? Brave, brilliant Andrea. Had I learned nothing of my limitations?

Instead he comforted me. "Did I tell you," he asked softly, clearing his throat, "did I ever tell you how grateful I was for everything you did? The dinners, the movie nights–the tweets and Facebook posts and all the energy you gave? I know I laid it on heavy in the end. I had to—that was also important. But I never told you the other side. I am so very grateful to you. You really did try to show everyone a bit of *Yiddishkeit*." He chuckled lightly, removing the pen from his mouth completely. "If it wasn't condemning you to cruel and unusual punishment, I would again say you would make a very good rabbi."

I laughed. Me? Seriously? No. Chance. Ever.

"You're sweet," I said. Then, "I miss you, you know." I had fought them for a while, but now the tears came easily. "You taught me a lot, and the rabbi here—well—his sermons are good, but just not the same." I tried to lighten up a little and wiped the corner of my eye. "And the cantor should be at the Met instead of in shul. It's all about the opera instead of getting people to join in. I know how much you love that."

He smiled. "No kidding. Yeah, not really my thing."

"I should go," I said. "Thanks for the chat. I'm glad I found you online." I was sure he wasn't so glad himself, but he was polite and still a pretty good actor.

"It was nice," he said. "You know you can always call. You don't have to wait to see me logged in. I still consider myself your rabbi. That means something."

It did mean something, but I was pretty sure this would be the last time I would randomly buzz in if I saw him online. It just hurt too damn much to see the transformation—the fading. I needed to remember him as he was when I got to Germany. I needed to remember the man that inspired me and got me to the *Beit Din* and could read my mind and that hugged me in shul and kissed my cheeks in a way that no American rabbi ever would.

"Hey," he said, stopping us both from saying the last goodbye. "I have thought about it a lot." His voice sounded cold and rehearsing, like a last run-through of lines before going off-book. "We didn't fail. I mean, I didn't fail and you didn't fail. It is just . . . I think I have recently come to understand that Stalin did much more to destroy Judaism than Hitler did. I mean, Hitler killed the Jews, but the Soviet system destroyed Judaism for the Russian Jews that stayed alive. We didn't fail. Really. There was nothing we could do. There was no foundation to build on. Take care, Andrea. We'll talk soon."

Goodbye, Rabbi.

I cried for a while, and then spent months thinking through those last words—examining and trying to figure out how to interpret what he was trying to say.

My journalism focus for my Master's degree had become steadily less satisfying until I applied for and was accepted into a Master's program in Jewish Studies, also in the greater D.C. area. That choice proved instantly more satisfying and better. D.C. was starting to feel like home, especially as Sabrina came to visit about every six months. I visited her when she and her Doctor from Berlin got married and I traveled to Berlin to hold up one of the poles of their *Chuppah* in a beautiful ceremony led

by one of the newly graduated and ordained liberal Rabbis—
Liora. Natasha spent the week with me and I paid for her hotel
even though her life had become much more secure of late as she
had gone back to school after she had begun dating an older
attorney with two children of his own, and who was by all
accounts a massive improvement over her previous spouse. We
held hands walking down the *KuDamm*, window shopping
Bulgari and Cartier, enjoying what it meant like to have a
friendship that felt strong no matter how many months or years
went by. Stephen and I tried the long distance thing but only
half-heartedly. I still needed to act out some internal drama with
real life people in the present and so much of Stephen still forced
me to look in the mirror in ways I was not yet comfortable with.
Maybe he was more of an aspiration for the partner I might
become in the future rather than a partner with whom I could be
in dialogue in that moment. But the memories I have of our time
together strengthen me. That is something.

More grad school, more visits back to my parents when
possible. My mother was diagnosed with breast cancer during
my second summer in Israel, and had already had a mastectomy
when I had returned. Neither she nor my father had said a word
so that I would not come back before the end of the summer
yeshiva sessions. So while I talked about Uriel, the newest love-
of-my-life for the summer, my mom played the part of happy
mother while she suffered and my father played the part of half-
stern half-proud father as I blathered along.

Out of what I am sure was mostly guilt, I took a semester
off, spent time with my mother and while she slept I slowly
worked on my thesis. The cancer had been way too advanced,
and as had been feared from the very beginning, the cancer cells
had found their way outside of my mother's motherhood and into
cells that would betray her and eventually cause a type of pain

323

and then drug-induced numbness that I am choosing now to block out so that I do not have to hear my mom's slurred speech in my dreams.

My father continued working. The medical bills, even with insurance, were barbaric. My dad went from work at Temple to the hospital cafeteria to my mom's bed while I took a break to the liquor store and then to bed with the bottle as he numbed himself against something that he as well had no desire to comprehend. I tried to channel every bit of rabbinical compassion I had ever seen from Rabbi Appelbaum and then Rabbi Theresa and then Rabbi Isaac. How did they speak to people in pain? What does my tradition say? What wisdom can I find that will sound like wisdom and not like some scared girl trying to quote the Talmud so I don't have to look up and see my parents wasting away, both in their own pathos. I tried to be cheerful, read books out loud as a good voice actor might, bring pretty looking and smelling things to my mother's bedside, and tell my dad with my eyes and my voice that I loved him, I understood, and that he wasn't alone. When she died with my hand in hers I ripped open my shirt and wailed my pain across the hospital bed, and then before the funeral I once again tore my blouse, much to the consternation Rabbi Theresa who had agreed to perform an atheistic burial service with Jewish symbolism, but had been preparing to hand me a symbolic ribbon to tear instead. My eyes told Rabbi Theresa that I had changed, and my father followed suit, letting his grief finally rise above his own numbness.

After we had both shoveled earth on my mother's grave–the Reform community had a separate fenced-off yard where interfaith couples could be at rest side by side–we walked off hand and hand. The two of us, me without a sense of irony, finished up a bottle of Ukrainian vodka sitting on the floor of our house, and then wallowed in tears and covered mirrors for a week as friends and Rabbi Theresa and the odd distant cousin brought nosh and paid respects.

As it became clear that my dad had decided to start living again, I went back to school and re-immersed myself in the pursuit of the type of academic excellence that would remind me of the confidence that I had lost as I was being proverbially locked outside the gates of my adopted Jewish community.

I once repeated to the campus Hillel rabbi what Rabbi Isaac had said to me—that Stalin been more successful than Hitler. The rabbi, barely older than I was and squeaky naïve in a New York island-of-Judaism-sort-of-way, was upset. Ok– "upset" may be stating it lightly. I stepped on some third rail and found myself thinking fast, trying to explain to the ever more bulging veins in his neck:

"Yes I know death camps are something else, but that is not what I am talking about.

"When I went to Germany and became active in the Jewish community, I saw the empty seats at shul even though the community had thousands of members and just assumed that everyone simply hadn't been properly exposed to the Jewishness of Judaism. You know–it doesn't really matter how secular someone is—when you have someone–a rabbi or youth group leader or Birthright *madrich*–who just has that shining Jewishness, you suddenly get that Judaism is relevant. Torah is real and a part of your today. And you know that if you let that light shine—the discussions and the singing and Shabbos and Sukkot and Pesach and trips to Israel and even fasting–that if someone can just be a part of those authentic moments it will all be fine. The community will be strong. People will flock. When that connection is made, then something happens to a Jewish soul and we get it. No questions, we just get it."

I knew I was parroting one of Rabbi Isaac's sermons, but wasn't that ok? Hadn't he said we build our own spiritual temples with the words of interpretation upon the foundations of all our teachers' and teachers' teachers' interpretation? Didn't he say that the presence of God is that which only comes today in the midst of struggling with the words of our past to make room for the interpretations of our future?

"I thought that by being that light, or maybe just doing the things that the rabbi couldn't himself do or didn't have time to do–that if I set up Shabbos dinners where we sang after the meal and talked and just were–you know Jewish–that between that and the rabbi that people would come to shul and that what we have here in America would be something they could experience and their Judaism would be like mine–cool. Important. Self-evident.

"But that is what Stalin did. There was nothing left to touch. Every bit of passion came out and tried to find a Jewish soul and then failed. No one came. I mean not no one, but maybe one out of a hundred. People weren't waiting for a good rabbi. People had lost any connection to what a rabbi was. People weren't waiting for a great *davening* experience. Prayer was meaningless–there was nothing left of Judaism but the stamp in the Soviet passport that said: 'Nationality: Jewish.' That was the beginning and the end of the Jewishness."

I wasn't sure who I was really trying to convince, so I started reading more Jewish texts beyond my studies, trying to see if there was another way to understand what had happened. It couldn't–it just couldn't be so that there was nothing left to reach—that Stalin had destroyed the Jewish soul in the same way that Hitler tried to stamp out Jewish lives. My Fulbright project had become my Master's Thesis and the Master's Thesis had become a comprehensive study of what happened in the Soviet

Union to Soviet Jews—historically, psychologically, sociologically and led to my Ph.D. There simply must be an answer. I needed to keep on learning—to come up with a plan.

Maybe in Chassidic philosophy there would be some story—some ritual or song without words that would be the cornerstone to reaching that tiny spark that must—must still be there. Maybe instead Kabbalah–perhaps mystical teachings would hold the key to finding the holiness that we are promised is in every aspect of the creation. Maybe if I simply went deep enough in the mirrors of the Talmud and Torah I would find the right story or law or prophetic goad to speak at just the right time to the right people or maybe the children of the right people and then I would succeed where the great sermons and music and services and dinners and movies and social celebrations of all-things-Jewish failed.

Maybe I just didn't try hard enough. Maybe I can still do it. There must have been a reason that I had been exposed to all the pain in failure. There is no way that such trials are in vain. That doesn't make any sense. *Kol Yisrael arevim zeh lazeh.*

At some point, you start realizing that you are just looking for reasons to do what you knew all along you were going to do. You start visualizing all the trials that brought you to your knees and then seeing if dialogue with your tradition can pick you back up again. On the other side of that struggle sits Herr Grossman and Herr Adler and Platt and Engels and the Czar. Maybe they're laughing or maybe they were just the angels that you needed to guide you to the moment where you become yourself. Yeah, Stalin is also sitting there and so is Hitler but their job is to be the adversary that tells you that they won—that there is no way the damage they inflicted can be undone. Except you saw those moments that say otherwise—Natasha mourning as a Jew and Sabrina transformed after her *mikvah*—Rafi standing up for justice and Rabbi Isaac seeing the solution and trying so hard even though he didn't know how to protect his body and soul. And you realize that allowing all of these people to become a part of you obligates you. At some point they either need to be ignored or their challenge needs to be accepted. At some point you either stand up to Hitler and Stalin and yes even the *Zeitgeist* that drives the most destructive moments of the Czars and the Grossmans or you grant them all a posthumous victory. You either selfishly ignore the world or you understand your own obligation to heal it based on the lessons from your teachers— both those you have loved and those you have hated. And as you are writing out your applications for rabbinical school in Germany and then traveling to Berlin for interviews and answering the spoken and unspoken questions as they look at your eyes, skin and hair you realize that there is a very real possibility that you will fail. The task is that big, the day is getting that much shorter and the job is that overwhelming. But then again you might just be exactly where you are supposed to be doing what you are supposed to be doing. You might just be in the only place you can be, doing the only thing that is to be done.

Acknowledgements

There is a reason that the city of Rabbi Isaac's community is never mentioned. It doesn't exist in any literal sense. No similarity to any *Einheitsgemeinde* in Germany is meant or should be inferred, and all characters, be they loved or loathed by Andrea, are as well works of fiction. In a very real sense, however, many of the struggles that Andrea witnessed are based on quite literal struggles, even if the characters that Andrea encountered are amalgamations of many dozens of these fascinating people.

As a first-time novelist, I am probably more indebted than I even realize for my editors and advisors, Sandra Andrews-Strasko, Katrin Bergmann, and Dr. Lisa Gaufman. Whether it was helping to zone in on the real history of FSU Jews and how and why that manifested as it did in Germany, or whether it was understanding the complexity of the relationship between Germans and the returning Jews in their midst, or whether it was just pointing out when something didn't work, these three remarkable humans made this novel what it is. The first manuscripts were heavy on my ego and it took their collective efforts to help Andrea emerge as one far wittier than the author. Without them, Andrea could not exist as she does and thus in many ways Andrea, luckily, contains much of their talents and goodness.

I am also grateful to Dr. Lewis Mandell for his invaluable guidance and advice on the processes through which a first-time novelist must go. Finally, I thank my teachers and mentors that pushed me, put up with me and honed me. If you don't know who you are and why I love you, I have failed.

71210664R00196

Made in the USA
Middletown, DE
20 April 2018